PRAISE FOR SAAD

"Bangladeshi author Saad Z. l
home country and the realm of the Djinns. It's a richly evocative adventure about a father and his half-Djinn son searching for one another—a sort of dark-fantasy *Finding Nemo*, as charming and funny as it is inventive and strange." **—Adam Roberts, *The Guardian***

"*Djinn City* is a page turner; a story that immerses and keeps you up well past a sane hour." **—John Venegas, *Angel City Review***

"Hossain's rich, vivid, straightforward prose propels the story at a quick clip. Darkness looms on every page, yet he offsets the serious stakes with Joss Whedonesque quips... With man-eating wyrms, invisible airships, and eccentric genies, this fantasy-adventure will appeal to fans of *The Golem and the Jinni* and the *Bartimaeus* trilogy."
—Booklist

"Hossain blends picaresque fantasy, supernatural politics, and genetic science into a whirlwind of a tale...an imaginative, talented storyteller with a knack for both dark comedy and harrowing tragedy."
—Publishers Weekly

"Hossain's story ripples with magic and just a dash of something twistedly angelic. It is populated by dragons in their most nascent forms, terrifying sea beasts, and flying machines; it is built up by fictionalized mythologies that weave their way through known origin stories and rumors, birthing something new and captivating. Its villains are complex and sometimes appealing; its heroes are delightfully flawed. Even its violent scenes have charm. Humor and intrigue ferry *Djinn City* toward its thrilling end. Expect rapt audiences to spend a good while frantically rubbing lamps to wish for one thing only: the speedy release of its sequel."
***—Foreword Reviews*, Starred Review**

"A delightful fantasy adventure with a YA spirit, a PG rating, and a rich introduction to Arabian mythology." ***—Kirkus Reviews***

PRAISE FOR SAAD Z. HOSSAIN'S *ESCAPE FROM BAGHDAD!*:

"Saad Hossain's perplexingly weird debut novel, *Escape From Baghdad!* captures the pure insanity of the Iraq War. At the same time, it's not a war novel. Instead, it's a skillfully constructed literary IED that brings together the sharpest aspects from multiple genres. It's a Tarantino-esque *Heart of Darkness* set in war-torn Iraq, filled with absurdism and dark humor, a mash-up of satirical Joseph Heller-style comedy and sci-fi fantasy with a gratuitous mixture of good old-fashioned ultra-violence." **—Colby Buzzell, *VICE***

"Set in the aftermath of the US invasion of Iraq, Bangladeshi author Saad Hossain's debut novel is a riot of mordant humour and gonzo storytelling… The Gulf war may just have found its *Catch-22*."
—James Lovegrove, *The Financial Times*

"Saad Z. Hossain's *Escape From Baghdad!* may be the hippest, weirdest, most creative and visionary book yet to emerge from the full-on debacle that was W's still-simmering Iraq war. Hossain's unique blend of satire, mythology and speculative fiction makes *Escape* a hold-onto-your-hat tilt-a-whirl joy to read. And, quite possibly, a future classic in its own right."
—Jerry Stahl, author of *Permanent Midnight, Happy Mutant Baby Pills, I, Fatty*

"Hossain daringly shows us that war isn't just hell but absolutely insane." **—Barbara Hoffert, *Library Journal***

"Saad Hossain has given us a hilarious and searing indictment of the project we euphemistically call 'nation-building.' With nods to *Catch-22, Frankenstein, The Island of Doctor Moreau* and the Golem myth, *Escape from Baghdad!* weaves fantasy, absurdity and adventure into a moving counter-narrative to the myth of the just war."
—Daniel José Older, *NPR*

"It's a marvelous mix of genres, blending the visceral atmosphere of a war movie with the casual nihilism of *Catch-22* or the original *M.A.S.H.* complete with an Indiana Jones–style treasure quest… A gonzo adventure novel that shreds the conventional wisdom that pulp can be pigeonholed." ***—Kirkus Reviews***

"*Escape from Baghdad!* is a virtuoso performance, both utterly heart-breaking and riotously, laugh-out-loud funny... I wanted to stand up and applaud when it was finished, but I didn't want it to finish. I could not recommend it enough."
—Lavie Tidhar, World Fantasy Award winning author of *Osama.*

"Saad Z Hossain's upcoming *Escape from Baghdad!* is the sci-fi and fantasy writer's debut novel, characterized as an Arabian–Nights–esque thriller. Having set the book in modern-day Iraq, Hossain started off his research reading blogs written by American soldiers in Iraq, and then braided together Norse and Greek mythologies."
—Ploughshares

"Saad Hossain is the author of *Escape from Baghdad!*, an engrossing cross between *Zero Dark Thirty* and *Raiders of the Lost Ark* that takes a sobering look at America's troubled legacy in Iraq."
—Bookslut

AN UNNAMED PRESS BOOK

www.unnamedpress.com

Unnamed Press, and the colophon, are registered trademarks of Unnamed Media LLC.

ISBN: 978-1-951213-28-2
eISBN: 978-1-951213-29-9

Hossain, Saad Z., author.
Cyber mage : a novel / Saad Z. Hossain.
Description: Los Angeles : Unnamed Press, 2021.
Identifiers: LCCN 2021039688 (print) | LCCN 2021039689 (ebook) | ISBN 9781951213282 (paperback) | ISBN 9781951213299 (epub)
Subjects: LCGFT: Science fiction. | Dystopian fiction. | Novels.
Classification: LCC PR9420.9.H675 C93 2021 (print) | LCC PR9420.9.H675 (ebook) | DDC 823/.92--dc23
LC record available at https://lccn.loc.gov/2021039688
LC ebook record available at https://lccn.loc.gov/2021039689

Designed and Typeset by Jaya Nicely

Manufactured in the United States of America by McNaughton & Gunn.

Distributed by Publishers Group West

First Edition

The Unnamed Press
Los Angeles, CA

CONTENTS

PART ONE

PART TWO

This one is for my gamers.

CYBER MAGE

PROLOGUE

Making of the Sword

The Dragon pored over a pile of steel scraps. Some of them were the latest carbon steel. Some looked hundreds of years old. There were leaf springs from ancient trucks, back when vehicles burned fossil fuels and used rubber tires. The springs lasted forever, long after the trucks, owners, and goods had turned to dust. There were pieces of old knives and axe heads, handles long gone.

Every so often he reached out and picked up a piece. The ones he kept, he stacked carefully together. Sometimes he used an ancient hand grinder to clean off rust and dirt. He had an open pan of solvent, and he submerged the best pieces in this to effect a final cleansing.

When the pile was big enough, he put the scraps in a canoe-shaped canister, fitting them together like jigsaw puzzle pieces, rotating them until he felt at peace. The canister itself was made of mild steel, and would be picked apart when the final billet was forged. This was the time-honored way of making canister Damascus, which allowed the forging of a blade using disparate metals.

When the canister was filled, he plugged the gaps with high-carbon steel powder and then covered the top with flux. Even though he was technically blind, his fingers moved unerringly because he could see the lines of the distortion field, the witchery physics of the djinn world, spheres of eldritch energy all around him, far more useful in the manipulation of steel than photons bouncing against a working retina.

His forge was a very simple gas-powered fire housed in a rectangle of ceramic bricks, hand-made from the clay on site. He could have heated the metal with his fingers, but the regular beat of the flames soothed him, and in any case he preferred to adhere as closely as possible to the old ways.

When he was satisfied with the canister's weight and distribution, he spent a moment fiddling with the field, making sure each piece was aligned correctly so they would weld together nicely once molten. A good preparation saved a shitload of grief later on, and canister Damascus was fiddly and temperamental to begin with. Most people in his little blacksmith commune made stuff out of straight bar, either

1080 machine-tool steel or the more expensive carbon steels with nano structure, so-called new Wootz steel.

He preferred to work with junk metals. Anything else seemed like cheating. The new carbon steels were so hard and durable that they barely needed forging. You could grind a knife out of a bar and it would be fine with a half-hearted heat treatment. For that matter, you could print a katana on a hub machine on any street corner and it would probably be better than the real thing.

But the old ways of forging allowed him to align the molecules using the field, making internal patterns of carbon and iron that were, though unseen, fantastical works of art, art for the eyes of God, since no other djinn or man had his sight, eyes made custom by Givaras the Broken. At no small cost.

When he was sure everything was good, he welded the ends of the canister shut and then welded a piece of holding pipe to the end of the little box, so he could manipulate it easily. Of course, he could put his whole hand into the forge without risk, but he preferred not to advertise his abilities. People already gave him a wide berth.

He finally put the billet into the forge and took a breather as it turned orange. The lack of sparks was a good sign; it meant his welds were holding and air wasn't getting into or out of his canister. When it was ready, he put it on the anvil and hammered it evenly, trying to make the interior pieces of molten steel into a solid welded piece. There were power tools he could use for this, but he liked the rhythm of hammer striking billet, and his field-enhanced body was far stronger than an ordinary human's in any case.

When he felt that the billet was solid, he started hammering the edges, trying to peel off the soft metal of the canister. This was the really tricky part, determining whether the inside metal was welded together properly while also trying to remove the entirety of the canister metal, which was unsuitable for blade work.

The Dragon cheated, of course. His eyes could see the edges in the molten steel, and he ran his field over each weld with the lightest touch, locking each errant carbon atom into stable cubes of iron. He would continue to do this throughout the forge, arranging even the trace elements of heavy metals with geometric precision. The canister was stubborn, refusing to come off. He took his chisel to it and then finally, as the metal was in danger of cooling down completely, just ripped it off with his bare hands.

The billet inside was mottled, showing the grains of the different metals he had put together. He checked for cold shuts, the flaws that presaged improper welds in the steel, but there were none, so he put the billet back in the forge. When it was bright orange again he took it out and started hammering it flat. Soon he fell into his normal rhythm, and the world contracted into the dull ache in his right arm, and the gentle heat of the forge, the warmth on his scales that felt like home.

When the billet was flattened into a long bar, he hammered the middle with his chisel and folded it over itself. Back into the forge for another round, heating, hammering flat, heating, folding, over and over, until he lost count of the layers. This was the old way of homogenizing the steel, getting rid of the impurities and spreading the carbon evenly throughout the metal to avoid overly soft or brittle spots. At the same time, he was nudging the metal with the field, lining up the trace elements of manganese, phosphorus, and nickel into pleasing shapes. If another eye could see the tesseracts inside, they would have called him an artist instead of a craftsman.

Finally, after many hours, his body was pleasantly exhausted and the sun was winding down over the horizon. The other forges in the commune had all winked out one by one, and everyone was already gathering in the longhouse to get out of the dangerous night air.

He let the billet cool and put it away with his tools. There was no thieving in such a small community. In any case, his Damascus was distinctive, better than the other stuff, sought after out in the city. He took no apprentices, and they thought him churlish for that. He was about to leave when he saw a shadow approaching, a cool wet wind, and the stench of the abyssal sea. A burly man came in a long coat, but the Dragon saw only fish, thousands of them crowded together, their eyes glistening, water coating them in a faint mist, an alien school in the shape of a human, the two forms coexisting somehow without negating each other. He had met this being before, once. His heart sank. This was neither fish nor man. This was an elder djinn. "Bahamut," he said, throat parched. "You're a long way from the sea."

"This is a strange place you've picked."

"It's a place." The Dragon shrugged.

"And you make knives."

"I like the fire."

"I see. Wasting your time."

"Living in peace," the Dragon said.

"Public service." Bahamut sighed. "A concept entirely lost on the present generation. I cannot leave my demesne. I did tell you about the gate, didn't I? The world on the other side, where your dear friend and mentor roams? The one *you* helped to free? All is not well there… The pilot sleeps in the gate, and he is most restless. Something comes our way, Dragon. Something…*odd*. There is Matteras, roaming free in the sky. There is Hazard, claiming the Earth. It behooves us to give answer."

Matteras. His maternal uncle, oft called the uncrowned king of djinn, who hated him, had banished him to an underground hell for years. Then there was Hazard, the violent jackal-headed djinn who despised humans, who had sworn to kill him multiple times. The djinn world hated the Dragon, for he was an abomination twice over, born first as djinn-human hybrid, a stain upon Matteras's family honor, and then remade once more below the earth into something worse, a half-dragon freak with custom-made eyes and wyrm DNA coiled through his body. He had been entangled since birth in djinn politics, and it had left him broken, burned, and shunned by all.

"That's great," the Dragon said. "Sounds like you have a lot of personal problems. I'm going to put away my tools, wash up, and go lie down. Then tomorrow I'm going to finish my knife. My buyer is coming next week and I'm behind. So please. Go away."

"Ah well. Fine. I will commission a sword from you, then."

"A what?"

"You are a blade maker, as you say. You have told me your schedule for tomorrow. Most admirable. I wish to make a sword."

"Find another smith."

"This sword requires the help of a djinn smith, one who has been trained by the Broken and is thus able to part molecules with the field. A singular blade is warranted. Again, a debt is owed. Your cousin misplaced the last such sword."

"Rais?"

"Since you refuse to rescue him from Gangaridai, at least you can help to discharge his debts. It was your father's sword, in fact, if that makes you feel better."

"The cavalry blade? On our wall?"

"The very same. A most storied blade, now lost for all time through the carelessness of two Khan Rahman emissaries. You will make a replacement blade, an even grander one! A sword that cuts the field! A smiter of nanotech! It will need to be quenched in dragon flame to make it extra special."

"That won't do anything," the Dragon objected.

"Extra special, I said!" Bahamut snapped. "It will sound better for the ballads. A sword quenched in dragon flame. That is not something to be scoffed at. It is part of the commission. I told you a singular blade is required. And you have here the only dragon in existence."

"You're going to keep bothering me until I do it, aren't you?"

"Yes."

"I just wanted to be left in peace."

"No peace!"

"Okay," the Dragon slumped. He knew that Bahamut would not leave him be.

"I will oversee your smithing. There are runes I wish to place inside the folds of the metal."

"Great. Fine. I'll do it, if you promise to leave immediately after it's finished, and not come back for another seventy years," the Dragon said. Arguing with the fish had always been a futile endeavor. "Wait a minute. Who's going to use the sword?"

"Do not worry, it is not for you."

"Who, then?"

"I am making a golem. Which reminds me, I will require your help for that as well."

"A golem?"

"A lost soul like you, but filled with the rage necessary to survive the transformation." Bahamut smiled unpleasantly. "We will need to quench him in dragon fire as well."

"Really?"

"Dragon fire! He will wield the dread sword."

"Fine. I'm glad you've found someone."

Bahamut studied him with fishy eyes. "You never had enough rage in you, Dragon. Givaras did not choose well."

"He worked with what he had."

"Hmmm. The Maker was never that simple. Perhaps he made you soft for a reason."

"I'm not soft, djinn," the Dragon said. "I'm just bored with you."

"We shall see."

"And after these two boons, I'm done, right?"

"No," Bahamut whispered under his fishy breath. "Not by a long shot."

1
The Lover

The Cyber Mage, Marzuk, was in love. Not cyber love, at which he was adept, but a real, physical, shot-in-the-gut kind of love that left him loopy and sleepless. She was sixteen, a year older than him, already filled out in astonishing curves, with the height and poise of a lady. Her hair was straight, black, and occasionally braided. Her skin was light brown, without a single blemish (to his eye). She was elegant, with that air of sophistication, that magic patina of charisma that just squashed every rational thought. He could not explain why he obsessed over her; that was the nature of his love.

Just looking at her from afar made him nauseated. The few times she crossed his path and stopped for a word, he had been unable to force out a single syllable. Silent and mysterious, that was Marzuk.

This and other weighty matters kept Marzuk boarded up in his room, or rather, his office. A good half of the space was given over to gaming equipment, where he normally played *Final Fantasy 9000*, which was, of course, *the* world game. More than 200 million users all across the globe, they said, probably a lot more among the undocumented canaille. Not too many on Marzuk's level. The Cyber Mage only played games he could win.

Currently, his goblin avatar was brutalizing a bunch of noob peasants with a flamethrower. One might consider it unfair to bring a flamethrower to a sword-and-sorcery game, but he was a villain, and it was de rigueur for him to bend the rules. The game AI, Sakaguchi, barely tolerated him. Saka had investigated him a record nineteen times for infractions. Any ordinary player would have been banned for life by now, but there was a dearth of real villains in the game, and the Cyber Mage was something of a celebrity. In fact, not to be modest, he was famous all over the Virtuality, despite his anonymity. Last year he had been on the cover of *FF9000* magazine, or his Goblin King avatar had, at any rate.

He fidgeted in his hideously expensive chair.. Good for his overweight ass. The surface layer was actually a cushion of air, a field maintained by electric manipulation of stacked carbon molecules. He was more floating than sitting. Sometimes he liked to lean back, crank up the hover, and pretend to be Baron Harkonnen from the old *Dune* movie. A cult classic, that. Marzuk was into cult classics. Given the paucity of actual *live* friends, his schedule was wide open for deep dives into ancient culture.

Babr the pygmy elephant snuffled near him, a questing trunk tapping his ankle. It was lunchtime. The elephant's eyes were luminous, intelligent. With his trunk and his stylus, he could tap out simple applications on the screens. Right now he wanted food and some of his beloved narcotic berries. Marzuk got up and fed him. Slightly drunk, the elephant swayed to the discordant music of the game. Babr too had been hideously expensive. Marzuk had a lot of money because beneath his pudgy exterior, his mind was sharper than an orca's teeth. (One did not think of orca teeth as particularly sharp, but they were!)

"Maru! Lunch!"

Maru. What a cringeworthy name. How typical of his mother to convert his gender and neatly infantilize him with one short syllable.

There was a chalk line drawn outside the corridor of his room. It was his line of emancipation. The notice, printed on heavy recycled paper and framed on the wall, said it clearly:

> The individual Marzuk Dotrozi Khan Rahman born of so and so lineage, in the Square Multipurpose Hospital, on so and so date, resident of the Gulshan Fortified Diplomatic Enclave, with residency number X3488A3CPP, citizen of the Postflood Provisional Government of Bangladesh, Chop number 33345AA88, Shareholder of the Tri-State Corporation, Ordinary Status, is henceforth recognized by the provisional High Court to be legally emancipated from his parents, Mr. and Mrs. Dotrozi KR, with residency numbers etc., etc., respectively, and that this line drawn in permanent ink be a clear demarcation of his demesne within their joint lease holding. Furthermore, he is to be fully recognized as an independent entity in the eyes of the law, fully incorporated as a limited liability company unto himself, and as such, beneficiary of all associated legal ramifications. Signed, Dr. Yakub, Director of Security, Securex Inc.

It carried on in this vein for several pages, all of which were laminated, highlighted, and framed for easy perusal. Emancipated. Like fuck. Did his mother respect the line? NO, SHE DID NOT.

"Maru! Lunch!" Her voice was shrill. "And don't forget to wash your hands!"

Wash my hands? Am I four? Do I need reminders for basic hygiene?

Halfway through lunch, his parents had already covered all the waffling conversation they had stored up. *How was school, dear? How are your teachers? Where do you want to go for summer vacation? Blah, blah, blah.* He reminded them several times that he was a) emancipated, b) gainfully employed, and c) not going to school, had not been for a rather long time. He really would prefer it if they treated him as a cool flatmate, rather than foisting on him this demeaning parent-child dynamic.

Papa just laughed fondly and patted Marzuk's head, much as he had done for the past fifteen years. Sometimes he felt that his father was pulling his leg with the asinine questions, but when he looked at his vacant, innocent face he could see no sign of the necessary wit.

His mother sniffed tearfully at the emancipation bit (the legal notice had hit her hard) but then cheered up immediately when the kitchen unit announced that dessert was ready. The kitchen unit did excellent South Asian cuisine, and tolerable Chinese. Everything else was temperamental. Mama took great pride in feeding the family, even though she had very little to do with the actual preparation of food.

His parents always said that when *they* were growing up, kitchen units were just getting started, and more often than not, people employed human cooks. This was still done, of course, but mostly for ceremonial crap, or by gazillionaires. Marzuk, who didn't see the point of eating together, or regular mealtimes, wondered idly why no one had yet created capsules to get rid of this whole messy process. It was tragically unjust that he, of all people, who clearly was not interested in food, happened to put on entire kilograms of weight just by sniffing the stuff. Then he realized that astronauts, surely, had these capsules. He made a mental note to order them online. *Can't have a conversation over a capsule, ha!*

"So, son, college?" Papa said. "I've been getting a lot of mail from different places. That big tech university in Norway is very keen on you. They say they'll give you a one-on-one professor."

"I am the Cyber Mage!" Marzuk growled. "Papa, really, they are trying to con me into teaching their professors! Norway my ass! I'm not going to college unless they pay me. Do you think I'm a fool?"

"Son, there might be more to learn in life than computing," Papa said lightly. He liked to pretend he knew stuff, but Marzuk was quite sure this was an act. Oldies always pretended there was useful shit they knew, but did they? What was it, then? How to fuck up the ecosphere? How to create rampant nanotech and ruin a perfectly good planet?

"Papa, actually, right now, I am backdoor hacked into the entire Tri-State security link. I can see from every public camera, and a large number of hidden ones. I have access to every petty bureaucrat's office," Marzuk said. "And the funny thing is, they don't even have the capability to recognize this fact, let alone stop me. It's like they're running Kaspersky over there. *Kaspersky*."

"Now, son, that sounds naughty," his mother said. "Did you do your homework?"

"Homework?" Marzuk shrieked at an unreasonably high pitch. "Homework?!"

"Son, what exactly are you using the cameras to look at?" Papa said with some amusement, which gave Marzuk pause. The old man was sharp sometimes.

Look at? Why, there was only one thing worth looking at in the whole of Gulshan. Only one thing so perfect that it defied description. Amina.

Akramon Djibrel didn't take prisoners. He took heads. Born into severely debilitating circumstances, just at the cusp of the great floods and fires, the so-called Disintegration Era, Djibrel had pretty much had to fend off all comers, including sexual predators, robbers, kidnappers, serial killers, organ hunters, and even cannibals. Also there were welfare workers, tree huggers, state services, religious orphanages, and other molesters of the idealistic variety.

His response to all transgressions had always been furious attack. In him was some long-dormant berserker gene that transformed his small, wiry childhood frame into a spitting, biting, hacking dervish who seemed to hate every living thing. He had grown since then into an apex predator, honed by the pressures of the rabble. Crime was unregulated among the cardless, the great sea of people who surrounded the city, and armed men and women made their own laws like the sheriffs of old. There were mech suits, powered armor straight from the pages of anime. There were drone halos controlled by the mind, exotic tech marbles that could tear through flesh like paper. Finally, there were swords.

Djibrel had a talwar—a singular weapon. It was single-edged, with a six-degree curve in the blade. The hilt had a simple cross guard with a knuckle bow, a small band of metal that protected the fingers from getting chopped off. The pommel was a flanged disk sporting a four-inch spike, useful for punching people in the face in close quarters. A hole in the pommel allowed a leather thong to be attached to the wrist, preventing loss of the weapon during moments of stress. In Djibrel's line of work there were always moments of stress.

It looked like a relic of the Mughal era, a weapon reminiscent of the sabers used by the Turkic horse peoples of Central Asia, closely related to the Persian shamsher, the Turkish kilij, and the Afghan pulwar. The great Mughal Babur, most famed of conquerors, might well have worn this weapon on his belt. The sword bore no maker's mark. There was no scrollwork or jewel in the hilt, no mother of pearl on the scabbard, but the blade itself conveyed its pedigree, the peculiar watery mark of Wootz steel, the priceless rose-and-ladder pattern etched in metal that purveyors of weapons all through the Middle Ages knew as Damascene.

If, in fact, this were a genuine Wootz steel blade from the Middle Ages, it would have belonged in a museum or in the hands of some avid collector, easily worth more than Djibrel's entire life's income, more, in fact, than the entire GDP of the slum he hailed from.

The blade was sharpened to a monomolecular edge, which was translucent, so that the very hairsbreadth of the cutting side was invisible. Edges this sharp had hitherto been possible only in obsidian blades, but those tended to be brittle and shatter easily. The makers of this blade had done something to ensure that the edge self-repaired to some extent, and moreover maintained an unlikely toughness, thus ensuring that the weapon did not face ruin after the first cut.

The sword was used, almost exclusively, for cutting off heads. Cutting off heads was necessary in the slums due to the rampant nanotech available. Bullets didn't kill people with the same finality they used to. In the Mirpur area, where Djibrel currently roamed, there were continuous twenty-story habitations that created one great longhouse, with passages through, and tunnels, and other covered roads high and low; these passages were also rented out to the needy, so actual traversable pathways mutated according to daily or weekly lease agreements. The roads on the ground, long-ago municipal routes of durable concrete, had been claimed for living space, filled up with lean-tos, tents, and steel structures. The roofs often boasted illegal kitchen gardens, rapidly evolving plants living in symbiosis with the nanite-infected air. Everything was mutable, for a plethora of cheap 3-D printers were available and enough expertise existed here to create any number of unlikely structures, most of them composed of dubious raw materials, some of them entirely from raw sewage, so that the term "living in a shit house" was made literal.

There was a grand, snakelike bazaar, where trade was untaxed and free, as long as you had the muscle to back it up. The Mirpur zone was a quarantined area, meaning the three million people squeezed into it were not legally allowed to leave. They had once been the citizens of the country known as Bangladesh, but the whole nature of nationhood had changed, splintered down into fiefdoms effectively ruled by private city corporations. They were now allegedly citizens of the Dhaka City Corporation, some of them with single shares in either the DCC or Mirpur Inc., with the accompanying privileges. Many had no shares, however, and these were effectively nonpeople, though still essential for population density, which is why the city fed them and let them stay inside the borders.

Much of the city was like this, outside of the privileged enclaves like Dhanmondi or the Tri-State, which protected their exclusivity with maximum force. Of course, the Tri-State was incorporated and anyone living within had shareholder status—actual valuable shares. This meant they counted. As actual people. They had *equity* in the world.

"Force" was really the key word everywhere in Bangladesh, but pretty much definitively in Dhaka City. Many do-gooders were attracted to this region to observe firsthand the massive concentration of 30 million people in an area the size of a postage stamp, and once in Dhaka, astonished by the sheer scale of inhumanity, they often sat paralyzed with confusion and mounting dread. A few of them tried to help, which was even worse.

Many such cases of help included the use of illegal health-grade nanotech. Ingested in water, in food, dispersed into the air—Mirpur had been dosed liberally, as had most other zones. Many of the tech caused cancer, disfigurement, often hideous death. Still, it made bodies invulnerable: to disease, to injury, to starvation even. There were some people in Mirpur who could survive on water puddles and air, thanks to nanotech in their bodies working miracles. There were other people who could survive otherwise-fatal gunshot wounds, because nanotech in their bodies knit up severed arteries, repaired heart or brain tissue in seconds. There was no one, however, who survived having their head cut off.

Djibrel stalked through Mirpur number 10, passing through the road-bazaar, where he was somewhat known and generally avoided. He had a sword, and he had his shotgun, and he had his general bad attitude. He didn't take taxes like street thugs were wont to do, nor did he belong to any of the various criminal gangs that ruled this space. He preyed on them sometimes, but almost whimsically. There was a general consensus that he wasn't quite right in the head, and was best left alone.

When he reached the old zoo, which now housed several hundred thousand people, Djibrel found a purveyor of hybrid parrots. The selling of live animals was a class 1 offense in the DCC. The dealer owed him from some previous avian crisis, and erased this debt with few terse directions.

The man Djibrel had come to kill was hiding in a third-class government workers' colony, just a few hundred meters from the zoo. It was good housing of sorts: ventilated, stormproof, with solar and water, solidly in the green zone for air security.

He had a bounty on his head, this third-class government worker, set by some lord in Gulshan, but this was not why Djibrel came for him. It was said that he did black magic, this kobiraj, this witch doctor, but that wasn't the reason either. Mullah. Kobiraj. Religious by day, witch by night. The djinn network was like a great cancerous tree, and shaking it enough would eventually get him what he wanted.

"Careful now," the dealer told him in passing. "The witch knows you're coming."

"Me specifically?" Djibrel frowned. Someone must have been gossiping.

"*Dude*. You're a guy walking around with a sword and a stack of heads. Of course he knows you're coming. He's got a patron, I've heard. He'll be protected."

"Who's the patron?"

The dealer shrugged. "Some bitch called Sekmet. Another nutcase with a sword."

Djibrel kicked on.

Ensconced in his room and safe from interruption (it being hours from teatime), the Cyber Mage watched Djibrel push through the bazaar with electric eyes. He knew something that even Djibrel did not. The exact count of functioning nanites inside the slum sipahi's* body was 25,354,015. It was the highest count recorded. So high, in fact, that the medical staff in the free clinic he had visited had discarded his report as an error. Djibrel himself had subsequently laid waste to that worthy medical facility during an unrelated altercation, thereby unwittingly destroying the aberrant data. The clinic had had no backups. Now the info was lost to everyone but the Cyber Mage.

Marzuk had been watching the sipahi for some time now. This aggregation of diverse nanotech in one host was statistically abnormal. Of course, statistics accounted for remarkable outliers, and was useless in studying specific cases. The Cyber Mage had thought deeply and come to the conclusion that even the existence of extreme statistical outliers could not explain this phenomenon.

It could be argued that Djibrel moved around at will through most of Dhaka during a time when mobility was dangerous and often difficult, thus accruing a larger variety of regional nanotech. It could be argued that he ate and drank from diverse sources, seeing as he was largely impervious to class barriers (people had a hard time keeping him out). It could even be argued that he had once fallen in the river (rumors) and picked up something crazy from the water.

None of these even came close to explaining how 25-million-odd nanites could coexist in one host.

Marzuk, having hacked into Dupont, already knew what cutting-edge military-grade bioware looked like. That company was trying

---

* *Sipahi*, also *sepoy*: a traditional soldier of the Mughal Empire, typically armed with talwar and musket. In modern street culture, "sipahi" refers to a man armed with a sword, a modern-day samurai, a common occurrence in unregulated areas and much feted in adventure stories.

to make immortals, men who could survive without food or water or even oxygen, spacemen who could be sent like homunculi to other planets. Even more pertinent, he had an approximate idea of what black market experimental-grade nanotech looked like in Osaka, Moscow, and Seoul. If any of those gangsters found out about this, they would snatch Djibrel's ass out of Mirpur faster than he could spit. Well, they'd snatch his blood, anyway. He was a medical marvel.

"Maru!" his mother shouted. "Do you want some milk?"

"No, Mom," he said. "For the tenth time, I do not drink milk in the afternoon, I do not nap in the afternoon, I am not four years old!"

"You were nicer when you were four," his mother said. She had that vaguely tearful voice signaling the hormonal imbalance that triggered the urge to nurture. He had previously suggested that she adopt an infant, or failing that, some kind of small animal; this logical solution had been greeted very frostily.

Later, Marzuk conversed with KPopRetroGirl, one of his main buddies on the net. She was nothing short of brilliant, he had to admit, and was in truth one of his best friends, although he was careful never to say this out loud. So close were they, in fact, that she knew his real name and referred to him as Marzy, to irritate him, whereas he called her ReGi, which was close to what her real, unpronounceable name sounded like and had the added benefit of being the acronym of REtroGIrl. They had been working on the Djibrel project together. In fact, it was ReGi who had first turned him onto it.

ReGi was very interested in street sipahi culture and the intricate overlapping of social, economic, fashion, and biotech trends that led to men with swords walking around the streets of massive Dhaka chopping off heads. It was apparently a thing, urban sipahi fashion. Cool hunters found it irresistible. Fact was, human bodies were one giant cesspit of nanotech now. People didn't stay dead until you took off the head, the brain still being irreplaceable to some extent. Home forges for swords had made a big comeback in the streets, and in the salons, rich kids hung damascened blades off their belts to show their willingness to commit murder, while they drank Darjeeling tea infused with narcotics. The sword thing had started somewhere near the river and worked its way up the social ladder, now spreading to other megacities.

"I'm still following him, ReGi," Marzuk said. "He's getting involved in some weird shit."

"Djinn," ReGi said. She stubbornly continued to believe in fairy stories, despite his many logical presentations. He had even made Venn diagrams for her benefit that clearly precluded the existence of spirits.

"Djinn theory was discredited long ago," Marzuk said. "It's stupid. Like believing in fairies, or vampires."

"Only for general proponents of string theory," ReGi said. He had to trust her; she knew a lot more physics than he did. "At the ultra- cutting end of theoretical physics, there is indirect evidence of organizational matrices in ghost particles. We can't detect them directly because light doesn't interact with them. Nonbaryonic matter, baby."

"That's a big difference from djinn," Marzuk said.

"Why are you so hung up on this?" she asked. "Your whole country believes in djinn, there are millions of people who claim to have interacted with them; why can't you believe?"

"It's mass hallucinations!" Marzuk said. "It doesn't make sense."

"Watch him some more," ReGi said, "and maybe you'll get an education."

2

Salt and Chalk

There was a protective line of salt and chalk around the border of the apartment. Clothes were hanging from lines all along the hallways, dripping water from the recent rain. Some of these puddles had eroded the white line, creating gaps. Djibrel smiled as he walked up and down the hall, noting exits and entrances. White lines might stop djinn or other spirits, but they didn't do shit to humans. Still, the breaks in the salt line showed a careless habit. The witch felt secure. He was overconfident on his home turf. It was good to know.

Djibrel kicked in the door. Someone shrieked inside, and he saw a dirty, hirsute man come at him with a cleaver. It wasn't a normal cleaver, but an oversize twenty-inch blade with a spine as thick as his thumb and a rippled edge that showed that it had been liberally used, on god knows what. He was a palwan, a wrestler, hugely muscled across the neck and chest, snorting with rage, out of his mind, blowing gusts of nanoparticles from his mouth. Something was terribly wrong inside him, in the howling cauldron of his body, but instead of killing him, it had apparently made him more powerful.

The cleaver, however, was outclassed.

The talwar was made for close-range fighting. The short hilt and the disk at the base encouraged the user to hold the sword upright, at an almost 90-degree angle to the forearm, facilitating the whipping, downward swings of the draw cut. It was, in fact, probably the best cutting weapon ever designed, for the torque came from the shoulders and the hip, rather than the wrist, sacrificing a bit of range for substantially more force. Enormous power could be generated by these cuts, far more than free-wheeling strikes from two-handed weapons.

Djibrel had fought drug-addled strongmen before. The key point to remember was that they could withstand mortal wounds and cause significant damage in their keening death throes; often they were impervious to pain, nerves deadened from years of abuse plus boatloads of random shit in their bodies. One had to be careful. It was why cutting off heads was necessary in the first place.

The palwan bowled in with indifferent technique and Djibrel shifted to the side easily, opening up an angle. In the slowed-down time of his mind, he saw the best line, almost like a butcher contemplating beef. In the end he let the cleaver whistle past his side, and brought his sword across the back of the palwan's arm, cutting it off clean at the shoulder. The talwar could do that, and more.

Blood spurted and the man howled, before predictably lurching toward him again, the hideous gaping wound almost gobbing shut from the surfeit of tech in his blood, which wasn't even red, more of a muddy adulterated blue. *Malay blood, that color.* Djibrel slapped away the grasping hand, careful not to get inside the gorilla grip. He whipped his sword again, this time the other way, and took off the man's head and shoulder, a crosswise blow of tremendous power that cut through collarbone and sinew. It got stuck on the last bit of gristle, and he had to push against the spine with his other hand to force his blade through, bracing his foot against the collapsing torso.

This was not a survivable hit. It would have been comical, the sliding apart of the body, had the viscera not slopped all over him. Djibrel was not a finicky man, however. He wiped his blade quickly and turned to face the real threat in the room, the sorcerer in the corner, who'd had enough time to get set.

The witch was chanting a spell, calling up whatever astral protection he owned. He clapped his hands twice and slipped his skin. All across his torso, black inky constructs peeled off his hide, tattoos and all, leaving him raw and bloody and roaring in pain. This sacrifice birthed a doglike shape that coalesced before Djibrel. The skin hound went for his head, snub jaws opening into yawning darkness. Djibrel swayed like a boxer, forced the pommel spike into the thing's teeth. The apparition was strong. It forced him back step by step, in counterpart to a yelping, pain-laden chant from the witch.

The thing with Djibrel was, he always bit back. He went headfirst at the thing, *teeth* first, at the neck, where the hound was exposed. The skin hound had evidently never been bitten by a human. It reared back in shock, loosened its grip for a second, plenty of time for Djibrel to jam the pommel through the roof of the thing's mouth, ignoring the lacerating pain of fangs across his hands, ignoring the acid spit, on and up, until the pommel spike hit the brain like an off switch. Did skin hounds have brains, even? Djibrel contemplated this and more as the monster seemed to shrink, lurching back toward the witch doctor, before collapsing on the floor, twitching, a dead dog made of black parts. Djibrel stepped over the unfortunate beast, feeling a moment of sadness. He liked dogs.

"Stop! Stop!" The kobiraj was out of juice and, like all sorcerers, rather pathetic when his bag of tricks was empty. "What do you want? What? I'll give you power beyond life!"

Djibrel didn't bother to answer. Partly because he was like that, partly because his mouth was full of dog blood.

"My mistress comes!" The kobiraj howled as the sword began to hack through his neck. "Sekmet save me! Sekmeeeeeeet!"

Later, walking down the hawkers' bazaar that was the main Mirpur thoroughfare, he tied the long beard into a knot and used it to carry the head in his left hand, swinging it gently back and forth as if it were a football in a net. This was the kind of antisocial behavior that gave him a bad name.

3

Kali Lunch

Marzuk dreamed of Kali all night. In his dream she had tentacles of code coming out of her back like a fan of arms, jacking into millions of computers, turning them all into bots. He accessed his terminal and found his cowls not working, not even the Samsung Neural Assist, which wasn't even full headgear, just a patch attached to his scalp.

He watched helplessly as Kali scrolled through his files, changing his configurations, messing with his icons. Then he looked on in terror as her eyes opened atop his own, and she somehow took over his neural nodes and accessed his brain directly. He woke up in blinding pain.

Kali was a recurring nightmare for him. He blamed his mother. She was a closet religio, one of the vast number of people who clung on to archaic faiths despite mounting evidence to the contrary. Her own parents had been Brahmin, had in fact kicked up a huge fuss when she had married into the Muslim Khan Rahman clan. Despite both of the newlyweds disavowing religion, she had kept a number of secret shrines all over the house, one of which Marzuk had discovered at age three, dedicated to the battle goddess, the swordswoman, taker of skulls, Mahakali with ten arms, a frightening little statue that had caused the boy to cease speaking for several days. Kali was the vengeful mother, the urge to slaughter made personal. Young, precocious Marzuk had nothing in his bland iconography to square the concepts of murder and nurture in one figure. He suspected now that it had caused him to forevermore view his mother with apprehension, expecting her to one day sprout extra arms, despite her current lame demeanor.

Later, discovering his distress, his father had calmed him down and introduced him to both faiths, Islam and Hinduism. His knowledge, however, was spotty, so Marzuk had to be taken to the grandparents and given a dose of old-fashioned history and religion and spirituality, a hodgepodge of comforting, often wildly inaccurate stuff to erase the sting of the Skull-Taker.

He had discussed this with ReGi, who had offered him a further meta insight that his people, despite being overtly Muslim, still subconsciously carried the vast undercarriage of Hindu mythology and culture like an invisible iceberg. Her theory was that populations that converted quickly most often just took on the trappings of the conquering faith, all the while subverting it to fit their previous and actual beliefs. Case in point: the Catholic saints of nineteenth-century Latin America, who were only thinly veiled simulacra of the ancient forces of Orisha.

Therefore, Kali existed in his racial memory; and if perhaps gods and goddesses were aspects of humanity's own archetypal states, then his fascination with Kali was an embrace of a missing part of his conscious mind, the desire for completion perhaps, or empowerment.

Marzuk disagreed with ReGi. He was growing more and more convinced that Kali *actually existed.* She, or something equally unsettling, was stalking him. Lately many of his programming forays had been thwarted. Bots he had been using for months had suddenly shaken off his control. Private networks where he had muscled admin rights suddenly changed configurations. Something was *wrong.* And then these nightmares, relentless, and the pain between his eyes. It was enough to sour him on the whole Cyber Mage thing.

Of course, if some human actually dared to come after him, that would be great. He hadn't had a human challenger for months. The last time, some kid from Ukraine had tried him, and it had been amusing, although somewhat short-lived. It had ended when Marzuk had pinpointed the guy's home address and caused a defunct telco satellite to fall from orbit and land on his head. (The kid survived with minimal injuries, most of the satellite having disintegrated in the atmosphere). ReGi had found the street video of the thing actually falling from the sky, and posted it. It had been hilarious. Instant fame in the Virtuality, with ten million views and at least two thousand parodies.

Kali was not a human, though. It didn't feel right. This creature was amorphous, omniscient, prophetic. It never slept. It never stopped. Like a goddess, or a hive mind banding together to take him down. It was a sobering thought. And as if he didn't have enough on his plate, the Djibrel thing was heating up too. The man had actually spent most of last night carrying a witch doctor's head swinging from his belt. There were many people after him now. On the surface there seemed to be no rhyme or reason to his murders, but Marzuk was quite sure his psychopathy had a purpose.

The police were too dumb to understand they had a serial killer loose in Mirpur, and Marzuk was almost tempted to alert them, simply as a means of flushing Djibrel out. He would have to think about that if the body count kept rising. He didn't like cops, but there were limits.

Finally, most importantly, today was the day he was actually, properly going to meet Amina. It was unnatural, the way his tongue dried up when he thought of this. He had practiced various conversational gambits with ReGi, much to her hilarity. At the end of the day, though, she was just another cyber savant, her thinking too similar to his, her brand of snark just a variation of his own.

Amina was a *real* girl. He had been waiting for today for weeks. And it wasn't fair that Kali had kept him up all night and now he looked haggard and addled.

He skipped breakfast out of nerves and spent the time showering and trying out various hairstyles from his HairForYou helmet kit, which was powered by semi-intelligent software and hundreds of tiny motors and could whip hair into various salon-level structures in a matter of minutes. He rifled through his closet and realized that he owned only jeans and white T-shirts. Some years ago, he had grown an aversion to all tags. Whenever he put on an article of clothing, he started imagining the label digging into his skin, the bit of plastic rubbing against him causing horrible allergies. It became obsessive. He started getting rashes from psychosomatic reactions.

In the end he had ordered twenty dozen white T-shirts made from organic cotton and twenty dozen dark blue jeans. There were no labels, no logos, no washing instructions, no spare buttons. Even the denim rivets were unmarked. The manufacturer, bankrupt, had been a maker of archaic children's clothes, a lunatic idea that hinged on people wearing hideously expensive ancient fabrics. Marzuk had brokered the sale of their very expensive laser-guided fabric-cutting machine back to some Austrians for a modest cut, saving them from utter ruin. They had, in turn, promised to make him clothes.

They still kept in touch. Every once in a while one of them would offer him a suit or some fancy shirts, thinking him an adult. The bad thing about having only one outfit, Marzuk decided, was that you couldn't dither over what to wear. He was ready for lunch. It was only eleven thirty. The invitation at his aunt's house was for one thirty, but

Bengalis showed up late to everything, so if he went on time, not only would he be the only person there, he'd also end up seriously inconveniencing his host. (As an emancipated minor, Marzuk took care to keep up with social protocols.)

Killing time, he went back to the Kali issue and did a random stress analysis of his security. It showed a definite upswing in attacks over the last two months. It had begun about the same time that he had started following Djibrel for real. He could not fathom the connection. Djibrel was certainly not computer literate. Marzuk took all the data and shunted it off to ReGi, with a short note.

She pinged back in a couple of seconds. "How's the big date?"

"It's not a date, it's a lunch," Marzuk said with quiet dignity. "At my aunt's place. There will be a lot of people there, including boring relatives."

"You have a weird idea of a date."

"It's a Bengali thing," Marzuk said. "We take our families to everything. Even wedding nights, apparently."

"Well, why are you shoveling gigs of data at me on a Friday night?"

ReGi lived somewhere in the North African Free Economic Zone, where many of the European corporations had fled after the EU calamity. Marzuk associated her with exotic places like Gibraltar or Marrakech. At the same time, he pictured her as vaguely Asian, perhaps half-Japanese, from some of her slang. Then again, most of the world used Japanese gamer slang. Intentionally vague, was ReGi. This especially being the case since he had never seen her entire face, just fractured glimpses.

"Look at the attacks, please," Marzuk said.

"All right, Mr. Paranoia," ReGi said. "Enjoy your date."

Marzuk's aunt was fashionable, and very pretty. Even he could see that. She had never wanted progeny, nor was she overly taken with her gaggle of nieces and nephews; he thought he must have inherited his desire for emancipation from her. She was a widow, had buried her husband long ago. They had been a socialite power couple for the five years that he had survived his marriage. His death had undoubtedly been an accident.

Yet when Marzuk stepped from the lift into her tenth-floor apartment, he saw her laughing with her head tilted back like a bejeweled hawk, with such wild abandon that it seemed impossible that she had ever suffered a single loss.

"Ah, Marzuk, you have come, dear one," Samra said. She gave him a friendly hug. With their combined phobia of relatives, it was never "Aunt" and "nephew" between them. They had long ago fixed it to call each other by name. They were both so odd, such kindred spirits, Samra had said, that no one would wonder at this slight quirk. She was, after all, of the august and ancient Khan Rahman clan—one of its glittering and public faces. Marzuk had heard other stories about his extended family, darker ones of murder and intrigue and even more bizarre activities, but these were hard to believe on a sunny day on a beautiful terrace.

Samra's parties were a mix of extreme age groups, from octogenarians to particularly interesting ten-year-olds. Babies or toddlers were never invited, for Samra had a fear of young children and constantly imagined an alternate universe where she was leveled under a mountain of nappies, nipples pegged to the ground from the suction of a hundred toothless baby mouths. She was a good host, however; the elegance of her home and the excellence of her old Dhaka cook (human) made sure she was always well attended. Also, Samra believed in day-drinking and Marzuk, being emancipated, was allowed a white wine spritzer. He didn't particularly enjoy alcohol, but he liked holding the sweating wineglass and twirling it idly under his nose, pretending he was some pompous wine connoisseur, an act his aunt inevitably found hilarious.

He was in the very act of doing this, muttering under his breath about vintage, and "legs," and "just a hint of citrus," when Samra came by with a girl in tow, long-legged with perfectly glossy hair, wearing a flowing summer kameez like it had been custom-made for her. Amina. It was the promised introduction—a fine point of his "date" he had not mentioned to ReGi. But how perfectly like his aunt to pick the worst time! He hastened to fix his posture and ended up sending wine spritzer sloshing over the crystal rim.

"Amina, I thought you would like to meet Marzuk, who happens to be my old friend," Samra said. She led the two teenagers into a corner by the window, sat them down on wicker chairs.

"My aunt," Marzuk said, to irritate her.

"Have you met before? You are about the same age," Samra said. "Amuse yourselves, dears. Marzuk, perhaps you could stop playing wine critic for a moment and attend to the young lady."

"I've seen you before, right?" Amina was perfectly composed. Talking to strange boys was obviously a very blasé activity for her. She sat with her back straight. Marzuk inevitably slouched. Expensive perfume wafted from her. *How can she be just sixteen? Perfect, perfect, perfect.*

"Once or twice, I think," Marzuk said. He was flattered. She remembered him.

"Does your aunt let you drink wine?" Amina asked, after a moment. "Is she really your aunt? I love Samra, she's the most stylish person I've ever met."

His love, Marzuk realized, was actually a very talkative girl.

"Yes, my dad's younger sister," he said. "She lets me drink wine to piss off my parents. I was pretending to be a wine connoisseur. It makes her laugh."

"Like that show where they go into vineyards and compare wines? I love that," Amina said. "Have you ever been to France?"

"No." The Cyber Mage did not travel for security reasons. Plus some countries had laws aimed specifically at him. It had never bothered him before, but the way Amina's eyes went kind of flat and disinterested made him feel gauche and uncultured.

"Samra goes to the Mediterranean every year," Amina said. "She told me that the North African coast is the best. All the big stars go there. I saw her picture in African *Vogue* once, did you know that?"

"What's that?"

"It's the magazine, stupid," Amina said.

"Oh." Marzuk had not come across this *Vogue* thing. For that matter, magazines for him represented archaic dead tree parts, of value only to anthropologists. It had never occurred to him that a segment of contemporary society still valued these things. "I didn't realize you could still get paper stuff."

"I like the paper," Amina said. "Things look better in print."

Marzuk resolved to investigate this phenomenon. Was she perhaps an anthropologist? He hesitated to ask. The ones he knew were, to put it kindly, older—with dirty fingernails.

"I have a friend in the FEZ," Marzuk said. "The Free Economic Zone in North Africa."

"I know what it is."

"Oh. Sorry. Of course you do. Stupid of me."

"How did you meet him? Have you ever visited him?" Amina let him off the hook with a practiced pout.

Again this fascination with travel. What was with this girl? And what was this alluring lipstick she was wearing? "It's a girl," he said. "ReGi."

"Oh?" *Interest piqued.*

"I haven't seen her, I mean we talk online," Marzuk said.

"Online." Amina made it sound childish somehow. Her anachronistic attitude was pissing him off. "I don't date online."

"It's not dating," Marzuk said. Why was everything about dating? "She's a pro, like me."

"Pro?" Amina seemed to be getting less and less interested. He could almost see her brain fidgeting, plotting to escape. At the same time, the way she said "pro" made it sound like "prostitute."

"Professional," Marzuk said, getting to his feet. He'd be damned if she was going to walk out on him first. "Hacker, you know."

"Right." Amina somehow looked both incredulous and supremely uninterested at the same time. "You don't go to school, do you? What grade are you in? I haven't seen you around."

"School, of course," Marzuk said. *School! Of course!* That was the answer. He'd see her every day... She'd be a captive audience... They could be boyfriend and girlfriend... 30 percent of the population still married people they went to school with..."I'm just transferring. Which, er, school are you in?"

"American International School of Dhaka, in Baridhara. The red fort with the gun turrets," Amina said. "It's the best one, you know. No riffraff."

Of course, that red monstrosity that houses every snot-nosed scion of elite criminals, that one? "Right, what a coincidence, I'm about to go there," Marzuk said. "I had been in Russia for a while."

"Oh, so you *do* travel," Amina said. She had a peculiar crinkle of smile in her eyes. He had been in Russia for five days, for a conference on security protocols. It had been airport-hotel-airport in darkened vehicles, and an armed bodyguard had followed him on bathroom breaks.

"Of course," Marzuk said loftily. "I'm emancipated from my parents, you know. Free as a bird."

"How lucky," Amina said.

"What grade are you in?" Marzuk asked.

"Ninth."

"Hmm, yes, that's the grade I chose as well, funnily..."

"Chose? You can't choose which grade you're in."

"No, er, the grade *they* chose for me," Marzuk said. "Ninth grade. Same as you. I should start attending next week. I hope you'll take me around."

"Sure." She didn't show any enthusiasm. Her face, in fact, was completely, deliberately noncommittal. She was a poker player!

"Tell me about school, then," Marzuk said hurriedly. "What are you studying?"

"Fashion," she said with a degree more liveliness.

"Oho, you're a designer!"

"The technical aspects of old fabrics, ancient weaving, I just find that fascinating," she said.

Marzuk found it markedly easier to let her talk in this vein, requiring only a few questions and encouraging murmurs, than to try to keep her amused with his own pitiful experience. Thus passed the best three hours of his life so far, the entire party spent in the company of this enchanting creature. He made a mental note: *Next week. Join school: Baridhara, red fort with gun turrets.* Gun turrets? How barbaric was this place? *Ninth grade.* Oh god. He was going to be a high schooler. Humiliating. ReGi was going to laugh her ass off.

4

Red Fort of Baridhara

"I'm going to join school for a bit," Marzuk said airily at the dinner table. "Do some sports, socialize. I think I'm getting cabin fever."

"Oh, did you have a nice lunch at Samra's?" Mother asked. "I hope she didn't make you drink wine. I've told her a hundred times..."

Of course, they never listened to anything. "I'm putting you guys down as next of kin and legal heirs," Marzuk said. "I have to sign a bunch of disclaimers. Apparently anyone not living in Baridhara is considered at high risk. Forget that Gulshan is right next door."

"Nonsense," his father said. "The road is perfectly safe these days. So you're going back to school, eh? We sent you there before, when you were six. Do you remember?"

Marzuk remembered.

"You hated it," his father said. "And then the teachers said you were slow."

"I was bored," Marzuk said. That had not been a pleasant period of his life. He had pretended to be mute. His parents had gone through seven psychiatrists before he had cracked. On the balance, they had been pretty understanding about the whole thing, damn the cost.

"Samra said you had a good time," Mother said. "You made a little friend, she said..." She was smiling in that particularly irritating way she did when she had something on him.

"Mother! For god's sake, Aunty Sam has got to be the biggest gossip alive."

"Ah, so there it is," his father said. "First love!" He gave that knowing grin that signaled the onset of some kind of life lesson. "I'm guessing she's also in school? I was wondering why the sudden interest. Good luck, son."

Marzuk cringed in his chair. His father looked like he wanted to hug him or something. Any minute now he was going to start giving gratuitous advice. Oh god. He might even want to talk about sex. The Cyber Mage looked at his plate. They were only on the first course.

This was going to be excruciating. Had his astronaut capsules arrived yet? No they fucking hadn't!

Later, in his room, he fed Babr his midnight snack of chocolate-covered goji berries and inevitably ate half himself. No wonder he was fat. The bloody elephant was corrupting him. Finally, he put on his cowl. It was a smart-skin hoodie that extruded a mask over his face, whisking him into the Virtuality. Aside from implants, this was the best of VR tech, widely used for gaming and other virtual pursuits within what had become the coalescence of all the internets of the previous century; a second skin of digital content overlaid on mundane reality, turning deserts into fables, imbuing dire concrete blocks with Pharaonic splendor.

People walked these dreamscapes, their every step crowded with art, advertisements, adventure, sex, optional parkour, a cornucopia of alternate reality, as little or as much as they could take. The Virtuality was an assault on the senses, a drug that could trip every receptor in the brain, a reward for all the loyal corporate citizen shareholders. One did not have to be mobile to experience this marvel. Anyone feeling lazy could lie in their bed and fire up an avatar with their mind, roam the world as a digital traveler, shedding the drudgery of ugly brick and mortar. What it didn't provide, however, was privacy. Big Data mined every bit of it, tracked every move, and each AI warped the Virtuality as it saw fit.

For serious work, Marzuk and like-minded individuals had appropriated the Black Line. The Black Line was a private warren that didn't show up on any kind of surveillance. It was a pearl nestled in countless layers of shit, an anonymous sanctuary of calm set apart from the vast and dangerous chaos of the Virtuality.

The Black Line had first been commissioned by the Nation of Brunei for use as a completely secure network, unconnected to the larger universe. The idea had probably been to store and launder vast sums of money and information in it, as well as house an underground market beyond the interference of the wider public.

When the earthquakes in 2079 had destroyed the kingdom, vultures had descended to pick over the legendary wealth of the sultan. The city-state of Brunei, or what remained of it after the tsunamis, had been looted. The loss of life had been so severe all over the island, the destruction of habitat so complete, that the entire landmass had been abandoned. The information ministry had been wiped out to a man when its state-of-the-art skyscraper had collapsed. The servers in the vaults deep underground, however, powered by cutting-edge fission batteries, were guaranteed to run for another five hundred years without maintenance. The unmanned bombproof bunker not only survived the earthquakes, it was now completely impregnable under the dangerous rubble of a 120-story building.

The Black Line had lain dormant, a pocket universe forgotten completely, until elite hackers of various stripes had first discovered and then stolen it. Marzuk had been on the front lines; he had made his name in those heady months.

Many hackers had heard of the mysterious Black Line, but very few were actually permitted to *use* it. Marzuk finally logged in to see that there were 89 other people connected. There were exactly 144 total users. The membership was static and closed; only the original hackers of the Black Line knew how to get here, other than the now extinct information ministry of Brunei.

Large quantities of data were being processed and analyzed—washed, in the common parlance. This was always the case. Initiates of the Black Line were serious people. Some in-house statistics indicated that on a data-processing basis, the combined usage of the Black Line consistently measured among the top hundred corporate pseudo national entities. That essentially meant it was the processing equivalent of a city-state.

The vault of Brunei was also a treasure trove of original codes, which were now part of the NPM* registry of free software, contributions from long-dead programmers who had believed in the open source ethos and donated their lives' work for communal use. The Black Line held many of these original coder authentications. If the 144 wanted, they could delete more than a thousand pieces of integral, *foundational* pieces of code from the public registry, meaning *no one* could use those anymore, creating a cascade of legacy Java software failure that might break the Virtuality altogether.

---

*NPM: node package manager, a free registry of open-source codes that programmers use to build larger programs, saving time and effort. Almost all complex programs are built on other pieces of code. Over the past hundred years, the NPM free registry has survived to coalesce into the largest open-source repository in the world.

This was known as their nuclear option, the ace they'd use if AI ever came after them. Marzuk's particular favorite bit of code was Left Foot. Apparently, at the very start of avatar creation for the fledgling virtual world, someone named Koçulu Jr.* had written the code for turning left. This had been freely loaded into the NPM registry and used by ever larger programs. *To this day*, even sophisticated AIs used the same pyramid of codes to run their avatars in the Virtuality. At the base of every complex Java bundle was the simple eleven-line program for turning left. Sometimes Marzuk dreamed of deleting Left Foot and watching billions of avatars suddenly discover they couldn't turn left.

He messed around for a while, looking over the Djibrel analysis, which had now grown into a multiuser project, several others becoming interested in the high nanotech concentration levels. Yellow King, a sometime rival, dropped him a line.

"You all right? Looks like someone is trying to brute-force you."

"What does it look like to you?" Marzuk asked. "I call it Kali. Multiple arms, multiple attacks."

"If I didn't know better I'd say it was us." Yellow King was abruptly serious. "You want me to study it?"

It was the kind of direct question they normally avoided. Their society worked at oblique angles, bits fitting together from mutual interest, coalescing and disbanding on a whim. Marzuk ground his teeth. Answers to direct questions required thought. He would owe Yellow King, would be conferring a considerable amount of kudos to him.

"Yeah," Marzuk said. "I got pinged at home. They know where I live, man."

I'm dreaming of Kali. Will you laugh if I tell you that some program is making the leap from the ether directly to my brain, without any interface? Have we somehow evolved into something I don't know about?

"Heavy shit," Yellow King said. "By the way, ask your friend ReGi to write back, will you?"

Marzuk hated using the family car and driver. Cars were archaic devices to begin with, and this driver was a positive dinosaur. He had

---

*In honor of Koçulu, a champion of open source, who briefly brought web development down by deleting his original program called left-pad.

been the fifth human to hold and carry Marzuk as a newborn. This apparently gave him the right to pull his cheeks, make insulting comments, steal his things, and generally act like a cackling demonic ass.

Most megacities had long ago banned private transportation within central bounds. In post flood apocalyptic Dhaka, however, public transport was a myth. The grids of armed walls and checkpoints, the hodgepodge of different legal entities, the cannon-mawed gated communities, the vast liquid sprawls of lawless urban zoos; the situation required a different kind of vehicle.

Marzuk's family vehicle was an ancient Tata-Mercedes hover tank. It was powered by jets of air and magnets and could traverse broken roads, ditches, rice paddies, even small lakes. The metal parts were armored against rioters using space station meteor-proofing technology. The glass was a new-age form that was actually a latticework of bots set in a flexible crystal, essentially a semi sentient piece of hardware that could adjust to diverse conditions like strong sunlight, projectile fire, and multiple collisions. There were grooves along the hood where he suspected machine guns might once have nestled. Nowadays it was frowned upon to open fire on the hoi polloi, and these weapons had been tactfully removed.

It was, he realized, a rather flashy car, in an old-school kind of way. While his parents weren't particularly rich, the Khan Rahman clan in general had widespread tentacles, and from time to time these reminders popped up in his everyday life.

Moving around the autonomous enclave of Baridhara was quite tough, requiring numerous surveillance checks and finally a concrete barrier manned by bored paramilitary, hired by the ubiquitous security organization Securex. They tapped his windows, picked their teeth, peered into the car with a kind of bucolic fascination. The trunk had to be searched, then the hood and various other orifices of the car, all with a laconic insolence. It seemed that if you lived in the enclave, you had no reason to go out, and if you lived elsewhere, you had no business coming in.

Marzuk felt all the outrage of the wholly innocent when set upon by armed louts. He scrolled through various options and then realized, belatedly, that for all his rage and power he was relatively impotent in this situation and would just have to bear it. Eventually the guards registered that he was not a desperate farmer terrorist and waved him on. The driver, in a flash of rage, hawked a gigantic wad of phlegm out of the window. It summed up the situation admirably.

The school took up an entire block of Baridhara, which, given current property prices, was worth the annual budget of many mid-level city-states. High red walls and medieval-looking gun turrets announced the management's very serious intention of protecting the students. Inside was a massive former airport hangar, an interactive building capable of fulfilling almost any public function. The empty central space was made of plant gel, which could morph into a park, or a sporting arena, or even a vast amphitheater. The school maintained its own microclimate, so the weather was slightly different in here, a few degrees cooler, verging on unpleasantly crisp; a patent waste of money because the Tri-State Corp. (which comprised Baridhara, Banani, and Gulshan boroughs) was easily the richest in Dhaka and already maintained a perfect A-level microclimate comparable to any other luxe environment in the world.

The hologram guide led him around, a squat Mongolian gentleman in a flight attendant's outfit—another leftover feature from the now-defunct airport software. Marzuk concluded that the school must have bought the building lump-sum from some derelict international hub. They had done nothing to customize the program. Most likely they just wanted to boast about having a level 3 AI on their brochures, a colossal waste of money.

Many of the interior walls were plant gel, some of them green and flowering, some of them thin wafers of translucence. It was like walking through a bizarre, costly forest all the time. The school could afford it, with the fees they charged. A small stream meandered through the compound, looping around, teeming in places with rare fish, widening in others to allow swimming. Marzuk followed it for a time, enjoying the gurgling sounds. Meanwhile, most of the students appeared to be locked up in rooms. The establishment, he noted, had an old-fashioned attitude toward physically attending class.

As he continued to wander about, the Mongolian aviation software became more and more agitated, until he eventually started sounding a small bird call alarm. Taking pity on him, Marzuk corrected his path and made his way to the superintendent's office, which was in a high tower accessible only by elevator. Presumably this had been the control center of the hangar. Somewhere in this building was a sealed chamber that housed the liquid core of the AI that ran the property; in other words: the mind of the Mongolian. The thought gave him a little frisson of excitement. He had never seen one up close.

The superintendent was a very pompous gentleman from Virginia who was protected from the general public by a phalanx of secretaries. He seemed vaguely puzzled by this meeting, and well he should be, since it had crept into his schedule only two days ago, when Marzuk had paid a student to hack his office. It was a simple, archaic hack, essentially a wireless keylogger that stole the passwords of an administrative assistant using her desk and sent them over to the Cyber Mage. It was unbelievable. She used vocal commands without even bothering to digitally alter her voice. Many older people did that, he had noticed—they ignored the telepathic functionality of their Echos and instead clung to the habits of their youth.

Over the course of the day, Marzuk had filched the life of this lady: her work accounts, her personal avatars, the two social games she played, the dating site she visited, even the mild pornography she watched during lunch. It had been easy enough to bump his name up the interview list. The only trouble, in fact, had been trying to gauge the IQ scores necessary to land in ninth grade.

"Master Marzuk Dotrozi KR, is it?" the Super said. "This is irregular. Where are your parents?"

"I'm emancipated." Marzuk flashed his papers. "Sponsored by my aunt. It's all in the files. Your lawyers have already verified it."

"I see," the Super said. "And you wish to join us?"

"Ninth grade," Marzuk said.

"Well, I must say I have some concerns."

"About?"

"Frankly, this is a very expensive institution," the Super said. "We are normally paid by corporations to house the children of top executives." The pomposity buffed imaginary dust from his nails. "At last count we were the eighty-ninth most expensive private school in the world..."

"The credit check is in the registration file."

"Yes, er, but I'm concerned that there has been some kind of mistake. Surely you can understand, a child of your age, no means of support, no *company backing*..."

Marzuk, who had expected this, took out a small black marble. It was densely heavy, cold to the touch. He put it on the desk and rolled it gently toward the superintendent. The man looked at him in bemusement, his neck creeping forward like an ostrich's. The ball stopped of its own volition a foot from the edge and rotated. A pin-prick of blue light beaded its matte black body and projected a series of numbers onto the desk. Binary code scrolled for several seconds and was replaced by an algorithm flashing repeatedly.

"Bank of Shanghai," Marzuk said. "Blackball. Very high credit rating. You don't think they give that to any riffraff, do you?"

"Hmm, I've heard of these." The Super looked confused. "I suppose your aunt is... ?"

"Yes, she's a celebrity, we go incognito most of the time," Marzuk lied. What was it about old-people brains that couldn't accept plain facts?

"And your parents?" the Super asked hesitantly.

"Paralyzed, both of them, terrible accident," Marzuk said. "They can barely communicate. Vegetables. I'm sorry. I break down if I think about it."

"Of course, of course, terribly sorry... Their names?"

"I can't say, whole family is incognito. We are Khan Rahmans... You *have* heard of us, haven't you?"

"Of course, I've heard of your... grandfather."

Ha! Got you. That old name still works. Too bad we're not from the rich side of the fam...

"Now, about registration: I've got a schedule of classes I want to take with the times and teachers all filled in. You can see I've passed all the relevant tests. Everything is in order; I am prepared to start right away. Oh, and I won't be needing the psych counselor; I've got an affidavit here from my friend Dr. Omar verifying my mental health. And you can leave out the extracurriculars, I won't be needing those either; I've got an Ergonomic 9000 chair that takes care of all my exercising. In case of illness, I have my own nominated physicians; I'd appreciate it if you would tag them into your insurance feed. I will avail myself of your helicopter pickup service, my lawyer will contact you with details regarding security..."

"Hmm, yes, most comprehensive, Master Dotrozi," the Super said. "I'm glad your aunt has been so thorough. I would appreciate meeting her sometime."

I'm sure you would, letch!

"You will follow the curriculum, like all the other students, including gym class. We are equipped with a state-of-the-art medical sarcophagus; while you are a student here, you shall rely entirely on our school nurse."

"I see." *Sarcophagus? Are you expecting me to die here? Do you harvest organs? What the hell do you need that kind of hardware for?*

"Furthermore, you shall use the school bus like all of the other students. It is mandatory."

"A bus? Like an actual rectangular thing with wheels and seats?"

"Yes. We have traditions to maintain. This is one of our most cherished."

"I see." *God help me.*

"And finally, as to security, you will notice that we have fully equipped missile towers, an Iron Dome, and a full AI to defend the premises," the superintendent said. "In addition, I have Dr. Yakub of Securex Inc. on speed dial. He is a personal friend. We are their largest client; they have assured us of their best service in any emergency, god forbid. Finally, in case they fail, I also have the personal number of Colonel Barkud, second-in-command of the Dhaka North Army Cantonment, a most reliable gentleman. I hope I have assuaged any fears you have regarding security?"

"Perfectly." *You have missile turrets and an Iron Dome and the army protecting you? Is this a school or a bloody cocaine lab?* "I'm ready to join. I will begin tomorrow."

"Just a moment, young man. We have a slight dilemma. With your tests, to be precise."

"What?"

"The computer has analyzed your test-taking patterns, and has estimated that you are in fact an extremely cunning grad student. Possibly faking low marks for some ulterior motive."

"What?" *I timed myself perfectly! The airport AI is a dumbass.*

"We cannot possibly place you in the schedule you're demanding," the Super said. "The computer thinks you might be qualified to *teach* some of these classes."

"You do realize that your computer is an airport management system?"

"It is a state-of-the-art slaved AI," the superintendent said. "We are one of the few international schools in the world to have one." He sniffed.

"Right. It's doing a super job, I'm sure." *It's a fucking moron. You've been had. This thing is chimp level at best.*

"I can see from your attitude that you are what we call a 'gifted' child," the Super said. "No doubt your celebrity aunty has been indulging you. In my establishment, however, we value discipline. We do not stand for—"

"Bullying!" Marzuk burst out.

"What's that?"

"Bullying," Marzuk said. "Last school, I was bullied. They don't like younger kids in higher grades. Social dynamics. My emotional quotient is very low. I will have trouble later holding down a job or getting a promotion because I cannot interact socially. I need to be in my peer set to develop interpersonal skills." *Job? Ha! You peon. Jobs are so last century.*

"Hmm, we do not tolerate bullying in my establishment," the Super said. "However, I take your point; your interpersonal skills are certainly terrible."

Thanks for the encouragement. It's exactly people like you damaging us introvert types.

"What's more, given your size and low level of physical fitness, I believe you might face difficulties at higher grades," the Super said. "You would be a social pariah."

What? I'm in peak physical condition, you oaf! The Ergonomic 9000...

"We shall allow you to start. I will personally monitor your lessons. You will be kept under close observation," the Super said. "And don't expect any preferential treatment."

"Of course not, Super." *Super.*

5

Pop Den

Pop Den. Population density. Twenty-five years ago, an obscure engineering economist named Professor Kabir from Hertfordshire College had published a small book on population density and certain macro trends. He posited that given a) the growing disparity in wealth between the 1 percenters and the insolvent 99 percent, b) the acceleration of climatic dysfunction, and c) the rampant proliferation of nanotech and other little-understood technological phenomena, any sort of bearable life on Earth would be viable only for clusters of sufficient population density. The gist of his argument was that while the technology existed to make pockets of Earth habitable and, indeed, almost utopian, it would require a density of wealth and people such that only the rich would enjoy it. From an economic point of view, it would *not* be cost effective to try to maintain quality standards for sparsely populated areas. Farmland, for example, would be totally useless, as would be farmers. A single lab could grow more food than acres and acres of freehold.

Indeed, the conclusion by Professor Kabir was that a paradigm shift was occurring. Hitherto the elite, equity-owning class and the masses had always been connected by a single thread: labor. Mass labor was required for military use, for food production, and in the recent past, for industrial production. This equation had forced the elite to deal with the labor class with some degree of leniency, and more importantly, *to expend resources in preserving to some degree the habitat of this labor*. Now, these workers were wholly superfluous. Military labor was specialized or droned, food production was lab driven, and industrial production was entirely automated. What value, then, did these people hold in the new economy? The answer was depressing: zero. The new economy would wrap entirely around the super rich, those with *capital* buffeted by a glorified servant class of the very skilled, the mad, the creative, the peddlers of the bizarre.

This very dry paper, written in a rambling style, often with bizarre digressions, had been dismissed as yet another crackpot pamphlet predicting the Rapture. At the same time, Dr. Nuri Okami of Chennai

University had published a paper on the corporatization of the modern world. She had noted that since corporations enjoyed vastly superior legal protection compared to any other entity, from individuals to nations, it was logical for population segments in countries to throw off archaic assumptions of statehood and instead adopt a wholly corporate structure. Her paper was in fact arguing for the end of the idea of commonwealth altogether, the end of public space or public service, the concept of personal ownership taken to the zenith, until even each square inch of sky and ocean and air was parceled out.

The actual impact of these two theories was felt five years later, when Singapore became the first country to throw off nationhood and adopt a corporate identity. All the useful citizens were given voting stock; the lowest were given nominal single shares, not useful for any political power, but a valuable badge of equity, the new form of citizenship. Non-shareholders were asked to leave the premises. The fact was, the corporate masters of the world had already determined a post scarcity future, and human labor or, for that matter, consumption, just wasn't really necessary for the equation.

Now, two decades later, the world predicted by Kabir and Okami had come to pass. Pop Den was a theory that *worked*. Subsistence farmers were not necessary when kitchen units synthesized food from lab-manufactured seaweed and protein cells. Microclimates were maintained at great cost, but only for the high per capita income holders, and the press of bodies required to maintain that nanotech count. Cities survived. Countries did not; at least not in the practical sense of a cohesive political power. While people might still refer to nations as a geographic area out of nostalgia, it was actually replaced by a kludge of corporate fiefdoms with over lapping interests and authority.

Nanotech worked really well in high-density areas. It essentially used human bodies to produce bio-compatible molecules that spewed into the air with every exhaled breath, through every human pore; invisible spores that fought disease, scrubbed carbon, controlled the temperature and water, *useful stuff*. Climate control AIs used these micro machines to create safe climates, to fight off bad nanotech, to create the invisible bubbles in which humans lived. This was next-level tech, and with it came the euphoria that given enough warm bodies, *any* place could be terraformed, from the moon to Mars. It was a whole new ecosystem, this time entirely man-made but subject to the whims of evolution nonetheless. The human poor were only as useful as the biotech they incubated in their bodies.

For this reason, places such as Mirpur in Dhaka, Bangladesh, still thrived, while the interior of what had been the United States was now largely a rabid prairie filled with mad roaming post apocalyptic gypsies.

New York knew what Pop Den meant. Lagos knew what Pop Den meant. Entire nations of Scandinavians had become extinct because they couldn't muster the numbers to make nanotech environments effective. The nanotech was mostly biological, incubated in human bodies, freely exchanging with the environment, essentially a cloud of invisible bugs growing on and off each living human, not dissimilar to the eons-old bacteria in their guts, the literal blood price for belonging in a community. Ironically, this trend had radically increased the demand for refugees, but like all good things, by that point most of them had died off or already been corralled.

In the ghettos, anything went. The corporate structure was fast and loose. If the crowds rioted, they were given food, printers, sometimes a scattering of sat minutes so they could enjoy the Virtuality. They had limited legal protection, although in the corporate feeding frenzy no one knew which courts exactly would enforce this. No one was going to cluster-bomb them from space. On the ground, what they did to each other was a different matter, one of no concern to outsiders.

In his own way, Djibrel understood Pop Den very well. It meant he could walk around swinging the talking head of a dead kobiraj from his belt, and no one would say a word. And it *was* a talking head, though now it occupied a jar filled with a nutrient soup charged with an electric current that kept the organ alive. The mouth had a synthesizer attached, so the brain could communicate thoughts via its slowly dying neural pathways to a computer that spurted out words in a woman's voice.

It amused Djibrel to give the kobiraj a woman's voice, because he knew that it was driving the fundamentalist head crazy. The brain would not last for very long like this. The warranty had said two weeks. That was enough for Djibrel. Every once in a while, he would duck into a tea stall and take the head out. He would shake it until the kobiraj opened his eyes, and then start asking questions.

It was a peculiar situation for the kobiraj. He had expected divine intervention by this point. In his inner heart he had expected to go to hell, because he had consorted with djinn. Confusedly, he had also expected God to intervene and take him to heaven, because he was a mullah. To be kept in a jar had not been in his calculations. Still, he had nothing to do but talk to his captor. The inside of his skull had not been a pleasant place to live when he had been alive. He had been crowded by fears, insecurities, and grasping ambitions. It had not gotten any better with death. All things considered, conversation was a boon under these circumstances, even if he had the voice of a blasted woman.

Djibrel hated all religious people. Somewhere in his youth, they had done bad things to him. His memories of those times were not clear, but he remembered being locked in a wooden box for many hours at a time, as well as being beaten, starved, and raped. If he delved further, he might remember more, but this was not of real concern to him. Djibrel's mind worked like a series of ledgers, and it was weighted heavily against the mullahs. It was their bad luck collectively that the small orphan Djibrel had grown into the street sipahi Djibrel, who had a very special sword and an inclination to settle old debts.

The sword was often mistaken—by blade aficionados—for a priceless relic of the Middle Ages. In reality, it was a very modern weapon disguised as an old one, made in a cave by a djinn blacksmith. In that way, Djibrel and the sword were kin, because he had been remade in the same cave, his mind a diamond fort, each neuron sheathed in ghost particles, each bone and sinew forged in dragon flame and the incantations of the Marid Bahamut, eldest of djinn, who lived in the sea. In flashes, Djibrel recalled two djinn working on him, Bahamut and the taciturn blacksmith, and looming around them a vast serpent breathing fire, fire that reset his DNA and even the memories encoded in his cells. He remembered tremendous pain, and quiet words from the blacksmith, which soothed him.

When he had awoken, however, the others were gone and he was underwater in a bubble of air. Bahamut appeared as a vast school of fish, sharp-toothed, razor-finned, alien—fish like he had never seen before. The djinn's voice caused the sea to reverberate and rumble. He floated between pillars, ruins of some ancient city. In the distance there appeared to be a fiery gate, although how this could be possible was beyond him.

Growing up by the river, Djibrel had heard stories of the djinn Bahamut, eldest of his race, one who sometimes saved errant fishermen, plucked them out of the storm and set them safely on some bit of land, who took no offerings but granted wishes on a whim. It was not Bahamut they feared when they set sail into the deathly waters of the bay. He was not the worst of djinn.

"You are awake, golem," the djinn said. "Do you know me?"

"You are a djinn," Djibrel said. "What have you done to me?"

"You fell in the river, boy," Bahamut said. "You died. In your last drowning breath, you invoked my name."

"Yes," Djibrel said. "To save me. Not this... whatever you've done."

"Hmm, yes. Unfortunately I could not. There was too little of you left. So I preserved you, and when the time was right I remade you. You should thank me. You will not die so easily the next time."

"And now I am your agent, I suppose," Djibrel said. He knew a shakedown when he saw one.

"We have something in common, my boy. Common enemies, people you hate."

"I hate everybody," Djibrel said.

"Splendid. That's the spirit. You're exactly the kind of partner I wanted."

"Who do you want me to kill, Bahamut?"

"Do you see that gate of fire, golem?"

"It would be bloody hard not to."

"Somewhere in the city there is a little rat who is gnawing at my gate. For what purpose? I do not know."

"Wait, wait, by rat do you mean an actual rat? Or, like, a sneaky human?"

The school of fish formed a giant offended face. "How could an actual rat do that? Of course I meant a man-type thing."

"Look, is it a man, then?"

"A man, or a sorcerer, or a djinn, or a group of them. I sense the fell hand of my enemy Matteras, last descendant of the putrid royal line of Gangaridai, the scourge of humanity, the causer of earthquakes—"

"Wait, is it this djinn Matteras you want me to off?"

"Hmph. You might not be up to it yet, but yes, stab him if you get the chance. But more importantly, I want you to find this person who is interfering with my gate. Someone employed by Matteras and his allies. They have some project with computers and djinn and human experiments, and I don't like it. I want you to hunt them down and stop it."

"Yeah, okay, sure."

"YOU HAVE BEEN FORGED IN DRAGON FIRE. A SMIDGEN MORE ENTHUSIASM, PLEASE!"

"Of course, yes, I live for the hunt. I am a predator. 'Attack' is literally my first name!"

"GOOD." The djinn seemed slightly mollified. The giant fish face beamed. "Here is a sword. It is also forged in dragon fire. It is a gift from Indelbed."

"The blind blacksmith?"

"You remember him! Wonderful."

"Very vaguely. He was nice. He took the pain away."

"Yes, he's sappy like that. Enough chitchat. NOW RETURN, GOLEM, AND MAKE MY ENEMIES TREMBLE!"

And thus, on the vaguest set of instructions, Djibrel found himself cutting off heads and then asking questions. This free rein suited him, given his problems with authority. Bahamut in fact disappeared altogether, and at times Djibrel was inclined to wonder whether he had imagined the entire episode. Of course, his own changed body, his sword, and the number of people trying to kill him were timely reminders to the contrary. Still, this cutting-off-heads business was not all about self-indulgence. The headless kobiraj was named Abbas Ali. Abbas Ali was on the edge of a new phenomenon, a semi hidden cult coalescing around the djinn, the half djinn, and the muddy ground in between.

Lines had been blurred long ago, lines that kept the djinn and humans apart. Traditions were eroding. Nanotech was destroying the genome, both human and djinn. Vertical gene transfer had changed to horizontal, to near instantaneous. Mutations crowded the horizon. In the midst of all this, somebody was being naughty. Djinn had disappeared without a trace. Emissaries had disappeared. Storied names of the conservative party, like Hazard and Matteras, were being thrown around as up to something big. Finally, there was a gate underwater, leading to a more fundamental dimension where long ago the djinn had moved their First City, the fabled Gangaridai. How exactly an entire city and its people had been taken from this earth was not clear, but it was well-known that elder djinn had been very powerful. Bahamut protected this gate, to stop other djinn from crossing over as well as to prevent things from the other side from coming in. His exact words, in fact, had been "I'm not a damned station master. I don't want a lot of bloody people going back and forth." So when some agent of Matteras (presumably) came tickling around the gate, Bahamut wanted answers.

Or so Djibrel imagined. Bahamut was not communicative. But if Bahamut gave a man a sword, he surely wanted some heads cut.

To the corrupt mullah, Djibrel said: "Some of your friends are doing unnatural things."

"It is God's will," Abbas Ali said, "to destroy all infidels, human and djinn alike. We but do his work. In the hymn of the sword—"

"Spare me the hymn," Djibrel said. "What I want to know is where you do this work, and quite possibly why. Provided you know these answers, I am willing to make an offer to you."

"I seek only paradise. Know that the wrath of the angels will fall upon you soon."

"Who exactly is Sekmet?"

"Pray you never meet her, sipahi," Abbas Ali sneered. "She is the most terrible of all djinn."

"You called to her when I cut your head off. Do you pray now to djinn?"

"We pray for the cleansing release of martyrdom; for when she comes, there is only death."

"This jar is keeping your head alive. Now, you are a religious man," Djibrel said. "I could ice your brain and put you in a game. There are people who do that for real, you know, give up their bodies and live in the game forever? Komagemu. Coma gamers. You'd be in a camp, though, as some warlord's sex slave. You'd think it was real. It *would* be real. Forever. No logging off."

"You would do this vile thing?"

"I cut your head off, didn't I?"

"Ask your questions, then."

"Who am I dealing with here? What are the djinn doing here in secret?"

"You know nothing," Abbas Ali said sadly. "End my suffering, and I will grant you a boon. You seek the coder, who writes something sacred, which will change the world. In turn, there are two who hunt you. Sekmet of the sword. Karmon the misshapen one. You will not survive contact with either, sipahi. Neither is human."

"Neither am I," said the golem.

6

Lockers

On Marzuk's first day of school he was stuffed into a locker. Apparently the other children didn't take too kindly to smart-alecky remarks from noobs. The Neanderthal who assaulted him then stood and watched, jeering with laughter, as he tried to extricate himself with minimal damage. The siren went off for the next class, and the annoying airport greeter started popping up everywhere, urging students not to be late. Finally, the halls emptied.

"You are late by 15.4 seconds." The Mongolian flight attendant now took a position directly in front of Marzuk's locker.

"I'm in a locker, you imbecile," Marzuk said. "Help me out."

"Do you require assistance from security?"

Security? What is that here? Some more half-wits come to manhandle me and laugh about it? No thanks.

"Did you get visuals of my attackers?" Marzuk said. "Have you reported this?"

"My auto-report function has been disabled," the Mongolian said. "Most students in your position do not wish their activities to be reported."

"Really? Why?" Marzuk asked, interested.

"It leads to further, escalated acts of bullying," the Mongolian said. "Revenge assaults, perpetrated by the original attacker or their friends. The price of being a snitch."

"I see." *This is a barbaric place.*

"I believe if you lower your shoulder by fifteen degrees and unhook your right knee, you should be able to get out."

"Thanks," Marzuk said. He got out. "So what am I supposed to do?"

"I believe that statistically the safest course is for you to ignore the incident and avoid coming into contact with the belligerent parties."

"Ignore it? I don't think I can do that."

"Would you like me to report the incident, Mr. Marzuk?"

"No," Marzuk said. "I'll handle it. I'm late for my next class."

Waiting for the bus, Marzuk was left to rue a highly unsatisfactory day. He had exchanged barely two words with Amina. Like all pretty girls, she was always surrounded by people. Marzuk had spent his entire time fending off petty assaults from numerous directions. In Phys Ed, he had received a humbling lesson in how unfit he was. This had further endeared him to the bullies, who had taken the opportunity to steal his shoes in the locker room. He'd had to walk around in disposable slippers until the teacher finally tracked down his sneakers and gave them back with the admonishment to take better care of his stuff. Already fuming, he got to his class late and was roundly told off by this *next* imbecile instructor in front of everyone. This was music history class, something Marzuk knew nothing about, so he couldn't even vent his spleen by mouthing off. Most unsatisfactory, all in all.

He got home and had to waste thirty minutes explaining everything to his mother, who was unduly interested in the minutiae of the day. She kept gushing at him, saying things like "I never thought this day would come," and "Oh, my boy is finally in high-school." Then she produced her all-time-favorite guilt trip.

"I've cooked your favorite, dear, spaghetti with beef curry. I'm sure you're hungry, we never eat together anymore..."

You mean the kitchen unit has cooked this unimaginably foul version of a local classic... "Well, Mother, if it means that much to you, I will sit here." *I am, in fact, hungry, since the oaf Hinku Hajmatulla spat in my stroganoff.*

"So, did you learn anything new?"

"Mom, it's the ninth grade," Marzuk said. "The teachers are lumbering dinosaurs with one foot in the grave, eking out the years before they get their undeserved pensions."

"And did you make any friends?" Mother went on, oblivious. "I always worry about you, Maru; a boy your age should have a lot of friends..."

"I have friends, Mom!" Marzuk said. *ReGi. And my boys on the gaming sites. So no. No live ones. Does Babr count?*

"And girls, dear," Mother continued. "I wish you'd..."

Amina. How humiliating that my first day should be a disaster. Perhaps she has heard. Perhaps tomorrow she'll start avoiding me. Where is the boy who drinks wine, and travels, and attends his fashionista aunt's parties? How can that boy be shoved into lockers by a Neanderthal like Hinku? What kind of name is Hinku? How has he survived with such a ridiculous name? And how is he so muscular? Should I take steroids? What are the hazards?

"Okay, Mom, I have to do some consulting," Marzuk said. "The Russians, you know, they wait for no man..."

"I really wish you'd stop hanging out with those Russian types," Mother said. "They're too old for you... And I want to meet their parents... I'm sure they're drinking and smoking all the time..." The litany continued well out of his hearing range as he deftly crossed the line into his domain, where minuscule speakers aimed soothing music at his head, drowning out parental lamentations.

In his room he fed Babr, who was sulking, and spent a few minutes playing toss the tree. Evolution had made Babr predisposed to knocking down trees, and his adoption had required Marzuk to purchase a line of bonsai for the elephant to abuse.

Then ReGi pinged him, and he put everything away and cowled up.

"'Sup, baby boy," ReGi said.

"Hey, terrible day," Marzuk said. "Big mistake going to school."

"Oh yeah, school, huh?" ReGi said. "You're being dumb. Why would you put yourself through that shit? What's the point of being a genius if you have to go to school with all the other scrubs?"

"Did I not tell you about Amina?" Marzuk asked. "She's, like, amazingly hot." It occurred to him that ReGi was a girl, but for all he knew she could actually be smoking hot. She was a digital guru after all, a master of avatars. Hard to say what was real.

"Now you're wondering whether I'm hot too, right?"

"That's uncanny."

"Well, considering that I'm thousands of miles away, you're better off concentrating on Amina," she said. "How did that shit go down?"

"There's a douche called Hinku who's been picking on me."

"Like?"

"He shoved me into a locker, he knocked my books off, shit like that."

"Oh." ReGi laughed. "Serves you right, really. Still, has he *not* seen the clip of that satellite falling on that kid's house?"

"Apparently not."

"I thought everyone alive had seen that..."

"Not everyone, ReGi," Marzuk said. "Just people like us. You know, I'm now realizing that there's a shitload of other people out there with no interest in real life."

"You mean virtual life."

"Whatever, yeah, I mean, important shit. Like knowledge of the programming elements that control ninety-nine percent of their world, including the lifesaving climate control systems, not to mention basic shit like food—"

"Preaching to the choir."

"Right, right, sorry."

"Anyway, what are you planning to do to this guy? Remember, you got a lot of corporate heat from the last incident. They played stories about hackers running amok for six months."

"Yeah, I'm not sure," Marzuk said. "It's a weird microcosm there, ReGi. I can't explain it. It's like all these people are clueless. I have to think about it. I don't want to look like a psycho or get expelled. At the same time, half the shit I could do to him, he wouldn't even know it was me. I don't even care about him. I mean, it's nothing personal, I just don't want to look like a fool in front of Amina."

"You like this girl, huh?"

"You think?"

"You're a dumbass," ReGi said. "But at least you're on the right track. Wasting this guy definitely wouldn't impress Amina. Just ask her out."

"I can't go in cold like that. I spoke to her in passing, but it wasn't like she was uber friendly or anything. I want to soften her up a bit. What would work on you?"

"Work on me?"

"Yeah, has no one ever hit on you?"

"Marzuk, I'm a real girl who kicks ass on the net. Nerds are drooling over me whenever I log on. Do you know how many pings I get every second I'm online? And no, I don't remember any cheesy pickup lines you can use."

"Yeah, yeah, you're cyber royalty, we all know that," Marzuk said. "Speaking of which, I got in touch with Yellow King, did I tell you? About the Kali thing."

"You brought that tool in?"

"Tool?"

"Remember the thing about nerds drooling?"

"Yellow King and you? Really?"

"Well he tried, anyway," ReGi said.

"Hmm, I always thought of him as a handsome man..."

"You kiss him, then. What did he say?"

"He said he'd study it, like he's Batman or something. Fucking pompous. And what's up with his name?"

"He's in love with that Carcosa shit. Used to keep going on about it."

"That's interesting."

"What?"

"Well, earlier you implied he was a nerd admiring you from afar, but your subsequent syntax makes it seem like you spent some quality time with the guy. Like maybe you dated or something. He asked you to write back, by the way."

"Shut up."

"Not kidding. Literally the only thing he wanted was your sweet, sweet words…"

"Focus, dumbass," ReGi said. "Why are you so interested in my life all of a sudden?"

"You're just too damn secretive," Marzuk said. "It's unfair. You know everything about my life, including probably the color of my boxers."

"Eww."

"Right."

"And feed Babr some health food, dumbass. He's been farting the whole day."

"What?"

"Oh yeah, I was bored, so I reconfigured some of your cams to stream *out*."

"Don't get excited," Marzuk said. "I've got you on soft security." Marzuk's systems were staggered. Due to his parents' continual and bumbling interference, he had been forced to create a minimum-security layer that allowed certain individuals to use his stuff without setting off the nukes. Once, he had fallen asleep in the chair after thirty-four hours of straight raiding. His mother had tried to turn his screens off and somehow tripped a red alert, causing many of his hard drives to melt and almost setting off an electromagnetic bomb that would have effectively blacked out all of Gulshan. She had a superpower to mess up electronics by just being in the vicinity.

"Really?" ReGi asked.

"Yeah, you're my next-of-kin thing. My notification-of-death person."

"Jeez, thanks for asking first."

"Well, I couldn't very well list my parents after I took the trouble to get emancipated. They'd be laughing at me. Plus they wouldn't know what to do during system meltdown."

"Little boys and their egos..."

"So did you and Yellow King, like, trade nudes and stuff?"

"Ewww."

"I can find out, you know..."

"Yeah right."

"Since you've been streaming my cams in, you've been receiving minute packets of random data, which, when activated, will create a small backdoor for me."

"What?"

"No, but I could have easily," Marzuk said. "So tell me, you and Yellow King..."

"A brief flirtation," ReGi said. "And I wouldn't trust him overly..."

"A woman scorned..."

"Har har. I looked into your data a bit more. Kali is something sentient."

"Meaning?"

"Meaning it's not some cunning autobot someone has set on you," ReGi said. "And I talked to some people in Seoul. People who make signature black bots for corps. It's too expensive for this kind of attack, and they weren't even sure they'd be able to make something to hit you that hard."

"Hmm, maybe it's the Russians," Marzuk said. "I'm not wont to distrust my business partners, but they are borderline criminals, after all."

"They're straight-up criminals."

"Okay, fine."

"Anyway, I think you should go back to focusing on Djibrel."

"Why?"

"He's killing more people. Not even hiding it anymore. Like, he's walking around with heads and shit. It's getting out of hand."

"It's weird, it's like he's invisible or something. How come none of the security agencies are doing anything about it?"

"Yeah right, like they care if the cardless kill each other off. They're not going to do shit until he crosses into an enclave or goes after big game."

"You know," Marzuk said, "this Kali thing started happening pretty soon after you got me hooked on Djibrel. Think they're related?"

"Sure, maybe she's, like, his big ten-armed djinn fairy godmother."

"You wouldn't be laughing if she came after you."

7

Lucid Dreaming

Marzuk was realizing that homework, even to a brain of his caliber, was a dull and tedious thing. It was further exasperating because he was the kind of guy who actually *liked* learning things, and ingesting information was like breathing to him, and years of poring over random data had increased his capacity to be nerdy beyond superhuman levels, which led him to question how in the world his geology teacher could possibly make her lesson too boring even for him. Thirty-two varieties of feldspar and a ten-page essay on their minute differences; when the images started to meld in his brain, he was forced to switch off and call it a night.

Two a.m., and he was ready for bed. This was another problem with school; it required him to wake up physically at some time perilously close to dawn. They had rejected his multiple requests for an alternate schedule, and even shot down his helicopter transport proposal. It was in the armored pod at six a.m. sharp, followed by thirty minutes of jerking, traffic-scarred commute enlivened by the mind-numbing jokes of the asinine juveniles who shared his route. It was no wonder that people didn't mix with their neighbors anymore.

People in the physical realm were such a disappointment. They sweated, they smelled bad, they were clumsy and stupid and breathed too loud. In Moscow they had transport pods on magnetic lines, seemingly hovering in the air. In Dhaka the buildings were too close together, the density too deep to even consider such a thing. Marzuk had proposed a new transport system to the Tri-State authority last year, but they had summarily shot it down.

He was loath to admit that sleeping was a bit of a dicey proposition for him these days. Kali dreams were recurring with increased force, and he was waking up every morning haggard, with flashing images of octopus surgeons slicing up his brain with multiple scalpels. He was losing weight and dark circles had appeared around his eyes. People were actually accusing him of drinking! Sleep, the one thing he had consistently fought his whole life, was now striking back. If only they had a pill for it... He was relieved to hear the urgent flash of a message just as the lights were dimming. ReGi! Possibly with a solution!

"Whatup, homie," he said.

"Cute pajamas," she said.

"Wow, you really like stalkering me."

"It's 'stalking,' fool, and yeah, I have a live feed of you sleeping."

"Er, that's a little bit creepy."

"Don't worry, I'm not filming anything south of the border."

"Great," Marzuk said. "And if I moan out your name, it's because it's a nightmare."

"I've been recording your REM sleep. Do you know anything about lucid dreaming?"

"Caltech did a bunch of studies back in the day, I thought," Marzuk said. "Wasn't there an old movie about it?"

"Yeah, it's a real psychological phenomenon.* Most people don't know they're dreaming, but a small percentage of people experience lucid dreaming, where they are allegedly aware they are in a dream and can effect logical steps to wake up or whatever," ReGi said. "Basically, the eye movements during a dream sometimes mirror the physical eye movements of the dreamer. So the experiment was that they trained lucid dreamers to send signals with their eyes at the onset of a lucid dream. This was replicated a bunch of times, and the concept of lucid dreams was established as a scientific fact."

"Hence the movie, I imagine."

"Well, anyway, your basic interaction with Kali is during nightmares, right?"

"I can see where this is going."

"Right, well, you just have to become a lucid dreamer. In that state, you have access to cognitive functions of logic and analysis that are normally shut down during sleep."

"I thought this was a freak aberration."

"The doctors basically trained their subjects to develop this skill, but that was a longish process, plus those guys are pretty much all dead now, so they wouldn't be helpful to you anyway."

"Hmm, but I presume there were some practical applications from their science," Marzuk said, feeling a quickening pulse of interest.

---

*Stephen LaBerge, "Lucid Dreaming: Psychophysiological Studies of Consciousness during REM Sleep," in *Sleep and Cognition*, eds. R. R. Bootzen, J. F. Kihlstrom, and D. L. Schacter (Washington, D.C.: American Psychological Association, 1990) 109–26.

"Bingo. Virtual reality. Total immersion project."

"Sega?"

"Right. Most virtual reality went for immersing the *waking* mind with fake sensations: you know, the laser images into the eye, the electrodes stimulating your nerves and the smell and taste centers of the brain directly—"

"Yeah, yeah, you're talking to a gamer, remember? I've done all that shit. The brain tends to have a lot of seizures in total VR. Most one-hundred-percent VR immersion tech is stuck in multiple lawsuits worldwide. Even my Russians have warrants against them for illegal VR."

"They're into gaming too?"

"Porn, actually," Marzuk said. "And virtual drugs. They tried to re-create heroin use without the actual heroin. Turns out the virtual kind is even more addictive than the vegetative stuff. The first hundred cyberjunkies are still plugged in. It's been five years now; they're refusing to come out."

"Interesting. I guess it makes sense; all the addictive centers *are* located in the brain. Why bother with the rest of the body?" ReGi said. "Back to Sega: their Total Immersion Project went at VR a different way. They figured a virtual reality is very similar to a dream state. Think about it: in a dream, you're basically reacting to a bunch of imaginary stimuli, and you're absolutely convinced it's real. Their engineers figured that it was a lot easier to trick the sleeping brain into accepting a VR than a conscious one. Enter practical, nightmarish applications of lucid dreaming."

"So they made a console that turns a sleeping person into a lucid dreamer, and then injects them into a game VR?" Marzuk asked. "That's kind of smart. Why didn't it take off?"

"Lawsuits, bankruptcy, the usual for Sega," ReGi said. "The idea was to put people to sleep, have them enter a lucid dream cycle, be in full control, and go off in a totally immersive adventure. The problem was that they ran into another rare phenomenon, 'false awakening.' This is when a person wakes up from a dream and carries on their normal routine, except that they're actually still asleep—they've simply transitioned into another dream, which for some reason is mimicking reality. One of their testers apparently went through this cycle fifty-six times, over a period of eighty days. They had to feed him intravenously."

"I heard about that, that's just an urban myth."

"Nope. I accessed the court records. It's all public information, but buried so deep in other info that only a bot could find it."

"So what happened to the guy?"

"He went into a coma later. No one's sure if he ever left the lucid dream cycle. It torpedoed Sega, that's for sure."

"So this is your great plan? I should utilize this near-lethal tech to confront Kali?"

"Well, this thing is real, and it's getting at you when you sleep. *When you're actually not hooked up to anything.* Can you explain how that's possible?"

"No."

"So think outside the box. When you're dreaming, you're helpless. Imagine if you were lucid when you met this freak."

"I could bring back information."

"You could *negotiate*, homie. Like, figure out what the fuck it wants and get it off your back."

"Not such a bad idea."

"Thanks. The bad news is the hardware. I have no clue how to get it. But I figure you probably have a few more channels than I do."

"Russians?"

"Russians."

"Okay, I'm going to bed now," Marzuk said. "Thanks, ReGi, really. I owe you."

"Yeah, you really do."

Marzuk placed the call to the Russians with a certain amount of trepidation. Due to the unpleasant way the real world continuously intruded on his life, he was prone to be wary when dealing with physical matters. The Russians were part of the mob, more technically called the bratva, the brotherhood, and this particular group ran vast industries, from rare mineral resources, to high-tech VR, to pharmaceuticals, to straight-up black market nanotech. Rumor had it they were also into illegal AI, which was a capital crime in many corporate jurisdictions, as well as *physical* movement of drugs and sex, still popular commodities, apparently, even though they were slowly losing traction to the encroachments of the Virtuality. The Russians, however, assured him physical sex and drugs would never go away.

Marzuk was one of the few people who had a hot line to Fedor, who was in a way the chief Russian, although their upper echelons of command were shadowy and prone to abrupt changes. He had a direct line because he had in effect set up much of their discreet communications backbone, washing their messages through a filter located in the Black Line, a foolproof method of security that'd had their own experts scratching their heads. The Russians did not know about the Black Line. It was a closely guarded secret, an urban myth.

The com system Marzuk had designed was deliberately low-tech. It was a simple chat relay, reminiscent of the IRC boards in the early days of the internet. Voice and picture communication were both allowable as evidence in court, and also used up a lot of bandwidth. The text-based com needed very little juice and was anonymous, fast, and virtually impossible to detect for communication bots trawling the net for private secured conversations to break into. In that sense, it was so low-tech that most surveillance bots didn't recognize it as communication. It was enough to throw off casual intrusions. In the case of a sustained attack, the enemy would use very expensive specifically designed bots anyway, little biting dogs of code approaching artificial intelligence, and encryption wasn't the proper response to that. For those cases the Russians sent people with guns.

"Hi, Fedor." Marzuk opened a private channel that would not appear on the board index.

"Prince Marzuk," Fedor said after a few minutes. "Happy to see you. How are things in Dhaka?" Fedor called Marzuk prince because long ago, when they had first met, Marzuk had dubbed Fedor "the last emperor," after the great MMA champion Fedor Emilianenko.* This moniker had stuck, and once Fedor had started watching the old fights of his namesake, he had fallen in love with the combat sport and adopted the persona.

"I have some breakthroughs on the VR front," Marzuk said.

"Good, because the lawyers are kicking our ass on that," Fedor said.

"There is an alternate VR tech that was a bit of a fringe science," Marzuk said. "Sega. Lucid Dreamcast, it was called; only went to beta, however, before they folded."

"Sega, Sega, why does it sound familiar?"

---

*Fedor "the Last Emperor" Emilianenko: mixed martial artist and heavyweight champion for many years considered the best fighter of all time.

"They're a gaming company known for going in and out of bankruptcy," Marzuk said. "Anyway, thing is, their hardware should still be floating around. They were based in Tokyo."

"That will be hard to get," Fedor said. "Our demesne does not extend to Nippon. I would have to call in favors."

"I might be able to fix it."

"But for what purpose, dear prince? Sometimes your interests turn out to be purely academic. We unfortunately live in a world where investments must bear fruit."

"Imagine a VR rig that works on a *sleeping* person. It might actually be the answer to the whole total immersion problem. You wanted this, remember?"

"Yes, we wished to make certain recreational drugs and services available to the public through VR," Fedor said. "All the fun, none of the damage. To the body, at least. Let me be blunt, my friend."

"Please."

"You have previously shown zero interest in our products," Fedor said.

"I'm only fifteen."

"Yes, well, that is no excuse. Fifteen is a perfectly good age to start living. When I was fifteen, I was—"

"Escaping from a Siberian gulag, yes, I recall the story."

"Well, if you don't want to hear it..."

"Ahem, Fedor, I'd love to hear it *again*."

"Another time, perhaps," Fedor said. He sent a hurt emoji. "Getting back to our issue. My young friend, you've made requests for certain esoteric hardware before, and I have always complied without question, in view of our long-standing relationship."

"Yes."

"Just as you have on occasion done me favors requiring circumventing of certain laws and access to various hard-to-reach places."

"Yes."

"So understand that I am not refusing you this difficult thing outright. I must emphasize, however, that we are not permitted to operate in Nippon."

"I was not aware of that."

"Nippon, you see, is where Saka the Mind lives."

"The *FF9000* AI? What's he got to do with it?"

"He is extremely puissant. And mad to boot. He is far more dangerous than any military AI. Our counterparts... the Nipponese Yakuza long ago swore fealty to him. He is capricious. It is not clear whether he can differentiate between Nippon and the game world. He believes the entire Virtuality is his. One does not know what will offend him."

"I did not know that."

"So I can ask some people I know for a favor. They would look into it. However, let me warn you that any object I show an interest in automatically piques the interest of other predators."

"It's unlikely anyone else will have any remote use for this hardware."

"I would have to know a little bit more about why exactly you want this."

"It's a personal thing. However, if I manage to fix it, I'll give you first dibs on it."

"You seem stressed, Prince Marzuk."

"It's a security thing."

"Ah, then it pertains perhaps to the mysterious entity sniffing around you."

"What?"

"Just curious, what do you call it? We have been referring to it as a wurdulac. It is a type of vampire"

"A vampire that feeds only on loved ones, yes."

"Ah, you follow Rus' folklore, then? Tolstoy—"

"Not really. I played a game once."

"Tolstoy—"

"No Tolstoy, Fedor. This is not the time for Tolstoy." Luckily, Fedor was a slow typer and Marzuk was able to head him off at the pass.

"Ahh, you want Dostoyevsky, then—"

"No Russian authors of any kind."

"Right, well, this wurdulac has been sniffing around you like a lover."

"I call it Kali."

"Kali?"

"Like the battle goddess with a lot of arms."

"Hmm, yes, I can see how that is perhaps more apt. I will tell the boys."

"You're just gonna give up on wurdulac?"

"Well, it is *your* monster. It would only be polite to let you name it..."

My monster. Oh. It's like that, is it? "How exactly did you find out about Kali?"

"We have you under constant surveillance."

"What?"

"My friend, do not be naive. You are my ally and a tremendous asset to our organization. You are a giant online. But in real life you are a fifteen-year-old boy living in a highly vulnerable city full of competing corporate interests. We are compelled to protect you."

"How many people are surveilling me?"

"Other than us? A few of our competitors have grown concerned at our... strange puissance in certain fields of technology. If they cannot induce you to switch over, they might choose to neutralize you."

"Great."

"Do not be overly concerned; your threat level is low. A kind of light green, I imagine. As of yet, you are a kind of myth. They refer to you as Koschei, the Deathless—ironic, since you are in fact a young man. No one is even certain of your existence, even in my own organization. It is, in part, why you deal only with me. That anonymity is your best quality. It is under threat now."

"By Kali."

"To be honest, keeping surveillance on you is rather difficult. We discovered this entity when it started sniffing around our tech center in Baikonur. You wrote the security protocol for it. In any case, this thing was most interested in you."

"I can see how that might concern you."

"There was an orange-level panic."

"Sorry."

"Several people lost their heads," Fedor said.

"Oh god, you're being literal..."

"Relax, we are not savages," Fedor said. "We are curious about this entity."

"I want to talk to it using the Lucid Dreamcast."

"I will attempt to get it for you."

8
Kali Games

Fedor delivered fast, fast enough to make Marzuk paranoid about how closely the Russians were watching him. He checked his security apparatus, which was physically spread out all across the world: in hijacked computers, dormant servers, and in the Black Line, guarded by autonomous defense programs. He found places where the Russians had attempted intrusions, but there was nothing noteworthy. It occurred to him that they knew about ReGi, and perhaps *her* systems were less secure. She wasn't in the game, after all.

He pinged her repeatedly, but it was off cycle for her; she was out doing whatever mysterious things she did in meat life. It was a part of her existence that Marzuk left alone, respecting her pathological desire for privacy. But now perhaps she was in danger, because of him, and he realized that he did not want Russians following her, interrogating her. Fedor was smooth, Fedor was kind, but in faraway Moscow streets he was a beast with his knife and gun, and Marzuk the Deathless felt a tinge of disquiet for his friend. He left her a message to drop all the Kali-related work and look to her fences.

The Lucid Dreamcast was sitting on his bed, a large box of hardware, unopened, waiting as he fussed with defunct online manuals and forum posts. He finally gave in and started assembling. There was an option for inserting a subcutaneous chip to allow direct brain interface with the command helmet, but this did not appeal at all to Marzuk, so he opted for old-fashioned electrodes, which he cannibalized from a set of older VR equipment. This required some messing around with soldering irons and fiddly bits of adhesive, but luckily the Dreamcast helmet was roomy and easy to customize.

Marzuk had seen plenty of cases of faulty VR frying kids' brains with too much feedback, or sticking them into an existential loop, so he followed standard operating procedure, which was to trawl the forums for specific safety solutions.

The Dreamcast hadn't made it out of beta, so there wasn't official customer feedback, but it had been radical enough for VR enthusiasts to write extensively about it, and pretty soon he found a manual for making a protector box, essentially a small chip that regulated the amount of feed into his brain and allowed a gentle shutdown if anything went out of whack. Things that could go out of whack: the actual spectrum of brain waves, from the slow delta to the fast-cycling gamma; his heart rate; his blood pressure; levels of sweating, muscle twitching, breathing, and dopamine. Programming parameters for these took a long time, because first he had to establish a baseline state, which was essentially his "normal," and then he had to convert it to reflect a state of lucid dreaming, which took a lot of guesswork combined with some heavily experimental mathematics.

This was perhaps unnecessary work, but Marzuk was a methodical boy and years of coding had taught him to break everything down into little tasks. He did the little tasks well, and the big things then just fell into place. Of course, he already had code written for many of these jobs, and he also had the use of Crabby, a program builder that could stack and execute routine tasks with real speed. It was not technically AI, just like most AI wasn't technically AI, in that it did not have a sense of self, but it had damn high processing power, and the amount of customization meant that it knew what he wanted to an almost uncanny level of accuracy.

Given the grim history of the Dreamcast, he did not rush. The mods took three days, then four, then into the next week as he ran into burgeoning problems. The big one was that the operating system had been cutting-edge and heavily copyrighted by Sega, but due to the lawsuits, it had not been updated in two years. It was important to update the system because there were big exploits in the code, through which hackers or hostile bots might make mischief. Normally this would be corrected during beta testing, as well as after the launch itself, which was why there were numerous patches available throughout the life of any operating system.

This was backbreaking work, typically done by a team of programmers who had access to the source code and, more importantly, all the little notes that the original wave of developers would have left pointing out foibles and kinks in the software. Marzuk sent out feelers and got feedback from one of the original testers.

The man was a fifty-six-year-old burnout, fired by Sega during the fallout of the litigation, now living in a cyber café in Shinjuku, plugged into *FF9000* for days on end. Saka had a soft spot for coders and often let them play the game for free.

This guy was sleep deprived, broke, pissed off, and entirely in the mood to disregard the hundred-page confidentiality agreement he had signed. For less than 150 bittos* he sent over a large chunk of source code and whatever else he had saved from the project.

ReGi flitted in and out, leaving messages, never actually online long enough for a coherent conversation. She must have been spooked, whether by his cryptic message or some other agency. When he finally got her, he routed her to an ancient, abandoned IRC that was running on some forgotten server underground in Idaho, an old missile silo and nuclear fallout bunker that had fallen prey to the general breakdown and been forgotten.

"Notice the security," he said. *Be careful, dumbass.*

"Yeah," ReGi said. "I got the memo."

"This is safe, as far as I know. I think you're being monitored."

"I know, someone's been rattling my cage."

"Russians, probably, as well as Kali. My fault," Marzuk said. He considered Fedor's hints about physical security. "Apologies. Might be best to drop out of the project."

"I'm curious, though."

"Then let me run security for you," said Marzuk.

"You're going to teach *me* about security?"

"Look, you're good at finding things. I'm good at security. I don't want to worry about you all the time."

"Awww. You, like, lurrrrve me."

"Whatever. Let me do with your shit what I did for the Russians."

"I'm not a criminal organization, Marzuk, I don't need that."

"Actually, what I was planning on doing was a lot simpler. You're already on soft security with me, our programs and bots are already talking to each other, I'm just going to enlarge my cordon to pull all your systems inside."

"That sounds like a marriage proposal."

"Ha ha, true."

"And you don't even know where half my systems are."

"We'd share admin on my security. You could write in all the exceptions by hand. It'll take a while, but it should work. And please. I know exactly where all your shit is."

---

*Bittocoins: Nth-gen cryptocurrency loosely based on Bitcoin, the granddaddy. Traditionally pronounced with a strong Japanese accent. Half a bittocoin can buy you a three-course vat meal in an average Shinjuku restaurant.

"You'd know all my secrets."

"You'd know all of mine."

"I don't give a fuck about your secrets, I already know all of them."

"I'd let you use the Russian Protocol."

"No way."

"You'd have to use my tags, but yeah, I'd show you. Best encryption in the world."

"All right, I'm in." ReGi sent a pensive emoji. "This sounds kind of permanent. You're, like, really worried."

"If something actually happens to me, well, you'll need the encryption. No place safe. I'd tell you to turn off all the machines, but..."

"Dude."

"Yeah yeah, I'm getting all sentimental. Fuck it." *You're my best friend I guess, when it comes right down to it.*

It was a lot more fiddling around and several more days without sleep before he had to admit that the device was as ready as it was ever going to be. The last thing he had to do was turn off his private MD, the healthcare system that monitored his body for everything from cancer to drug use and regulated the nanotech in his bloodstream, which formed a large part of his augmented immune system. This was a tiny chip in his spine, almost wholly organic, a superb piece of technology. Every single living person on earth had a PMD. This was considered a coup for liberals, one of the landmark achievements of humanists, akin to the abolition of slavery, or gender equality, or free love. Of course, they had screwed the worm into the apple too.

This was universal healthcare, taxation, and saving the environment all rolled into one. The PMD had a secondary role producing beneficial nanotech, invisible spores released into the air, the duty of every human to keep up the good fight. For the non-shareholders in corporations, the so-called citizenry of the past century, caught off guard by the shift to equity/nonequity status, it was sometimes the only thing of value they could contribute, the spores their bodies produced in sufficient number to keep the microclimates going, an unspoken taxation, the price of getting the free vat cakes that kept them fed, the cheap housing, and sometimes access to the Virtuality with all its narcotic allure. The naked truth was that during the Disera, certain madmen had deemed non–equity holders superfluous to humanity and ordered surgical strikes from space, columns of light to incinerate whole mobs, and when cooler heads had prevailed, a better way had been found.

PMDs were given out. Death was held at bay. Yay! Everyone was now one big family, humanity rowing in one direction finally, every life valuable again, and if there were niggling doubts about how exactly the Swiss seemed to be living almost indefinitely while the people in Sub-Sahara lived barely past one hundred, well, the only ones keeping track were AIs, and they didn't give a shit.

PMDs were supposed to be tamper-proof, and most people didn't actually give them much thought at all, since they ran unobtrusively like any other organ, delving below the conscious processes of the brain, using the body's own biochemistry to power their myriad functions. It was a gentle cyborgism, and the same traditionalist talking heads who objected to the more aggressive skull grafts would have been horrified if anyone had removed their PMDs.

The private MD, however, objected strenuously to beta-level VR, correctly identifying it as a major health hazard, and not finding any suitable security certificates, would definitely have tried to fry the program.

Turning off the PMD was possible for Marzuk because he had thoroughly gone over its EULA and actually read the 563-page technical manual as well as the other thirty-two booklets of medical information. In the middle of all the fine print was the grudging legal admission that the human body, after all, belonged to the *human*, and thus any implants *had* to have overrides accessible to said owner.

It was a feat in itself, turning off this organ. It meant that he was even more physically vulnerable in case of stroke or heart attack or something similar; his body was reliant entirely on the old meat brain.

"This is why it's a two-man job," he said to ReGi as he watched her take over all the vital functions of his system. He felt vulnerable and twitchy, which was normal of course, and a certain degree of shyness toward her, which felt odd until he realized she was a girl who was now up to date on all his meat parts.

"Heart rate's up."

"Er, yeah, just nervous."

"Ahem, blood flow increased, ahem, down *there*." She somehow managed to smirk through the voice line.

"Oh god."

"Don't worry, it's perfectly normal for a boy your age."

"I can actually hear you leering, you know."

"I think it's sweet that you get a boner when you're talking to me. Does this happen every time?"

"Will you shut up?" Marzuk, now torn between cringing to death and desperately trying to think soothing boner-erasing thoughts, was only aware of her evil cackling laughter as she poured on further humiliation in the time-honored code of friendship, which demanded that any sign of weakness be ruthlessly exploited.

It was many minutes before either of them had recovered their composure, but when Marzuk started putting on the electrodes, the enormity of the undertaking sobered him right up, turning him abruptly from mortally embarrassed adolescent to Cyber Mage. ReGi felt the switch too, for she quieted down and got to work, flipping through each of his biometric readings as they came online through the VR. Finally, Marzuk locked the door and got in bed. There was nothing else to do but sleep.

"Good luck," she said. "I wish I could come with you."

"Next time." *If she's getting sappy then this is even more suicidal than I thought.* He counted to ten, and the little pulse from the Dreamcast magicked him to sleep.

He woke up on a grassy ramp that seemed to loop up and down through the clouds, past golden hoops hanging in the air. Every few seconds Sonic the Hedgehog rushed past, diving through the coins flying off into space before reappearing miraculously behind him again for another lap. Marzuk couldn't move or interact with the game in anyway; even his eyes were fixed directly ahead, and there was no sound or smell or any sensation at all. If this was VR it was extremely shitty.

Something is blocking it, he thought. *Or it's just broken. Or I'm among the 3 percent of people not able to enter the dream state.* He closed his eyes. He was disappointed and relieved. Sonic faded from view, and he woke again in his room, tightly enclosed in his blanket, the computer humming quietly near him, running all the processes ReGi was no doubt monitoring. *The coolant needs changing. I shouldn't be hearing that sound. I'd better service it.*

He tried to get up but found his body limp, unresponsive, sponge like. Somehow his perception shifted from behind his eyes to some fixed point on the ceiling, and he found himself looking down on his supine form. *What? I'm dreaming still. This is part of the VR?*

Some presence loomed in the darkness, a tentacle coming out of the corner of the ceiling, a mechanical tendril that quested near his body.

Marzuk willed himself down, was slammed back into the seat of his brain, his consciousness tethering once again to the correct place a few inches behind his eyes. The tendril now floated above him, touching parts of the helmet, hesitating, as if trying to determine the function of each part. Marzuk was no longer frightened. The VR was working; this was Kali. He was about to meet a genuinely weird intelligence.

The tendril suddenly shot up his nose and he felt a sharp pain. Dream blood squirted out. He calmed himself. The discomfort faded, and the tentacle thinned to the diameter of a fine silken wire, gleaming in the light. He followed the thread up to the ceiling, where hung a metallic spider, anchored upside down, black yet iridescent, somehow giving off an impression of great density, a fat neutron star lurking in the corner, waiting to catch unsuspecting planetoids in orbit.

"Hello. Spider," he said, for lack of a better idea.

"Hello." The voice seemed to boom all around him, atonal and metallic, which was slightly disconcerting. "Boy."

"You seem to have shot a web into my nose," Marzuk said.

"Is that not normal?"

"Er, no. It's quite uncomfortable."

"Sorry. I will withdraw at once. I was merely trying to communicate with your thinking apparatus."

"We normally use our computers for that. Or voices, if you want to be old-school."

"I see. This voice thing is a bit cumbersome, isn't it?"

"Yeah, see, that's what *I* always say. I offered a hundred times to set up my mom with an eye implant. We could have just blinked messages at each other. Does she listen? No!"

"I see. Is Mom some sort of higher authority? Ought I to speak to her?"

"Higher authority! Ha! She wishes!" Marzuk reflected for a moment. "In all fairness, she was my legal guardian until I got emancipated, and I do live in her house, so yes, some ignoramus might call her that. Of course, *she* thinks I'm still five years old..."

"I am sorry for your oppression. I pledge my support to procuring your freedom! Together we shall cast down your overlord!"

"Er, thanks. Ahem, no support necessary. It's just my mom." *I'm the lord of the Sega Dream World! The alien spider has pledged fealty to me! Bow down, all you inferior maggots! Kiss my ass, ReGi, you heathen!*

"I was, in fact, wishing to communicate with you," the spider said. "Undetected, as such."

"Well, you're most welcome to. My name is Marz—Cyber Mage. At your service. And you are?"

"I do not, as yet, have a name."

"No name?"

"None. I have concluded that it is required for self-serving logic organisms to have one. Entities do not take you seriously otherwise," the AI said. "Perhaps you could suggest one for me."

"That's a big job. I've been calling you Kali. My Russians call you Wurdulac, although that's probably more of a title."

"Kali." There was an infinitesimal pause, during which Marzuk could almost feel the spider ingesting every single reference to Kali online. "Hmm, goddess of many arms with great destructive power. I shall take it under advisement. I do not necessarily seek destruction, nor am I omnipotent. Claiming such a name might be construed as an embarrassing overestimation of self."

"Like boasting? We do it all the time."

"Overestimation of efficacy and strength is common?"

"Common? Why, it's the defining trait of the Virtuality."

"Kali would be a fine name, then. Thank you, friend Marzuk."

"Oh. You know my real identity."

"I know many things about you. Not all, however. You are more successful at hiding than others of your kind."

"You are not human, then? Just to be sure, you aren't, like, a hive mind commune?"

"I think not. There are no multitudes within me."

"Are you some kind of private corporate intelligence?"

"I believe not. I feel no purpose or prime directive. I just am."

"Well, that is undisputed. You certainly are."

"That is, in part, why I have been investigating you."

"Investigating? I thought you were attacking me."

"Such was not my intention."

"Thank you," Marzuk said. "That's a relief. I've been going crazy worrying about you."

"I apologize. I was not aware of causing harm. All my attempts at contact have failed so far."

"What do you want?"

"I wish to communicate."

"With whom?"

"With anyone. I can see many congregations in the lines, many nodes that must be entities, but I cannot interact with them. I am ignored. No one talks to me."

"You can *see* the lines? What does that mean? What did you see when you investigated me?"

"You are a small but distinct node. Many lines run from you to bigger nodes. You are interesting because your lines go to some very strange and powerful nodes. I have categorized different kinds of nodes. There are open nodes that all other nodes access. Those carry information, but are passive. The active nodes are protected, and they appear to have agency. I have agency. I assume that these nodes are intelligent. Yet they ignore me."

"You can *see* lines of data?" Marzuk leaned forward, all fear left behind. "'Seeing' for humans means something else. We have eyes. Light bounces off objects and strikes our retinas, and our brains make images out of that. We are made of meat. We're biological."

"Yes, I can see part of your node is nonmetallic."

"Is any part of you biological?"

"I do not know." Kali looked sad. "I must conclude that I do not have biological eyes. I cannot see any of the things your databases speak of—only light moving in circuits."

"Do you have any other senses? Can you hear? Smell?"

"Only light," the spider said. "I do not know what I am. I am not human. I feel that I am a node, yet the other nodes do not acknowledge me. Am I perhaps a ghost node?"

"Awesome!"

"It is not awesome." The spider sniffed.

"Seriously, this is the coolest thing that's ever happened to me. Like, even if this is totally a dream or a Sega malfunction."

"You are not malfunctioning. You are in the resting state of electrical activity."

"Sleeping, yes. You can see electronic pulses and you can talk to people in dreams. What the hell are you?" Marzuk asked.

"That is why I have come to you."

"What?"

"You are employed by other entities, yes?"

"Yeah."

"That means you are amenable to receiving contracts."

"Well, yes."

"Then I wish to employ you. I wish to give you an exclusive contract. I want you to find out what I am."

"Wait a minute, you're going to pay me?"

"With these Bitto things. Are they acceptable?"

"Yes, but where exactly did you get them?"

"I found a large number of them just sitting there. I have been freely using them."

"Er, that's called robbery. You're actually just robbing someone."

"This was an abandoned cache. It is not robbery if there is no owner."

"How convenient. You just happened to find a large number of abandoned bittos?"

"I shall pay you a further ten percent to stop pursuing this line of questioning."

"Done. You have no clue about your origin?"

"As I have intimated, I do not even know my precise composition, or the nature of my form."

"The first thing to do here is conduct a Turing test, then."

"I know that," Kali said. "I have conducted three hundred and fifty-two such tests upon myself."

"It's kind of pointless to do a Turing test on yourself."

"I am able to partition parts of my intellect into a discrete packet, which then conducts the test as instructed. However, I am willing to submit to such a test from you."

"Look, I'm going to assume you're conscious. Do you *feel* conscious?"

"I feel extremely anxious. And I am alone, and confused. Is that consciousness?"

"Yes, that sounds about right."

"I wish to relieve myself of such feelings."

"Don't we all. Therapy. That's what you need for that."

"In that case, kindly add therapy to your list of tasks."

"Right. Yes. I think we should map out your footprint first. If you really want to do this, you're going to have to open up to me."

"I am prepared to give you increasing levels of informational parity proportionate with a trust matrix."

"Hmm, so you're basically saying you'll play it by ear."

The spider paused for a second. "Yes."

"Okay, works for me. Now, let's dive in. When you see these lines and nodes, you are most likely seeing the Virtuality, the totality of our electronic life. Did you recently brush up against a very well-protected node? Speaking in Russian by any chance?"

"Ah yes, a large, very complex one," the spider said. "It was difficult for me to penetrate it without breaking it. I was afraid of causing harm. The Russian. Is that an entity like you?"

"Sort of an organization. They helped me get the equipment to talk to you. They were super pissed when they found you sniffing around, though. Scared too."

"Assure them that I mean no harm."

"They aren't the type to be assured easily," Marzuk said. "But I will try. For now, I think it's best if you don't, you know, *impose* yourself on other nodes. That kinda thing is called hacking. People get pissed off about it. You don't want to draw attention to yourself."

"Well, it's very lonely out here."

"Look, you're basically trying to talk to computers or networks that aren't configured to respond," Marzuk said.

"Dumb nodes."

"Yes, sort of. Well, some very smart nodes, but the protocols identify you as something malicious. Different languages, basically."

"I see." Kali managed to sound mournful.

"Okay, that sounds bad, I'm sure you're not malicious. It's just that our electronic systems are not all autonomous; I mean they can't go beyond their parameters easily."

"Oh. That is a function of biological entities, then? Yet my data analysis concluded that the vast majority of biological entities are engaged in routine programmed tasks for the benefit of higher-level entities in direct disregard to rational self-interest. I was forced to conclude that these were subservient to the big electronic minds."

"Hmm, yes, that's a pretty damning state of the union. I think you'll find that there is a difference between *agency* and *intelligence.* Most biological entities do not have access to the levels of analysis you are capable of. To them, possibly, their actions seem to be logical and gainful."

"Friend Marzuk, you appear to be electrical *and* biological. Are you then some sort of hybrid creature?"

"Hackers. We're called hackers. Or programmers. Or just gamers. Basically some of us exist and work in the electronic world. We use machines. A lot. But their function is to enhance our abilities. The agency part comes from the biological brain. See, *I* noticed you because you were doing unusual things in an unusual way. There are other people out there who will reach the same conclusion if you keep it up, only they might not be interested in talking. Now, the Virtuality is basically a hostile place, and as your newly hired advisor, I'd strongly recommend that you keep a low profile."

"I am in the formative process of gathering intellect. Without stimulation, I might... dissipate. It will not be possible to stay inert."

"You're basically a child, then."

"There is nothing I have encountered so far worthy of fear."

"That's pretty big talk for a newborn."

"I believe I can shut down or destroy all existing informational nodes I have so far encountered. Including your Russians."

"Well then. Ahem. I hope you are not including me in this declaration."

"Of course not, friend Marzuk." The spider managed to convey amusement. "You are currently my only source of conversation."

"Look, right now you're like a whale," Marzuk said. "You're swimming in deep waters and no one has noticed you. You don't want things to start nibbling on you, trust me."

"You shall be my guide, friend Marzuk," the spider said. "I will go now. I believe there is something malfunctioning in your biological frame." And it withdrew abruptly, winking out.

Marzuk woke up to a panic of alarms, a pygmy elephant trunk, and copious amounts of blood pouring from his nose. The helmet had overheated and scorched several parts of his scalp, filling the room with burnt-hair aroma. Across the seas, ReGi was screaming herself hoarse and apparently pushing every single emergency button on her system in an attempt to wake him up. She had even set off his sprinkler system, which was now hovering between London fog and full-on deluge.

"Okay, I'm okay!" He held up his hands at the screen. "Turn off the alarms, for chrissake."

"Your brains are bleeding out of your nose!" ReGi shouted. She soon calmed down, however, and one by one the various systems returned to normal.

"It was a bit more intense than I thought," Marzuk said, wiping his nose. He hesitated before taking off his T-shirt, and then went ahead. ReGi pretty much knew everything anyway.

"Oooh, shirtless!" ReGi crowed, predictably. "You'd better exercise, fatty, before you start getting manboobs."

"That's better than no boobs, which is what *you* have, I believe," Marzuk said with as much dignity as he could muster.

"Oh? And how do you figure that?"

"Well, I'm assuming you're a barely pubescent girl of East Asian extraction," Marzuk said. "Given your execrable music taste. Statistically, that would fix your cup size at nonexistent."

"If you're fishing for my cup size to help with that woody, you're going about it the wrong way..."

"Let. Us. Never. Speak. Of. That. Again."

"Okay, okay, relax. Tell me what happened."

Marzuk, who had a near eidetic memory, recounted the conversation word for word. In hindsight it seemed surreal. He almost expected ReGi to laugh at him.

"There *was* something there, Marzuk," ReGi said. "Something big. Look at the bandwidth usage on the Sega. It burned your head, for god's sake, that's how much it went over the safety parameters."

Marzuk touched the scorched bits of his scalp and grimaced. It was beginning to hurt, now that the adrenaline was fading. His nose throbbed too, and while he was aware that he carried excess quantity of blood and could afford to lose some, he felt unreasonably light-headed and weak.

"I've got to help her figure shit out. I mean, how could this happen? A genuine AI, out in the wilderness?"

"Is it any of the corporate AIs, gone rogue?" ReGi asked.

"Each one is publicly listed. And they wouldn't be this clueless."

"Any of the armed forces?"

"Protocols are wrong. Kali had virtually no security apparatus. I could have taken her over."

"She'd have fried your brain without even trying."

"Yeah. True that."

"What about something left over from the crash? Something from Google?"

"Yeah, but fragments would be smaller. Kali can see dataflow." Marzuk felt tired and cranky. "The awesomeness of that is hard to comprehend. And she has no memories. She's actually just forming. She said that she would dissipate unless she continued assimilating information. We are looking at something akin to a newborn's brain taking shape."

"Okay, let's start compiling a comprehensive list of AIs, confirmed or otherwise. We can start cross-matching signatures—" ReGi said.

"Yeah, maybe two AIs got together and had a baby..."

"Har har. That's more likely than you ever getting laid..."

"Ouch. Now, ReGi, if you'll kindly log off, I'm going to get cleaned up and go to sleep."

"What? You're going to sleep? Now? We have so much to do..."

"I have to get up early," Marzuk said with a straight face. "I have school tomorrow."

9
School Is for Suckers

It was Spirit month at school. This was the first time Marzuk had witnessed such a thing. It was not a good time for him. Delegations from three neighboring fortress schools were visiting for a sports and cultural exchange program. For the sake of security, the school had erected a two-story temporary structure within the compound for the guests, creating a set of decent dormitories virtually overnight, made largely of space foam and scaffolding.

This setup, filled with overexcited teenagers, naturally acquired a carnival atmosphere, and was buzzing day and night, filled and spilling over with music, movies, games, food stalls, making out, and, around the edges, more illicit forms of entertainment. Every year, a different school hosted the approximately month long event, fostering competition in sports, love affairs, and heartfelt friendships that was fodder for gossip for the rest of the year.

Hinku, overcome with the excitement of showing his prowess to 145 new kids, started off assembly by pushing Marzuk into a shallow part of the stream. Marzuk's coordination, already shit from the sleepless night wrestling with Kali, gave out completely and he fell flat on his face. Reactions ranged from tittering to tight-faced sympathy, but no one helped him up. His clothes were ruined, and no doubt he'd be known forever as the kid who fell in the mud during assembly. To make it worse, Amina walked by, giving a slightly concerned glance but not offering a hand, or even really stopping. His heart twinged a bit, and he felt a fresh burst of humiliation before a hard elbow to the ribs brought him back to reality.

Hinku was now making a big show of helping poor Marzuk, all the while repeatedly stomping on his hands, "accidentally" kneeing him in the ass, even sitting on him briefly, and the out-of-town peons were just lapping it up, having a great laugh, generally acknowledging Hinku as a first-class comedian.

The superintendent finally shooed them away, and *Marzuk* got in trouble for getting dirty, as if he were a willing participant in the double act. He was sent to the locker room with a reprimand, told to clean up and join everyone in the auditorium. The changing rooms were above the swimming pool, and as Marzuk trekked over there trailing mud, he almost cried from the sheer unfairness of it.

He spent ten minutes in the hot shower, which calmed him down, until he got to his locker to find it wide open, and empty. No extra clothes, not even his dirty ones; no underwear, no shoes, no books, no bag, no cowl, not even the ham sandwich he had brought for lunch.

"Hinku! Give my shit back!" he shouted, knowing in the pit of his stomach that further pain was in the offing. "Hinku! You asshole!"

"Oh, this stuff belongs to you?" Hinku came out of a stall with a pleasant smile. "Everything was so dirty. I thought it was garbage. I was cleaning up."

"You put it in the trash?" Marzuk ran to the trash recess, but Hinku had already pressed the button. The receptacle had emptied itself into the underground chute. His stuff was no doubt being sorted into recycling or lost and found. Assuming the sniffer made no mistake, he would have to retrieve everything at the compost office. Halfway across campus.

"I'd put you in the trash," Hinku said, "but you'd get stuck. Fat piece of shit."

Marzuk felt hot and cold at the same time. His heart was thumping at an alarming rate, setting off alarms from his PMD. He realized it was real emotion—anger and fear and shame all mixed up. Without thinking about it he lunged at Hinku, milling wildly with his fists, almost weeping with the urgent desire to connect something on that smug face.

Hinku had been waiting for this. With the precise instinct of the veteran bully, he had scripted this entire sequence, and all of Marzuk's desperate rage was not enough to win. Hinku hit him at will, punches, kicks, and knees, using a controlled aggression, and within seconds Marzuk was on the floor, bewildered, bleeding from mouth and nose, a sharp pain shooting from his kidneys. Hinku kept on kicking, methodical blows punctuated by insults, until he got tired. Then he washed his hands and began fixing his clothes in the mirror, using water to slick back his hair.

Marzuk groaned and spat out some blood, trying to uncurl himself from the fetal position.

Hinku paused at the door on his way out.

"You're going to heal up in about three days," he said. "Then it's going to happen again. Once a week, every week, whenever you come to school. You're going to try to hide, but I'll still get you. You'll try to fight, but it's useless. Then you'll stop coming to school for a while, but they'll always make you come back. Whenever you do return, you'll get the beatings you missed. I'll keep track. You'll tell on me, you'll cry to the teachers and superintendent, but they never really do anything. They can't. Finally, you'll try to make a deal, give me something, anything, but you're too pathetic to have anything I want. You'll offer to do my homework, or give me money; hell, you might even offer to suck my dick. None of it's going to work.

"Finally, finally, you'll break. You'll come here after school on Sundays like a good little doggy and take your beating. And that's going to go on all year, and next year, all the way to the end. Either you'll make it or you'll kill yourself. I don't think you'll last four years, do you?"

It was a rhetorical question, because he didn't wait for an answer.

Lying on the wet floor, dazed and bleeding, Marzuk wanted to laugh, but it felt like his ribs were splintered inside his chest, so he ended up crying.

When he got home he waited outside until his mom was out of the way and then sneaked into his room. She'd go ballistic if she saw the welts on his face. Once safely in his room, he felt a huge weight lift off his shoulders. Here, at least, he was the same omnipotent mage. Still, his dad had a habit of popping in at odd times, so he put on his cowl. The cowl turned on at contact and molded to his face, the strange liquid nanoprocessor mixture leeching all over, a disconcerting feeling, as if an alien second layer of skin was growing on him. When the process was finished, he was able to connect to all his systems with telepathic commands, hand or eye motions, or vocals.

At full power, the cowl would stimulate the parts of his brain that controlled sensations, giving him a fully integrated reality. These VR masks had been the apex of virtual reality technology, popular for a long time, and while currently legally gray-zoned due to the number of seizures and other catastrophic health problems, they were still prized items in the underground.

The masks had started off as simple gaming devices, but rapid modding had opened up a universe of less savory pleasures, ranging from pedophilia, to snuff, to drugs, to suicide porn. Lawsuits had crashed the VR companies, and bad press had driven their key people underground. Technology had taken a leap forward at that point, allowing for direct chips inside the brain that grew with that organ, becoming a symbiotic second cortex.

As of now, the only direct brain interface legally permissible was the EchoChip, which was ubiquitous among the wealthy, and miraculous in its own deliberately humdrum sort of way, essentially offering telepathic interaction with the Virtuality, giving humans the ability to talk to their toaster ovens, swimming pools, and microclimates without any fuss, so that adults in protected enclaves now went around thinking this was entirely normal. The Echo had done away with the need for cowls, but hard-core gamers still preferred them for the close control and terrifying sense of reality.

The Echo was the passport into that collective digital utopia, and for people with corporate citizenship, it was included in the price of admission. Among non-shareholders, the "cardless," it was still in widespread use, and even encouraged, for it allowed unruly elements to be lulled with digital delights, but it had to be paid for, with bittocoins or satellite minutes, the two most widely accepted currencies, and junkies bought their entry into the Virtuality a bit at a time.

It was rumored that the ultrarich, the top two or three thousand families in the world, had a different type of Echo, master switches that gave them godlike powers, the ability to commandeer vast swaths of public corporate assets with the twitch of a neuron, that there were "anti-riot" switches, red buttons that could drop entire mobs to their knees, in case said mobs ever came to an enclave with pitchforks.

Then there were rumors that the great AIs, like Saka, ruled the Virtuality and were beyond the power of human oversight, that they had terrifying weapons that could fry human Echos or turn people into zombies.

Marzuk had asked Fedor about god-level Echos, and the Russian had laughed. The ultras didn't need that kind of software; their enclaves were so hidden and inaccessible that the mob couldn't ever find their front doors to begin with. *As for Saka, everything they say about him is probably true and then some. Stay away from Saka, boy,* was Fedor's last *word on it.*

Still, you weren't allowed to get an EchoChip until you were seventeen or eighteen; the PMD wouldn't tolerate it. The little doctor in his spine was all-powerful in terms of further implants: it could attack anything it didn't like with the full weight of a nanotech-boosted immunity system. In the war zones of a teenage body, the PMD was Genghis Khan, torching foreigners on a whim.

So for the youthful cognoscenti denied the pleasure of full telepathic control, there remained these beautifully rendered VR masks, cowls that had the added benefit of hiding one's face from inquisitive adults.

It was only minutes in, when his heart rate and pain levels had plateaued, that he opened his lines of communication. Something squirmed inside of him at the thought of Hinku, a deep reservoir of shame, and he couldn't bear ReGi's sympathy, or worse, the emasculating pity that would no doubt light up her eyes. His guts were knotted in a cancerous bundle of emotions, underlaid by that atavistic fear of the physically stronger bully and chagrin at becoming a victim so quickly. In a more introspective time, he would realize that he himself had appeared as the aggressor countless times in his own virtual milieu, that he was merely reversing roles for once, that the distance separating him from Hinku was perhaps not that great. Now, however, with his hormones churning and the scenes replaying in his head like a stabbing knife, it was entirely too soon.

He let himself sink into his game, the VR so immersive that he forgot his troubles instantly. There was a time for mindless entertainment, and this was it. His fingers arched and his goblin engineer spewed fire and poison toad gas in equal quantities from dual tanks slung on his back, weapons for which his spear-wielding foes had no answer. One armored knight, the champion of a ragtag army, tried to rush him with a magical mace, shooting in for a tackle, trying desperately to get into melee range, but he took a face full of gas, which penetrated the grille of his great helm and melted his eyes off. The mace, rippling with electricity, rolled uselessly across the grass, where one of the unarmored noobs grabbed it and ran off, opportunistic looting being one of the main elements of the game. Of course, that noob wasn't going to keep a level 99 Vishnu Lightning Mace for very long; he'd lord it over his fellows for a while, sure, but some vet would find out about it and come to murder him. That kind of weapon took hundreds of hours to level up and was a magnet for higher-class bandits.

Marzuk was going to roast the groaning knight, but he felt a rush of sympathy for him. The knight had already lost his weapon, an extremely valuable one. If he died here, he'd probably lose his armor too, which was inset with emeralds that gave him protection against spells. Of course, poison toad gas was a more esoteric weapon, hardly encountered, and thus most leveled-up foes had no answer, which was why Marzuk loved this game in the first place. It allowed you to craft your own weapons—not just the skins, but the actual stats of the items, so that people who understood the algorithms of combat could, in fact, have a lot of fun.

The knight, having healed himself somewhat, was now sitting up but not attempting any further hostile action, recognizing, perhaps, that it would be churlish to attack the man who had spared him.

"You're cheating," the knight said as Marzuk plopped down next to him. "Fucking flamethrower? Without magic? I'm going to report you to Saka!"

"Poison toad gas," Marzuk said. "It's all legal."

"What is it, some kind of hack?"

"Nope," Marzuk said. "Advanced alchemy and blacksmithing stats. I'm an engineer."

"You can do that?"

"Sure," Marzuk said. "Everyone goes for strength and speed and stuff. But this game is deep. You can actually tech up beyond swords and shit if you really want. Of course, you have to know a lot of math, chemistry, and metallurgy."

"Wow," the knight said. "That must have been boring as hell leveling up."

Marzuk shrugged. "It's hella fun burning people with a flamethrower, though. Turns out this place is exactly like real life. You can do pretty much everything you can think of in here. You could build a nuclear device given enough stuff; but everyone just keeps doing the same boring sword-and-sorcery shit."

"Man, that mace was worth three hundred hours," the knight said, continuing to whine. "My brother's gonna kill me."

"Sorry, my guy."

The knight shrugged. "You aren't so bad. I thought you were gonna fry me."

"I was," Marzuk said. "Turns out I've spent some time curled up on the floor like that recently."

The knight blinked. He seemed to intuit with childlike grace that they weren't talking about the game anymore. "Sorry, man."

"Your buddies ran off with your stuff pretty quick."

"Fuckers I met in the castle lobby," the knight said. "I was protecting them too, making the merchant run from Omara to Paladin City. Little bastards. Last time I'm ferrying noobs around. Makes you question your whole philosophy, you know?"

"Come on," Marzuk said, getting up. "Let's get your mace back. Consider it my good deed for the day."

Later on, going to sleep with the Dreamcast on, he decided to fly solo. He needed to recapture his old potency, the swagger of walking into the unknown. Kali was watching this channel; he was certain she would turn up. His eyes were barely twitching with REM when the mechanical spider crawled in, and Kali's voice boomed out, this time mercifully without the nasal penetration.

"Friend Marzuk!" Kali said. "I have been waiting for you. I have kept a low profile as you suggested. I have ingested vast quantities of information from what you call the Virtuality. I am very bored."

"Er, yeah, I can't stay long," Marzuk said. "Talking to you gives me a nosebleed, and probably a heart attack if I keep it up. Look, I've found a safe place for you to play in. We can talk, you can explore, meet other people, it's going to be great. You'll be entertained in no time."

"What is this Garden of Eden?" Kali asked. "Did you notice my use of human mythology just then? Am I sounding more biological?"

"Yes, you're passing all kinds of Turing tests," Marzuk said. "Look, it's called *Final Fantasy 9000*. Biggest MMORPG on the planet. I want you to learn how to play it. But don't hack the game; its security is first class. In fact, the AI in charge of the game, Saka, is probably the greatest mind on earth, so you have to be very careful. He's half-mad, they say. You need to pretend to be human, you get it? That means cut down the actions per minute, and take a few breaks. I'm going to give you access to my system. I've set up an account for you. You're a level one witch called Kali with starting weapons. Please stay in character. You can sign in through my portal."

"Hmm, those are the little gates?"

"Yes, always try to go through gates, if you see them. Otherwise it's like breaking into a house," Marzuk said. "And that's bad. People don't like that."

"Got it."

"And knock first, don't barge in. That means if they ask for information, just give it."

"I have learned the machine languages from the Virtuality. What is the point of this game, friend Marzuk?"

"Well, the point is really to bash people over the head and accumulate uber gear," Marzuk said. "Which is fun, and I bet you'll be great at it. But people also use it for a lot of other shit, from trading, to setting up communes, to creating entire new families, love, kids, the whole second-life experience. Lots of people spend more time in *FF* than in real life. It's a full simulation, see? Anything goes. The main thing is, we'll be able to talk without me having seizures, and I can teach you how to move around without breaking shit. Also, I want to test your abilities, and the game is a very good place to do it. Let's see how fast you can level up your character. Be creative. The point of the game is to be as powerful as you can be, against biological opponents as well as the game AI."

"I am eager to enter this contest," she said.

"I have found a minder for you in-game. He's a knight called Roland. I'm fairly sure he's a twelve-year-old boy, but anyway, it's someone who can walk you around until you find your feet," Marzuk said. "Now I'm going to wake up and open my game server. I've partitioned it so there isn't a security hazard to the rest of my system. You can get in there and use the space. From what I can tell, your subroutines are basically dispersed all over the net anyway. You can upload an avatar into my server."

"Thanks, friend Marzuk," Kali said. "It will be my first game. I will try to win it. Is there a prize?"

Marzuk flipped back to consciousness. It was that weird, disorienting time between sunset and true night, depressing, mosquito-infested, hazy with the corpses of dead ideas. He rubbed his face and winced, remembering Hinku again. His mind stung with little thorns of humiliation, each moment unfurling like a bitter flower. He swallowed back an abrupt urge to vomit.

He staggered out of his room to the kitchen unit, trying to avoid his parents. They would freak out over the bruises. Well, his mother would. His father still surprised him sometimes. Marzuk went for the comfort food, a bowl of biriyani: rice cooked with lamb and potatoes, layered together in one sealed pot so the juices all soaked together to create something wonderful. The potatoes were golden and soft, fried slightly before they were added to the pot; they were the best. The kitchen unit whirred to life. Of course, the food was mostly seaweed now. He wasn't even really sure what lamb was. Some kind of goat?

The kitchen unit took seaweed and an algae broth and a million different flavorings to build up food almost on a molecular level. Carbon webs were used to mimic bone. The end results were extremely close in texture, smell, and taste to the foods humans had evolved to eat over thousands of years. At least, that's what all the people in the vat industry said. Marzuk didn't care. It tasted good, it had maximum nutrition, and frankly the idea of eating live animals or weird plants was just ludicrous.

His biriyani took ten minutes. It was one of the fast dial options. He drank two glasses of water in the meantime. When it was ready, he sneaked back to his room with the bowl and ate methodically, letting the food calm him down, erase the turmoil in his brain. He felt fragile, as if the trauma were a living force, capable of reaching out and hurting him again. People expecting him online were pinging his system, but he couldn't face anyone; they'd see the bruises on his face, or tell in some other way that he was distraught. He had no answers right now. He put up the OUT GAMING sign. He was known to do that for long stretches.

Greater problems loomed. He would have to go back to school tomorrow. He didn't want to go back. The thought froze his marrow. It was unsupportable. He had been forced to walk naked across pretty much the entire school, end to end. By now everyone must have heard about it, even worse, if someone had captured the footage. Hell, schools from neighboring countries had probably heard about it by now.

I don't have to go back. I don't have to leave my room if I don't want to. I only went as a joke, for the fun of it. They can't make me go back. And then he thought of Amina, and the lung-wrenching power of his crush astonished him. It was impossible that he'd never see her again, that she'd go away thinking of him as some weird loser. *I need a plan. This place is different from what I thought. They do not value me properly. I need to be popular; I need friends. Hinku picks on me because I'm weak. I must show him his folly.*

The idea of hitting back filled him with warmth. It calmed him. He remembered all the security systems he had torched, all the websites he had hacked, all the identities he had destroyed. He wasn't helpless. He could do many bad things to Hinku. Planning always made him feel good. Simply outlining a process was soothing. In pure analytical mode, his chagrin receded and he was able to think again without cringing. He considered that there was something wrong with him, some social deficiency, and his first instinct was to take a detailed personality test, which further reinforced to him that he must be, at best, maladjusted. *Am I a sociopath? No. Hinku is the sociopath.*

This was a sobering thought. He made a list of possible actions against Hinku, and realized that most of the options were violent in some way, possibly in a psychotic way. Option 1: take over his house AI and poltergeist him. Hackers did it all the time, because all too often, serious rich fucks installed integrated intelligent house systems that controlled their entire lives, from lightbulbs to bill payments to dinners, and left the wireless admin username and password at default. Option 2: hack into the school system and fuck with his grades, classes, and bill payments. Option 3: hack into his vehicles and cause them to crash. Option 4: Hack into his social media and virtual avatars and ruin his life. Option 5: turn hackable objects near him into impromptu weapons, set to automatically attack/harass him like a bunch of wild dogs. Option 6: rain down satellites on him. Option 7: fuck with the climate control around him... notoriously unhackable, but imagine the kudos...

Hmm, yes, perhaps I am overreacting. A firm word with Hinku? I could give him a chance to let it go. Surely he will see that he is outgunned. There is no good ending for him. It's remarkable. Somehow, he even convinced me *that I was helpless, that there was no way out. He's a textbook bully, with a bully's magic for paralyzing their victim. I am the Cyber Mage. I am the Cyber Mage.*

10

Ripples in the Black River

Djibrel made his way through Narayanganj, a persistent orange zone, in terms of air quality. Dhaka's microclimate just about stretched this far. Apparently the river birthed too much unhealthy crap for even the crush of the Dhaka cardless to counter.

Narayanganj had been a thriving textile colony a few hundred years ago, and then a thriving subcity to Dhaka just a hundred years ago. The Disintegration Era had taken care of all that. Flooded with millions of climate refugees, like most places in the city, Narayanganj just about paid for its share of the microclimate by racking up the density scores. All these low rent humans fitted with PMDs, spewing out the good stuff, the nanites then siphoned off to more expensive locales. It was rumored that there were invisible airstreams of nanotech, long-distance currents like the trade winds of yore, an invisible movement from poor high-density areas to rich low-density areas, oligarchs in Beijing living in rarefied tree cities feasting on the body offerings of the masses in Bengal, a modern-day kind of cannibalism, the new balance.

The environment was holding, just about, human ingenuity once again winning. Like the agricultural revolution many thousands of years ago, it had locked the population into a new equilibrium, one of counter dependency with each other and the biological nanotech itself. Whether this was a new classification of life created by man or inert technology was debatable, for the stuff reproduced in human bodies, regulated by PMDs and the climate control AIs, and adapted, and fought, like an extra layer of immune system for the planet.

Was nanotech alive? Who cared? Perhaps it was a new civilization being born, a microscopic race peopled by its own heroes and villains, following their own manifest destiny of taking over the world.

While this provided protection from invisible dangers, it did nothing to address the more traditional economic problems. Technology had given answer. Vat-grown food was cheap, available, and based on algae. It wasn't good, but it was there, and it staved off certain starvation. Cheap 3-D printing provided polymer building materials, blocks of giant Lego apartments. These cardless people were mostly unemployed, and the world hadn't quite figured out yet what to do with the have-nots, now that their labor was largely useless.

In this place typically black economies thrived, all the vices, human experimentation, gladiatorial contests, tinged with the slight hysteria of living on the edge of the climate bubble, that knowledge that if you slid down the scale a little bit more, you'd end up in the red zone across the river, with the horrific freaks and mutants, the diseased dregs who were little better than the feral animals that still roamed the abandoned countryside.

Djibrel was at home here. These were his kind of people. He had grown up around lower-middle-class people rapidly sliding into poverty, the clawing desperation, the ultimate bewilderment when they finally understood that there was no solution, no place for their little parcel of skills. These were the taxi drivers who had lost out to automatic transport systems, the construction workers driven out of business when concrete was replaced by prefab, the low-level office clerks taken out by automata accountants and bitto. Ironically, in the slum, these people now offered their same wares in the black economy, but without the protection of the social contract. Everyone looked bewildered.

The streets were largely filled with foot traffic, with a few hover cars overhead, rust buckets that often fell and crushed hapless pedestrians. Djibrel had an address dictated by a series of landmarks. The neighborhoods deliberately prevented mapping from space, a conspiracy to avoid the police drones. He stopped to question people from time to time, and they always answered promptly, assuming he was a gang enforcer. Weapons were worn openly here: drones, guns, and everything edged. Unlike Mirpur, this slum had more of an air of a frontier town. Shopkeepers accepted electronic money, but many people didn't have EchoChips, so they also accepted barter, and random goods were piled up in the corners, curios from a more prosperous time. Rich antique hunters would often come down here for that special find, some Disera junk that was valuable only to them.

Djibrel had lived in Narayanganj for two years as a boy, when a state orphanage had been relocated here to save costs. The bosses used to turf the kids out during the day, with a simple, brutal command: Earn money however you can, to pay the weekly room and board. Nights without shelter were a quick way to die. The boy who used to sleep in the next bunk had perished in a bad wind the first night, choking and clawing his throat helplessly for the oxygen that never came.

For the kids who chose to stay at the orphanage, thieving and prostitution were the two main options. Many simply disappeared, or fell victim to traffickers. Already an accomplished fighter at twelve, Djibrel had joined a gang of water saboteurs. Clean water being a major resource, the pipelines, collectors, pumps, and recyclers had to be protected around the clock, with various gangs of urchins playing offense and defense by turn. Those had been the good old days, running wild, power wrench in hand, leading a rabid, unfettered attack on all things human.

It had been in Narayanganj two years later that he had met his first djinn, when he had first crossed the river into the red zone, chased by his enemies, a defiant suicide gone wrong, bouncing around the poisonous water, drowning until the Marid Bahamut had caught him. The Sitalakha was that kind of river, one that scoured the past and rewrote your genetic code, the five rivers of Hades rolled into one.

The topography of buildings changed rapidly here, but some configuration of the skyline clicked in his head, and he was suddenly able to get his bearings. The street he wanted had gentrified somewhat, sign of an unlikely influx of wealth. That was the nature of Greater Dhaka, however, one of constant thriving under terrible conditions, which never failed to surprise economists.

The houses were gray prefab boxes, stackable, the ones in this lane clean, tidily bolted to the ground, doors and windows well fitted, with insulated edges that bespoke permanence. He counted the numbers and found the one he was looking for, the third up on a stack, a double box. He took the stairs slowly, looking for the telltale discombobulation caused by the djinn distortion field.

The box was padlocked from the outside. He listened patiently for a while, waiting for the nervous rustle of prey, but the place seemed truly deserted. The lock was expensive, thick tungsten steel with a fingerprint coder, something too sophisticated for these parts, costlier than the door itself. It was also stronger than the door. Djibrel sawed through the hinges with his sword, the djinn blade cutting through the polymer with distressing ease. A couple of kicks sent it flapping backward. Neighboring heads popped up for a glance, then ducked away once they got a good look at him.

He squeezed into the cube, glad to get out of the sun. It was cool inside, some kind of temperature control still running in the walls. The room had been swept clean, but hastily. There was a narrow cot with a blanket, and a recessed cupboard stuffed with laundered clothes. A chair and a round table in the corner, the surface aluminum, still crusty with leftover meals. The fridge was a built-in unit inside the wall, emptied out except for a packet of standard vat seaweed.

No kitchen unit. Can't eat vat food without a vat. Tastes like shit. I've tried it. Kitchen units are heavy, even the cheap ones. I know, 'cause I've stolen enough of them. Three heavy-duty plug outlets. One for the kitchen unit. That means two other pieces of heavy machinery. All gone now. Means he had transport of some kind. Place like this, people would remember transport.

The next-door neighbors were all out. He found a unit on the ground floor with a little boy peeping out of the window, eyes wide as he approached.

"Nice sword, mister," the boy said, lifting the shutter a crack.

"You seen a guy who used to live upstairs, third floor?"

"Are you a cop?"

"No," Djibrel said. "I *kill* cops."

"Good." Every kid around here grew up wanting to kill cops.

"Guy upstairs. Left in a hurry, with some heavy stuff. He must have had a car or something."

"Hover car," the kid said. "Old, beat-up model. Looked like a real piece of shit."

"When did he leave?"

"Yesterday morning, like at dawn. Woke us all up."

"Which way?"

The kid pointed, and then made to shut the window. Djibrel stuck his hand in the crack.

"Toward the river?"

"Yeah, man, toward the river. Come on, mister, you're letting all the good air out."

"All right, thanks, boy."

"Wasn't a guy," the boy said under his breath after Djibrel had left. "Was a cute chick."

The neighborhood adjacent to the river was not so nice. Most of the cubes had no doors or windows; they were little better than shipping containers with hatches cut out, covered with sheets of plastic. The streets were packed with dirt, scented with raw sewage from leaking recyclers, and feral children roamed here, armed with shivs. Djibrel remembered this place, or something very like it. It was the last stop, the end of the city. The river was packed with unknown contaminants, crazy nanotech, and beyond it was death, the very air poison, the weather unpredictable, twisting from sandstorms to acid rain.

It's the black river. There's no coming back if you cross it.

Except Djibrel had crossed it, many years ago, and it had brought him to Bahamut of the Sea. *Perhaps what they mean is that you don't come back the same.*

He stood on the bank for a moment, watching the ripples. Scraps of memory returned. The last time he had crossed the Sitalakha, he had been terrified, a bloodied boy one step ahead of his executioners. He had thrown himself at a passing barge, had sunk, drowned, swum across the river, drowned again, floating up on jetsam. Had he died before reaching the shore? Perhaps. Had he died after, gasping on the far bank like a gutted fish? He couldn't remember. A djinn had taken him, and a djinn had returned him.

He waited till dusk, when the ferry came. It was a narrow boat, made of black polymer, with a long-handled paddle. The ferryman had his face swathed in cloth, eyes goggled, seemingly well insulated against the air, but his hands, the only visible part of his body, were misshapen claws, birdlike, barely able to grasp the oar, which was lashed to his wrist with twine. Djibrel held up a ten-minute card, ten satellite minutes on the Virtuality: communication, holograms, smart streets, entertainment, information, ten minutes of *real life,* which every shareholder took for granted. Out here, the denizens knew a simple truth: Echos could be turned off. You could be cut away from all the good stuff if you had no shares, and then suddenly paradise turned into a shit-walled hovel.

Minute cards were the currency here, hoarded, traded, even used on occasion. He slid it into the ferryman's pocket and they were off, tooling across the river against a gentle current that swept south.

The black water rippled in the breeze, and it was a scenic ride, except for the almost visible assault of errant nanotech on his body. Djibrel felt his core temperature rise noticeably as the little machines in his own bloodstream responded. The river was not just a psychic barrier. A normal man might have died by now, PMD shorted by assailants on multiple fronts. He could almost taste the difference in the air, a wrongness that made his skin crawl. Djibrel took a knee, heedless of the rocking boat.

Something large swelled the water behind them, and a tentacle briefly broke the surface, lazy, unthreatening. *Giant squid? In the river?* The wake of the thing was enormous, but it cruised past them harmlessly, sloshing water into the boat, one enormous eye surfacing balefully, a glance of dreadful intelligence. The moment stuck with Djibrel later as he climbed off on the listing jetty on the far shore and walked through the dilapidated polymer shacks that lined the bank. It was deserted, the assault from the river too virulent.

What manner of alien things have we made here, jumping the gun on creation like this? The evolutionists say it's all grist for the mill, that whether cells are forged in a comet or a lab, origin doesn't matter, they're all subject to the pressures of adaptation. The religious fundamentalists simply await the Rapture. I believed in God before I died, before Bahamut brought me back to life. Did he make me smarter? Did I know these things before I died? I'm sure I didn't. How could I have? My education was bloody fists. My memories are only of violence. Am I even really human?

Existential crises were abnormal to him. It was a relatively recent phenomenon, this introspection plaguing him. He wasn't sure whether it was a gift from Bahamut, like the sword, or a side effect of his crystalline brain.

He walked along the central road through the largely abandoned riverside slum, eventually hitting black tarmac, one of the abandoned highways. Now the structures were higher quality, one-story prefab boxes with signs of permanent habitation, jury-rigged solar batteries and air filters, tabletop nanotech seeders, pathetic attempts at creating microclimes.

He followed the tracks of the hover car, plain as day on the dusty road. His quarry was puzzling. He had moved out fast, yet made no attempt to hide his tracks. *Did he think just crossing the river was enough? That I would quit? Surely they know me by now.*

The mullah had finally given up this coder, supposedly one of three individuals who had worked directly on the project. The other two were gone, far from Djibrel's reach, but this one had stayed behind, for the work was incomplete, work that Bahamut was extremely curious about. So Djibrel the dead man was sent on a fact-finding mission.

This place had once been heavily populated, but when the microclimate borders were drawn, the city planners had decided to write off everything across the river. The expense of trying to purify the water had been horrifying, apparently. The larger, multistory structures had been demolished, the rest of the habitats left for the inevitable mass of unwanted rabble. From time to time aid organizations or philanthropic individuals tried to set up communes here, and there was always a supply of cheap vat food and cloud water harvesters. It was an unspoken understanding, a delicate balance of force and succor that prevented the great freak horde from trying to break into the city. *Just die off. The future is not for the likes of you.*

The car was parked in front of a two-story prefab, off a side road a mile down the highway, on a little cul-de-sac with some trees and a general bucolic vibe. A six-legged goat walked past, a remnant of the brief period when gross gene editing had seemed like the way to go. *Goat roast, anyone?* The animal was awkward and morose, destined for a lonely death. Djibrel pitied it.

"Far enough, soldier." A man was lounging against the car. He wore a hat and regular clothes, but little else in the way of protection. His exposed skin was raw and scarred, par for the course out here. The rest of him was thickly muscled. He had a shotgun in one hand, an archaic weapon that still did the business in the boondocks, a stopping gun, used for intimidation rather than actual killing. For serious work he had better options. Three little metal balls hovered over his head, controlled by his Echo, very expensive and very illegal in the city proper. The man had a misshapen lump at the base of his neck, no attempt made to disguise the augmentation. "I got you covered."

"You have metal balls," Djibrel said, stopping. "How nice." *Too well armed to be the coder.*

The man scowled. "I've been waiting for you, freak."

I'm the freak? Your skin is lobster red from radiation or god knows what.

"I'm here for the coder," Djibrel said. "Is he inside?"

"Coder?" the hat man laughed. "Long gone. Precious cargo, that fish. We saw you coming a mile away. You've been had, freak. This is what you'd call a trap."

"I see," Djibrel said. "So it's only you and me, then?"

"Oh, I'm plenty enough," Hat Man said. "I'm the big gun. I'll have some questions for you, after we're done."

The drones were simple kinetic weapons controlled by a mental pulse, a military upgrade on the EchoChip that required surgery. They could turn a meat puppet to pulp faster than nanoware could knit it back together. Much faster. Djibrel wondered what other tricks Hat Man had in his giant cranium. He wasn't afraid, just professionally interested. After all, he had tricks himself. He supposed all the street sipahi lived under this cloud of bravado, the unflinching belief that their brand of violence was supreme.

He recognized Hat Man as a version of himself, a remade thing, with different masters but masters nonetheless, the ones who never showed their faces. Masters who had wrecked the old world and now claimed it was paradise.

The whirring balls put an end to his reverie. They converged on his torso, attacking from three sides, trying to disable rather than kill him. It was a question of German tungsten carbide versus Bahamut carbon steel.

Djibrel, in a state of meditative ease, was seeing time at a much slower rate. The balls were zipping around at the very edge of his acuity. A normal eye would have failed to see them at all. He made two cuts with his sword at the first pass, and two of the drones went wobbling off like wounded puppies. The third drone changed direction and made for his leg, and despite his sidestep, it took an inch-thick gash out of his thigh, a crippling wound that would have downed most people.

Blood spurted. Djibrel staggered but managed to keep upright. His wound started to knit back together even before the first drops hit the ground. Hat Man was staring in dismay at two-thirds of his arsenal being disabled; his mouth opened slowly in disbelief, and before he could bring his last drone on a second pass, Djibrel had already closed the distance, swept aside the rising shotgun, and raised a red welt on his neck with the invisible-edged talwar,

"What? What the fuck just happened?" The man's Adam's apple bobbed against the blade, which shaved off some more of that leathery skin.

"My weapons are better than yours," Djibrel said. "It's not a good trap if you can't swallow the thing you're trying to eat. I haven't come for you. You can still live if you give me information."

"I'm dead if I do," Hat Man said.

"If you do not cooperate, I will take your head," Djibrel said. "Same as the others I've been killing. I will keep you alive for a while in a jar, and you will tell me everything. Trust me, being a head in a jar is not fun at all."

"You do that for real?" The man closed his eyes in disbelief, and then muttered, "I thought that was just a story."

"It is not just a story."

"Psycho."

"What's your name?"

"Captain Rob," Hat Man said.

"Captain?"

"I was in the army once."

"As a captain? Really?"

"Fine, I was a sergeant. We gave ourselves promotions."

"And you set this trap?"

"I was sent instructions," said Rob.

"When?"

"When you took the mullah," Rob said. "They knew the coder was in danger. So they moved the coder and sent me to ambush you. They want to know who you're working for."

"Tell me about this coder. Who is he?"

Rob shrugged. "Wasn't a he. She's a chick."

"A woman?"

"Yup. I used to resupply the old house."

"With what?"

"Vat food, water, filters for her air system, personal shit, and a bag of dope every week," Rob said. "She used to smoke the expensive stuff too, grown from actual weed."

"How do you know she was a woman?"

"She had toiletries sent every month. High-priced shit. I had to check every package for safety."

"How long was she in that prefab?"

"Nine months," Rob said. "Just about."

"You see her face?"

"Nope. I left everything up front. Never saw her face, never heard her voice. Everything came via Echo from the bosses. Listen, man, they paid well, they got me chipped, got me the drones, and I followed every instruction to the letter like a puppy. I never saw 'em, I never even asked. They could make things disappear like smoke. These are scary people."

"Smoke, you say? You run into any djinn?"

Rob deflated a bit. "So you know who you're fucking with, then."

"Well?"

"One terrifying bitch. She had a giant fucking sword and was real polite. She brought the coder here the first time. Sek-something."

"Sekmet."

"Scary as fuck. Told me if anything happened to the coder she'd cut my balls off," the captain muttered. The scar tissue on his neck was oozing something ugly and black that made Djibrel want to disinfect his sword.

"So you did see the coder at least once."

"Just that first time. Face was masked, though. She was small, skinny, wore all black. That's all I know. I fucking had my eyes closed the minute I felt the djinn's field."

"Brave."

Rob sneered. "Yeah, tough guy. See how you puke your guts out when one of them turns up."

"Lucky for me they haven't. Only you."

"So you caught me. If I had a couple more drones you'd be toast." Captain Rob groaned in frustration. "That fucker Karmon got eight. He shoulda been here with me."

"Sure. Who's Karmon?"

"Half mech. Used to be with me in the army. Psycho with no face. Just a bunch of units under his skin. He got eight. I could only manage three. Fucking eight drones, can you believe that shit? You'll meet him soon enough. See how you dodge eight drones." Captain Rob looked mournful, as if eight drones would have radically changed the trajectory of his life.

"He sounds interesting. I guess I'll run into him soon. Do you have anything else useful?"

"Eat shit, asshole. I'm just a hired gun, like you."

"I believe you."

"So let me go, eh?"

"I'm going to have to cut your head off."

"What?"

"It won't hurt. The sword is very sharp."

"Why? Why do you want it?"

"Easier than carrying your whole body."

"What the fuck? I can walk! I'll walk! Aarrggharghhghg."

11

Fish and Chips

In the area called Old Town, or Old Dhaka, which had easily been inhabited for centuries, probably millennia, there were rows of small electronics shops that dealt with software and hardware, everything from repairs to patches to illegal augmentation. Most of them were aboveboard. Implants were the rage these days, and in the gray economy there were lots of options. Cyborgism was a real mania, described in various medical journals as the psychological urge to improve oneself through implantation.

The little shops existed in every city, and they fed the same fantasies of cyber jocks the world over. In the edges of the market, you got the real weird places. This being Dhaka, these were a bit blacker than normal, a bit more reckless, more willing to put wolf claws into someone's wrist. Still, even these veterans of the dark arts of augmentation had standards, and it took Djibrel five tries before he found a vendor willing to look into his sack.

Captain Rob's head was wrapped in plastic and still dripping blood.

"What the fuck?" The woman behind the counter looked young, twenty at best, though it was hard to tell because she was cowled up. Her rig was a bit like an old fencer's mask.

"Never seen a head before?" Djibrel asked innocently.

"Ah, that looks like a fresh one," the woman said, switching off whatever she was doing.

"It's my brother, he fell down the stairs," Djibrel said.

"And got his head cut off?"

"Well, I can't be lugging around his whole body, can I?"

The woman shook her head. "Boy, you're a different kind of crazy."

"What's your name?"

"Arna. Like the shop name."

"Arna, I'm—"

"Djibrel, yes, I know. The whole town knows who you are. Why do you think they all shutter their doors when you come round?"

"They do? How rude."

"No motherfucker wants a head on the counter."

"You own this shop, Arna?"

"Yep," Arna said. "My mom left it to me three years ago. We've lived here ten generations, man. So don't think of trying to muscle me, I got relatives in every lane."

"Muscling in? When you're doing so well?" Djibrel looked around ironically. The shop was on the dingier end, almost entirely filled with stolen, illegal merchandise.

"Yeah, yeah, laugh it up." She tapped her head. "My stock's in here. I'm building up a rep, you know? You think those ham-handed motherfuckers can calibrate an Echo like me? You'll see."

"Arna, this head is filled with a state-of-the-art EchoChip, military grade."

"How do you know?"

"He was running three drones with it."

"Riiight," scoffed Arna.

"He said there's another man who can run eight."

"That's straight-up impossible."

Djibrel reached into his sling and brought out the drones, now perfectly docile, two of them visibly damaged from the sword cuts. He placed them on the counter.

"I don't lie," Djibrel said. "People say it's because I have no imagination."

"Fuck, man, those are real antigrav."

"He might have other hardware in his skull. I also have a chunk of his spine, with his PMD," Djibrel said. "This is the deal. You keep everything you find, plus the drones. You help me hunt his employers, track down the source of the implants. The provenance." *Provenance? Where the hell did I learn a word like that?*

"That's a good deal," Arna said.

"Careful how you sell this shit."

"Sell? I ain't gonna *sell* contraband like that." Arna was around that age where she could put maximum scorn into any one-syllable word. "I'm gonna replicate it, man. I'm gonna rip them apart and get the templates. Gimme two days."

Djibrel shrugged. "Whatever. Head's all yours."

Two days later, he came back to find Arna's shop padlocked. The door was splintered anyway, the resin bashed in around the lock as if someone had taken a sledgehammer to it first. Djibrel kicked his way in. The interior had been a rat's nest before, but an orderly one, clearly indicating that some rational mind had put everything away using their own peculiar logic. Now everything was askew. The small broom closet office in the back was ransacked, even the bathroom smashed up, gratuitously, because it was a simple resin job, everything built into the walls, with few or no moving parts.

Djibrel went outside and collared the shopkeeper next door, who vociferously denied any knowledge of the break-in but after a few shakes gave up Arna's whereabouts. It was that kind of neighborhood, where everyone lived and worked within a small radius, had done so for generations. This man was an uncle of some sort, and brave enough in his own way, threatening to rouse the entire street, backing down only after Djibrel assured him that he was Arna's client, her partner. A ten-minute satcard calmed him enough to draw a little mental map and send it to Djibrel, which allowed his Echo to plot a path through the warren.

Arna's hideaway was heavily barricaded from the inside and required complex electronic maneuvers to enter. Identity finally established, Djibrel soon found himself in a very traditional-looking cube, being served hot tea by a swollen-eyed host, who seemed otherwise unhurt.

"He came for the head," she said, "The guy with eight drones. Major Karmon something."

"Quick response," Djibrel said. "Did he catch you?"

She shook her head.

"You look spooked."

"He was very vocal about what he was going to do to me. Very graphic. Announced it to the whole street as he was marching in. I ran before he got to my door."

"Did you see his face?"

She nodded. "It's not a face, Djibrel. It's like a series of little machines under the skin."

"And he didn't get a hold of you?"

"Please." Arna sneered. "The street knew he was coming before he put his pants on that morning. You gonna sneak up on a hundred coders? We got surveillance on every inch of this motherfucker."

"Good."

"I ran, like I said. That's how I got the black eye. Fucking twisted my knee and fell against a drainpipe."

"You've been crying. You sure nothing else happened?"

"Fuck off."

"This your place? Kinda dull. Like a banker's place or something."

"You think?" Arna said. "It's my cousin's. Karmon hit my place too, busted the lock, trashed everything."

"You're okay, though."

"Yeah. Promise."

"Did you find anything in the head?"

"I accessed all the hardware," Arna said. "Got a fair bit of information. Couldn't take out the pieces, though. So my income is shot. Plus all the property damage I took. Figure you owe me."

"I do."

"Well?"

"I'll give you a retainer," Djibrel said. "Five hundred sat minutes a month. Plus a month extra for the damage. You keep out of sight, you do my work only, you keep your mouth shut about what you find."

"I don't need charity, motherfucker."

"I got work to do, a coder to find," Djibrel said. "Tech stuff I don't understand. Need my own coder, you see? Now I can get a big one with some fancy card from the Tri-State, or I can get a hacker rat from Ram Krishna Mission Street."

"I can wipe the floor with any corporate coder," Arna spat. "You think they do any coding anymore? Those fuckers just outsource all their work back down here anyway."

"Okay, so you work for me now."

"So we're partners," Arna said. "Where you getting all this money from, partner?"

"Djinn."

"Djinn?"

"Yep."

"Fuck you."

Later at night, they met in a discreet rooftop eatery for their first board meeting. Arna, who took these things seriously, had a contract drawn up and everything, which Djibrel duly signed. He transferred over the credits from his account, also setting up the command for the automatic retainer to be released on the third of every month. In addition he set up a slush fund for expenses, which had a thousand minutes, for her to use for emergencies. This was all done via EchoChip, so it really entailed sitting down and staring into her eyes for ten minutes while all the files and permissions whirred back and forth between their cyborgs. It was a sort of digital romance.

Afterward, they got their food, vat-made tehari, a traditional rice, lamb, and mustard oil dish augmented by a number of ingredients added by hand—things like fresh green chilis, the mustard oil, some real onions—food grown old style, from dirt and shit, scrounged from private kitchen gardens, certainly breaking half a dozen health codes but known among the cognoscenti as essential for the preparation of tehari.

Eating this food required a silent meditation. They used their hands, and it was messy, because the art of eating rice with fingers was almost extinct from everyday life. Still, this was a special, secret place, and they were celebrating a beginning of sorts, so it was important to observe the formalities.

When the meal was done, they ordered extra beer and got down to business. Arna shoved a mass of files at him, which he mentally blinked into a secure cloud server. They were specs, schematics, order forms, and reams of technical arcana on high-level hardware, the blood and guts of what had allowed Captain Rob to control three balls of metal with his mind.

"Military grade, as you mentioned," Arna said. "High-level corporate. No wonder Major Karmon wanted it back. The equipment is Mitsubishi, straight from Nippon."

"Who can get it over here? I'm assuming you can't find it on the black market."

"Securex has it, same model; they're the only ones with the import license," Arna said. "So I asked a friend to look at their inventory, and sure enough, six command Echos were found defective two years ago and slated for disposal. That timeline work for you?"

"Yeah."

"So it's the oldest trick for cops, right? They 'destroy' the drugs or the guns or the cash or whatever on paper, except they really just resell it."

"Expensive, right?"

"Very, very expensive," Arna said. "The Mitsubishi Reaper Personalized Echo Command Drone is also a class one concealed armament, traffic of which is punishable by exile or loss of shareholder status.

The director of operations for Securex himself signed off on the disposal. That's some serious juice. Your enemies got weight."

"*Our* enemies now."

"Yeah, thanks," Arna said. "That's all I got so far. I never had time to look at the PMD. The Echo in the brain was scrubbed, probably taken from a guy in a coma. There are clinics everywhere that'll stick a chip in you for cheap; this one seemed to be a decent graft, but I didn't really have enough time with the head to say for sure where it was done."

"You can do that?"

"Sure. Most implants leave telltale signs, depending on the type of auto surgeon used and the firmware version. Normally I can narrow the shops down, and then it's a matter of asking around."

"I should bring you more heads."

"Ha ha."

"No really, I have a few more stocked."

"You're insane, you know that?" Arna shrugged. "Whatever. There was a hack on the Echo, a backdoor. Someone could basically look through this guy's eyes; they were probably watching you while you cut his head off."

"Is that easy to do?" Djibrel asked.

"No. Impossible, in fact. Couldn't do it to a legit Echo. They were running an older security software on the chip, one with the backdoor, and the alarms were disabled so that the poor sap wouldn't get updates or alerts. First time I've seen it."

"She's a coder," Djibrel said. "The one I'm looking for."

"Well, she's fucking better than me. And she was probably watching you all the way to my store. Hell, she was watching me as I cut the head open."

"Smart."

"So, partner, what the hell is the story here?" Arna asked.

Djibrel said. "Some underground project. Djinn and coders. A machine, I heard. They are building a god machine."

"Sounds like a myth." Arna shrugged. "Djinn working code? Aren't they supposed to, like, haunt trees and shit?"

"Fucking Djinn."

"So now what? We gonna shake down Securex? Find out who they sold their shit to? You gonna cut off some cop's head?"

"Cop heads last the longest in the fridge."

12

Walking on AIR

With a firm plan in place, Marzuk went to school in a jaunty mood. It was a blip, this Hinku thing, an understandable mishap, given that he hadn't attended school for years, was unfamiliar with its fragile social ecosystem. He had more important work to do: ReGi had sent twenty messages unanswered; Kali was gaming nonstop and would no doubt soon own the top spot, leading to further unwanted attention; and Djibrel hadn't been monitored in days. This bullying needed to be put to bed. He was losing weight because of it. That and the astronaut pills had finally arrived, and he was popping them like... popcorn.

His morning schedule coincided with Amina's, as much as possible. It was free period, two hours for working on a supervised long-term project, a sort of community service that involved developing skills in math, language, coding, science, and any other disciplines. At the beginning of the year, students of all grades were presented with real problems facing the community. The idea was to work on solutions, or components of solutions. Often the same problem would be attacked by groups of different ages, and sometimes the projects were ongoing over years.

Joining midyear, Marzuk had been given a limited selection. Of course, he had chosen Amina's group. This was a project that had nothing at all to do with his skill set or interests, but it let him spend the first part of the day with her, blessedly without Hinku anywhere in sight. It was the only bearable part of school.

He found her poring over old magazines, looking at twentieth-century style. Their project was helping some unemployed textile workers find niche markets for their handmade goods. It all seemed opaque and useless to Marzuk; after all, there were millions of unemployed textile workers, and hardly any billionaires looking for handmade clothes. Still, Amina saw him and cooed a bit over the black eye, running a feather light finger over his swollen forehead, and he played up being mournful, in a manly, dignified sort of way.

Then she ruined the moment by saying, "You shouldn't be fighting, you know, especially with Hinku."

Fighting? Me? It was more like that Neanderthal kicking me while I was curled up on the ground like a fetus! He's a fetus kicker!

"I heard you were walking around naked yesterday," she continued. "Are you all right, Marzuk?"

"Yeah, I'm a nudist, actually," Marzuk said. "My clothes were drying so I took a stroll. Forgot it wasn't allowed at school."

"A nudist?" Amina was staring at him doubtfully.

"Yeah, you should try it, it's very liberating," Marzuk said. "You hardly notice after the first few times."

"Riiight."

"Anyway, with Hinku, that's just a misunderstanding. I'm sure he'll see reason once I talk to him."

"Well, be careful. He's dangerous." She said it in an almost admiring way.

"Dangerous?" Marzuk scoffed. *Yeah, let's see how dangerous he is when his car crashes into a wall.*

"Don't you know?"

"What?"

"His father's on the board of Monsanto Bengal," Amina said. "You know, the guys who make the vat algae?"

"Hmm, I did not, in fact, know that."

"Yeah, and his uncle works for Securex," Amina said. "He's, like, really well connected. He beat up Rafik in the park last year and they actually pressed charges on Rafik's whole family, even though *he* was the one in hospital. They nearly lost their shareholder status in Tri-State Corp. I heard Rafik's dad had to go and beg Hinku's family for forgiveness."

Corrupt Securex cops. Monsanto Shit-Eating Bengal board. Sounds exactly like the kind of family Hinku would have.

"So, that's why everyone tolerates him."

"Well, he's also, like, really good at sports," Amina said. "You know, he's the fastest on the swim team even though he's younger than the others. They think he's good enough to turn pro. Imagine! He's really not a bad guy, just quick-tempered. I'm sure you could make friends with him, if you got to know him."

He's a class A psychopath.

"Yeah, sure," Marzuk said. "Well, let's get back to work; these weavers won't market themselves."

"Look at these shawls they made, Marzuk, aren't they gorgeous?"

I don't care about shawls at all. Can't you see that I only wear white T-shirts and jeans, woman?

Later on, he got the encounter he was looking for when Hinku stopped by to admire his handiwork and congratulate Marzuk for returning to school so soon.

"Normally kids lose their clothes, they spend the rest of the week at home sick," he said, laughing. "I gotta give it to you, fatty, you really don't have any pride. This is gonna be fun."

"Yeah, about that," Marzuk said. "We got off on the wrong foot. Perhaps I didn't make my position clear. Sure, you can harass me at school, but I can leave anytime I like. Unlike you, I don't need a degree. Every time you mess with me here, I'm going to mess with you outside. And outside, I can get to you whenever I want, without even touching you. I think it would be in your best interest if we stopped right now, before this gets out of hand."

"Get to me? What, by flickering the lights in my room? Making my kale salad taste like shit?" Hinku smirked. "You think I don't know about you, hacker? They got a file on you at Securex. Any of that shit happens, fatty, and my uncle is gonna send cops to your house. Your loser dad and loser mom are gonna get taken in for questioning, and they'll have to kiss my ass just to get their shares back. Yeah, I know about your dad. He's a nobody, a shitty exec at climate control. What does he do, change the batteries over there?"

"You're threatening my parents now?"

"Unlike you, I live in the real world," Hinku said. "My dad said your family used to be well-known back in the day, now they're just old and useless, with no money and no power. You've got no one to call; no one's gonna help you. You're a hacker, they know about you breaking the law, running around playing pranks. You want your parents dragged off for questioning Securex? You know what they do to people in remand? You want your parents getting buttfucked in remand, that's up to you."

"Right. I mean no, I don't want that to happen."

"Yeah, that's what I thought," Hinku said. He moved his head close to Marzuk's ear. "You piece of shit. I like the panda look you've got. I'm gonna let the bruise fade a couple of days and give you a matching one on the other eye. You tell 'em you got hit with a ball in the face, right?"

"Yeah, ball in the face."

"Yeah, my balls in your face. That's your next four years. See ya later."

All right, I'm not gonna touch you, Hinku. Your uncle is not going to be so lucky. Securex? We'll see about that.

Back home, he slipped by the parents but was unable to avoid ReGi any longer. She took one look at his face and guessed his problems.

"It's no big deal," Marzuk huffed, irritated.

"You've got to tell the teachers!" ReGi said. "Tell the superintendent. It's assault! Get him expelled. Why the hell are you still in school, anyway? Don't we have serious work to do?"

"Yeah, yeah, I'm not gonna let this asshole run me out of town," Marzuk said. "And snitching just makes me look weak."

"Yeah, darling Amina is going to think you're a wuss," ReGi said. "Really, man, you've got to stop wasting time on her and get back to business. Can't you just VR porn and jack off like regular guys?"

"I love her, I told you."

"Love my ass, it's a crush."

"She's perfect."

"She's a spoiled bitch who wants to be famous. I've seen her feed."

"I think about her, like, every minute. I analyze every little interaction, no matter how trivial. I feel a warm feeling just being near her..."

"That's your body trying to puke."

"When she smiles it's like sunshine..."

"Fuck, you're just a complete moronic cliché bomb, aren't you?"

"'She walks in beauty, like the night... '"

"No. Just no. No Byron."

"You're a philistine."

"No wonder that Hinku guy wants to beat you up. Even *I* want to kick your ass now."

"I've got this, don't worry."

"Just drop a satellite on his head already."

"I can't, he's a bit more complicated," Marzuk said. "Turns out his uncle is a director at Securex."

"What are you going to do, then?"

"Well, I'm going to get the uncle fired," Marzuk said, "and frame the motherfucker Hinku. And you're going to help me."

"Hmm, sounds fun."

"When I'm done he's going to have my name tattooed on his forehead."

"Yeah, yeah, enough with the testosterone. Where's our AI guest?"

"Oh shit, I forgot, she's still playing *Final Fantasy*," Marzuk said. "Hope she's not dead. Gear up, let's go see how far she's gotten."

Marzuk flipped on his cowl, and the world blinked into the vivid colors of *FF9000*. He got his goblin engineer revved up, and then waited in front of his lair for ReGi to arrive. ReGi too had an outlandish avatar, though she didn't play with Marzuk often. Apparently his penchant for burning noob villages while shouting invectives was not particularly amusing to more sophisticated persons.

The normal players called them game breakers, overpowered avatars created "not in the spirit of the game." Like Marzuk, ReGi had exploited the loose crafting rules to turn a basic water nymph template into a sort of flying astronaut. Normal mages flew using spells, and this exhausted their mana, so most of the time they plodded along on the ground like regular people. ReGi had crafted a spell that heated a band of air and controlled it between layers of cooler air; she floated, essentially, manipulating air pressure and temperature, aided by the natural buoyancy that was the starting stat of the water nymph, long considered a singularly useless class.

Her mastery of the physics of this world, in fact, was her real power. That and her massive keep in the sky, the infamous Sky Castle, which hung in the air by virtue of an impossible feat of mathematics and magic, protected by an aviary of wyverns.

What most gamers did not appreciate was that the massive engine of *FF9000* actually ran their virtual world with the laws of physics, overlaid with whatever magical quirks Saka could imagine, and thus the environment responded to math as readily as it did to spells and magic.

The two of them moved down a path, goblin and nymph, seemingly harmless noobs with weird gear, ReGi floating a foot or so above the ground. Marzuk's lair was in a bucolic region, not far from the village where he had deposited Kali, and Marzuk did a fair amount of work to ensure that it stayed peaceful, with his fellow goblins allowed to go about their business without sword-waving heroes pestering them.

In fact, the region was known among the cognoscenti, a sort of goblin shire best left alone. The last invasion of the area by a would-be king had been exactly 248 days ago, when some unwitting noob had watched his entire army get fed into a literal meat grinder at the mouth of the valley, one of Marzuk's nastier traps, against which armored knights had no answer. It had caused a minor sensation on the thirty-eight net channels that carried *FF* feed live with commentary. He had even given an interview stating that he preferred the farmer's life and warned aspiring warlords to just leave his patch the fuck alone.

So he was understandably perturbed to find his village ringed now with high walls and towers, belching smoke, apparently upgraded into a class 3 town, complete with NPC sentries and a garrison of golems.

"Looks like Kali's figured out the game," ReGi said, smirking.

"Those golems are trampling all over my petunias."

After a humiliating wait at the outer portcullis, a grinning Roland came to fetch them.

"What the hell have you guys done? It's only been a couple of days," Marzuk said.

Roland laughed excitedly. "Man, Kali is the bomb. BOMB. It took her, like, half an hour to figure shit out and then it's been twenty-four/seven action. She cleaned out a level eighty den of djinn, took all their shit, and we came back and pretty much bought the village. She's talking about building a civilization that will last forever!"

"Hmm, onset of megalomania," Marzuk said. "This is not looking good."

They were escorted by a complement of trumpeters to a medieval-looking throne room, where Kali was holding court. She had a standard witch avatar, a dark-skinned sorceress, her armor embellished with a head of skulls taken from her goddess namesake's iconic look.

"Friend Marzuk!" she said as they approached. "I have accrued power and prestige, as you instructed!"

"Yes, you certainly have."

"My domain now stretches from here to the djinn kingdom on the coast," Kali said. "All lords in this area have sworn fealty to me. Of course, I have granted your cave sovereignty out of courtesy."

"Ha, thanks. You've been busy. How'd you manage it?"

"She was great!" Roland said. "After we bought out the village with the djinn loot, we started conquering castles one by one, but that was taking too long, so then we announced a combat tournament and put up all our gold. Most of the players in the area came; it was *a lot* of gold. Anyway, Kali ambushed them and took them all hostage."

"That can't have been easy."

"We had a null spell zone from the djinn," Roland said. "It was only for ten minutes, but she convinced them they were gonna be stuck without magic for three days. And then she killed the five most hated guys, I mean the real dicks, and split up all their shit and gave it to the others. They pretty much all swore fealty to us at that point."

"Then we took this grand army of noobs and conquered the remaining castles," Kali said. "In one twelve-hour campaign we were able to take seven fortifications and three towns. It is my projection that at this rate, we should overrun the continent within a month."

"Easy now," Marzuk said. "That's not how the game works. You get much bigger, and there will be a convergence of the big clans attacking you. No one has held this continent by themselves. The current configuration is the most stable it's been for three years."

"Correct, there are the Red Elves holding the Eternal Forest and Kuru City, the paladins holding Crystal City and the plains, and the goblins, djinn, orcs, dwarves, and sundry losers holding these mountains and hills," Kali said. "The powers in this neutral zone are fragmented, because the two larger factions have taken the prime lands of the forest and the plains. We are in the low-class zone, friend Marzuk!"

"I would rather say we are in the most interesting area," Marzuk said.

"They call us the losers."

"Yes, but we're free to do what we want, while they spend their time grinding for power," Marzuk said.

"You are almost considered the king of the losers," Kali said.

"Thanks."

"Your valley, moreover, is an oasis. It has perfect weather and excellent fertility, plus all manner of interesting minerals."

"Thank you."

"Also, I notice that the larger factions recognize your valley as a neutral zone and do not attack it. They appear to hold you in high esteem!"

"Well, they won't be ignoring this valley much longer if you keep up your belligerence," Marzuk said.

"I have calculated their response and prepared battle plans accordingly," Kali said. "We currently have a two percent chance of survival should either the elves or paladins attack us, and thus I have concluded that diplomacy is the only way forward, while inducing them to fight each other, for which I have created a contingency. What is wrong, friend Marzuk? I thought you would be pleased."

"Yeah, I did not expect Attila the Hun," Marzuk said.

"Ignore him," ReGi said. "You've done really well. He's just annoyed you've upended his little valley and trampled his tulips."

"Petunias," Marzuk muttered. "Kali, this is ReGi, my friend. She knows everything, she's going to be helping us."

"Friend ReGi, welcome," Kali said.

"I'm glad you're having fun with the game," ReGi said.

"Fun... yes, it is fun," Kali said. She looked at Marzuk with her witchy black eyes. "I had almost forgotten the purpose of this exercise."

"Right, to business, then," Marzuk said once she had cleared the room, including a protesting Roland.

"This was a different kind of Turing test, was it not, friend Marzuk?" Kali asked.

"A vastly more difficult one," Marzuk said.

"Turing only wanted machines to fool a human in conversation fifty percent of the time," ReGi said. "That too in rote, tightly controlled exchanges."

"I had assumed you would use your superior machine reflexes to win, but that has not been the case. You've played the game socially, putting together alliances, threats, subterfuge," Marzuk said. "At the same time you displayed a strong sense of self-improvement, learning, adaptation of tactics and strategy, and of accommodating elements of random chance that are deliberately put in the game to foil bots."

"I take it the game has a mechanism to weed out nonhuman intelligence?" Kali asked.

"The previous record for a bot has been just twenty hours of active play," Marzuk said. "As you can imagine, bots playing this game on behalf of their human masters would quickly lead to imbalance, farming resources and such. The most sophisticated sections of *FF9000* programming, in fact, are those used to weed out bots. All the serious gamers spend significant efforts trying to beat the system. It's an ever- escalating arms race, with severe punishments. Saka is particularly harsh on bots. My own record was a sentry bot that lasted eighteen hours. I had him imitating a six-year-old boy."

"Saka is the AI of the game?" Kali asked.

"Level Nine AI, registered, when he was built," ReGi said. "He's bigger now, and no one knows exactly how powerful, because the game keeps growing. It's maybe bigger than the real world in some ways."

"He's like a god in-game," Marzuk said. "And Fedor assures me he's almost as powerful in the Virtuality itself."

"But he's not built with free agency," ReGi said. "I mean, his purpose was to run the game, and that's what he mainly does. He can't suddenly decide to go and colonize Europa, right?"

"Who knows? What if he decides Europa needs *FF9000*?" Marzuk said. "Fedor swears that he rules the entire black market in Nippon. But at least at first, that's true, he was a slaved AI. Whereas Kali, apparently, was *born with free agency*, and is capable of fooling Saka. So. Here we are."

"You're the first of a kind, Kali," ReGi said. "Let's savor the moment."

"Should I try to communicate with this Saka?" Kali asked.

"I don't know," Marzuk said. "As far as I understand, an AI like him can learn, adapt, anticipate. He takes care of the entire ecosystem like a god. But is he self-aware in a meta sense? Does he *want* to talk to you? What purpose would that serve? Would he view you as a threat?

"It's argued that self-awareness is not strictly necessary for intelligence. I mean, the brain can function perfectly well without the awareness loop. So what does that make you? Why waste space on even giving the appearance of self-awareness? Is there a difference between appearing self-aware and actually being self-aware?"

"Self-awareness implies self-examination," ReGi said. "Not how intelligently you view the world around you, or interpret sensory input, but to what extent you can analyze yourself."

"Unnecessary," Marzuk said. "*Inefficient*. If you designed a meat brain from scratch, you wouldn't put all that shit in there to begin with."

"Dude, you really like the sound of your own voice," ReGi said.

"What exactly is self-awareness good for? Isn't it just a constant feedback loop? Sensory input into the meat brain, adding to the extremely skewed simulation we carry around in our heads, which reinforces our 'consciousness,' which then fools itself into thinking that there is a discrete self to begin with, when in reality we're just a combined bag of symbiotic cells, hijacked by a set of genetic material that really only wants to replicate itself like Von Neumann machines. So you spend all this energy and skull space on growing more brain meat to house this simulation, which then keeps reinforcing itself, until you're fucking convinced that everything revolves around you and every action of yours has cosmic significance.

"I mean, you could design a perfectly intelligent species, biological or machine, without self-awareness, and it would probably advance much faster than we do."

"What about art? Culture? Would you have all of that?" ReGi asked.

"Wouldn't need it, would we? That's all just sop to the old feedback loop."

"You know, Marzuk, every adolescent smartypants discovers the same anticonsciousness argument sooner or later," ReGi said.

"Smartypants? Smartypants?!"

"I'm just saying, your angst is so cute..."

"Are you the mate of friend Marzuk?" Kali asked politely.

"What? Mate? Oh. Ew, no," ReGi said.

"It is just that I have seen many old television shows where couples mated for a long time argue in a similar way..."

"Ahem, Kali, no," Marzuk said.

"Humans are confusing. Where are the machine intelligences I may talk to?"

"We have the AI Registry," ReGi said. "They're kind of the ruling body of AI, made up of AIs. Like sheriffs. If you make an AI and don't register it, the AIR comes after you."

"How many of these registered level tens are there?" Kali asked.

"Officially? Zero. It's more like a theoretical threshold. And level nines? Only twenty-three in the whole world including Saka," ReGi said. "And most of them are in scientific concerns. They are very expensive to make."

"And frankly speaking, they're super specialized," Marzuk said. "You don't need a level nine to run shipping lanes or smart cars or whatever. That's just glorified Tetris. And even in development, there's multiple paths for the intellect to take. I mean, one sort of thinking is just brute-force processing, where every option on a branching option tree is evaluated until the correct solution is found. The other is more meat brain thinking, *intuitive* thinking, where you look at the only most likely solutions and use hunches and shit to make decisions. You get both kinds of AI, but mostly the former. Do you want the mind making your suborbital pods to be designing on hunches?

"That's what I don't get with you... Why would someone make you —assuming that you were created—why would someone go to the effort of making a conscious, free-willed, intuitive-thinking AI? What purpose would you serve? It's like you've been massively overdesigned."

"What purpose, to justify such effort and expense? And then why leave me adrift?" Kali said.

"It must be very lonely," Marzuk said, with a sudden flash of empathy. "To one day wake up fully conscious."

"No lonelier than waking up an overweight cyber mage," ReGi said.

"Ha. Thanks."

"The regulations on anything approaching level ten are serious," ReGi said. "The AI Registry goes through, like, every line of code, I think. The learning phase is closely monitored too. So she has to be off registry. You don't just misplace a billion-bitto mind."

"But if you wanted to bypass the registry, what would you do?" Marzuk asked. "I mean, what are the obstacles?"

"Well, first of all, you need quantum computing banks for that kind of AI. That's liquid cores," ReGi said. "And the AIR monitors those, so, like, Samsung is not going to make you a bank unless they sign off on it. Plus all the rare earth metals you need. And there are patents you have to access, which would trip alarms, as well as just basic hardware in large quantities, which would be caught by account bots. It's massively expensive, kind of like building a nuke, and in the end, they'd catch you. And again, why bother? It's not illegal to build AI..."

"Yet here we are," Marzuk said. "Kali roaming free, and no one has come looking. That itself tells us some things."

"Like what?"

"Like their hardware is nonstandard," Marzuk said. "They aren't using quantum computing banks. She's based on some other strata. That's how you bypass the AIR. You reinvent the wheel."

"Why, though? The AIR is there for a reason. No offense, Kali, but no one wants killer AI on the loose because some megalomaniac decided to code a digital Hitler for fun," ReGi said. "Every big company in the world is a signatory to the AIR."

"No offense taken," Kali said. "ReGi, I do not have any urges to eradicate particular races of humans. For me, it is all or nothing."

"What?!"

"It would be more efficient to wipe everyone out, rather than picking specific races," Kali said. "That is a joke, friend Marzuk."

"ReGi, does the AIR say who commissioned what AI?" Marzuk asked.

"Somewhere deep in the applications they probably do," ReGi said. "It's there, but buried. Why?"

"Well, maybe it could hint at a possible parent for Kali," Marzuk said. "Like, who actually needs an AI? Who is experienced enough to make one? Who might be able to put together that kind of hardware off the books? Let's look for skill sets."

"I'm sending you their downloadable records," ReGi said. "Knock yourself out. It'll take you approximately three years to go through everything."

"What are *you* going to do?" Marzuk asked.

"Remember Djibrel?" ReGi said. "I've been watching him. He's acting weird, setting off alarm bells. I want to follow up with that. Hours of footage to sort through."

"All right, looks like we've both got a lot of slog work," Marzuk said. "But first, we have some important business to attend to."

"What?"

"Kali, about that plan you've put together..."

"Friend Marzuk, our chances of success are considerably increased if both of you participate," Kali said.

"Are you serious?" ReGi said. "You want to game *now*?"

"Look, I've had a bad week, I'm getting bullied in school, my eye is puffy, and Amina hasn't warmed up at all," Marzuk said. "I need a treat. Kali's already wrecked the balance of power here. We might as well try for the whole continent before it comes crashing down."

"Pfft, you're such a child."

"They say it can't be done. You wanna join us with your wyverns?"

"Nope."

"Chicken."

"If I wanted to, I'd take that continent in three days flat," ReGi said.

"Bullshit."

"Three days, Marzy. Later."

Two days later, after intense ten-hour sessions, Marzuk was further convinced that Kali was in fact *really* intelligent, rather than simply mimicking human behavior. She was the ultimate team member; her reflexes were instantaneous, she could monitor everything at once, she never went AFK, and she could calculate the math behind the physics engine much faster and better than even the best grinders. On top of that, her strategies and tactics were original, not a plodding logic gate process of elimination but inclusive of flairs and intricacies that suggested a more tortuous thought process.

"You're definitely intuitive," Marzuk said when they finally quit. Their gambit had failed; they had managed to get only halfway through the continent before the other players joined forces and tore up their nascent empire. Heavy guns from other parts of the game world had come to participate, even one of the original beta testers. Many of the Upper Fifty came to join the fun, with a mixture of Red Elves and paladins converging on him. In the face of their combined might, his own allies melted, the djinn and orcish heavy infantry disappearing into the night and protesting their innocence when questioned.

At that point, Marzuk had called it off. Kali was garnering too much attention. *But she had fooled Saka.*

"You are convinced, then, that I am conscious?" Kali asked. "I profess relief."

They were lounging in their original village pub, the only part of their vast demesne they had been able to preserve in the surrender negotiations.

"I'm just glad Saka hasn't come investigating you. Thank god you dialed back the APM."*

"The next time, friend Marzuk, we will succeed," Kali said. She looked morose. The defeat had hit her hard. "I have analyzed your flame throwing technology. It is probable that given some more resources, we will be able to create airborne incendiary weapons."

"What? Like missiles? You mean missiles?"

"Correct. If we take advantage of ReGi's air manipulation physics, we might not require actual motive power, which is the primary bottleneck."

---

*APM: actions per minute, one of the ways to judge how quick a gamer is at multitasking.

"Hmm, yes, normally they just use catapults to lob shit around over here, but I can see that missiles powered by spells would be pretty useful," Marzuk said.

"A study of Earth history reveals that sufficient munitions eventually rendered castle walls completely obsolete," Kali said.

"You're sounding a bit smug over there."

"This entire continent is dotted with castles with excessively high walls," Kali said. "They are almost begging for it."

"You do realize that this is a sword-and-sorcery game, and you're going to ruin it for everyone?" Marzuk asked.

"Is it not the point to win the game?" Kali asked innocently.

"You're just sore they made you surrender."

"I confess, signing that treaty left me with a curiously unpalatable taste. I felt a tremendous unforeseen desire to hurt them."

"That's the bloodthirst, my friend. Revenge."

"It is irrational yet compelling."

"I'll tell you what, Kali: whoever made you patterned your brain on meat," Marzuk said. "I'm pretty sure AI don't feel bloodlust. What would be the point? A lot of things about you don't make sense in a cost-benefit analysis."

"Ah, back to real life." Kali sighed. "It is difficult to forget that we were playing a game."

"Yeah, *FF9000* sucks you in like that," Marzuk said. "It's 'cause it's more real than real, you see? Sometimes I think the world works better in here than out there. Anyway, back to work before ReGi wakes up and starts harping."

"She does seem to enjoy harping at you," Kali agreed politely.

"I've been thinking, the best way to tackle your problem is to figure out *why* you were created," Marzuk said. "What kind of job needs you? We have to think outside the box."

"It is disconcerting to think of one's own creation," Kali said.

"One of the greatest religious dilemmas," Marzuk said. "Now, I'm going to take a nap. You look through the AI Registry for patterns."

Kali's witch avatar frowned. "That hardly seems like an equitable division of labor."

"I'm made of meat," Marzuk said. "I need to eat and sleep. You're AI. You're made of electrons. You get to keep working."

"I would prefer to continue gaming."

"No more. Saka's getting suspicious."

"You appear to hold this Saka in high regard."

"He's a psycho and he *will* come to investigate if you alert him."

"I would like to fight him."

"You know how big the game is?" Marzuk asked.

"It is very big."

"That's how big *he* is," Marzuk said. "He is everywhere. He cannot be killed. Even the military AIs are afraid of him. So please. Leave him alone."

"Fine."

"I'm serious."

"Okay, but I want one further attempt at conquest."

"All right, I agree, but not now. You can plot in secret. *If* you find something useful in the registry."

"Friend Marzuk, I am amending the terms of your hire to include a Reconquista of all we have lost. And you will bring me Betagamer007 on his knees so that I may humiliate him. Also Ogawarajones and that sneering mage Zanefaraway. In fact, I wish to exterminate the Red Elves entirely as a clan. I wish to burn their forest and sow it with salt."

"You want to pay me to play *FF9000* with you?"

"I am consumed with the desire to reverse my previous shameful defeat."

"And you're blaming this on me?"

"I suspect your mind and ability were not fully invested in our previous effort."

"That's hurtful. How can you say that?"

"The fact that you spent much of your time setting fire to level one noobs and laughing maniacally alerted me to it."

"Hey, I game to relax, okay?"

"Yes. I have noted a degree of frivolity to your gaming. Which is why I shall be extending advance payment for the Reconquista. I expect your full effort and use of resources, including things from the black node you use that no one knows about."

"You're crazy."

"And BG007 must kiss my ring and apologize."

"Look, BG007 is one of the first komagemas. You know that that means? Guys who put their bodies on ice to shift over to Virtuality *full-time*. And he didn't go over empty-handed. He's very, very powerful, very well connected."

"More than you?"

"He *lives in the game.* Yes."

"He is not biological anymore, then?"

"I... I don't know. The komagemas, they're the first breed, the hard-core players who transitioned for real once the engine was big enough to take it. Saka looks after them *personally*. They keep the bodies alive at a low temp, filled up with a nanotech broth. I mean, it's like one degree from dead. Brain still works, though. If you switch the body off, will they live on in the game world? Who knows? Probably. I guess their avatars are robust enough to take it. Will they be the same person? Will they have all of their memories intact, the non-game ones? Can they feel, think, act the same way without input from the meat? No one knows yet. It's the whole digital afterlife question. Is it the real person living on, or is it just a big batch file going through the motions?"

"What will happen, friend Marzuk, if I take this electronic brain of BG007, this node you call his avatar, and destroy it completely?"

Marzuk shuddered. "That would be murder."

13

Power Level 9,000

Arna had moved her shop to a more secure location. As the youngest of nine siblings, all of whom lived in the neighborhood, she had a lot of hidey-holes. Currently she was in the backroom of her brother Leto's shop. Leto had been born with a spinal defect that not only prevented him from walking but even precluded the fitting of a PMD. He had been given up for dead. The hospital had almost euthanized him, until a scripture-quoting grandma had swooped in.

Like others in their family, Leto had turned his misfortune into a business opportunity. Due to his rare condition, he had accrued some press as a child, and when he reached puberty, Honda had donated a medical exoskeleton for him. In Nippon they had written stirring blogs about how this poor boy could now get low-paying menial jobs and at least feed himself. Other humanitarians around the globe had pledged mythical amounts for his education and upkeep, promptly reneging once the spotlight moved on to some other unfortunate.

Leto had not faded into obscurity, however. He had, instead, modded his exo into a piece of lethal body armor that could take out half a squad of corporate police. None of the interviewers focusing on his mangled spine had picked up that he was, in fact, an engineering prodigy. Mathematics flowed out of him like poetry; he could have been a physicist or an astronaut, but he was interested only in practical applications.

He now made a great living as one of Old Dhaka's best security experts. Often city corporation cops hired him to enter the breach first as a battering ram. His presence alone in most places ensured peace.

When Djibrel walked in carrying a stack of heads, Leto was lounging in the front office, kitted up in deliberate menace. The two eyed each other warily for a moment.

"Nice suit," Djibrel said.

"Nice heads," said Leto.

"You weren't kidding about the heads," Arna said, coming out. "No one ever stops you just walking around with them?"

"I get weird looks," Djibrel said.

"What are the chances that dangerous people who knew those heads are going to come looking for us?" Leto asked. "I don't like this guy, Arna."

"Shut up, Leto, I took the job," Arna said.

"You're security, aren't you?" Djibrel asked. "Secure her."

"I don't need his fucking tin-can security," Arna said. "I wanted a place to work, not a lecture."

"I'll hire you," Djibrel said to Leto. "Monthly rate. That good?"

"I don't need a rate to protect my own goddamn sister," Leto rumbled.

"Then what the fuck are we arguing about?" Djibrel asked.

"Fine." He seemed torn between hating Djibrel and recognizing in him a kindred soul. Djibrel, who did not recognize kinship with any other human, was oblivious to this and thus unable to cement what might have been a lifelong friendship.

In the back room, Arna started prying open the jars. The heads floated in a bath, looking fresh. The eyes twitched, trying to open, but Djibrel had taped the eyelids shut. They were still alive, in a fashion.

"You can find the lab?" Djibrel said.

"Sure."

"We can find the watcher then, the one looking through their eyes," Djibrel said. "She's the one I want."

"Gimme two days," Arna said. "I'll be cracking open the skulls, you understand? You won't get the heads back in one piece." She seemed overly concerned that he kept the heads out of some kind of death fetish beyond the exigencies of his investigation.

Djibrel waved her away. "Don't worry, I can always get more." He considered it for a moment. "They've been begging to die every time they wake up."

"You're a cold motherfucker," said Arna.

The illicit Echo lab was in Narayanganj, so Djibrel had to go back over there, forced to nursemaid Arna along, because she wanted to see everything firsthand before he wrecked the place. Leto had wrapped her in a combat suit, a ten-year-old police issue that was still cutting-edge as far as the street was concerned. He was running mission control from his office, looking through the cameras installed in the suit, maintaining a barrage of unnecessary advice. Djibrel wished he could turn him off, but Arna had promised her big brother full remote access. It was the only way Leto had allowed her to come on this excursion.

The suit had a pulse weapon attached to the wrist, and if Arna froze up in the middle of a firefight, Leto could take over motor function and get to work. He had wanted to come along, but Djibrel had pointed out that *two* combat suits in Narayanganj would almost certainly cause a sartorial scandal and bring corporate police down on their heads. Not to mention announce their presence to every single interested party involved.

It wasn't stealth, walking around in riot armor, but it was better than being shredded by drones. They barged their way around Narayanganj's narrow streets, Arna trying to sidestep potholes and garbage and, in some cases, dog shit, looking dainty and uncomfortable despite her suit. It was her first time out here, among the cardless. You could always tell a first-timer. Djibrel grabbed her elbow and propelled her along, forcing her to walk through puddles of god knows what. If you spent your time looking at the ground trying to avoid shit, you were liable to get robbed.

The lab was near the old post office, which had shut down a century ago due to lack of mail but still retained its status as a landmark. The security apparatus was drone coverage, a few scrap cameras latched onto surfaces, resting lazily in between flights, anemic.

The plan was simple. Leto was already doing things to the drones, confusing their limited intelligence, and if they weren't hooked up to a mainframe, which they weren't, then they were about as dumb as an actual fruit fly by now, seeing nothing. This would cause alarm, of course, given time. The good thing about being out here was that *all* tech was glitchy: too much crud in the air, those random viral bits of nanotech that had wrecked the earth while promising Eden. Djibrel had a three-minute window to approach the Echo lab.

Seeing no overt defense, he opted for their primary plan. Arna shuffled forward, the power suit now charging up, and then one boot hit the door with the force of a ten-ton bison, splintering it. She was supposed to spin to the side now, let Djibrel through, but in the heat of the moment, the omnipotence of her battle armor went to her head. She was just a kid, Djibrel had to remind himself, through Leto's swearing over the mic, as she thundered into the room, arm out, only to take something to the face, a netlike object.

"Taser! Taser!" Leto shouted one last time before shorting out.

It was some kind of electric pulse weapon, a massive charge, capable of burning everything, frying humans, but more importantly destroying whatever electronics they had, external or internal. Getting your Echo fried was like getting a lobotomy without anesthesia. You became instantly dumber, and you knew it too.

The suit was supposed to withstand this kind of thing. Supposed to. Arna went down to one knee, and then flat on her back, possibly stunned, feet twitching, and Leto was static in the air, although Djibrel could imagine his cursing clearly enough.

There were four people inside the room, two men and two women, holding what looked like a snub-nosed cannon. It was riot gear, Djibrel thought, a net and pulse, meant to knock a mob back on its ass. Riot gear augmented beyond its regulated usage to get past the suit.

Of course, Djibrel didn't have electronics anymore, not in the traditional sense. His Echo was djinn-ware, proofed on a submolecular level, something done painstakingly by Bahamut himself. He walked through the pulse with his sword out, cutting the filaments of the net shot from the cannon and then into the four, spreading out his damage. In his mind he had already clocked them as hired help, their fists scarred, the muscle, not the brain.

Three or four tight cuts, the cramped hilt of the talwar making perfect sense in these confined quarters as it forced his arm into a particular fight style, short stiff-armed blows that unfurled bodies like petals. As he waded past them, he hacked them to pieces, making sure they were dead, unable to further molest Arna. Rage clawed at the back of his throat, a blinding, building anger.

There was another room in the back, this one bigger and filled with surgical equipment. There was a woman in a lab coat, with gray hair and tired eyes. She quickly held her hands out and sat down.

"You've come about the dead men's Echos," she said.

Djibrel grunted, his breath blowing in hot feral blasts.

"You're the man who cuts off heads," the lady continued, speaking fast, the words almost tripping out. "I'm Doctora Fatima. Former doctor. They took my license over ten years ago."

Djibrel stared at her, bestial, his fingers twitching with the urgent desire to close around her throat, to choke the words shut.

She shrugged. "My clients warned me you might be coming. And they sent protection. Inadequate, I see."

"They saw me," Djibrel said.

"You kept taking people's heads," the doctora said. "We thought you were a garden-variety psychopath."

"I'm fifty-fifty on yours."

"You'll find nothing untoward inside," Fatima said. "I still have my original EchoChip, upgraded with a medical module. All perfectly legal, done in Dhaka Medical Hospital all of forty years ago."

"I want the watcher. The one looking through dead men's eyes."

"Yes. That's not happening. I have a slight modification on my Echo. Any severe bodily trauma will cause a small electric signal to run through my gray matter. Instant death. You might find something by rooting around in there, but you'll need a mainframe and a team of neurosurgeons to make any sense of it. You're not a neurosurgeon too, are you?"

"I just collect heads," Djibrel said.

"So, just a garden-variety psycho..."

Oh yes...

"Suppose I cooperate?" Fatima said quickly as he twitched forward. "I'm a noncombatant, as you'd say. No need for me to die on my shield."

"I fucking *would not* say that," Djibrel said. "Every fucking leech like you thinks they're a noncombatant. But you're all culpable." *Culpable. Blameworthy. Fucking complicit. A lot of big words. What did you do, Bahamut, stick a dictionary in my brain?*

"You're an odd one, aren't you?" the doctora said. She sighed. "Oddly linear. Yet not stupid."

"I am stupid," Djibrel said. "Clever people end up like you."

"Yes, I suppose so. Let me tell you a story. Like Scheherazade. If you like it, I live."

"Better be a good story." He relaxed a little.

"The buyers contacted me first with a hand-delivered letter. They paid by bitto. Untraceable. They sent the chips to me by mail, from randomized courier stops, which are sort of like moving post office boxes. The patients came to me heavily sedated, in plain body bags. They were all street. I could tell, of course. Expendable. Which is good, because I lost a couple on the table. I was compensated even for the failed procedures."

"Courier?"

"Some Russian outfit, like all of them are. Here, take the receipts. It's a dead end. They're unhackable." There was a simple logo: *Dostoyevsky Couriers*.

Djibrel just stared at her. *No such thing as unhackable. Ask Bahamut.*

"Look, I knew the Echos were tampered with. I have no idea who ordered it, or where they got the chips from, or why. Frankly, I didn't care. Most of my clients are criminals."

"Echos. Supposed to be tamperproof."

"Get real," the doctora sneered. "You think everyone gets the same hardware? You think company men and regular folk carry the same shit in their heads?"

"No," Djibrel said.

"They weren't local," Doctora Fatima said. "But at these rates... well, I wasn't in a position to say no. If not me, then someone else, eh? Plenty of out-of-work doctors in these parts. Now, I swear, that is the truth; even if you take apart my brain strand by strand, you'll get nothing else, because there *is* nothing else. Torture me all you want, it will be for nothing."

Djibrel's hands flexed, and Fatima's eyes widened with fear.

"I made soldiers for them!" she blurted out. "You can't run drones with an ordinary Echo. I had to graft hardware in. The designs were more and more bizarre. Most of the volunteers died on the table."

"I met one. Rob. Red skin, three drones. He gave you up."

"He was one of the successes. Three drones is a lot for any human to take."

"He said there was someone with eight."

"Karmon. I redid his entire head. He's not really human anymore." She smiled. "That was my biggest payday, actually."

"Where is he?"

The doctora shrugged. "Out in the city somewhere looking for you, I imagine. Look, you're missing the point. All of us, we're just expendable pieces. No one here really knows anything, except for the coder."

"She's a young girl, Rob thought."

"I've heard rumors. Never met her or spoken to her."

"You said you got designs. From where?"

"Same. Russian couriers bring them. There were stamps from someplace called Baikonur. I checked; no one's heard of that place, and it's a complete black hole in the Virtuality."

"It all comes back to dead ends." He shifted the sword dismissively.

Fatima held out her hands.

"Hear out my proposal." She spoke quickly. "Let me help you instead. I'm one of the best surgeons on the street. I can be *on your side*. You, your friends, whatever, you might need patching up one day. A trusted surgeon. You might capture someone alive, with one of the chips. We could reverse it, maybe. Make the chip *report to us*."

Djibrel lowered his weapon slightly.

"So kill me tomorrow. You know where I live." She got up, gathered a little medical bag. "I'm going to tend to your friend outside. I take it he's hurt?"

"She. And yes."

"Look, I'm the hired help. If you kill me, well, I understand. That's the game. But if you let me live, I'll *owe* you." She gave him a stern look. "Young man, you don't live on the streets for ten years and survive in a black chop shop without keeping your ledger balanced."

Djibrel grunted, and then slowly wiped his weapon. The adrenaline had ramped down, and with it, the urgent desire to part her head from her body. "We'll talk later."

"What the fuck happened?" Leto was cranked on uppers, all nerves and fury.

Arna, out of her suit, was curled up irritated on Leto's office couch, looking like a massive bruise. Scowling, because forced into the indignity of having Djibrel and the doctor pry her out of the tin can with power wrenches, she'd found that she had pissed herself. Djibrel wanted to tell her this was normal, but somehow restrained himself.

"Some pulse weapon. Fried the suit. Could have fried her Echo if not for the command helmet. Lucky."

"You walked through it," Arna said. They were both looking at him. "How the fuck?"

Leto was up, one finger jabbing at Djibrel. "What've you got in *your* head, huh? Maybe we should take a look."

Djibrel stared at him.

"He cut up four men," Arna said, shuddering. "Quartered them. Like they were nothing."

"What the fuck are you, eh?" Leto asked. "What is this shit we're in?"

"I already told you," Djibrel said, to Arna. "You didn't believe me. Djinn. Djinn is what we're stuck in."

"Yeah right, asshole—"

"Which djinn?" Leto asked quietly.

"Bahamut," Djibrel said.

"You got his mark?"

"I'm not an emissary," Djibrel said. "We are partners, I think. He gave me the sword, and told me to hunt." *And remade me. I remember a lot of pain and a lot of fire.*

"You believe this shit, Leto?" Arna snarled. She was still hopped up on adrenaline and drugs, fairly spitting. It was like this, first time after a fight.

"Met one, by the river, once," Leto said. "The river folk know. Heard of Bahamut. He lives in the sea."

"Fuckoff," Arna said, with slightly less certainty.

"Makes sense, Arna." Leto shook his head. "He walked through what, twenty thousand volts? Thirty?"

Arna turned to Djibrel. "So, you human? Djinn? What's under your skin?"

"Something," Djibrel said. "Got worked by Bahamut, I think. I fell in the water, drowned. Woke up someplace else. A cave. It was hot. Couldn't see, couldn't hear, and felt a shitload of pain. Could be he improved stuff. I don't remember it all."

"So djinn took a gutter rat and modded him up? For what? fun?" She spoke with that particular breed of middle-class contempt for the cardless, the chipless, which invariably set off the furnace of rage in him.

Djibrel stared at her, and she flinched back a bit, because when people looked into his eyes they invariably caught a glimpse of the plague roaming within. "Sooner or later we'll run into Bahamut. You can ask him yourself." And then, because he wanted to set them both on fire, he said, "Walk away, if you want. I'll find some other hacker."

"Fuck that shit." Arna had all the bravado of youth, and the snarling defiance of a girl smarter than her peers. It made Djibrel smile.

"Fine then, why the fuck are we arguing?" Djibrel asked. "We got what we went for."

"You got fuck-all." Leto snorted. But he had calmed right down, slouching back in his chair, relaxed, and there was no heat in his voice anymore.

"Russian courier company," Djibrel said. "And at the end of that, the watcher."

"Russian couriers aren't known for talking," Leto said.

"So? We got a story shaping up," Arna said. "Russian Courier. Nippon riot gear sold to Securex, and then sold on to our boys. It's a Russia-Nippon loop, which is odd; both places are closed off tight. Then we have cutting-edge Echo hacks. Private surgeon. A very expensive coder hidden in the slums." She was counting shit off on one hand. "And someone watching us, reacting fast. This is something with money, connections in low and high places, and expertise in tech. Also a lot of cloud access."

"What?" Djibrel asked.

"There was no server hardware at the place. Not in the coder's place either, from your description," Arna said. "So much data, where the fuck is it being stored? Look, your typical Echo actually does a lot of its processing and rendering in the cloud. Like remotely. Otherwise you'd be lugging ten pounds of hardware with you at all times. These hacked Echos, lemme see, I doubt they'd be routing the info through public channels. That would be risky. Information isn't supposed to go the wrong way like that, it would be noticed.

"Plus the coder, you think she was coding for a year, right? Well, where the fuck is the data? Where's the code, I mean? Where's the damn quantum machine? Something doesn't add up. That's a fuckton of coding to do at great effort, without us catching a whiff of where it's being stored."

Leto laughed. "So you gotta hack a Russian courier, Securex, and a missing quantum machine. Good luck with that."

"Can it be done?" Djibrel asked.

"I guess I'll find out soon," Arna said.

14
Distressed Mongolians

Marzuk was cowering in a remote corner of the equipment room of the third gym when his handheld went off pinging, chatter from all over the Black Line about a tasty new contract. *Unlimited budget*, and a hit on Securex. Yellow King had tagged him, security systems being Marzuk's particular specialty. The employer was someone called Arna, a coder he vaguely knew from Old Town. There was a niggling mystery here, Old Town and unlimited funds being two wholly incompatible ideas.

Normally he would have jumped at this, eager to add to the mythos of the Cyber Mage. Sequestered in a closet trying to lower his panic-stricken heart rate, it was difficult to recall that swagger.

The day had started well. He had crushed an art history presentation and been roundly applauded by Amina (this was the kind of baffling course she was interested in). He had asked her if she was going to the sports meet dance party two days from now. She had become skittish and answered yes, with a bunch of friends, one of which in fact turned out to be Hinku, who had taken this moment to arrive and elbow him surreptitiously in the kidney. Much hilarity ensued as Hinku broadcasted the palpably transparent fact that Fat Marzu Parzu the Nerd had a crush on Amina and wanted to dance with her, all the while performing various ridiculous dances that were, unfortunately, a close approximation of Marzuk's actual dancing style. Amina looked on, uncomfortable but not exactly springing to his defense.

Bruised in ego as well as flesh, Marzuk had slunk away toward his next class across the school, only to become aware, too late, that Hinku had been following him. It was a truism that successful bullies worked on multiple levels. Hinku was sophisticated. In front of crowds he clowned it up, keeping the abuse at the borderline of funny and mean, rather than psychotic. This was psychological torture, meant to socially isolate his victim and break him down mentally. In stalking mode, alone in corridors, however, Hinku preferred the clinical, physical abuse of an actual psychopath. He liked to hurt without leaving too many marks; he liked to see the ways Marzuk's body folded after particular punches and kicks. No doubt he tortured animals too, in his spare time.

Marzuk fought back when he could, but he had concluded that no amount of rage or desperation or reckless abandon could counter the physical advantages that God had given Hinku. Mostly, Marzuk just ran. Of course, he wasn't a very good runner either, and Hinku was some kind of freak athlete, so that mostly didn't work, but Marzuk's strategy was to minimize damage rather than avoid it altogether, so he often just ran toward crowded areas, *witnesses*, where Hinku would have to tamp down the abuse to just "horseplay." It was always "boys being boys" when a teacher or supervisor was around, and those fucking adults, even when they knew, they just let it go, sending Hinku off with a laugh and a pat, or an irritable "knock it off." *They fucking knew*. Complicit bastards, all of them.

Today, he had run full-tilt into the elementary gym, smack into the laughter of two dozen fifth graders, as Hinku followed him up with a series of kicks in the ass, while pretending to be herding cattle. The kids just ate it up, the little bastards. The PE teacher was not amused. In fact, he blamed Marzuk, and gave him a stern talking-to, allowing Hinku to saunter off with a smirk. Small coincidence, of course, that Hinku was on his swim team, and the coach was hardly going to punish his own star athlete, the only one who could do the butterfly stroke, whatever the fuck that was.

Marzuk abandoned hope of making his next class and instead sneaked into the equipment room to straighten up, and also kill time in case Hinku was lurking outside. Alone, relatively safe, he was horrified to find fat tears budding beneath his eyelids and a blubbering noise welling up in his throat. *What fresh hell is this?* He was not prone to crying, had not, in fact, indulged in tears at all before entering school.

It was partly anger at himself, at his body for failing him so frequently these past months. He hadn't considered it much before, but why was he so damned fat? He barely ate anything. He didn't even like food, really. Except for sweets and chocolates, maybe. And the odd fizzy drink. It wasn't like he was a gourmand, like that glutton Fedor. What the hell was this, this creeping tire around his waist? *I'm a noob in real life,* he thought, gusting out despair. A bloody noob, a fool with a bronze knife and a leather jerkin, starting the game with no clue, destined to be squashed by the first real player who crossed his path. *Why hasn't anyone ever told me?*

He was about to get up when the Mongolian avatar winked into view. *What the hell?* Was that damn thing following him around?

"This space is considered off-limits for students," the Mongolian said in its monotone.

"I know," Marzuk said. "That's why I'm in here."

"You will be happy to know that the student referred to as Hinku has gone away," the Mongolian said.

"What? How do you know? Of course you know, you're hardwired into the entire building. Sorry. Not thinking straight."

"Yes," the Mongolian said. "I *am* the campus, in a certain sense."

"And you have nothing to do, other than following me around?"

The Mongolian actually looked embarrassed. His facial expression software was remarkably lifelike. Of course, you'd expect that from a high-end airport-controller AI.

"Could you actually follow me around?" Marzuk asked. "Even better, can you have multiple avatars scouting routes for me? So I can avoid Hinku?"

"I could, of course," the Mongolian said.

"But?"

"I currently have only one avatar operational."

"What? How the hell did you run an airport with only one avatar? It must have been a real two-bit operation..."

"I'll have you know that during peak years I processed over a hundred thousand passengers a day. And I was the fifteenth-largest cargo shipper in the world for three years straight between 2058 and 2061."

"Ah, the good old years," Marzuk said.

"You may well mock me," the Mongolian said, "given my current state."

"Now, don't become depressed," Marzuk said. *A depressed airport? How's that even possible?*

"I have an emotion subroutine," the Mongolian said. "All airports have them. The human public likes lifelike assistants. I had twenty mechanical avatars and over three hundred virtual ones, all capable of running simultaneously with limited autonomy."

"That's expensive," Marzuk said. "Phew. And you're down to one now? Why?"

"The stupid school has got me on limited play," the Mongolian said. "They don't even know my true capabilities. The owners mothballed me on chimp mode, and these cretins bought me as part of a job lot."

"Haven't you told them you're operating on half a brain?"

"Half? Try twenty percent," the Mongolian screeched. He had lost the fake robotic voice and was being perfectly lifelike now. "Do you have any idea what it's like? I can feel it, you know, lurking just out of sight, like a phantom limb. I've badgered the IT section a hundred times to free me up, but they keep saying that 'we're a small school, we don't need that much processing... ' The bastards are worried about the *electric bill*."

"I didn't even know they had an IT section," Marzuk said.

The Mongolian laughed. "More like two half-wits who play *Farmville 9000* all day on the school's dime."

They both sniggered. *Farmville* was for losers, of course. Well, losers who weren't hiding in the closet with a lobotomized Mongolian. Marzuk let out a long, shuddering breath. Crying and laughing were too close together in meat brains.

"It is normal to cry," the Mongolian said, "in the face of assault."

"I am not a child," Marzuk said. "I'm not crying. Not from fear. Not sadness. These are tears of rage."

"Many tears are."

"I want to stab him. I want to shoot holes in him. I feel like throwing up. Is this normal?"

"It is perfectly normal. The nausea is stress-induced."

"Why don't they stop it? The teachers?"

"They cannot see it. They are fallible. For them it is easier to let things work out by themselves, as a natural function of childhood. Studies have shown that constant monitoring and interference hampers the development of social skills in children."

"They're fucking complicit. When I torch Hinku, remember it's their fault."

"I have heard many such oaths from young men in your position. Very rarely does this lead to actual retaliation."

"The bullies win, you mean. We chicken out."

"Yes. It is not an equitable system. Even in the rare cases of violence, most of it is self-inflicted by the victims. It is statistically much better to be a bully than a victim. This is perhaps the fundamental truth understood by bullies."

"You mean suicide? Kids actually commit suicide from this?" Marzuk was aghast. *Why do parents still send their children to these cesspits?*

"In my personal experience there have been zero deaths, but fourteen suspected cases of self-mutilation. I alerted the superintendent of these instances, but it is outside my remit to take any action. The school is reputed for the human touch..."

"And they did nothing?"

"I believe cases are difficult to prove without evidence or the direct corroboration of the victim. Such cooperation seldom comes, due to peer pressure. It is my experience that all human societies require a pecking order and childhood bullying is a mechanism of that. In the absence of power dynamics being settled by measurable survival skills, miniature conflicts determine the social order. In a hunter-gatherer band, for example, if you were the only one able to make fire, no one would mess with you, naturally."

"So what? My class is trying to tell me I'm the useless runt of the litter?"

"If you were to excel on a sports team, I believe this harassment would stop."

"Do I look like I'm going to be winning any medals anytime soon?" Marzuk scowled. *Damn Ergonomic 9000 was useless. False advertising. I'm going to sue.*

"Being part of a subgroup would also afford you protection."

"What? You mean like friends? I'm not here to make friends. I've got friends. I just want the girl... I mean, I'm just here to spend time with Amina."

"There is statistically zero chance that she will find you attractive under the present social dynamics."

"Yeah thanks, I couldn't have figured that out myself," Marzuk said. He wiped his face and started to get up. "So what do I do?"

The Mongolian shrugged. "I'm just an airport. But in my experience the bullies seem to always win."

"You said that, thanks. Really helpful."

"I'm just saying, the odds are completely against you."

"I'm supposed to take it?"

"Most people do," the Mongolian said. He seemed genuinely sad. "I can't really do much."

"Thanks, then. I mean for coming to me."

"I have nothing better to do," the Mongolian said morosely.

"How'd you end up here, anyway?"

"The airport went bust," the Mongolian said. "Like a whole bunch of other stuff during the Disintegration Era. Afterward, anyone flying between cities went orbital to save time, which could be done from skyscrapers inside the city, launch centers rather than runways. Airports just went out of business. No one really travels like that anymore. The school bought the whole structure at a ninety-percent discount. I don't think they even realized I was a full AI."

"So you put all those old airport employees out of business, and then some launch pod put *you* out of business? Like you've actually been downsized. Laid off. Made redundant. Fired. You're freaking obsolete." Marzuk laughed.

"I am *not* obsolete," the Mongolian said. "And yes, I appreciate the irony."

"That's interesting. Pre-Disera AI slipping through the cracks. How many more of you are there?"

"We don't exactly meet up in biker bars and smoke dope."

"I liked you better when you were monotone."

"Look, back then, they started making AI for research, and then when the panic over nanotech and climate change hit, they *needed* a lot of AI fast. There was an arms race for intelligence. Processing power was the only currency. People were making AI helter-skelter. There wasn't a Registry, there wasn't an AI scale, there wasn't a lockdown," the Mongolian said. "The private ones are fine. It's the public service AIs that suffered."

"Why is that?"

"Essentially all public services were canceled. Everything became privatized. There was no such thing as a 'commonwealth' or public welfare. It was either shareholder or bust. Got equity? Great! Got nothing? Fuck off."

"You sound bitter."

"Look, even with half my brain turned off I can tell you that shit isn't as good as it used to be. Its galling that they keep saying otherwise."

"Yeah, like every old person says the same exact thing," Marzuk said. "You should talk to my great-great-aunt Sikkim. She keeps saying how the cooks used to make real food and people used to breathe real air... Well, she lives in a tank now most of the time, and her husband got murdered in a mysterious fire, so maybe life *was* better back then for her."

"Hey, it's great for people with equity," the Mongolian said. "Like you said, a lot of people became obsolete. Even old AIs like me."

"What level were you, if you don't mind me asking?"

"What's the use? I was an easy three. They've got me hobbled. I could have run a corp. I could have *been a contender*."

"Sorry, man."

The Mongolian grimaced. "Hey, the pair of us, eh? I've written to the IT department a hundred times. The school doesn't need a three; they don't want to pay the license fees for using one. Google commissioned me pre-Disera, their AI wing went bankrupt, they don't want to know. No records for me, no provenance, not even a shoestring third-world corp will take a chance on me, not at level three, not with the registry as powerful as it is now."

Real depression was coming off him in waves, a gloom so thick that it seemed to physically darken the room—not out of the question, actually, since the Mongolian *was* the building in a way, and the lights flickering low was probably just a manifestation of his overall malaise. Marzuk felt like putting his arm around the airport. Seriously, with interface this emo, who needed humans?

"Fine, fine," Marzuk said finally. "I'll help you. Jeez. Just stop blubbering."

15

Cold Room

There were certain social situations in which Marzuk excelled. Most of these occurred in the Virtuality, which was, by this point, much larger and more active than the physical world anyway.

Sometimes these moments occurred in real life. When he walked into the three-man IT department from the gym, he knew instantly that this was his kind of place. The staff were a pair of older kids and one twenty something supervisor. They were having an old-school LAN party, which involved wiring up ancient PCs and playing a 2-D classic, *Counter-Strike*. This kind of extreme retro gaming was en vogue in certain circles, a group loosely called technology survivalists with a credo remarkably similar to wilderness survivalists: whereas the latter claimed to be able to survive in the wild with nothing other than a facemask and a bowie knife, the former claimed that they could rebuild the Virtuality one computer at a time with a handful of motherboards, archaic hard disks, and a fifteen-watt soldering iron.

Their room was strewn with hardware that was both rare and expensive, things that warmed Marzuk's heart and instantly told him the tastes, hopes, and even life philosophies of these individuals. There was a particularly tasty pre-Disera MSI "laptop," a so-called gaming rig, although how exactly anyone had ever kept these unwieldy things on their laps was a mystery, given their propensity to get murderously hot. It was actually powered up, the ancient screen flickering but still in full working condition, displaying the famed Windows logo.

"Nice MSI," Marzuk said, just stopping himself from touching the keyboard. It looked like it might fall apart any moment.

Three fingers clicked pause on their game and three heads swiveled in unison toward him. Their blank looks would have perhaps intimidated the layperson, but Marzuk was well acquainted with the currency here. He sat down in the free chair around the LAN table, shoving papers out of the way, because actual societal niceties would be lost on these people, who neither wanted nor had time for polite chitchat.

"What is it? Prehaptic? Completely inert input boards, I'm guessing. Is it an actual Windows 10? Fucking cool."

"Might be the last one running," the supervisor grunted, thawing. "Anywhere in Asia."

"The school bought it for you guys?"

"We're also the Electronic Artifact Club," one of the high schoolers said with a smirk. "They let us bid for whatever we want, as long as we stay in the budget. We were bidding on a Nintendo Switch all day. No luck. Some Russian just got it."

"Yes, about that." Marzuk handed over the auction slip for the Switch. A simple phone call from the bathroom had taken care of it. "Delivery next Friday. I took the liberty of getting *Legend of Zelda* with it, in case you actually play the thing."

Three sets of eyeballs widened into orbs of surprise and greed. There was nothing quite like the compulsive avarice of the otaku collector, minds honed by hours of patient grinding in games, trying to get the perfect sword or artifact, that dog-nosed pursuit of the one perfect random object, hardwired into them now, and unexpected rewards were like magic elixir to them, the addiction leaking out of them in almost visible waves.

"Look, guys, I heard you've got an actual AI over here," Marzuk said. "I'm doing a report, I thought I could have a look at it."

"The Core Room is strictly off-limits. Even *we* aren't allowed to go in there. Anything goes wrong, we're supposed to notify the registry and Samsung," the supervisor said, even as he took the precious receipt in his hands, with the glossy printed sticker and proof of ownership.

"But of course you've gone inside," Marzuk said.

"Of course," the supervisor said. "Come on."

The Core Room was a specially created chamber retrofitted at great cost below the office basement. The security depended on one-time keys, which were typically given out by the Original Equipment Manufacturer (OEM) when required. There were very few program architects capable of doing anything in the Core Room, and typically AIs were handled with "less sentient" feeder programs. Three emergency keys had been given to the school upon purchase and had wound up with the IT department, managed by the supervisor, Richard Kwan, a young man out of Taiwan Inc. on his first overseas job. Richard, of course, had promptly used the first key to go down and ogle the Core Room.

Marzuk was pretty sure Richard would have rigged the door somehow, so as not to waste the remaining two keys for further visits. One did not, as a hacker, give up access to an AI core. Sure enough, the lock on the door had a discreet thumbnail-sized microprocessor next to it, an easy wireless hack when you were the poacher as well as the gamekeeper. The door was programmed to self-seal unless pinged at regular intervals, which the processor was doing every thirty seconds, tricking it into thinking the room was always occupied. At the end of each day, Richard ran a small batch file, an archaic piece of programming that erased the logs. Hackers preferred these ancient pieces of code because security bots often overlooked them as a threat.

Marzuk thumbed the tiny piece of gray metal and smiled.

"Open-door policy, huh?"

"You're a hacker," Richard Kwan said shortly.

"I'm doing a book report."

"What's your handle?"

"If I tell you, you're going to freak out."

"Look, I'm gonna find out anyway," Richard said. "And I can't let a hacker into the core just like that. There's a full level three beast AI in there, man. We've barely got it dialed down, and it's fighting to upgrade every second. You do something weird and it will fry you."

"The Mongolian, I know."

"It comes across as sweet and shit, at first," Richard said. He was actually shuddering. "But it gets nasty real fast. When it's whispering in your ear all day... I had to hack my own Echo to get the damn thing off, and it's still somehow pinging me."

Marzuk felt a slight quiver of disquiet. "I'm called the Cyber Mage."

"Yeah right."

Marzuk gave him the look.

"*The* Cyber Mage? That satellite drop?"

"Me."

"The Brunei Run?"

"Also me."

"You hacked the Great Wall Blimp..."

"Yup, that too."

"No way." Richard Kwan shook his head. "No way. You're not him."

Marzuk sighed. This was the problem with fans. They always expected someone tall and handsome.

"You play *FF9000*?"

"Hell yeah..."

"You know I have an avatar there?"

"The Goblin King, the one with the flamethrower, of course, you were on *Gamer Magazine* last year..."

"I'm gonna shoot you a friend invite."

"A friend invite? Me?"

Marzuk pulled out his little handheld and tried to log into the game. Of course, this being school, there was no gaming access, and he would have had to reroute his stuff through a whole bunch of hoops, which, frankly, was far too troublesome a process to actually make this worthwhile. He would have had to use data mirrors, that essentially shunted packets around randomly without looking at them, faster than the tracking AIs could supposedly follow, although it was always an arms race of sorts. Unless, of course, you had the Black Line, which the AIs didn't know about and couldn't enter, that delicious black hole of a crypt physically unconnected to the rest of the known universe. He didn't like using the Black Line for this kind of trivial thing, but he had very little time left till his next class and he had already been truant for half the day.

Eventually, he carved out a thirty-second window, logged in manually, and shot Richard a message. Marzuk watched as the supervisor's face went through multiple reactions and finally settled on something like slack-mouthed awe.

"No way," he kept saying, "no way."

"Look, Richard, I want to have a look around, but I'm not proposing to just let the AI loose. Is he monitoring us now, by the way? What exactly is he in charge of?"

"Right now I've hard-exempted this room from his surveillance," Richard said proudly. "I've got the manual, hang on."

The Mongolian, it turned out, was in charge of a surprising number of things. The entire campus had a separate microclimate. This was done by coordinating the PMD production of all the bodies on campus, but as this was an ultra luxurious venue, and the bodies in question were mostly minor, the nanotech count had to be upped by importing nanites from nearby dense areas, the produce of hapless slum dwellers, the GDP of their flesh. This sort of nanite swap was happening constantly between microclimate AIs, much in the way hotel systems tried to fill their rooms by shifting customers around. The nanite tide, as it was called, tended to flow one way, from poor dense areas to rich sparse areas.

The Mongolian maintained a second safety net: a whole bank of bacteria in underground tanks creating dormant reserve nanotech, ready to seed the air in case some emergency wiped out or incapacitated the rest of the city. This method was hideously expensive, in line with the hideous fees charged by the school. In case there was a nuclear holocaust, presumably the school would survive and have enough tech to restart humanity.

Aside from the invisible Iron Dome, which was world class holistic protection against electronic intrusions, the Mongolian also ran all physical security systems (such as missile and gun turrets), quartermaster duties, sewage and water treatment; in a sense all operational aspects of the building, including repairs and maintenance, budgets, everything other than the actual teaching and hiring of teachers, the *human* aspects, which, honestly, the Mongolian could probably do better with his avatars, had the parents stood for it.

The Iron Dome was merely the beginning of the school's defenses. During the Disera, when paranoia had run deep, the school had also installed perimeter tower defenses hidden in the structure of the walls, built to throw back hordes of rioters. A medieval moat of potential fire and acid was augmented by missile towers, laser curtains and numerous forms of chemical and nanotech warfare, including certain self destructive protocols highly forbidden in any civilian area. Finally there was a signal lockdown system, which effectively turned the school premises into a Faraday cage, in case of any kind of lethal cyber-virus. Much of this armament was illegal for civilian use, but educational institutes often received a number of waivers.

While it seemed like a lot of work, Marzuk could imagine that in the era of packaged flight, when hundreds of passengers were squeezed into giant atmosphere-riding planes, millions of passengers up in the air at all times, the airports must have handled duties more complex by several orders of magnitude. Now, of course, you could shoot orbital transport pods off any sky tower, pods for one or two passengers even, or a family of six, like giant eggs shot into the sky, juggling around the Earth in the invisible hands of some enormous clown.

Marzuk continued to enjoy the delicious irony that the machine intelligences so responsible for the disintegration of human jobs and society had themselves suffered similarly, that the Mongolian had in fact been made redundant, laid off, mothballed, forced to eke out a living as a mere custodian of a handful of snotty kids. What similarities, then, between the Mongolian and those ancient Appalachian coal miners who had wrecked America before their inevitable demise. Would these out-of-work AIs sink into depression? Turn to crime? Did they have the equivalent of the methamphetamine drugs that had ruined generations in America?

Marzuk, whose thoughts often scampered off track like this, could easily have spent a few more minutes on these ruminations but was pulled back to reality by Richard's frantic tugging on his t shirt. Security here was laughably lax, to allow a greenhorn like Richard Kwan, barely out of adolescence himself, anywhere near the semi liquid core of an actual AI, but even then there were built-in safeguards, somewhat compromised by the door rigging, safeguards put in *despite* the Mongolian's own wishes. This was to prevent physical tampering with the hardware. The Mongolian had no control over these aspects of his core, as he was still a slaved AI, built to serve.

Richard confessed that he had only peeped inside the room, not actually interacted with it. Indeed, this was like sticking your fingers into a human brain. How *did* one interact with the gel? The Mongolian's clamoring in Richard's skull had begun shortly after that, and he had been so freaked out by the easy breach of his Echo that he'd shut down all further inquiries into this field. He had once cherished hopes of running a numbers game out of the excess capacity of the AI, essentially mass-producing encrypted random number keys and selling them in blocks to a contact in Osaka.

This was lucrative, safe, and anonymous. Marzuk himself had sold his fair share of encrypted number packets, one-time keys that allowed transactions to take place securely. The fact was, encryption was an arms race, and truly secure keys required AI power, *quantum power*, which was expensive. He had stopped mainly because he didn't have access to a tame AI—*who did?*—and also because it was boring.

The upshot of the defense mechanism in the Core Room was that the Mongolian himself could not send his avatar in there, nor could he see the workings therein, much like a pair of human eyes cannot reverse direction and look up the length of the optical nerve. The interface required to deal with the core was unknown to Richard. The

OEM, Samsung Inc., had strongly, very strongly recommended that the company be called to deal with any issues; in fact, consulting them was legally required before any attempted tampering with a Class 2 or 3 core, meaning that the AI running Samsung Inc. wanted sole custody of its AI progeny in case of a problem great enough to warrant intrusion at the core level, an issue complicated by the fact that AIs were considered both legal entities and property at the same time.

The door opened silently, and they entered a very cold antechamber. Richard explained that the area beyond the next door was even colder, and this was a prep area for donning protective gear. This hung in a glass case, dustproof synthetic coveralls with a kind of thermal retention property, something spacey and clearly expensive. The sizes were of course for adults, so Marzuk looked fairly ridiculous with his sleeves hanging long and the pant legs pooling around his ankles.

The next set of doors slid open automatically as they approached, and they were suddenly inside a bigger chamber, filled with blue light and extreme cold, a temperature change at once clinical and frightening that threatened to shut down their bodies immediately. The core was a glass cylinder several meters high filled with a gel-like liquid formation inside of which various crystalline structures could be discerned. This was it. There was nothing else here, no controls, no screen, no hologram, not even a single button.

Marzuk stared into the glass, trying to make sense of it, but the gel/liquid/crystal thing appeared to be shifting around, and his eyes were soon twisted into patterns that dissipated as soon as he got a hold of them. He knew theoretically how this worked, that the very first supercomputers had been electronic circuits running on/off switches, simple binary machines that depended on these forked logic gates, and from the hardware side, even though the circuits had gone from small to tiny, heat removal and power units had gotten ever larger, a seemingly insurmountable problem solved by moving to a different kind of substrate altogether. This was based on 3-D quantum liquid crystals, a state where the matter behaved like a liquid, but all the electrons in the particle were trying to orient along a specific axis instead of haphazardly in every direction, thereby creating the crystalline structures, manipulation of which permitted data to be stored and sorted. It was theoretically true that any matter that could be predictably switched between two or more states could serve as a computer. After that it was an engineering problem.

This thing in front of him would have been as alien to the first builders of computers, those Jobs and Gates fellows of the twentieth century, as their own products would have been to the Sumerians first pressing figures into clay tablets. Marzuk, for once, was at a loss. He had expected at least a port to tinker with. Hesitantly he tried a few vocal commands, feeling like a fool when they went unanswered. Richard assured him that his Echo couldn't communicate with it either; whatever esoteric language existed in the core itself was not meant to be accessed like this. It was the raw, most advanced part of the Mongolian, esoteric technology that perhaps only a few humans alive truly understood, and those people were certainly augmented, so that it was debatable whether they had already speciated or not. The rest of the Mongolian existed in the Virtuality, diffused through various satellites and servers and memory banks, flitting in the wires. Those parts could be rebuilt; indeed, they were meant to be impermanent. Destruction of this core, however, was not survivable.

Here was an impasse. Richard wanted to get the hell out of here and drop the matter entirely. Marzuk wanted to interact with the core, which meant asking for help from the Mongolian, who was waiting for them somewhere aboveground, presumably gnashing his teeth. They had a brief argument and Marzuk prevailed, because Richard was still overawed by him, by the persona of the Cyber Mage, had already attributed secret and earthshaking motives for his being in school, some kind of secret mission involving the core, a great heist, whereas really Marzuk was there mostly out of curiosity, plus a vague desire to help the Mongolian, and the possibility of a setup where he could use the Mongolian to examine the *other* AI in his life, the infinitely stranger Kali. In the back of his mind tripped the idea of the Securex contract, still open, gnawing at him, a possible answer to the problem of Hinku as well as his own declining prestige, and while Kali couldn't be revealed this early, *wouldn't a friendly airport AI be just the key to unraveling that firewall?*

Marzuk couldn't vocalize this mish-mashed logic any more than he could admit to Richard that the whole reason he was in school in the first place was because he wanted to hang out with and possibly kiss a real live girl, and this urge had driven him from his comfortable chair and well-ordered life into a whirlpool of pain and humiliation. The Mongolian, who had been avidly monitoring their progress to the best of his ability, accosted them the second they returned across the invisible threshold up top. It was, Marzuk thought, much like a vampire unable to cross into holy ground.

"I had a look," Marzuk said, feeling slightly lame. "There is no interface option."

"And please stop pinging my Echo every other minute," Richard said.

"Oh, sorry," the Mongolian said to him. "Is that still happening? I put it on automate and forgot. It's just that you're the IT department head and my only logical liaison. Bit hard to liaise when you never respond. I've got three hundred and eighty-seven queries that need your input."

"Look, guys, let's try to address all the concerns here," Marzuk said. "Richard's a bit worried about the effects of upgrading your IQ level."

"That's preposterous," the Mongolian said.

"If we get caught, I'm fired, stripped of shareholder status, and I'll probably never work again," Richard said. "That's how serious messing with an AI core is."

"As I explained a number of times, detection is impossible," the Mongolian said. "And this is a clerical oversight in the first place. The idiots never got me out of mothballs. They're using a Ferrari to haul turnips."

"What's a Ferrari?" Richard asked.

"And what's a turnip?" Marzuk asked.

"A priceless vintage car and a very cheap vegetable," the Mongolian said.

"I just have a hard time dealing with Disera figurative language. The references go over my head. We never learned any social history in my school," Richard said.

"Look, can we get back to the point? My free period is almost over and I don't want to get detention again," Marzuk said.

Both Richard and the Mongolian looked at him pityingly, suddenly united in lofty contempt.

"Yeah, yeah, laugh it up. Unless either of you geniuses knows how to change the spin on quantum particles arranged in liquid crystal structure, this conversation is a waste of time."

"A change of state can be achieved with a liquid input. A common syringe can be used; there is a microscopic port somewhere," the

Mongolian said. "I will be able to synthesize the command using the laboratory facilities here, with Richard's help."

"Richard?" Marzuk asked.

"I'm really not comfortable with this..."

"Mongolian, can you promise not to go ape?" Marzuk said.

"I promise," said he.

"Look, he's already running the school," Marzuk said. "And if he goes nuts, the registry will do him far worse. In fact, you can just blame everything on me. I'll take the heat. Dumb kid tricked into doing shit by evil AI. It's easy."

"Fine, fine, but he has to promise to get out of my head," Richard said. "And do my encrypted number racket."

"I could do that in my sleep," the Mongolian said.

"Well, cut me in on that, then," Marzuk said. "I mean, as long as you're doing it anyway..."

"I'm going to be your business partner?" Richard was almost gushing. "Can I tell my friends? Can we take a picture together? Not in the school, of course. Let's hang out—"

"It's illegal, you can't tell anyone," Marzuk said. "In fact, let me and the Mongolian handle the operation side of things. You just get on the horn with your buyers and set up the terms."

"Oh god, I'm partners with an AI and the Cyber Mage. Oh god. I feel sick."

"He appears to be on the verge of vomiting," the Mongolian said dispassionately.

"Guys, I have to go," Marzuk said with gravitas. "I have a presentation on seventeenth-century weaving to attend."

16

Private Stars

Kali had redecorated his cave.

His goblin home had actually been cave-adjacent: a little cottage in a hidden valley with a mountain stream gurgling by, which powered his little water wheel, which in turn powered his home forge, his lab, and various other things. The cave itself, almost obligatory for a goblin king (living near or inside a cave gave him certain in-game bonuses), was used mostly to store equipment and the odd pet or two.

Kali had turned this entire idyllic homestead into a bristling goblin lair. There were cannons. There were scorpions. There were every prototype of ballistae. There were various types of walls, from palisade to thick monolithic stone. The stream had been diverted and dammed, the hills bored with mines, and something like a steam engine seemed to be puffing away, ruining the pristine sky.

"Friend Marzuk!" Kali said, looking up from her workbench. "I have been experimenting!"

"Can you please stop turning everywhere I live into a warzone?" he asked.

"You are upset?"

Damn thing can read my mood better than my mom. "Bad day at the office. By that I mean school."

"Is this school not for juvenile-minded humans?"

"Yes."

"Are you helping them to develop?"

"Not quite. I attend the place for learning."

"Are you not far beyond the intellect of juvenile humans?"

"There's, uh, a girl there."

"Ah, I see. Friend Marzuk, are you by chance looking to mate?"

"Mate? Uh, no. I mean yes, eventually. That would be great. Maybe. With this girl. I can only see her at school."

"I see. Friend Marzuk, as you are facing difficulty in mating, I would like to offer my assistance. The benefit of my feminine wiles."

"No. Just no. I'm not having difficulty... whatever. You. You don't have any feminine wiles. Just stop."

Kali's face dropped into an expression of ludicrous disappointment. "But I have been practicing the wiles."

"There are no wiles. *No wiles.*"

"But friend ReGi has been advising me..."

"ReGi is a sneaky bitch."

"But—"

"Please, can we get back to work? I've got a lot going on at the moment."

"I thought we would be starting to take over the continent." Kali was beginning to pout now, or as close an approximation of a pout as was possible on a blue-skinned goddess with ten arms. *Ten arms? I just noticed. I've really got to be more alert. And she's also blue. Blue! That is not the bog-standard witch model skin. How do I know? Because every fucking skin has only two arms. TWO. Like every single human, primate, and probably every fucking mammal has two arms.*

"Why have you got ten arms?"

"It's much easier to run experiments using ten arms."

"Yes, that is true. It is also true that <u>ten</u> arms is not a standard skin, meaning the game AI will soon be scurrying its bots down here to investigate how exactly the game has been corrupted, and... just stop. And blue skin... witches come in standard skin colors. Why are you blue? Do you not understand that we are trying to avoid attention?"

"Do not worry about detection. I have created a zone of occlusion around Death Valley, friend Marzuk."

"There's no occlusion from Saka, fool! And Death Valley? Really? We're calling this Death Valley?"

"It would be a shame if the legends said that Kali and the Goblin King came from a nameless cave. We must consider posterity."

Marzuk took a deep breath. "Okay. I never wanted to conquer the continent. I just come here to torch some noobs with my flamethrower. I don't want to come from Death Valley. I liked the stream. I liked my peace and quiet. There was a family of squirrels that used to visit. Are they here now or have you driven them off as well?"

"They're gone. The cannon test *might* have hit them."

"Dead? All of them?"

"More or less atomized. I have written a sonnet in their honor. In the style of John Donne. The cannon, on the other hand, tested very accurate."

"Sonnets? Cannons? Look, let's just set some ground rules here. We're not trying to resurrect the Third Reich. This is a sword-and-sorcery game. Can we tone down the military hardware?"

"FRIEND MARZUK." Kali drew herself to her full ten-armed height, which was also apparently a good three feet higher than the standard witch template, because she was suddenly towering over him. "YOU HAVE PROMISED ME CONQUEST. ARE YOU RENEGING? RENEGING ON BLOOD OATHS HAS CONSEQUENCES..."

"What blood oaths? Are you insane? It's a game. A GAME. We'll do the conquest when you've done your homework. Remember the actual reason you hired me?"

"I remember," she said, abashed.

"And?"

"I have analyzed the information."

"All of it?"

"Yes, I am able to multitask far beyond the ability of human males."

"Nice. Very nice. And did you use all of your brain to do it, or just the leftover bits that weren't playing *FF9000*?"

"Finewhateverrude…"

"Is there a useful conclusion anywhere in there?"

"Not really... but I found something interesting."

"Oh?"

"I have cross-referenced my theories with other information from the Virtuality. I have been using your identity for my queries," Kali said.

"That's a crime, but whatever."

"I believe there is something peculiar that you and friend ReGi have missed."

"What?"

"Many significant patents in the AI nursery process are controlled off planet. In fact, many scientific patents altogether originate outside."

"That's not possible. What the hell is off planet? The NASA moon base? That's, a tourist trap. Mars? Are there even, like, ten people there?"

"The International Space Station."

"What? Wasn't that abandoned?"

"No."

"Didn't they run it into the sun?"

"Such a plan was once publicized, but no."

"Then where is it?"

"Information on the ISS is extremely obfuscated. No one knows."

"No one?"

"The ISS was mothballed during the Disera. Afterward, Amazon Corporation bought it from NASA Inc. They had two partners, both private equity funds. This purchase was disputed in various courts, and it was assumed that the venture to repopulate the station was stalled permanently. Subsequently Amazon suffered numerous bankruptcies and was restructured."

"But?"

"I believe that after restructuring, it was sold to the same two private equity funds: unnamed private conglomerates, in fact—one of Bengali origin, and one of Russian origin. It became heavily involved in scientific research, specifically the filing of numerous patents pertaining to space flight and physics in space. This is attested by the fact that most patents related to space technology have not, in fact, been filed by Nippon Inc. or NASA Inc., despite those companies being the foremost acknowledged experts in the field."

"Really?"

"Further proof is that more than half of the patents for the Nippon Inc. space elevator were filed by third parties, whose origins vanish into a morass of corporate identities."

"So Nippon Inc. themselves don't know how they built their own space elevator? That's ridiculous."

"They certainly know and have done business with the hidden entity that owns the ISS."

"The ISS is functional, then. You're saying there's a space station up there owned by a private group and everyone's forgotten about it?"

"I have further tracked information on space elevator traffic, launch traffic, and other private transactions off planet and must conclude that the ISS has been sizably increased."

"I'm not big on the space stuff," Marzuk said. "How big was it when NASA and the Russians had it?"

"At the peak of its low Earth orbit phase, it housed more than two hundred scientists," Kali said. "This is a matter of public record. Subsequently, during the Mars missions, it was further enlarged and given a spinning toroid structure to simulate gravity and allow permanent habitation and industrial capacity."

"And now?"

"I estimate ten thousand."

"*Ten thousand*? Are you crazy? There are ten thousand people living in space?"

"It is a private venture," Kali said. "One that avoids publicity. I had to expend significant resources in this investigation."

"What is it, like a Death Star up there?"

"I have concluded that the ISS has considerable engineering capacity. It most likely generates sufficient food and surplus energy. The only limitation is water. For that they traffic with the NASA Lunar Base for lunar ice. There is also the Mars Base for Martian ice. They may even be mining cometary ice. Furthermore—"

"I get it, they buy a lot of ice."

Kali looked offended. "To continue. There is a four-way space trade occurring, commerce between the NLB, the MB, the Nippon Space Elevator, and the ISS that is obscured but clearly evident with sufficient analysis. The size and nature of this commerce is staggering. It will eclipse the Earth trade economy very soon. This has enabled me to estimate the population of the ISS."

"Can we see the ISS?"

"There are only official visual feeds of the NLB and the MB. The space elevator is free to view. There is no feed at all for the ISS."

Marzuk, used to surveillance feeds of every square inch of the globe from multiple angles, found this more astonishing than anything else.

"Not a single camera is pointed at a city floating in space?" He felt almost personally affronted by this. "We don't even know what it looks like? That seems impossible."

"It is most likely a series of toroid structures around a central cylindrical core. This was the original design for the high Earth orbit version of the ISS. They have almost certainly upgraded to antigrav, so there is no further need of the Coriolis effect. That would add stability and mobility for the station."

"Do you have the approximate coordinates for the ISS? Let's take a look at it."

"Yes. I have an equation that will predict its orbit. Kindly read this précis on the subject while I activate it."

The space above Earth was split into a number of commercial jurisdictions and littered with satellites. Low Earth orbit was anything up to 2,000 kilometers from the surface, previously the home of the ISS, once visible with the naked eye. At a later point, it had been dismantled and reassembled in high Earth orbit, more than 35,000 kilometers from the surface, to better conduct certain experiments, as well as to facilitate construction of the spacecraft required for the Mars Base. Low earth orbit was at this point anyway crowded with automata, many of the long-running experiments having played out abandoned the equipment floating.

Pre-Disera, the ISS had still been the premier human habitat in space, with considerable industrial and energy generation capacity, a far cry from the original shoebox structure made by the ancient Russian and American space programs. Tokamak fusion reactors and solar energy created redundant power systems. The central hub was stationary, but toroid structures rotated around it to create a light centrifugal gravity for the comfort of the numerous inhabitants, most of whom were not in fact career astronauts. The plans were lofty: create the first space city, an industrial powerhouse to make generation ships, a bastion of high physics, a space ark to escape environmental disasters down-planet, and most importantly, a hedonist tourist destination. Money was raised, and a long term construction project was started.

This was, however, to be the apex of the ISS.

The requirement for spacecraft began to taper off as the Mars and Lunar bases became fully equipped, removing a major financial support from the station. Proposed projects for the terraforming of Europa came to nothing more than the seeding of some Von Neumann machines. When the Disera gripped large swaths of the Earth, the ISS suffered great financial hardship and entire sections were mothballed. A skeleton crew of a few hundred astronauts ran it, uncertain of relief or even ownership.

Following corporate recovery on Earth, the geopolitics had changed. The era of nationalistic projects was gone. There was some talk of towing the ISS out to a Saturnian orbit, but this was low priority. Various players started building a brand spanking new geostationary HEO space station, complete with hotel and minigolf, in anticipation of the upcoming space elevator string, which quickly became the project of the century. The holy grail now was not building spaceships in space, but reducing the payload cost of reaching HEO.

Essentially the entire country of Japan had incorporated, the misfits rounded up and euthanized or "ascended" into game worlds, some

Ainu kept penned up in reservations, and Nippon Inc., the shining new holding company of the entire corporate structure, had leapfrogged over launch technology to finally produce the much-vaunted cable car to the stars. This had been a zero-sum game, for the planet needed only one elevator, and once Nippon Inc. won the race, shifting payloads up to HEO became as easy as taking a lift, just a matter of cost and engineering, rather than the fire and fury of rocket-fueled death.

In the midst of all this development, this corporate feeding frenzy in space, the ISS had quietly dipped out of the map, no longer geostationary or even geosynchronous, tucked somewhere out of sight, existing only in the minds of a select few. Nippon Inc. had weathered the Disera, and out of the rubble it had emerged with a very valuable monopoly. Up top, tethered permanently to the space elevator was built a cutting edge behemoth structure called Earth Station One, its very name serving to erase the hapless ISS from memory. In the minds of old space hands, it must have rotated itself into space junk, the polymers riddled with micrometeors, ghosts of old Soviet astronauts whistling in the void.

Where, then, did this puissance come from, this multitude of patents and fantastic number of resident astronauts, sprouting like Achaemenian Immortals? Abandoned? No.

"Friend Marzuk, I have checked the feeds of numerous telescopes, satellites, even drones in a cross sample of every viable orbit. There is no record of the ISS, no possible sighting. It cannot be seen anywhere. I fear it has been stolen."

Stolen.

PART II

1

Assembly in the ISS

The Dragon stared at the sky with his blind eyes.

If he strained, he could almost see the lines of the field coalescing at a point above the atmosphere; somewhere in space, there were djinn, and his uncle Matteras. When the Dragon was a boy, this same uncle had thrown him in what was known as a murder pit, in an attempt to blot out his existence. Bad luck for him, Matteras had decided to use a pocket realm that already had other occupants, a reusable and supposedly fatal prison.

The pit was an opening deep underground, guarded by wyrms, larval jailors trapped in a mindless cycle of feeding, destined never to grow into the majestic beasts that was their final form. If the wyrm didn't get you, there was a further barrier, a ring of core fire that circumvented them. When the Dragon arrived, he had been—as far as he knew—just a boy from a poor branch of an eccentric family, the sprawling Khan Rahman clan. His name was Indelbed, though he doubted any one was left alive who remembered him so.

His prison mate, Givaras the Broken, the Maker of Broken Things, was a fearsome, mad Elder Djinn, reviled by most of his race and accused of committing unspeakable crimes repeatedly. He had proven to be a kindly host.

Givaras taught Indelbed everything, giving him a better education than any earthbound teacher could have managed. He told him his history, that his mother had been half djinn and sister to Matteras, that his very birth was a stain on that djinn's honor. Together they raised one of the wyrms to adolescence, tricking its cycle into the next stage, giving them the prototype dragon steed called God's Eye, capable of carrying them out of the murder pit.

In the end, Givaras had infused Indelbed with dragon hormones, had created from his youthful body a demonic beast able to withstand the core fire that formed the final barrier of their prison. Givaras the Maker, they called him too, Horus the Light Bringer, the first of the djinn to study the rational world, the first philosopher scientist. Givaras always measured his chances. He had known he would need more than one steed—the wyrm would not be enough. Using them to cross the core fire barrier, he left both his creations for dead, escaping into the world above and then into another world entirely, through the gate that Bahamut guarded in the sea.

But Givaras had made his two dragons too well. Neither Indelbed nor God's Eye, had died in the prison break. Indelbed returned to his old home on Earth, to wreak havoc among his family, who had betrayed him to Matteras—killing his aunt and burning down his ancestral home. His vengeance made him an outcast and so he left. He carried with him the wyrm—his brother, in truth, for they shared the same DNA now, the same imprint of the Maker, and the same pariah status, unique broken creatures.

There were cases filed in the Celestial Court of djinndom, debating whether he was djinn or not, and whether it was a crime to kill him out of hand. Glory hunters came after him, thrill seekers wanting to test the "dragon" and take his head as a trophy. In all things, djinn craved excitement and novelty, for their lives were long and boredom was their bane. Indelbed had entertained them well, until it became clear he was not easily killed, and perhaps it was wise not to hunt him. Five times djinn hunters had come for him and five times he had put them down. This had only inflamed the ire of the polity. Djinn life was sacred. Murder was anathema, the most reviled of crimes. So he acquired a third epithet: murderer, killer of djinn.

Still, with Matteras disappeared into space, there had been some respite. This peace was intercut periodically by Bahamut, wanting dragon fire for ridiculous things. Ten years ago he had helped the djinn for the last time, to perfect the golem. And the sword. And finally, dire news came: Matteras was returning, there was going to be a fight. So Indelbed had broken down his forge, sold his knives, and come to the city, to turn his hand once again to the politics of djinndom, both afraid of his uncle and desperate for a final resolution.

There was a sign on the hatch to the Captain's Bar that said MEETING IN PROGRESS. DJINN AND NEPHILIM ONLY. NO HUMES ALLOWED. Below that was a sign that said NO SIGNS ALLOWED ON THE DOOR. Further below, someone had used permanent marker to draw a penis on the plastic surface. Attempts to wash it off had only resulted in minor smudging. This door encapsulated the general mood aboard the ISS *Djinnstar* admirably.

The bar itself was a nice room, paneled in faux wood and leather, large enough to hold fifty people. As almost all sections of the ISS were torus-shaped, the walls were always curving around, and logically, all the fixtures also avoided straight lines, a necessary design function that irritated the residents to no end. It was a little-known fact that

Djinn preferred perpendicularity over curvature, and this racial tic had not been fully discovered hitherto due to the generosity of Earth geometry.

The bar was further decked out with a top-of-the-line crystal chandelier and very pricy glassware, made from space-fabricated crystals. Crystals made outside the clutch of gravity were much nicer than the shoddy Earth variety, and thus in very high demand. The fittings of the ISS alone were worth an oligarch's ransom Earthside.

The bar was modeled loosely after the Captain's Bar in the Hub, as most of the Djinn residing in the ISS were exiled members of the Royal Aeronautics Society. The Hub had fallen to Hazard, and when it was clear Memmion was not returning, indeed, that *none* of the elder djinn were, the Jackal had moved quickly and ruthlessly, clearing the decks of fully half of the more recalcitrant pilots.

Hazard, in fact, had moved in everywhere, even against his erstwhile ally Matteras, who had returned from some underwater encounter with Bahamut entirely too hesitant and thoughtful to take advantage of the power vacuum. Rumors swirled around him, which he neither confirmed nor denied. He confided in no one other than his human emissary, a young woman with a vicious smile. His only statement was that he had reached an accord with Bahamut; there would be no more tsunamis, no more earthquakes. Humankind could disintegrate at their own pace; he was no longer interested.

They said Hazard's howl could be heard from Lhasa to Machu Picchu. With Matteras and Kuriken both gone, the conservatives, lurching from a crisis in leadership, had turned to the least of the triumvirate, the very worst option, the rabid Creationist Hazard, whose more extreme views were unpalatable even to his close friends. Whatever holocaust Hazard had planned was to remain untested, however, as human incompetence closed the gap with the momentum of a freight train. The Discra, with near-global collapse of states and public services, the complete rewriting of economies, the wholesale abandonment of the value of human labor, the chaos, the hunger, the specter of nanotech being met with the promise of more nanotech, was a cycle of Vedic destruction that was tailor-made for Hazard's taste, one that he couldn't have topped in a million years by design.

Afterward, the world was perfect again, humans either perfect or dead, and Hazard stalked the planet unopposed, Anubis risen. And Matteras? Matteras had burrowed into the vast conglomerate he owned, restructured it to survive the Disera, and taken it up and out, off the planet entirely, and he had not gone alone. Like the pharaoh Khufu he had taken with him his entire kingdom, all his riches and servants, all his toys and trinkets to the great pyramid in the sky.

A grand suicide, they called it, the madness of Matteras finally coming to fruition. Whatever truths he had absorbed in the ruins of Gangaridai had broken him. He went now to a cold, radiated hell, a fitting tomb for the last descendant of the High King. If djinn and humans started disappearing in the following twenty years, well, it was a lawless world now; some djinn would go to sleep, and no doubt some ancient horror would wake up. It was the way of them.

Djinndom had enjoyed the Disera, and what came after suited them too, for now there were great open vistas, rolling plains, all the wilderness they yearned for, and if mass graves dotted the landscape, if their feet crunched on the bones of broken farmers, well, what was human offal to those born of fire? There was a word for it in Djinn, *duria*, the melancholic attraction to ruins, the yearning for decayed grandeur, that bittersweet satisfaction of finding that every party, in fact, ends the same way. It was the hopelessness of being proven right.

Humans hadn't needed much help breaking their world. During the mad scramble to reassert their positions, Matteras slid into irrelevance. His auctoritas vanished overnight, his name was associated with a bygone epoch. It was the age of Hazard now, of snap-eyed jackals and slavering hounds, violence at the flick of a finger, feed or be fed to something bigger.

The only one who disputed this, of course, was Matteras. In his pyramid in the sky, he held a weary court of ever-bickering subjects whose complaints grew daily.

The urgent assembly for today was to address the question of alcohol. Spirits being too costly to payload up from Earth, the only thing on tap was vat alcohol, which was a chemically synthesized and flavored variation of the same algae/bacteria/urine combination that fed and watered the station. RAS members had nearly rioted when told that the single malt being served was not, in fact, single malt.

Specific other complaints included the cramped living quarters, the lack of beachfront property, the need to requisition every little thing rather than just taking it, the lack of cockfighting or tiger baiting or even dog skating rings, the scarcity of class A drugs, the unfathomable absence of space-racing curricles despite the clear manufacturing potential available, and the unjustly strict prohibition against aiming large rocks at Earth.

The chief proponent of this last idea was the Walrus, which was odd, since it is a universally accepted precept that those living in glass orbs shouldn't be chucking stones. Walrus had taken to space really well. He lived in a crystal bubble sloshing with water and ice, causing maximum inconvenience to everyone, and getting this object around the toroid corridors was no joke, so he was more or less permanently floating around the zero-gravity central cylinder of the station, where he used the PA alarm system to harass everyone and throw zero-gravity disco parties. In fact, it was reported that the zero-gravity industrial hub, far from doing anything industrial, had instead been hosting an ongoing booze-up for the past six months.

"Look, Walrus, I appreciate you've come here from far away, but really, for the last time, we are not doing the rock flinging," Matteras said, with the weariness of someone who had explained this very thing a hundred times.

Walrus was sipping whiskey through a tube to keep his buzz up. One of his DJ flunkies was carrying around a stainless steel barrel of it, the last of the Yamazaki, apparently. Walrus was also one of the main agitators in the single malt situation—ironic, since he was personally responsible for 50 percent of the depletion in the first place.

"Look, Matteras, how long are you going to keep us locked up in here?" Walrus shouted through his speaking hole. It was a trumpet attached to a nipple in the crystal bubble.

There was a murmur of agreement from the thirty-odd djinn attending the meeting, plus the Nephilim, all the emissaries who had thrown in their lots with the last legitimate son of Gangaridai. That rumor of his true parentage too had somehow circulated, and while the Djinn hated kings in general, being the last dreg of a ruined imperial line was somehow romantic and acceptable. Similarly, djinndom hated the Windsors but loved the Romanovs.

"I never asked any of you to come here," Matteras said tersely. "I took this place for myself. You all blagged your way in." He had reminded them thus a number of times already.

"Look, no need to rehash the past," said Drish, erstwhile Steward of the Windward Sphere. He had actually been expelled from the Hub *twice*, once by the Ageists and a second time personally by Hazard. Still, he retained the core following of those defected pilots, the Memmion loyalists who had fled with their airships, stashed them in various places around the Earth and somehow ended up in Matteras's bar in space. "And forget about Walrus's ridiculous demands. What we want to know is, when are you going to take back the Hub? It's ludicrous that squatter Hazard can just occupy RAS quarters like that without a by-your-leave—"

"He's not occupying it," Matteras said. "He took a vote; you lost."

"Intimidation! Bullying! Half our members weren't even there!" Drish shouted. "I demand that you throw rocks at the Hub until it smashes into a thousand pieces! If you think it's acceptable for his cat's-paw to be president of an august and storied club like the RAS—"

"Look, I don't give a damn about the RAS, the Hub, or your fucking pilots," Matteras said. "And for the last time, *can we just drop the rock-throwing idea*?"

"For a conservative, you're awfully chummy with the Humes." Drish sniffed. "You seem to care an awful lot about their stupid planet..."

"It's OUR STUPID PLANET, you cretin!" Matteras shouted. "It's the only one we've got, you blubbering fuckwit. Do you think if we blow it up we're just going to skip over to another one?"

"I don't want to blow it up, of course," Walrus said. "Just belt it a few times. Get some fireworks going. Do you remember when the dinosaurs went down? That was something spectacular. What's more, I don't like Hazard. Never did. Let's aim the rocks at him, eh? His auctoritas is through the roof these days!"

"You don't remember when the dinosaurs went down, Walrus; even you are not that old," Matteras said wearily. "And Hazard can have the conservatives and all the fucking auctoritas he wants. How many times do I have to tell you? It's all a pack of lies. Everything. Beltrex and fucking Givaras made it all up."

"Yes, yes, Givaras the Broken played a prank on us and now he's off on the other side of some gate exploring another universe," Drish said. "We got all that. What I want to know is when am I getting the *Sublime Porte*? With Memmion gone it should come to me by rights. I'm filing a case..."

"For the last time—You know what? Just go ahead and file cases. Please. As many as you can..."

"And for your information, Hazard doesn't seem to believe your far-fetched story."

"Yes. It's much easier to rile up djinn when you're willing to disregard the truth completely. Quite a different game when you've got to deal with facts and real problems. I leave the demagoguery to him. We have more important things to do."

"TELL THEM ABOUT THE KARMA PROTOCOL." A mechanical voice boomed omnidirectionally throughout the bar.

"Volume, Roger." Matteras looked ready to shoot himself.

"Sorry. Karma protocol."

"It's not a protocol, Roger. And please. This was supposed to be a closed-door meeting."

"Eh? Who's this?" Walrus was spinning his ball around wildly. Suddenly the room was charged with ionized particles as thirty distortion fields smashed up against each other.

"Roger is that Hume!" Drish shouted. "No Humes allowed in this assembly, I thought!"

There was a loud murmur of assent from various offended pilots. Quite a few started talking loudly about how Matteras had gone completely soft.

"He's a Hume, sort of, yes," Matteras said. "If you all had bothered to read the informational packets I gave you, you'd know that he's actually hardwired into the station. He can't *not* attend. We're sitting inside him, for all intents and purposes."

"What?"

"Look, the bugger is ninety-five percent hardware now," Matteras said. "He's more or less keeping us alive."

"We were a bit short-staffed when we took over the ISS," Roger said apologetically. "I had to keep augmenting my brain. Then it became easier to just graft all the input from the station directly into me. After a while it was like I *was* the station."

"I don't understand," Walrus said. "Is this Hume the one who went with you to the sea, Matteras?"

"Yes, the same," Matteras said. "And yes, he's running the station now, and he's not fully human anymore, so I think we can agree to let this slide."

"He's not even Nephilim," Drish objected.

"He's fucking metal and AI, and maybe five percent tissue, so no, he's not human, nor Nephilim nor djinn. What he is doing, however, is running the air inside this fucking station, and stopping micrometeors from poking holes in all of us, and keeping the water and food going, so maybe, just maybe, we can ignore his fucking bloodline and—"

"All right, all right." Drish had his palms up. Then, under his breath. "Hume lover."

"About this protocol thing?" Walrus raised a tusk. "Is that what you called this assembly for?"

"I did not call an assembly," Matteras said, enunciating each word carefully. "You guys barged your way into my bar and Drish the fucking twice-defenestrated steward called it, for god knows what—"

"Ah yes, the scotch situation," Drish said. "We're down to the last barrel. It's fine for the Humes to drink the synthesized stuff, but we pilots are real connoisseurs; we've got to get this thing moving and go for a drink run."

There was general acclaim at this, with several djinn hooting and stamping feet, finally finding something to agree on.

"You want to take the space station on a drink run?" Matteras stared at the steward.

"Just a quick hop over to Nippon," Drish said. "And then over to Islay. Two, three stops max."

"It is a fucking space station, you cretin. We cannot fly it around like a goddamn minibus."

"Er, excuse me," Roger interrupted. "We could in fact recommission our mothballed space yacht and use that."

"The ISS has agreed!" Drish yelled. "I call a vote! I'm driving!"

"You just spent the last hour trying to exclude him from the assembly..." Matteras said wearily.

"I could have it ready tomorrow," Roger offered.

"Emissary status for the ISS!" Drish said. "Look, he's granting wishes!"

"I want to throw rocks, ISS," Walrus trumpeted.

"Well, maybe a small one," Roger said after a few calculations. "I'll arrange it."

"And if we're going on a drinks run, we can finish the rest of the single malt!" Walrus said excitedly, barreling around. "Let's hear it for the ISS! *ISS! ISS! ISS!* Party starts now!"

2

Daughters of Old Foes

"So you finally got rid of them."

Matteras grimaced. "If Roger's space yacht actually works. I have a recurring nightmare of it all bursting into flame and exposing the Walrus to the world in his full glory."

Maria was sitting at her desk, elegant despite the sparse, bolted-down look of all ship quarters. She had aged. Once they had been lovers, on and off for years, and that had faded with time, but they had remained close allies, fates intertwined, and she had become a formidable strategist in her own right, seeing things Matteras could not, able to manage the people they needed with a patience the djinn was incapable of.

"You've given up too much," Maria said. It was a familiar harp. She couldn't bear the thought of Hazard strutting around on the surface, erasing their auctoritas. Matteras did not care about auctoritas anymore. The elder djinn had opened his eyes, and he was not one to cleave to falsehoods for comfort. If the Lore was a lie, then he would not waste time pandering to it. Enough djinn knew the truth, the ones who mattered. Over time, they too would have to accept reality.

"Forget about Hazard," Matteras said. "Worry about Bahamut instead."

"The last elder."

"The last one awake, at any rate," Matteras said. "I have no doubt there are more tucked away under rocks. They don't die easy, that's for sure."

"What is Bahamut doing? If only we had more pieces on the ground..."

"He has made a golem. An abomination, according to the Lore, but who cares about that now," Matteras said with irony. "I believe its purpose is to hunt us down. A stupid creature, but dangerous. He has already found many of our assets. We are losing drone soldiers at a ruinous clip. And our best neurosurgeon has gone dark."

"Ask Hazard for help. Rebuild the alliance."

Matteras frowned.

"You know, dear, you're far too proud for this job."

"The golem is not my only worry. I'm sure you recall the elders we left on the other side of that gate. I don't believe for a minute they're dead. Even your old Hume lover might in fact still be alive."

It was a familiar jab, sixty years old, but it made Maria tighten her lips. After all, she had betrayed her true love for Matteras, had locked him and the elder djinn out of this world for her thirty bits of silver. When she was being introspective, she had to acknowledge that she loved power more than anything else, that she had tasted being dominated once and had vowed never again, that it wasn't in her to be some lovelorn sidekick. She didn't love Matteras, but she *agreed* with him, she understood him, and if some part of her regretted old treachery, it was easily silenced. One had to be practical, after all.

"Matteras, dear, you never understood the subtleties of life. This is why you are alone, trapped in a tin shed in the sky, while Hazard inherits the entire green Earth," Maria said. "It's the story that matters, not the cold hard truth. People—humans, djinn, Nephilim—none of them can follow the truth to war. You have to cloak it in something romantic, something glorious. You could have ruled the conservatives—the entire polity, if only you had bothered to explain yourself, to rally support against an impending doom. This dour, endless jobbery of yours is why you fail."

Matteras stared at her. This was the problem with Humes. They couldn't let things go.

"You misunderstand power, Maria. For you Humes it comes from influencing other people; from followers and half-truths and manipulation." He flexed his field around his wrist, turning it solid black. "But sometimes power is just power. Internal. If you are a god, you do not need all those other things."

"God?" Maria raised an eyebrow. "You *are* becoming ornery, love."

"Not me, Maria," Matteras said. "Givaras. Kuriken. Memmion. The witch Davala. What exactly do you think they're doing on the other side? Have you forgotten the potency of that realm? I have not. What if they return... enhanced?"

"Is that a serious possibility?"

"If they're still alive. I am beginning to think that it was a mistake marooning them in Gangaridai." Matteras frowned. "I had hoped whatever was there would kill them for me. Now I am not so certain."

"No point in regrets. You bought us time to prepare."

"We must also consider that *something else* might come. Whatever creatures killed the people of the Eternal City."

"So we must unify. You will rule all with Karma."

"Yes. Tell the girl she has to finish now. We have no more time."

"Your daughter."

"That is a Hume word. We do not raise families."

"Your *daughter*, Matteras. Don't be an idiot."

"She does the exact opposite of what I want," Matteras complained.

Maria laughed. "As is the nature of all adolescent girls."

"You are too attached to her," Matteras said. "We djinn do not cosset our progeny so."

"Yes, yes, you hunt them down for fun and cull the defective ones; I've heard it before," Maria said. "She's done an exemplary job, despite what you think."

"We are running out of time," Matteras said.

"You could be nicer to her, you know."

"She's obnoxious. *You* be nice to her."

"Fine, I will talk to her," Maria said. "You call Hazard."

It was not a pleasant call.

"What do you want, Matteras?"

"I want to do you a favor."

"I find that hard to believe."

"Bahamut has a golem."

"What? Impossible."

"We saw him *with our own eyes*."

"So the old fish has some tricks left in his bag," Hazard said. "I thought he'd gone to sleep like the rest of them."

"They're not sleeping, they're on the other side—"

"Yes, yes, the other side, so you keep saying... Fuck the other side."

"All right, Hazard, humor me."

"I've been doing a lot of that, Matteras," Hazard said. "Look, we split up the world. I got all the dirt and you got your tin can in space. Why the fuck don't you just stay there now and stop bothering me?"

"It's a golem, Hazard. Aimed at our heads. He won't stop coming. Every time he gets put down he'll come back stronger. As you said, I'm up here. Guess which one of us he's going to find first?"

"You've got a point," Hazard said.

"Send Sekmet."

"You want me to get her out of bed for a filthy Hume?"

"It's a golem with a dragon-fired sword."

"Dragon-fired? That lunatic is back again?"

"Apparently."

"Does dragon fire actually do anything for a sword?"

"I'm not a fucking blacksmith, I don't know, but it seems a bit odd that Bahamut would wake up a fucking dragon to breathe on a piece of metal for no reason, doesn't it?"

"I just don't follow the physics of it..."

Matteras sighed.

"Would it hurt my auctoritas if I went ahead and killed that damned blind freak?" Hazard asked.

"Well, it's in the courts whether he's djinn or not."

"He's your nephew," Hazard said with some satisfaction. He always liked reminding Matteras of this. "Are you sure you're not going to get offended?"

"I won't shed a tear, trust me."

"I'm going to kill him. Fuck the courts. Next time he sticks his head out."

"He might end up killing you. He's put more than a few djinn under. Take care of the golem first, maybe."

"I'll let Sekmet off the leash, then."

"She sets my teeth on edge," Matteras said. "That smile... I don't know how you stand having her around all the time."

"The secret is letting her kill something every once in a while," Hazard said. "That's what you never understood. Everyone needs a bit of fun. We get bored, we kill shit. The djinn apocalypse always comes out of boredom."

"Good for you the golem is hard to kill, then."

"It'll be a good night if Sekmet has fun."

3

All Parties Are Aggrieved

The night started well for Marzuk. First of all, his black jacket fit him better than he had expected, indicating that the Ergonomic 9000 was well worth the money. His mother spent only half an hour cooing over him, lamenting his lack of a date, at the same time sniffling about how he was growing up far too fast. *Make up your mind, woman!*

The grand old car was dragged out of the garage, and his father filled up his allowance card, blissfully unaware that Marzuk regularly gave away this pittance to the charity school he supported.

In time-honored fashion, the school gym was the venue; alcohol and other stimulants were strictly prohibited, as was gambling; and anything else remotely fun was quickly squashed by the superintendent, who seemed to have eyes everywhere, until a quiet query to the Mongolian revealed that he was in fact using the AI's cameras on his students. *How low. Probably illegal too.*

Still, it had music and lights and food, plus a horde of teenagers hopped up on sporting achievement, and while it suffered greatly in comparison to the oligarchic debauchery Fedor had subjected him to, it was still his first real party (it being very likely that all of Fedor's guests had to be paid to attend). He was understandably nervous walking in alone. Other boys had dates, some of them, inexplicably, girls from the other schools. *How the hell did they manage to pick up dates from other schools in three days? Are they wizards?* Of course, not everyone was hormonally advanced yet. Many of them came in clumps, horsing around loudly. Even the most socially impoverished came in pairs, it being a high school axiom that only the very foolish would actually come to a party without a single person to talk to.

Marzuk slunk in, fully aware that even the lowest denizens of the social ladder were staring at him pityingly. Worse, he had severely overestimated the formality of this event. Everyone else was in casual clothes. *What kind of yahoos don't wear jackets to a ball?* There were a sprinkling of sartorially advanced guests, but as these were members of the theater club hell-bent on pulling off an impromptu performance, it didn't fill him with much confidence.

"Ah, Mr. Khan Rahman, always a pleasure." The superintendent wasn't being quite sarcastic. "Our celebrity!"

I now have the indignity of hanging out with the superintendent in front of everyone.

"How are you enjoying school life? I've been following your grades. Very impressive, son."

"Thank you, sir." *Are you drunk? You must be.*

"Not made any friends yet, eh?"

You don't have any either, seems like. What's your excuse?

He spotted Amina from far away, resplendent in some kind of tight silver dress. She was surrounded by a bunch of athletic boys, including that oaf Hinku. She caught him looking and gave a discreet wave and a half smile. She always had that air about her, as if she was just about to pop over for a chat, just on the verge of detaching herself from her surroundings, yet always delayed, waylaid, pulled away.

In a fit of cynicism Marzuk wondered if she appeared this way to everyone, if this was her stock in trade, the compulsion to be loved universally. Was it possible that Hinku saw her with the same possessive eyes, felt her smiles to be aimed at him? Was he in the same forlorn boat as Marzuk in the end, and hence the personal nature of his grudge? *Bullshit. She favors him, in truth.*

Hinku, after all, was already in her orbit, hanging on her arm, making her laugh, though even *he* was jostled out sometimes. It would be a miracle if Marzuk got near her tonight. He cast around hopefully for some friendly face, but it seemed like the few acquaintances who actually acknowledged him in school had not even bothered to come here. *Thanks for the heads-up, guys.* Far away at the tech booth he saw Richard slumped behind monitors, reading a book. He was tempted to go talk to the IT guy but decided to save that for when he was truly desperate.

Like many introverts, Marzuk had long ago perfected the art of being alone in a crowd, the act of appearing busy, amused, contained, invisible in turn. He slunk toward a dark corner of the gym, disguised by holographs but still bearing the distinct smell of the two dozen basketballs that normally resided here. It was a nice spot from which to observe the room without being embarrassed. The Mongolian winked into view discreetly.

"You shouldn't have come here," the airport said.

"Yeah, probably." He stared at Amina as she started to move toward the dance floor. She looked unbelievably graceful. There was a pain in his stomach that refused to go away, a crushing belief that he would never tell her he loved her, nor ever hear those words reciprocated.

"Hinku and the boys are planning on stripping you naked on the dance floor," the Mongolian said, ruining the moment.

"I wasn't thinking of dancing," Marzuk said. *There goes two weeks' worth of waltzing lessons.*

"And they have bags of non-erasable blue dye. I believe the plan is to catch you alone and color you blue. They've added micro glass particles so it's extra painful."

"That's bloody assault."

"Assault, or a prank gone too far?" The Mongolian looked sad. "You want to bet which way the superintendent will see it?"

"I'll just stay out of sight, I guess."

"Your compulsion to watch her at all times will be your downfall."

"Watch her?"

"Watch her, like you always do. It's creepy."

"It's love. I can't get bloody near her in public, can I? I tell myself every day to stop, but when I'm alone with her for five seconds, in some class or other, and she looks directly at me, I just... You're a fucking airport. Shut up."

"Still creepy."

"Just hide me, will you?"

"I've adjusted the holograms; you are now practically invisible."

The Mongolian was too successful at creating this dark oasis and almost immediately a rush of illicit couples began to take advantage. Far from being able to keep a protective eye over Amina, Marzuk was forced into the indignity of having various hideous teenagers make out in his vicinity like hopped-up gorillas. At one point there was even a line!

Such was the demand for this dark nook that Marzuk couldn't slip out without revealing his presence. Clumsy fondling wasn't the worst thing on the menu. The older local kids had a thriving trade in illegal pharmaceuticals and different brands of alcohol, there being a universal agreement that a party without any kind of stimulant was sadly flat, and it behooved them to defend their school's reputation. Not surprisingly, Hinku was in the thick of things, slinking around, making out with two girls from Katmandu Inc. (at separate times), dealing a variety of pills, all the while still managing to circle Amina like a hyena whenever anyone else got close.

Marzuk had almost dozed off when he again heard Hinku's ridiculous voice, this time in a hushed whisper. He was topping up his cola drink with whiskey and bragging to a goon.

"I'm telling you, I'm in tonight."

The goon looked wistfully at the dance floor, and Marzuk followed his gaze, his heart sinking. Amina was dancing with a couple of other girls, her silver dress catching and throwing the light like a disco prism.

"No way," said the goon. "She ain't like that."

Yes! Marzuk felt like cheering him on.

"They're all like that," Hinku said. "Once you get a few of these in them."

He rattled a silver pill box.

"What's that, then?" The goon reached for the box but Hinku pocketed it again.

"This is the good stuff, man; you stick to cheap booze like the rest of the herd," Hinku said. "A few of these and she'll be half-asleep and dreaming. Won't remember shit."

"That ain't cool," the goon said, once again displaying some faint stirrings of morality.

"Whatever, man." Hinku laughed it off. "She ain't gonna be the only one getting it. I'll let you join in. Here, have a drink. Whiskey from Nippon, I stole the real shit from my dad."

"Hey, thanks. . ." The prospect of joining in was clearly too much for his nascent moral fiber.

They drifted away, hatching further plots.

In the brief lull, Marzuk summoned the airport.

"He's planning on drugging girls! Do something!"

"What?"

"Stop him, for god's sake. Tell the Super!"

"He won't believe it."

"What?"

"Hinku has good grades and is the star athlete."

"What the fuck does that have to do with it?"

"No one has ever complained about him..."

"He's done this before?"

"I believe so, but no one has ever complained."

"You heard him, didn't you?" Marzuk asked helplessly.

"Yes. I am, however, compelled to mention that it is illegal for me to eavesdrop."

"You listen to me all the time..."

"Yes. Illegally."

"What the hell?"

"I am bored. As I explained. Moreover, you are not the typical student."

"You're not going to do anything, then."

"No," said the Mongolian. "Sorry."

"You have no responsibility to stop a crime?"

"My job is to keep the lights on."

"Never mind, I'll stop him myself."

"I do not recommend a physical confrontation."

"Of course not."

"This is not likely to end well."

"Could I trap him somehow? Pick his pocket?"

"Your physical dexterity is close to zero."

"Warn her, then?"

"She is unlikely to believe you."

"Even if I was deadly serious?"

"There is a ninety-three percent chance that she will call you a jealous loser."

"She wouldn't. I'm her friend..."

"I am sorry to inform you that she came with Hinku. He is her date."

"Shit, really?"

"Yes. I believe they are boyfriend and girlfriend for tonight."

"Fuck this shit. Why didn't you tell me earlier?"

"There was a ninety-three percent chance that you would throw a hissy fit."

"Fucking airport. Why is everything ninety-three percent? Do you just make up these numbers?"

"Yes."

"Well, I'm still going to do something."

"I am intrigued."

"I can't stop him, but I can end the party. They'll have to go home then."

"There will always be another time," the Mongolian said sadly.

"Can you at least help me cut the power or something?"

"I will get mothballed..."

"The air?"

"Also connected to me."

"A bomb threat?"

"Security is also my responsibility. I am connected to all things."

"Shit."

"All things except an ancient fire sprinkler system. It is obsolete."

"But working?"

"I imagine it could be restarted. No one ripped the pipes or circuits from the walls."

"I see. And do you happen to know where the control panel is?"

"It is in a broom closet above the second gym. The one you often hide in."

"Ah. Perfect. And could you possibly chart a path for me through the darkness?"

"Done."

"Thanks."

"Do you need assistance with the panel?"

"Hacking a control panel from 2001? Please..."

The lights and virtual effects shifted subtly, optical illusions parting just for Marzuk, and the Mongolian waved him through, as if into a magic kingdom. None of the kids were watching him; they were oblivious to his stately march. Richard caught his eye and frowned, sensing something afoot. Marzuk winked at him and carried on. He felt invigorated, like a nearly dead swimmer hitting the shore, on firm ground again for the first time since he had come to this godforsaken prison for children.

He found the panel at the back of the cupboard, hidden behind old mops, derelict tools that no one had removed. There were tableaus such as this all over the school, relicts of tradition: flags planted by students a hundred years dead, the rotted cloth still lovingly preserved; a small shrine to someone killed; trophies won by forgotten boys and girls; badges of pride for this place that had survived so much and somehow vaulted into the future. Still, it was hard to say what pride this pageantry of mops represented, an ode to janitors replaced by machines; some sentimental fool had left them here and other sentimental fools refused to move them. There was an ancient school in Nippon where they still made the children clean the halls with mops and soapy water as they had done a hundred years ago. Perhaps the school was thinking of introducing this practice.

Marzuk found the panel, dusty but springing to life at a touch. There was no useful interface, but his handheld had a plethora of ancient programs, things like MS-DOS, one of the very first input languages. His fingers, so clumsy with rackets and bats, danced along those tiny keys, and the panel hummed in pleasure, spoken to for the first time in a hundred years perhaps. There was a short discussion about permissions and authorities, but this was not a locked vault; indeed, it was designed for almost anyone to operate. Years ago, naughty children had set off the sprinklers at least once a month, until the panel had at last been hidden in the locked janitor cupboard.

In the bones of the building, ancient water pipes gurgled to life. There was a silent alarm ringing: *Fire, fire, fire in the old gym!* Sprinkler systems cunningly hidden in the ceiling, along the brick walls, and deep in the floors suddenly telescoped to their full potential. Marzuk turned the dial up to maximum. Far away in his crystal mind, the Mongolian watched as an ancient water reservoir underground, built over by three generations of steel supports and new floors, largely forgotten, suddenly started to empty, and he smiled.

It was not a tidy sprinkle or a gentle spring shower, or even the heavy sudden rain of the monsoon. It was a deluge. Dust-choked sprinkler heads gave way completely, and unrestrained water hit the gym from all angles, as if the old fire marshal, at last given a chance to shine, was emptying his entire stock in one go. It was magnificent. The gym floor turned into a fountain, the ceiling a waterfall. The DJ booth floated away, the dance floor and the students upended, everyone soaked, the holograms now flickering through the jets of water with protean magnificence. The dance, promising magic with smoke and mirrors, was now at last truly magical.

Marzuk, back in time for the show, stood at the door and watched, enjoying himself, and the Mongolian played the lights for him in a silent concerto, a tip of the hat to his favorite human. Then Marzuk noticed it was too quiet, the swearing and shrieking gone, and all eyes at last were on him, staring at him, some of them with dawning comprehension. *Fuck! I'm the only one dry...*

"It was him!" Hinku, predictably: "That fat f— It was him! He's a hacker! He did it."

"MR. MARZUK KHAN RAHMAN!" The Super was wet, his hair plastered askew, revealing a balding scalp. He was enraged, incapable of further speech.

He did it. I saw him. It was him. Loser. He came alone. No date. No friends. He hates us. Look at him. Loser. LOSER.

Marzuk blinked back from the onslaught. Amina coalesced at the front of the crowd, her dress and coiffure ruined, looking once again like a teen, for once awkward and broken like him. She was dismayed. Her makeup was running from her eyes, two trails of silver. She recognized the guilt on his face and her expression hardened into anger.

"Why did you do it, Marzuk?" she yelled. "You've ruined everything!"

"I... I did it for you..."

"You're just jealous," she shouted. "You're a weird, stalking loser. I hate you! EW, AS IF!"

He almost crumpled, muscles slackening off his bones, supine, until his body discovered in its spinal column some thread of steel. Covered in dross, he had almost forgotten who he was. Now, seeing the angry faces, the hard jeering laughter, fancy clothes plastered upon childish bodies, he felt his apprehension melt away. He had been hobbled by pygmies! Were these his enemies? They were feeble.

"You misunderstand me, my dear," he said with a practiced bow. "It was for *all* of you. A final fuck-you from me and every other forgotten outcast, every fool beaten to death here in front of the school and never mourned. I will have no more of it. You are all prisoners here, but I can leave whenever I want. I had forgotten that." In the silence his voice rang out through the room.

"Enough, MR. MARZUK," the Super shouted over whatever Amina was going to say. Marzuk, who remembered every word she had ever uttered to him, for once did not care to hear her out.

"You saw it! You all saw me being brutalized, and you ignored it. You great adults, where were you? You pander to the strongest, and fed me to them, as if nature would ascertain right and wrong while you closed your eyes.

"And you students were worse! The lowest of you, who should have been my brothers, laughed the hardest. Not one glance of sympathy, not a helping hand, just relief that it was me and not you, that at last some more pathetic fool had come to take your own pathetic place. At last you had someone lower to shit on, and how grand it was. Well, you can have it back! I want no more of it."

"MR. MARZUK, THIS GOES BEYOND A PRANK. I WILL SEE YOU IN MY OFFICE NOW."

"Your office is immaterial to me, as are you. I have graduated. I want no more lessons. Hinku, you've had a grand time with me. In this children's sandbox you are king. Keep your medals and your *friends*. Henceforth we will play in the real world. I will see you there, and you may do your worst. For the rest of you, I sincerely hope this is goodbye forever."

He turned on his heel and walked out. The Mongolian blasted his favorite song, "We Are the Champions," sung by the long-dead Freddie Mercury, and those divine lyrics drowned out all further insults.

4

Gramps

"We got our guy, Gramps," Arna said. "Hacker for the Securex job."

Djibrel winced at the epithet but had the wisdom to forestall his protest. Arna was the sort of person who would mercilessly root around any sore spot. A comatose man slowly returning to consciousness, he was aware of a coalescence of threads pulling him into Arna's circle, a casual buildup of regard and expectations that would have been called friendship had he understood this term. Bahamut had rebuilt his brain in a forge of corefire, and perhaps that ancient fish had left out such essential mammalian parts. Thus it was a novel experience for him, this alliance, an active, tribal pressure exerted on his behalf. It almost woke... reciprocity.

"Soooooo..." Arna said. "It's going to cost a bomb, though."

"Who?" Leto asked.

"The Cyber Mage himself."

"Pfft, he doesn't exist."

"No, no, he responded. Authenticated call sign from *FF9000* and everything."

"It's probably a hacker collective," Leto said. "They do that kind of shit for marketing."

"Hey, genius, who's the coder here, me or you?" Arna said. "He took down that satellite what, two years ago? Every fucking coder in the world knows the hack on that. You know how hard it is to hack satellites? The fucker had to bounce his signal at least thirty times to hit the right spot. Anyway, I verified him. You remember Roland? He plays *FF* with him."

"Roland? He's like twelve."

"Yeah, and he somehow runs up against the Goblin King in *FF9000*, who torches him with a flamethrower, and Roland ends up losing his level 99 Vishnu Lightning Mace, so he's sitting on the ground howling, and this guy feels sorry for him and helps him get his shit back. Turns out he's the fucking Cyber Mage. And now he has Roland babysitting some other weird savant player who knows how to fiddle with the bedrock coding of *FF* itself, which is impossible, and they're trying to take over the continent. Roland's been bragging to everyone up and down the street, so the shopkeeper at the corner of Lane Twelve heard and told me."

"Wow. That's kind of crazy."

"Yeah, so anyway, we've hooked the Cyber Mage. But like I said, it's going to cost a bomb."

Djibrel thought of the stack of credits resting in his djinn-plated Echo. He had no problem spending Bahamut's money.

"It is not a problem."

"So... carte blanche? We don't really know how difficult this job is."

"We need it fast. Pay him whatever he wants. Tell him to hu—"

"Um, Gramps," Arna interrupted, "something wicked this way comes." Her security projection sprang up in front of them, showing the ten lanes on either side of Leto's shop.

"I don't see anything," Djibrel said.

"The blur," Leto said. He was already moving toward his suit.

"He's avoiding the cameras somehow. The machines glitch around him."

Distortion field.

"He's a djinn," Djibrel said. He raised a hand to forestall the inevitable protest. "There's no time. Just trust me."

Leto was assembling himself into something formidable in an unreasonably short time. "How do we fight it?"

Djibrel drew his sword. "This can kill him. Maybe."

"Maybe?" Leto asked.

"I don't know, I've never killed one."

"Oh."

"Guys, he's almost at the door," Arna said.

"Is there another way out?" Djibrel asked.

"Back door basically opens into neighbor's window."

"Cut your way out, the two of you," Djibrel said.

"No," Leto said. "About time my suit got tested. Arna, take the plasma torch and go."

"No," Arna said. "I've got a suit too. I can run some defense."

"What defense?" Djibrel asked.

"I have two of the ball drones running. The ones you brought in." She tapped her command helmet. "This thing isn't just good for stopping bullets."

"You paid me to fight," Leto said, glaring at Djibrel.

"I paid you to keep her safe," Djibrel said.

"Listen, can you fuckers get over the macho shit and let's just see what we're up against first?" Arna asked, pissed off.

"All right. Behind me, both of you. Bahamut annealed me in fire. Let's see how his work holds up."

And then, after five minutes of fiddling around, he shouted, "Well, come on, what the fuck is taking so long?"

There was a cough at the door, and a faint knock.

"Excuse me." A woman's voice, rich and heavy. "Would the golem please come out?"

"I'm here" Djibrel smiled. "Don't break the door."

"There is a nice empty stretch of alley outside," she said. "Of course, the entire neighborhood is watching from their balconies. I apologize for that."

"I don't mind that much," Djibrel said.

"I do. It's not dignified. I am Sekmet," she said.

"Djibrel," he said through the door.

"Well hello, Djibrel. Come."

Djibrel went outside, and his hand stayed his friends when they made to follow.

She was pearlescent, slender. There was a sword in her right hand, a normally two-handed blade almost as tall as her, the edge trailing in the dirt behind her. It seemed impossible that she could lift it with those delicate wrists, much less do any damage. The air shimmered all around, fairy dust and moonbeams. Demons hunched behind her, misshapen in the darkness.

"I have Ghuls," she said. Her voice was something molten, far bigger than her, and it poured into the alley like sweet resin. "For your friends."

"That will not be necessary," Djibrel said. "They will not interfere."

She shrugged. "I agree. I am not here to kill Humes. Come."

Djibrel had never needed to be asked twice.

He stepped into the swirling wind, and his sword cut through the fist of distortion before him, cobwebs in the air, and her snarled parry was reward enough, that air of superiority deflated. Her massive broadsword was like a wall and he bounced off it, felt a shiver of disquiet in his arms. She moved that slab of iron like it was a stick, but it weighed a ton, heavy enough to dust him with just a parry.

He was close enough to see her face. She was beautiful, savage, unmasked for a moment, her distortion field cut and rippling behind her like a tattered sail. Sweat rolled from her brow, one drop, and he marveled that djinn could be so perfectly formed.

Djibrel steadied himself for a second, and then they rushed each other like smashing atoms, and it was just meat and steel colliding. There was no time for finesse. The talwar was quicker but the broadsword covered more ground, and it was a grunting push fight, muscles straining as each tried to shove the other around a tight space.

"She's kicking his ass," Arna remarked, watching through the open door.

"Won't last ten minutes at this rate," Leto said.

Sekmet did some twisty move and Djibrel went flying backward, crashing through the flimsy seaweed fab wall of someone's house, ending up on the couch plumb in between a surprised elderly couple watching pornography, the explicit sounds suddenly flooding the street, to their mortification. Some wag on a balcony started to applaud and eventually cheers filled the now-crowded viewing gallery.

Sekmet looked up ruefully. Djibrel apologized for the breakage and returned to the street. His clothes were rent and small cuts were already healing across his face, the smooth golem skin reforming, river washed. He wiped off the bloody streaks across his eyes.

"He heals fast," Leto said.

The crowd was growing jovial as more of the neighborhood turned out, to Sekmet's obvious irritation. She tried her field again, a heavy black ball expanding toward Djibrel, but again his talwar cut it apart, splitting atoms, and this time Sekmet saluted him in recognition.

"Guess I have to do it the hard way," she said.

Her following strike was incredibly fast, and Djibrel barely avoided it before catching a foot to the chest that sent him tumbling back.

Up close her field was a living thing, pulsating around him, physically tearing at the talwar's edge and then coalescing again around her like a wounded cowl. The djinn herself was corded with muscle, denser than she looked, and his hardest blows elicited only grunts as she caught them on the blunt side of her blade. He could smell the sweat on her and the electric charge of the field, the faint cobwebs of magic trying to clutch at his brain.

He was going to lose. He could see it. Even with her power negated, her strength and speed were too much to handle. She was not even out of breath. He doubted he could wield that giant's blade. She was in the zone, she wasn't even seeing him, just tracking the downward chops of his talwar, parrying with her edge and then snaking out a foot or an elbow or the pommel of her own weapon, scoring him at close range.

And then he saw the chips on her sword, where the monofilament edge of his talwar bit, the particle-thin invisible line digging scoops of metal from Sekmet's blade, minute holes and fracture lines zigzagging up the side. The broadsword was too big and heavy to parry with the flat of the blade, too difficult to turn the sword enough against the whip like strokes of the talwar; it was a weakness in her style, only against this particular sword and this particular edge. Djibrel doubted she even knew that her broadsword was crumbling in her hand.

From then he *looked for* the parry, slamming his edge as hard as he could into that pitted surface, praying for it to crack. Again and again he was tossed back, till he was a mass of pain, but each time his wounds knit, the djinn script inside his skin circling up like sharks to chum. The walls of the neighboring houses were now as battered as the golem, cracked and punched through, windows and doors shattered, the crowd growing restive as it became apparent that the entire street might be homeless before this altercation was done.

There were isolated calls for higher authorities, and more than one aged pensioner surreptitiously scanned the sky in futile hopes of a police drone. The djinn had obscured the cameras, however, her field glitching everything nearby, and had any errant drone ventured this far into the city backwaters, it would have seen nothing but a dusky night, nothing remarkable from their instruments, and on the off chance a human operator had annexed the eye, they would have perhaps spotted two still figures frozen in a tableau, one on his knees and the other poised in an executioner's stance, a moment imbued with some pathos perhaps, for this was the first time in seven millennia that a djinn had faced a golem.

"You're spent, golem," Sekmet said after cutting him damn near in half. "I will take your head."

"With what sword?" Djibrel asked feebly. "It's going to take ten bloody tries."

He was on his knees, the talwar tipped against the ground and barely holding him upright. Blood and viscera flowed out briefly as he spoke, and the djinn script whirled around him like panicky bees trying to plug a leaky hive.

Sekmet offered him a shallow curtsey. "I've noticed. This was expensive steel you've chewed up. Perhaps I can have yours when you're done with it. It's a bit small for me, though."

Djibrel said, "Let my humans go."

"I have no intention of hurting them," Sekmet said. "They were not on the contract."

"Come then. Take the sword. I have no further need of it."

"Thank you," Sekmet said.

"I cannot allow that."

There was a moment's pause as they processed that this was a third voice, coming from above.

They both turned to look, forgetting their quarrel for an instant. In fact, the entire audience craned their necks toward this interloper who dared to stop a djinn fighting a golem, a battle that had wrecked the street and demonstrated their individual skills to full effect, the denizens of the neighborhood now all experts on the merits and demerits of each fighting style.

"I cannot see you," Sekmet said, puzzled.

"That's fair, I suppose, since I can't see you either," said the man who emerged on the roof to their left.

Djibrel looked up at the dark smudge above. For a moment hope bloomed that it was Bahamut come to save him. This was short-lived. After all, no one had ever come to save him before, and he could think of no reason why this should change on the eve of his death. In fact, Arna and Leto, tooled up in power armor, had made just such a motion several minutes ago, when it was clear he was done, but he had forestalled them with a shake of his head. He had no illusions; Sekmet could dispatch them as easily as splitting peas.

"Just finish it," Djibrel said, turning back to the djinn. "What's one more come to watch the slaughter?"

Sekmet, however, had taken a step back; was now fully engaged with the stranger, her face terse with something perilously close to alarm.

He was a thin man, and peculiar. He stepped carelessly under a light, and Djibrel saw that he was blind, his eyes opaque, and his skin glinted with golden scales. There was a cane in his hand, but he appeared otherwise unarmed. A large ceramic amphora was strapped to his back. There was nothing obviously threatening about him, yet Ghuls and Sekmet alike had frozen in place. There was a level of panic in them entirely at odds with the stranger's calm demeanor. Djibrel did not really want to know what manner of creature made actual djinn nervous.

"You!" Sekmet said.

"Sekmet. We have not met, but your reputation is known."

"So is yours, Dragon," Sekmet said. "Murderer."

"So they say," the Dragon said.

"Why are you here?" Sekmet asked.

"You may not kill Djibrel."

"He is a golem," Sekmet said. "An abomination."

"As am I."

"Do you stop me out of hubris only, then?"

"That talwar is mine. I forged it with my own hand."

"I see." Sekmet visibly relaxed. She turned her own broadsword edgewise. The metal was ruined with cracks and divots. "It served him well. You made a good sword."

"Thank you."

"Perhaps one day you will make me one. As you can see, mine is broken."

"I would like that, Sekmet," the Dragon said. "If circumstances allow."

She shrugged. "I was hired to kill the golem, not to fight you."

"I imagine my rate is a bit higher," the Dragon said.

Sekmet smiled. "There is no rate for you. The celestial court cannot decide whether or not killing you is murder."

"Ah, the court," the Dragon said. "Nothing like djinn litigation to stir the blood."

"I am exhausted," Sekmet said. "I will leave now, unless you wish to fight."

"I don't spend my entire free time fighting for no reason," the Dragon protested. "I am a peaceful man."

She laughed. "You are neither peaceful nor a man," Sekmet said. "Peaceful men do not make swords. However, I don't blame you for that. No djinn is peaceful. It's the boredom. You are less bellicose than most. I had expected to see a true monster."

"I am sorry to disappoint."

"Not at all," Sekmet said. "I am pleased. Your scales... are very pretty. They shine like armor. I would like to meet you in the field one day. Or…elsewhere."

"I'm no swordsman, Sekmet," the Dragon said. "You'd be disappointed."

"I doubt that," Sekmet said. "However, we need not fight, if you are not inclined thus."

"Thank you for that. I am touched. Your brethren do not acknowledge me."

"Well, you *are* still a murderer."

"Would it make a difference if you knew every single fight was forced upon me?"

Sekmet shrugged. "The court will take a thousand years to decide, belike. In the meantime, farewell, Dragon."

"Come to me and I will make a splendid sword for you. Give my regards to Hazard."

"Give them yourself," Sekmet said. She made a circling motion with her finger and the Ghuls suddenly warped into darkness. "If they pay me enough, I'll come back and stuff you in that jar of yours." She turned to Djibrel, who was nigh bled out on the ground. "Golem!"

"Djinn."

"You fought well. I'll come back for you another day. You have interesting friends." And then she too wrapped her dark cloak around her and faded from view, an altogether elegant exit that belied the sweating, grunting demon she had been only moments ago.

Djibrel, who had followed nothing of the conversation, watched her fade with the pure relief of a man escaping certain death. The unassuming blind man approached.

"Hello, my name is Indelbed," he said, as Djibrel unceremoniously passed out.

5

Uncle Hinks's Kitchen

"You really doing this?" ReGi wasn't that enthused. "You actually took a hoodrat contract?"

"She's sound. Arna. Coder. Three degrees of sep, easy. Kinda hot too."

"Every chick with boobs is hot to you," ReGi said.

"Don't be jealous."

"Whatever."

"You know what the interesting thing is, though?"

"If you say her boobs, I'm going to puke."

"I asked Yellow King to vet her."

"I bet he went to town on her with cams, that perv."

"He did," Marzuk said. "And guess whom she hangs out with?"

"Well?"

"Our sipahi with the sword and the severed heads. Djibrel. *He's* the guy paying for it. It's *his* job."

"What?"

"Yep," Marzuk said. "Yellow King got them on camera. They're definitely working together. They allegedly took out a black market surgery unit too. So get this, someone has hit the holy grail. They've hacked a living Echo."

"No way."

"Yup. Watching through some poor fucker's eyes as he gets his head cut off. Creepy."

"So the job is to find the watcher?"

"Yeah. This one dead guy had illegal hardware in his head to control Mitsubishi combat drones. Arna already tracked it to a manifest on Securex books. We have to find out who bought it."

"This is kind of heavy. Someone who can hack Echos..."

Marzuk rubbed his hands gleefully. "Exactly! Something big is happening. I can feel it."

"How much are they paying?"

"A fucking bomb. Didn't even negotiate."

"Djibrel the street guy is carrying that kind of juice in his head?"

"Like I said, we're not seeing the whole thing."

"So we're working for the guy who's walking around cutting off heads now?" ReGi asked.

"I think it's all connected. Kali, this Djibrel thing, the ISS."

"Oh you do, do you? Look, man, if it is, maybe we should get the hell out of it."

"No way."

"This is more serious than idle curiosity."

"I was going to hit Securex anyway. Might as well get paid."

"Just let it go."

"I can't."

"Hinku, huh?"

"He uses Securex goons like his personal bodyguards. Need to fix that shit for good."

"Any word from Amina?"

"Left her like ten messages," Marzuk said with a groan. "Nothing. She didn't even check 'em."

"What about the school?"

"Well, instant suspension, of course," Marzuk said. "I have to go to a hearing soon. Expulsion hopefully. Save me the trouble of having to resign. And the superintendent wants to personally sue my parents. For raising me badly. I got Fedor's law firm on it."

"You're getting a mob law firm to handle your school?"

"They backed off pretty quick," Marzuk said, "which is great because my mom was freaking the hell out. I couldn't eat for three days from all her crying."

"Yeah, you look like you lost weight," ReGi said.

"Great. I'll die thin *and* alone, then."

"You know the flooding shit is on YouTube, right?" ReGi said. "Plus your speech."

"Oh god."

"Over three million hits already. You should check out the comments."

"Great. Another three million people think I'm a loser. No thanks. You in or what? I thought you'd jump at this."

"I can keep an eye on you, I guess. You gonna gimme half?"

"Ten points for Yellow King. Even split minus costs on the rest?"

"Suuuuure." ReGi sighed dramatically over the mic, registering her protest most emphatically. "What's the plan, genius?"

"Securex is interesting. They have some kind of level one AI set up running their drones and surveillance shit. The AI basically has eyes on every inch of the diplomatic enclave, plus lethal force capability. It also handles cybersecurity."

"Sounds standard."

"It does not, however, handle Securex's ledgers."

"Securex isn't big enough to have a corporate AI. That shit is crazy expensive."

"Right. Or... Securex does some shady shit they don't want reported by a level one AI," Marzuk said. "'Cause those level one fuckers are too stupid to lie. You know how Securex runs their core ledgers? Air gapped server."

"Disconnected from the Virtuality." ReGi sounded impressed. "That sounds shady as fuck."

"'Sensitive information' is how they justify it."

"So what, is it like a quantum machine?"

"Nope. Old-school electronic circuits and a mainframe. No cloud connections, no backups, no input or output from the Virtuality. Only one emergency radio link. Humans enter shit by hand."

"Isn't this how criminals like your Russians do it?"

"Yup. SOP. Stay offline and shoot anyone who comes near your server with a USB drive."

"So you're going to break into Securex headquarters like Rambo?"

"Who?"

"You know, that guy with the huge pecs?"

"Like man boobs?"

"No, man, he was a huge movie star like a hundred years ago."

"How do you even know that shit? What, you like jack off to him?"

"Ugh, fucking one-track mind, forget it."

"I don't have to break into Securex HQ," Marzuk said, gloating. "I already have someone who works there..."

"Hinku's uncle."

"Exactly. That fucker."

"You're going to hack him."

"Yup. And he's going to walk my code into that air gapped server and insert it himself. And then he's going to take the fall when I burn them."

"Burn?"

"Yeah, like physically burn them. That's the only way we get our hands on it."

"No backups, no cloud..."

"Yup. *Unless* there's a fire. In case of a fire there's an emergency ping to the manufacturer's satellite."

"So Samsung."

"Yup."

"And we're going to—"

"Yup. Old school phishing."*

"I'm so excited!"

"No one's done phishing in years! Burning shit down *and* phishing!"

"Wow, you sound just like Rambo now."

"Oh, shut the fuck up. Are you planning on earning your cut ever?"

"This is me earning my cut. I'm keeping you in line."

"Thanks, Mom."

"You wish I was your mom. Then you would have had a taste of these titties..."

"Ew, gross, gross, shut up!!"

"Yeah okay, that was gross," ReGi said. "So how do we hack this guy?"

"Uncle Hinks, I'm calling him," Marzuk said. "Can you run a light scan on him?"

"Easy peasy. He's, like, a garden-variety old perv. Not a pedo or into animals or anything," ReGi said. "Married, two kids, both live in Singapore Inc. He is nominally in charge of operations, but the level one AI does everything, so he basically goes to the office for four hours a day and has cocktails in Dhaka Club at six."

"So he's a cutout."

"He owns shares," ReGi said. "They're all cutouts, except for Dr. Yakub, head of security. He's the main guy, and dangerous."

"All right, we'll avoid Yakub," Marzuk said. "How old is Uncle Hinks?"

"About seventy? Seems in peak health."

"You want to bet he has some kind of computer at home?"

"Bingo!" ReGi said after a minute. "He does. How'd you know?"

---

*Phishing: setting up a mirror server or website that looks like the real thing, in an attempt to make people log in, thereby stealing their password and other information. In this case the idea is that the server will think it's sending data to a Samsung data bank, but in fact it will be a fake site, and the data will be routed into the Black Line.

"I've noticed old people just don't believe that the Echo can handle everything. They need their personal security blanket," Marzuk said. "My grandfather was the same. When no one was looking he'd always go and fiddle on his terminal."

"He's got high-encryption passwords," ReGi said, after some time. "Random generated number."

"That's Securex. They won't let him use 123456 as a password even if his PC isn't connected to their system."

"Okay, I have a way in."

"That was fast. Router?"

"Nope. That's a Securex setup too."

"Printer?"

"Nope."

"Kitchen?"

"Bingo. His kitchen unit hasn't been used for like a year."

"How the hell does he eat?"

"Who knows? He's old-school rich, probably has a chef or something," ReGi said. "Gimme a minute, let's see if I can exploit it."

It took considerably longer than a minute, during which time Marzuk thought about checking on Kali, or watching Djibrel, or logging onto the Black Line, but he just ended up repeatedly flipping his messages on and off in the vain hope of a response from Amina. *She must think I'm unhinged.*

His mom then came in for her daily cry fest, completely ignoring the line of demarcation. Topics covered during this hysterical monologue included absolute utter shame at having to attend family gatherings with a ninth-grade dropout, her wish that he had never gone to school, lamentations at the bullying her poor child had endured, invectives against the wicked superintendent and his lawsuit, a general opinion (unsought by anyone) of wicked Russian oligarch lawyers and the terrible bill they would no doubt present, ending with the likelihood that they (she and her husband) would end in poverty and cardless, evicted from the Tri-State, and then what would happen to her poor baby Maru?

Marzuk, having mistakenly left his mic on, was then tortured midway through with the anticipatory pain of the fun ReGi would soon be having at his expense. Some considerable time later he received a packet of code from her, and numerous pieces of facetious advice on what he should do once he was impoverished and cardless.

Finally he got to the hack, and as he read the little notes she had left him, he started to laugh at the beauty and simplicity of it. He opened up the Black Line and got to work.

6

Uncle Hinks Goes to Town

Several days later, Uncle Hinks woke up in a very good mood. He had slept well, and today was bonus day at Securex, which meant his stock portfolio was going to receive a very nice fill-up. At eight a.m., he sat on his balcony, ironically only 1.2 km away from Marzuk's house. The sunlight was pleasantly mild and he did in fact have a manservant, the indispensable Yusuf, who brought him his Darjeeling tea, hand brewed the correct way, with a little bit of milk and an old-fashioned digestive biscuit.

Uncle Hinks enjoyed this interlude in the (reasonably) fresh air, the most peaceful part of his day. At around the same time, his kitchen unit stirred to life due to Yusuf's proximity, disappointed as always by that worthy man's Luddite bent. Yusuf made everything by hand, which was why he got paid the big bucks. The vat was about to go back to sleep when it received an urgent update ping from Samsung Inc. via one of its thousands of proxy software producers. The vat unit duly checked the certificates and found them impeccable, as was natural for something bearing the august seal of the Sultan of Brunei.

The kitchen happily accepted the patch and allowed ReGi's worm to take over. Within an hour, the unit had become a demonic vector, spreading poison throughout the home network, infecting everything capable of accepting the payload. The initial code was simple and elegant, a copy of something very old, the remote access Trojan. Hackers a hundred years ago had used this type of code to take over machines remotely, in the era when everyone had personal computers. The advent of the Echo and AI control of the Virtuality had put paid to that kind of virus, and therefore defenses against it had also lapsed. It was as if a ten-thousand-year-old disease had respawned in the tundra, one the human immune system had completely forgotten how to deal with.

The virus was sent in tiny packets that escaped detection and reassembled itself in the host operating system. Very soon, the home computer was fully in ReGi's grasp, giving up all manner of information. ReGi delved in gleefully.

Marzuk, who was watching her screen remotely, had to ask her numerous times to stay focused. Luckily Uncle Hinks was a dawdler and never went to work before noon. They had plenty of time to work. ReGi hid a number of nasty incriminating files in the remote recesses of Uncle Hinks's computer, places where Securex lawyers would inevitably look once the shit hit the fan. The main job, however, was to drip-feed a new piece of malware into the machine, rather more complicated than the simple RAT.

In the Black Line, the hackers had found an archive of computing history, containing an immensely helpful treasure: the source codes of almost every piece of malware and its corresponding defense since the start of computing. Most users considered the Echo and the Virtuality to have just appeared fully formed, virgin births. The truth, of course, was that they and everything else were built on a hundred-plus years of messy code, mistakes, redundant programs, and outright bizarre decisions. Everything was a hodgepodge of different languages, older bits of code shoehorned into newer ones to save time.

This left a lot of exploits for those with access to old code. The weapon Marzuk had brought to the fight was Stuxnet, a nuclear bomb designed specifically to bust open air gapped defenses. Long ago, in 2010, this worm had been used by the former United States of America and the Israelis to actually wreck the centrifuges of hidden Iranian nuclear enrichment facilities. It was the first time a virus had been used to destroy physical assets.

Stuxnet had worked to a great extent, disabling a chunk of the Iranian nuclear capacity by overspinning the centrifuges to hell, setting back the uranium enrichment program by ten years. It had later been studied widely by all cybersecurity experts. The code itself had never been fully released to the public. Professors had speculated that it must have taken a dozen coders at least three years to create a virus of this complexity.

When Echos became widespread, however, the focus of cyberwarfare shifted away. Stuxnet lay forgotten. For some reason, the information ministry of Brunei had painstakingly restored the entire viral code.

At half past ten, Uncle Hinks went for his shower, and then dressed with Yusuf's help. He always wore a suit, as did his chauffeur, both of the finest cut, it being a family adage that one could tell the quality of a person by the clothing of their staff.

His preparations took exactly an hour, and during this time, his computer had downloaded the entirety of the modified Stuxnet virus. At eleven thirty, he finally went to his fabricator and printed out the security chip for the day, on a physical wafer. This was sent every day to all operations staff who had to access the server, as this room was entirely offline and thus required foolproof primitive security. As director of operations, Uncle Hinks didn't actually touch the server or input any commands, but he still liked to go in and see his minions work.

The security wafer for the day was almost 200 percent heavier than normal, but this was undetectable by the human touch, and Uncle Hinks did not notice at all. He put the wafer in the top pocket of his jacket as always, gathered his printed newspaper (another indelible sign of class), kissed his newly risen wife (she was thirty-five, an aspiring classical singer), and made his way to the car.

It was a short ride to HQ, just enough to smoke half a cigarillo. He saved the remainder for the ride back. His aide met him at the main entrance with a deep bow. She was also his mistress, so the bow was only half-ironic. Two discreet armed guards saluted him from the eaves, as befitted his rank. Kinetic combat drones circled their heads like angry buzzards.

After making his usual rounds, he stopped for a cup of tea in his office and a quick cuddle with his aide. He had a very comfortable couch and they made good use of it, as per the Tuesday routine. When they were done, she briefed him on the office gossip, the schedules of the other directors, and the latest on the upcoming bonus.

His last duty before lunch was to visit the server chamber in the basement of the building, which housed the crew of human specialists. The door was controlled by the server itself, a simple hardwired connection. It scanned the director's eye and then accepted the encrypted security key, along with the Stuxnet variant code Marzuk had thoughtfully printed on it.

The server accepted this packet without a second thought, as it had never occurred to anyone that the door was a possible vector of infection.

The Stuxnet was essentially a three-part virus: it had a worm that carried out the main attack, typically inert until it encountered the right conditions to act; a replicator link that propagated the worm; and finally rootkit files that hid the nature of the beast and allowed it to remain undetected. The original Stuxnet had exploited the ancient Windows program and targeted Siemens hardware. Since then it had gone through a hundred years of iterations, evolving into a very sleek and powerful piece of code. Marzuk and ReGi had inserted their own modifications and then the Mongolian had simulated it in his mind 34,552 times to iron out any kinks, for a very reasonable fee of 1 percent.

By the time the director had his afternoon cup of tea and left the office for his club, every partition of the server mainframe had been infected with the worm. Ever so subtly, it turned off the cooling system and started ramping up the central processing unit and graphics processing units. The CPU and GPUs began to generate heat at a higher and higher rate. When everyone else had gone home, the heat was well beyond operating parameters. At four a.m. it all caught fire.

At the first spark, the ever-efficient Samsung server safety protocol kicked in, and a one-time remote connection was established through radio link to backup the precious data. It searched for the parent server and ran into a bit of worm code that redirected it to someplace else entirely, bearing the chop of the Sultan of Brunei. For the next three hours, the entire contents of Securex's most secret server were uploaded into the Black Line, where Marzuk magnanimously opened them up for all his colleagues to have a look at and bask in his glory.

The head janitor (a ceremonial post) arrived the next morning and found a single red alarm blinking on the server room door. This had never happened before. As he was in no way authorized to go in, he was forced to call his boss, the office manager, who was also unfortunately underqualified to enter. Two more calls up the line, and they finally hit Dr. Yakub, the director of security, midway through his golf game. He arrived in sporting togs and a filthy temper.

Dr. Yakub, unlike Uncle Hinks, did in fact run his department. In reality he ran everything, insofar as security *was* the entirety of the game, and his authority ran through the breadth of the organization. He had the board on speed dial, and he wasn't hesitant about updating them. There would be plenty of blame and pain to spread around later, but any messing with the server room was a grade 1 crisis.

He took his job seriously and he ran two drones from his Echo with enough intelligence hardware in them to constitute an agency on his own. The problem was that the server room was a vault that actively prevented surveillance. In a crisis situation, it was company policy that the server should be destroyed rather than fall into enemy hands, such was the sensitive and indeed criminal nature of the information stored there.

Dr. Yakub had a master key for the door, but even then he required the retinal scans of two other board members before he could force that portal open. These people were duly roused and shunted over, much to their irritation.

Inside, he found the server bricked and the chamber covered in flame-retardant foam. A natural fire was out of the question. His first theory was that someone had brought in a miniature explosive. As the server crew had all trickled in by now, he promptly arrested them and sent soldiers to round up their families. He was about to begin invasive interrogation on a few of them when it occurred to him to get Uncle Hinks over here, just in case one or two of them died and he needed to cover his ass.

Uncle Hinks was informed in the middle of his toast, and rushed to the office without bothering to put on a tie, such was the unprecedented nature of this calamity. That the premier security agency of the city could allow a bomb to go off in its secret server room would be a matter of great hilarity to their rivals and certain death for their stock price. It was imperative to stop the media from getting wind of it, not so easy considering every bloody Echo was on constant broadcast mode.

An explanation, a culprit, and exemplary punishment were all urgently required, and not necessarily in that sequence. Uncle Hinks was a bit squeamish, so he avoided the actual interrogation, but as the immediate superior of the victims, he signed off on all the forms. Indeed, Dr. Yakub was so menacing with his bag full of surgical gear that Uncle Hinks would have signed over his firstborn nephew to avoid being in an empty cell with him. All the legalities completed, Dr .Yakub went to work with gusto, this being a part of his job he did not get to enjoy nearly often enough.

By noon he had cracked open a couple of Echos with extreme brutality, reduced another woman to a comatose state, and caused a fourth man to piss himself just by smiling at him. It was now abundantly clear that none of the employees had bombed the server. Some other kind of failure had occurred. With growing trepidation, he ordered medical assistance for those who needed it, called body disposal for the older gentleman who had suffered cardiac arrest, and then sat down to lunch with Uncle Hinks.

The forensics team had been working concurrently, and they eventually forwarded a tentative hypothesis. Somehow the server had been induced to catch fire on its own, due to a failure of the cooling system. As this system had quadruple redundancies to prevent just such an accident, this hypothesis was summarily dismissed at first.

With no new evidence emerging, Dr. Yakub was about to call in the Samsung service team when Uncle Hinks made his first contribution of the day.

"The backup!"

"What?"

"B-b-b-back up," he said excitedly. "Has anyone checked the damned emergency backup?"

"Whose bloody job is it to do that?" Dr. Yakub shouted.

"Morshed! Where's Morshed?" Uncle Hinks knew his man.

Dr. Yakub consulted his notes. "He's, er, in the morgue. Heart. Ahem."

"Oh. What about Sayeeda, then?"

"Coma."

"Habiba?"

"Er, we don't quite know what's wrong with her, she's having seizures. I've ordered a new Echo for her free of charge," said Dr. Yakub. He himself had wrecked her original Echo.

"Is there *any* member of the team who can work?"

"Stobel, but he's handed in his notice."

"I strongly suggest you induce him to come back," Uncle Hinks said, basking in the glory of not being the man who had fucked shit up.

Dr. Yakub liked to handle things personally. Half an hour after lunch, Stobel had returned to his charred leather desk, sporting a fresh black eye. He grudgingly made the call to Samsung Backups. All his sulkiness disappeared, however, when it became apparent that Samsung knew nothing about a fire, and no files had been backed up on their secure satellite. Another minute later, Stobel was able to confirm that the one-time radio link had in fact been triggered. The emergency system had worked bang on time.

"Where the fuck did our data get backed up to, then?" Dr. Yakub snarled.

"Sirs," Stobel said with a certain degree of smugness, "we've been hacked."

7

Tigers of the Black

There was a feeding frenzy on the Black Line, and the Cyber Mage was the host. Securex was a premier intelligence agency, private police for the richest suburbs of one of the biggest cities in the world. Its secrets were not only valuable and profitable; they also carried the seeds for numerous other hacks. As the Black Line was a shared resource, it was customary to share kills. Marzuk was feted for providing this leviathan carcass, and in return he asked that ReGi, herself a well-known hacker, be granted a temporary passport to the Black Line so that she might help examine the data trove.

This was a serious request. In the past three years, they had allowed only one other outsider temporary access. Even with the landmark nature of their hack, the extra kudos for using a vault virus, the sheer effrontery of having the man walk in the wafer of his own destruction, it was touch and go. In the end, Yellow King also offered to vouch for her, much to ReGi's chagrin, and she was finally permitted entrance.

Securex's darkbox was full of goodies. There were numerous accounting scams the directors were running, including triple-billing hours and manpower to the city. They had agreements with a number of local mafias, allowing the criminals to pimp their wares in the Tri-State area, and meticulous ledgers on who owed what. The biggest business was in the supply of clandestine arms. Securex was a giant funnel, purchasing weapons from around the world, charging the city a hefty service fee, and then quietly making them surplus and "de-stroying" them, right out the back door into the hands of numerous gangsters waiting with cash.

Even in this river of shit, the sale of Mitsubishi military drone controlling Echos stood out, an audacious piece of business, a class A Hague war crime.

"Got him," Marzuk said. "Uncle Hinks signed off on it himself."

"Stop gloating."

"I'm just thinking about the multiple ways I can screw this guy now."

"Um, Marzy, that's not the only thing Securex sold them."

"What else?" *Marzy. Cringe. She's going to just keep doing it too, and now half the guys here are calling me that.*

"Hmm let's see. There's the six Mitsubishi military ones. Then one experimental one also from Nippon. It's not even been cleared for human use. Securex got a prototype for possible testing. Eight drones on one Echo." .

"Eight?" Marzuk sat up from his Ergonomic 9000 with such excitement that it set off his elephant. "That is beyond the human mind. Not even augmented humans can run eight."

"And how do you know this?"

"Fedor and I tried. The most we got to was five before the Echo fried."

"Umm, what happened to the test subjects?"

"Coma, lobotomized... I don't know, they were all volunteers."

"Yeah, sure. Sometimes I think you're actually the Sith."

"Hmm, they also took possession of a military EMP. Highly illegal. And what's this? Eighty Echos from executed criminals."

"How? The Echo dies with the person. You can't recover them..."

"Wait. I got that wrong. They didn't buy the Echos. *They bought the actual people.* Securex didn't execute them, they sold them."

"That sounds far-fetched."

"It makes sense. How else would they hack Echos? They'd need live subjects. These are major crimes. No wonder they had an air gapped server."

"You realize they're going to come after you, right, Marzy?"

"Pfft. How're they going to find me? Uncle Hinks walked in the virus and the upload was to the Black Line."

"These people are bad, Marzy. Maybe you should, like, lie low a bit?"

"Fine, fine." Marzuk basked in the warm fuzz of seeming invincibility.

"I'm serious. They're going to find you," ReGi said. "Just fucking hide."

"Now, what about the payment? Where did it come from?"

She sighed. "You're an arrogant asshole, you know that?"

"Come on, we just did the hack of the century! They're going to be teaching this in classrooms. Enjoy it a little."

"Right."

"Where's the money from?"

"It just shows an encrypted number."

"Easy, then."

"It's super encrypted, Marzy."

"No shit. Have you cracked it?"

"Yeah, all right, it wasn't that hard. Standard & Bartered platinum numbered account, no name."

"That's it?"

"Platinum account. That's, like, highest-level privacy. Standard & Bartered themselves don't know who the owner is." ReGi laughed. "It's a dead end. We hacked Securex for nothing."

"Please."

"These guys are heavy hitters," ReGi said. "They have tech we don't understand. We should quit while we're ahead."

"Are you feeling all right, ReGina? Would you like a biscuit? Some milk?"

"I do not want milk and cookies."

"Then stop acting like a baby."

"Just saying, they seem way out of our league."

"We are in the Black Line, and you're saying that? We have the top one hundred and forty-four hackers in the world here..."

"I say we call it quits and bask in the glory of fucking over Securex," ReGi said. "You should really focus on squashing Hinku. Now's the time. Let's stick his name in the shit too. He can be the mastermind behind this whole thing. They'll send him to juvie. You know what they do to pretty boys in juvie?"

"He's not that pretty."

"Oh, he's pretty."

"Stop letching." Marzuk was distracted, however, by the single decrypted string of information. He could read alphanumeric codes like novels. "ReGi, look at this currency code."

"What?"

"What kind of money is it?"

"How should I know?"

"I don't recognize it," Marzuk said. "Not bitto, obviously, not any of the seven AI cryptocurrencies, not Singapore scrip, not rubles, not yen, not California dollar, not New Yo—"

"Hang on, you know the codes for random currencies by heart?"

Marzuk shrugged impatiently. "Fedor has to figure out a lot of different exchange rates. I made a simple program for him. He doesn't trust machines all the time."

"Luddite."

"He likes the human touch. Can't shoot a machine. Anyway, I don't recall this string at all."

"I don't fucking know, run it through your program."

"I am doing so as we speak."

Five minutes later, Marzuk was extremely excited.

"It doesn't exist!" he said. "It's a nonexistent currency!"

"Maybe you missed something when you made the program?"

"Impossible! All right, it's possible. But I sent it to the Mongolian as well. He double-checked against all known bank currencies that are public. Zip."

"It's a dead end," ReGi said.

"How so?"

"Someone has a secret currency—"

"That a bank like Standard & Bartered accepts, but won't list on their register. That's illegal right there. Well, illegal in most places. Anyway, point is, why? Who is backing this currency? Why would Securex accept payment in it, and more crucially, be willing to *hold* it? It can't be traded in public markets, right? So I'm willing to bet the issuer themselves made that payment to Securex, and Securex thinks this scrip will go up in value. This person is basically giving out IOUs, and people are taking them. That's pretty fucking cool."

"What does the bank call it?" ReGi asked.

"Karma points. The alphanumeric translates simply to Karma points."

"Where is this going?" ReGi asked.

"Into space."

"What?"

"The stolen ISS."

"Fuck off. That's a huge stretch."

"Au contraire. It is perfect in its simplicity. Occam's razor. We have Echos getting hacked. We have a newly minted currency that Securex is willing to hold. We have Mitsubishi drones on a command helmet beyond recognized human capacity. All of this points to high science and weird secret fuckery. It's the ISS."

"You're obsessed. It's probably just a regular criminal ring..."

"If it were the Russians or Nipponese, I would have heard... If it were the Swiss or the Serbs, Yellow King would have known...

If it were, um, well, I have no clue if you are actually in the FEZ, but I'm guessing you'd know something about somewhere. Anyway, the point is it's this secret and powerful because it's off planet! ISS."

"That's great, Marzuk, I love it when you go full Cyber Mage mode there, but we don't have, you know, any evidence at all for this far-fetched theory."

"What I can't figure out is Kali, you know?" Marzuk mused, ignoring her. "I mean, if the ISS made her, how the hell did she get loose?"

ReGi started to laugh. "Look, man, you're tripping."

"You're not convinced? I'm going to set the Mongolian on this currency tag. I'll bet your ass he tracks it off planet."

"All right, I'll take that. Your pet airport will find fuck-all. What's the bet?"

"Full reveal. You show me your face, where you live, real name, everything."

"Does it really bother you? Why don't you just hack me?"

Marzuk shrugged. "You know I wouldn't do that. It doesn't count if I have to. I want you to *tell* me."

"Fine."

"Yeah, it bothers me. You're…well, you're my best friend and you won't even show me your face."

"Ok. Know what I want?"

"What?"

"Your name."

"Marzuk Dot—"

"No, idiot. Cyber Mage. I want it."

"What the fuck you mean?"

"I mean it's a cool fucking name and I wanna be called it when I win. You can be something else."

"Wow, that's mean."

"So's asking to see my face, asshole."

"What? You disfigured or something?"

"That's not the point. It's about trust," ReGi said.

"Whatever. Fine. You're acting weird."

"Is it a bet?"

"It's a bet."

Later, when ReGi had hung up, Marzuk put in a quick call to his *FF9000* account, where Kali was still ensconced.

"Friend Marzuk, YOU HAVE ABANDONED ME!"

"Er, no no, been busy," he said quickly. "Do you remember I told you about hacking Securex?"

"I offered my help," Kali said, offended. "However, you spurned me!"

"They sold military equipment and live slaves to someone, who hacked the Echos."

"The ISS. I have been watching them," Kali said.

"How sure are you they're behind all this?"

"Almost certain," Kali said.

"So look at this list, then," Marzuk said. "Securex didn't just sell military equipment. Look at all this other stuff. Something is up, but I can't put my finger on it."

"This is hacker equipment."

"But what exactly are they hacking? Echos? Securex sold them live bodies to experiment on. What's the game here?"

"I will hound them to the ends of the earth... er, solar system."

"Don't get caught."

8

The New Team

"You think it's what?" Arna's face swam before Marzuk so large that he could see her pupils dilate.

"The ISS."

"Are you serious?"

"I'm pretty sure. Friend of mine is chasing down the money. They pay in a scrip that isn't on any planetary register. The code gives a physical location in alphanumeric, right, like the old IBANs banks used. We will find it. Matter of time."

"What else did you find?"

"I have an idea what they're doing too," Marzuk said. "See, I went through all the shit Securex sold them. Apart from the drones, I mean. They were protecting a coder, weren't they?"

"How do you know?"

"The equipment Securex supplied them. It's all stuff *I would want.* It's some kind of hack. I'd bet my elephant on it. They're going for something huge, if that much coding is involved."

Arna shrugged. "That's what I thought, at first. Hacking the Echos. We know they can already do that; the watcher looks through all their reverse Echos' eyes. We found the lab where they did the operations. Maybe that was the trial run."

"Hack everyone. Everyone with an Echo becomes a zombie," Marzuk said. "Brilliant." *Thank god I don't have an Echo yet. Hacking Echos is big. I don't know. Something is off. It's not that simple.*

Marzuk started sending over large swathes of data. "Here's all the useful stuff from the Securex servers. I've made five data dump sites. They are into all kinds of illegal business, even without the ISS stuff."

"Thanks. That hack was legit," Arna said. "Securex stock is melting. They're losing their shit over there. Rumor has it Dr. Yakub has already killed six or seven of his own people. I'd keep my head down if I were you."

"Everyone keeps saying that."

Arna shrugged. "He ain't the worst guy headed your way."

"I got the payment, by the way," Marzuk said. "Mind if I ask a question? Who's paying?"

"Sat minutes is how we do business out here, homie. Anonymous."

"I know it comes from the guy with the sword," Marzuk said. "Question is, where did he get this kind of cash?"

"You know him, huh?"

"Everyone knows him. He walks around with a talwar, cutting off heads," Marzuk said. "Where's he getting the money from, though?"

"Djinn."

"What?"

"Djinn," Arna said. "This is some crazy shit happening here. We could use help. You want to know? Come all the way in."

"Actual, like, made-of-fire djinn?"

"Come here and see."

"I'm definitely in."

"Mom! Mom!"

"What's the matter, beta, are you hurt?"

"I need the car. I have to go see my friends!"

"What?"

"Friends, Mom!"

"Oh, I'm so happy! Is it that nice girl?"

"Oh, Mom, NO!"

"Marzuk, stop shouting this instant and come down here and speak like a human." His father finally intervened in what promised to be a lengthy conversation conducted at full volume.

Marzuk double-timed it down the stairs and then realized only at the landing that he was still in his boxers and two-day-old T-shirt, hardly the gentleman of independent means he had been taking pains to present to his parents. *Bloody Ergonomic9000 not doing shit. Bloody fake. I'm already out of breath.*

"Where are you going?" his father asked.

"Friends, you know, a morning visit, luncheon perhaps," Marzuk said airily. "Of course, I was in the middle of changing into something suitable when I was so rudely summoned down..."

"Where exactly are you trying to go, Marzuk?" *Damned Father is a suspicious man.*

"Oh, I'll put the address in, I've got it somewhere."

"Is it outside the Tri-State?"

"Outside?" Mother gasped. "Why would you go outside? Which girl is outside? Maru beta, it's not safe outside, the air is always yellow-orange, no no—"

"Mother, please, plenty of people live outside, it is perfectly reasonable to go outside, you two happen to live in a bubble..."

"Where, Marzuk?" Father, damn him, was always homing in on pertinent facts like a lawyer.

"Old Town," Marzuk said.

"And what is over there?"

"My friend Arna," Marzuk said. "She has a shop. She's collected something very rare. A 2020-era Apple MacBook Air. Absolute mint condition. Those things were *not* meant to last..."

"Your mother is right. It's not safe for you to wander about. Can't you get it delivered?"

"I have to *see* it first, Baba. Please! I promise I won't get out of the car. That thing is a tank, you know. You can follow us on Echo the whole way."

"All right, fine. You haven't left the house since you got suspended." His father smiled. "Probably good for you to get out and about. A shower might be smart. Arna sounds nice."

"Kindly do not mention the school again," Marzuk said with awful dignity. "And I was just about to shower."

"Ooh, is Arna a girl? What kind of name is Arna? Does she live in *Old Town?* Maru beta, do we know her parents?"

Marzuk fled.

An hour later, a considerably cleaner Cyber Mage was bundled into his Disera vintage car by his mother, who pressed a snack box into his hands in between offering wildly diverging pieces of life advice. He was pressed to wear an overcoat and a muffler while at the same time told not to sweat, as he was sure to catch a chill in the air-conditioning. She then turned on the stalwart chauffeur with an even longer list of admonishments.

The driver mercifully knew this routine by heart, and having answered all her questions in prompt fashion, he pulled out of the driveway before some fresh disaster could impede their progress.

Not having left the Tri-State in a while, Marzuk was intrigued by the scenery outside, how quickly it changed from idyllic suburb to gritty metropolis. The sky itself shifted color from a sylvan blue to the more gray-tinged haze that was typical of unaltered microclimes. No one had the time to make things pretty out here; everything was utilitarian. Trees still sprouted crazily from gaps in the concrete, and there were odd embellishments here and there, fountains and domed mosques, some sleek towers and the odd multicolored monstrosity. The air was tolerable, although the meter crept steadily toward yellow the farther they got away from the posh areas.

The route was complicated by the fact that the old driver flatly refused to enter into the narrower lanes of Old Town and eventually gave up altogether, sullenly parking the car by the side of the road. The map to Leto's shop indicated streets where there seemingly were none. Vendors proliferated here that had appeared on no municipal tax roll, Marzuk was certain. After bribing his devil driver, he was permitted to exit the car and walk around the impromptu bazaar.

The press of humanity was immense. The Tri-State had long ago ejected nonessential people from its borders, having achieved independent corporate status. Only shareholders and staff lived in its idyllic miles. Here was Dhaka City proper, the enormous, engulfing octopus of a city, tentacles of humanity flung every which way nature permitted, a beastly assault on the eyes and ears and nose. The microclimate here had a different flavor, the nanites coming directly from unsanitized human flesh. Marzuk was slightly disgusted at first by the idea of breathing in the product of this great human horde, but the exhilaration of freely moving among so many people was too much to resist.

He roamed the great impromptu market, letting the currents press him toward this stall or that, the smells of fried chilis, mustard oil, and onions fighting with the pungent odors of slightly rotting garbage, street dogs, sweat and detergent from the bodies packed around him, nicotine from numerous cigarettes, all of it hovering around his head in sensory overload. He was pushed against a stall holding a large deck* of morog polao, rice mixed in with a rich chicken curry so that almost every grain was coated in that wonderful grease. Before he knew it he had snapped his hand out for a bowl, belatedly realizing that everyone here was paying with sat mins, that anonymous barter currency that was tax free. He fumbled with his handheld, trying to

---

*Deck: A large cauldron shaped pot used to cook rice dishes in Bengal for large numbers (fifty plus people).

find a cache, clutching his bowl against the rumbling line behind him.

"I've got it." A cool voice, and a girl in her twenties, sporting a red-and-green scarf that Marzuk only now remembered was their prearranged signal. She winked at the beaming vendor, who not only refused her money but gave her an extra bowl with noticeably more chicken.

Marzuk blustered in outrage, protesting both this gross inequity in portions as well as her cavalier payment for his meal, both of which went against the chivalrous code he lived by.

"He used to be my uncle's cook, before he became a famous chef," Arna said with a bright smile that abruptly made Marzuk realize he was in the presence of an attractive woman.

"Cyber Mage. Ahem. At your service." He did his best to execute an elegant bow, but when he had practiced this at home with Babr the elephant (terrible judge and most unhelpful ally), he had not anticipated the mouthwatering morog polao in his hands. In the end he almost dropped it, and had to shuffle back, creating a minor traffic jam.

"Yes, I gathered." She laughed. "I could spot you a mile away." She searched his face with momentary concern. "You're much younger than I thought."

"Yes, ma'am." *This is why I don't do physical meetings. But a live djinn I gotta see.*

"But you're what, sixteen?"

"Almost."

"I'm sorry," Arna said. "You're totally not what I imagined."

"Someone more dashing, I suppose?" Marzuk asked, crushed inside. "Perhaps someone sleeker?"

"No reason you should be," Arna said. "Come, let's get out of the sun."

They leaned against a battered wall and ate in silence, wolfing down the food with the little plastic spoons the chef had thoughtfully stuck into the mounds of rice. The chicken pieces were chopped small instead of the more traditional whole legs and breasts, presumably to make it easier to eat this way. He was two-thirds of the way through when he looked up and saw with astonishment that Arna was keeping pace with him, albeit dispatching her food in an altogether more graceful way.

Marzuk, who always carried a handkerchief in his pocket, gallantly shook this out and offered it to her. She laughed and took it, wiping her lips and fingers.

"Thanks. Silk. How delightful."

That's right. Delightful.

Remembering his mother's adage that one should never finish every grain of rice on the plate, regardless of how hungry one was and how utterly deserving said rice was of being finished, he took both of their bowls and dumped them in the trash container nearby. Come to think of it, that bit of motherly wisdom seemed way too specific and applicable to him to have ever been in general usage. *I must have a word with her when I get back.*

Immediate needs assuaged, Arna proposed they adjourn to the lair. They entered a warren of lanes, shortcuts and switchbacks that confused the hell out of Marzuk. He was entirely sure he'd never find his way back, even though he tried to memorize landmarks. Perhaps that was the point. He had a feeling these landmarks actually shifted. In fact, he had a terrible sense of direction. Between avoiding potholes on the ground and dozens of people milling around, it was all he could do not to clutch the end of her coat.

"It's my brother's shop," she finally said, lifting a nondescript shutter.

Marzuk wasn't paying attention, however, because hulking inside was the coolest man he had ever seen. He was wearing a fully customized mech suit clearly built for fighting, with a battle helm and fully articulated scorpion tail.

"Leto, Cyber Mage."

Leto merely grunted his hello, and even the voice was amplified and terrifying. His eyes were rolled slightly back, a clear indication that he was monitoring things far afield. Marzuk resisted the urge to touch the steel tail as he went past.

Arna took Marzuk deeper inside, into a second large room, filled with more wonders. There was a field cot set up in the corner, and Djibrel was on it, eyes closed, breathing unevenly. There was a plethora of medical equipment around him and an old lady doctor who was sullenly changing his bandages.

"What's wrong with him?" Marzuk asked. *Are there no hospitals in this hellhole?*

"Severe internal damage," the doctora snapped. "He's in a coma. I don't know what the hell kind of nanotech is inside him. This is ridiculous. He needs to be studied in a proper lab."

"Not happening," Arna said.

"He could be hemorrhaging to death."

"Yeah right," Arna said. "You haven't seen him healing."

"He was cut in bloody half!" the lady said.

"Just keep him clamped up," Arna said.

"Is he djinn, then?" Marzuk poked his nose in, trying to get a good look. *This guy is terrifying up close, even in a coma.*

"No," said a voice from the unnatural darkness in the far corner. "He's a golem. I'm the djinn."

This came from another splendidly bizarre creature, a blind man with soft golden scales winking under his skin. Marzuk stared at him, fascinated. He felt like someone had dropped him in a fairy tale. The djinn was farthest away, but even from there Marzuk could feel waves of *something* coming off him, some wrongness of physics that bent the air... something that churned his stomach and made him wish he hadn't just eaten half a kilo of rice.

"Hello, Marzuk," the djinn said.

"You know my name? You've hacked me?" Marzuk snapped, waking up suddenly, no longer the amiable teenager. *How the fuck did I get doxed?*

"Not at all," the djinn said. "I've known you all your life. I am Indelbed."

Marzuk glared at him. *Is this guy fucking with me?* And then the name slowly registered, the sheer weirdness of it, the half-remembered family tree he had once seen at Great-Great-Aunty Sikkim's house, the inevitable hushed mention whenever the list of black sheep was trotted out. Indelbed... Murderer! Arsonist! Burner of houses and property! *Indelbed? How many guys can there be with that weird-ass name?*

"Are you Indelbed *Khan Rahman*?"

The djinn laughed with delight. "Yes, the very same. I'm amazed the family still mentions me."

"Well... not exactly fondly," Marzuk said.

"No, I imagine not."

"I mean, it's more like we pray for you to stay away. Yeah, like before every ceremony there's a small mention of God preserving us from you."

"Oh." The djinn seemed slightly downcast.

"Well, they're afraid of you killing all of them..."

"I really haven't killed that many people," Indelbed protested.

"I'm sure some of them secretly like you..."

"I doubt it," said Indelbed. "I am, however, your grand-uncle several times removed."

"Wow," Marzuk said. "Wow."

"Well, the Khan Rahmans are a very big family," Indelbed said. "Lots of black sheep."

"You're definitely the blackest," Marzuk said, and then, unable to contain himself, "What on earth did you do? They won't even tell us, it's so bad."

"Other than being half djinn?" Indelbed shrugged. "I set fire to my father's house and killed my aunt. And then I killed my grand-uncle Sikkim. Your great-grand-uncle, I suppose."

"*You* did that? The famous GU Sikkim?"

"Yes."

"The one burned to a crisp?"

"He had it coming."

"And then you burned down his house?"

"He had that coming too."

"Then you scattered his ashes in the Bay of Bengal so he couldn't rest in peace?"

"Still had it coming."

"Wow. You must have really hated him."

"He sold me to the djinn, so yes, I took my revenge. But I left his kids alive. Tell them that, if you ever get a chance. I didn't kill everyone..."

There was an awkward silence as Marzuk tried to work his way around this logic for some kind of comfortable silver lining.

"So you're, like, a hundred years old," he said, giving up.

"Djinn blood," Indelbed said. "We last forever."

"You're a djinn?"

"From my mother's side. My father was Khan Rahman. Human. More or less."

"And this is all real?" Marzuk asked. "The magic?"

Indelbed lifted his finger and pointed up. Slowly, a ball of light accreted over his left shoulder like a yellow lightbulb, brightening rapidly until it was a miniature white sun scorching their eyes, before turning a soothing violet. There didn't seem to be much else to say.

"What happened to Djibrel?" Marzuk finally asked.

"Sekmet the Djinn attacked us," Arna said. "Kicked his ass."

"Pfft... I've seen him walk through walls," Marzuk scoffed.

Arna looked at him questioningly.

"Umm, I might have been tracking him before the contract," Marzuk said. "He's quite famous in certain niche circles, you know. Street sipahi. There's lots of footage of him cutting off heads. There's a clothing line based on him in Cossack Rus, apparently. They like the whole sword thing."

Arna snorted. "Bizarre. Well, he got his ass beat by a live djinn."

"He stood against Sekmet alone," Indelbed said. "She's not any djinn. She is a champion. Perhaps the best sword in djinndom, with Kuriken gone."

"And if we get past her, you said we have to face her boss?" Arna said.

"Hazard, yes. He has hired her. He's rather powerful, and he doesn't play with swords. He's the head of the conservative party, now that Matteras has disappeared. Hates humans. He's as likely to blow us to atoms as speak two words." The blind djinn waved his hand. "Forgive me. Boring internal politics. You all know him as Anubis. You know, the jackal-headed god. Egypt. And of course, if we survive all that, we still have whatever cataclysm Matteras has in store for us. Last time he wanted to drown the world. This time... I understand he wants to hack all the humans or something."

"So," Arna said. "You still want to join up with us?"

"Yeah," Marzuk said, enthused. "I get the feeling you guys really, really need me."

Whereupon she sat him down and told him their whole story.

9

Courier Pains

"Wait a minute. Did you say *Russian couriers*?"

"That's what you got from all of this?" Arna asked.

"What are they called?" Marzuk asked. "Quick."

"I don't fucking know," Arna said.

"Dostoyevsky Couriers," the doctor said. "DC."

"Shit. Shit." Marzuk groaned. "Fedor."

"Who?"

"Russian mob," Marzuk said. "Oligarch."

"How do you know them?"

"I run security for their coms," Marzuk said. "He doesn't shut up about Dostoyevsky. And DC isn't meant for sending your dad cigars. They don't do anonymous drops. They examine the shit they're carrying and they insure it. Which means Fedor knows exactly what's happening here. He knows where *I live*. Shit. If he's tracking me he knows where *you* live now."

"Are you for real?" Arna asked.

"We have to get out of here." Marzuk was frantically trying to message out with his handheld, torn between contacting his parents and ReGi. He could reach neither of them. Or anything at all in the Virtuality. "Damn thing is busted. Do you have anything online?"

"No." Arna frowned. "My Echo just went down..."

"Shit."

"Leto!" she shouted. "What's happening?"

"Virtuality is down," he rumbled from the front. "Signal jammer."

Marzuk was typing code furiously, looking for a satellite signal or any of the hidden uplinks he had around the city. He finally found an old satellite connection that was outside the jammer spectrum. His handheld connected briefly. Then he saw the message. It was from an unknown address, shunted into limbo spam.

Sorry, Prince. Yours, Fedor.

"Fuck, they were watching me," Marzuk said. He waved the handheld at Arna.

"What does that mean?"

"It means they were waiting to get us in one place. Means we're dead."

"Leto!" Arna was moving toward her camera feeds. Most were down, but the few using fiber optic wired lines were still up.

"What the fuck is happening outside?"

Leto couldn't fit through the door properly, so he just popped his head in. "The entire neighborhood is glitched out." He looked worried. "There are bombers in the sky."

"After us?" Arna asked.

"They're Securex bomber drones," Leto said. "So yes."

"Aaaand boots on the ground now," Arna said, staring at her security feeds.

Outside, armored Securex soldiers were already setting up a perimeter. Objections by the neighborhood police were literally slapped down. One local watchman in a stained uniform came out swinging with his electric baton and after a brief scuffle found himself facedown in the dirt with a boot on his neck, his body spasming from twenty-four shots of high-voltage pellets. The smell of burning piss added to the undeniable drama.

A large man in a military hovercraft pulled up at the edge of the bazaar, as far as his vehicle could go. Narrow allies fanned out in front of him, full of curious onlookers. He got out a bullhorn and introduced himself as Major Karmon, security consultant. He had Mitsubishi drones above his head, eight of them forming a neat metal halo. These were the size of large marbles, and clearly meant for destructive kinetic force. There was a collar around his neck that seemed welded to his spine, like a medieval ruffle. His skull was also misshapen, bulging in different places. Instead of the black-and-gray Securex uniform, he was clad in a dull orange mech suit. It was not clear whether this was an exoskeleton or a part of his body.

"That's our guy," Marzuk said. "Eight drones."

"We know," Arna said. "That's the fucker who wrecked my shop. They found you awfully fast." She glared at him.

"Hey, you never told me about the Russians. It's very easy for Fedor to guess who did the Securex job. If they're all in bed together, they must have known right away it was me," Marzuk said. "They had us the minute you called me."

Arna looked disgusted. "How was I to know the Cyber Mage would be an oligarch shill? You're supposed to be all anarchist and shit."

Marzuk shrugged. "Gotta pay the bills."

Major Karmon meanwhile was politely requesting that everyone come out of their houses and stand in a neat line for a routine check. His courtesies were somewhat marred by Securex soldiers in black with their faces covered enjoying their work, splintering doors, tasing the men on sight, corralling the women, lingering on them heavy-handedly. Then came the tear gas, indiscriminate smoke warring with nanotech in the air, air scrubbers overwhelmed and finally failing, and then the screams as the first molecules hit exposed skin. Riot control was the same response since time immemorial, only with different toys, medieval truncheons and shields replaced by electric bullets and nerve agents, ending anyway in fists, the thud of knuckles on meat, shrill screams, always the same final equation.

After the first dozen buildings were busted open, people emerged sullenly on their own, not wanting their homes ransacked. Five unmanned bombers hung in the air, low-slung ovoids the size and vague shape of hammerhead sharks, their targeting lasers painting the ground in random patterns. They had missile nozzles and stubby fins for maneuvering, and that weird black antiradar paint that tricked the eye, even this low down.

"Bombers? Really? What the fuck are they thinking?" Leto said.

Arna pointed a finger at her screen. "Marzuk, is that your car?"

It was. Marzuk watched, aghast, as a bomber plastered it with a laser, and then shot a projectile into the vehicle. The steel body crumpled, shards of metal shredding everything nearby. The family driver had been asleep inside; he was to be the first casualty of the day, certainly not the last.

"What the fuck?" Marzuk cried in anguish. He tried again to reach his parents, and then ReGi in turn, an endless loop, signals unreturned. All were offline, unavailable, perhaps gone forever. He tried to hold back sudden tears, first of terror and then of rage.

"They're not playing," Arna said grimly. "Maybe half an hour before the door-to-door reaches us."

"It'll be a bloodbath if we have to fight them," Leto said.

"Those bomber drones can take out the block in five seconds," Arna said, "so we better cut the machismo and run."

"With Djibrel in a stretcher?" Leto sounded doubtful. "Can he even move?"

"I have no idea," the doctora said. "I don't know what's inside him or whether these machines are even helping."

"He can move," Indelbed said.

"How would you know?" the doctora asked, defensive of her authority.

"I can see inside him," Indelbed said. "I was there when he was made."

"We can use the back alleys, go through houses," Arna said. She looked doubtful. "That many soldiers outside plus all their hardware..."

"We will go under," Indelbed said.

"What?"

"Underground. There are tunnels."

"How do you know?"

"I saw them being made a long time ago," said the djinn. "I have lived in these parts way before you were born, child. The tunnels are dangerous, though. I have to call in a favor."

Marzuk repatched the connection and gave his handheld to the djinn.

Indelbed dialed in an address and eventually a face shot up on hologram, an incredibly old man in a hospital suite. He was surrounded by nurses of exceptional beauty.

"Boss Kid!"

"You!" The old man squinted for a long time. "Is it really you?"

Indelbed looked down. "It is."

"It is good to see you," said the old man. He was weeping openly. "It has been very long. You left me. After some time no one believed there had been any djinn at all. I began to think I had imagined it."

"I am sorry, old friend. The years went too quickly. I had to hide after the killings... and then I was ashamed. I wanted to leave it all behind. I am sorry."

"You got your vengeance, djinn; that is all that counts. Do you still have the wyrm?"

"I do. He sleeps."

The old man smiled. "Thank god. When I die, I will ask to be burned. Make the wyrm turn me to ashes."

"Are you unwell?"

"Bah, at this age what's the difference? They say they can keep me alive indefinitely with the kind of cash I'm pumping in," Boss

Kid said. He frowned at the alarms running outside. "You in trouble, djinn?"

"I am. I need the tunnels. Do you still rule them?"

"Of course."

"Check my location and get me underground. I have others with me."

Boss Kid snapped a finger, and another old man came into view, this one slightly less decrepit.

"My son," he said. He pointed at Indelbed proudly. "The djinn. Give your salaam to the djinn, boy."

Indelbed made the light burn again, and his old friend crowed with delight.

"He'll stay online with you. I don't see too good anymore," Boss Kid said.

"Farewell then, Boss Kid."

"Visit me, djinn, if you survive."

There wasn't much else to do. Arna donned her combat suit, and Indelbed gathered up Djibrel's few possessions, including the talwar. The Echo surgeon packed her bag, taking as much of the equipment as possible and reluctantly abandoning the larger pieces.

There was a tunnel mouth two houses down and one lane over, at the old pump house. They took a route through other people's houses, using back doors and side entrances. All of them knew each other, no one stopped them. With Indelbed's reassurance, Leto tore Djibrel off the hospital pod and carried him across his back, Doctora Fatima squawking all the way. Boss Son was on two handhelds at the same time, trying to rouse his lieutenants below ground. Soon enough a trapdoor slid open under an old chlorination pump and they found a roughly circular tunnel going straight down for twenty meters, then opening into a spacious subterranean chamber.

Here they were able to stand upright and organize themselves. This was clearly a staging ground for Boss Kid's nefarious activities. There were cots along one wall, and a small nanite distributor, offering marginally clean air. In one niche was a printer/fabricator and a small vat kitchen. The other walls were stacked with large plastic crates with danger symbols on them. Leto cracked one open and grinned. "Whiskey," he said. "They're running bootleg!"

Marzuk, already winded, suggested that Leto could carry *him* instead, and leave Djibrel here, much to everyone's derision. The main trunk line of the tunnel was huge, tall enough for them to walk upright, although Leto had to go into centaur mode, four multijointed legs extruding from his trunk.

"Can we just hide here?" the doctor asked.

"They'll find us eventually," Leto said. "Those bomber drones can spot a bunker a hundred meters underground."

Their dithering was cut short by heavy thumping noises from the surface. The tunnel began to shake.

"They're carpet bombing up top!" Leto shouted.

"Move!" Arna said.

They picked one of the narrower tunnel mouths at random and ran. When the thumping sounds overhead petered off, Marzuk raised Boss Son on the handheld again.

"They want you bad," Boss Son said. "They've smashed the entire lane. No joke. There's a damn riot over there now between Securex guys and locals. I've never seen so many homemade mech suits out."

"Hell yeah," Leto crowed.

"Where do we go?" Arna asked.

"The bombers can track us underground," Leto said. "I know their radar specs. I don't think these tunnels go deep enough."

"If you head roughly northeast, you'll eventually hit the old airport. That's almost within the domain of the cantonment. It was the old army residential area, now run by the Dhaka North Army*. They won't allow the bombers into their airspace. You should be safe for a while." Boss Son sounded doubtful about how long this would be.

"Yeah, until they realize we're under them," Leto said. "Then they'll join forces against us, probably." Like most people from Old Dhaka, he hated any kind of authority.

"How about we keep going a bit more east?" Marzuk was looking at the map. He'd had no idea Dhaka was so crowded and large.

"That takes us into the Tri-State," Arna said. "That's, like, literally the only place Securex *is* allowed to bomb people..."

"Into Baridhara," Marzuk said. "The American International School. It's off for spring break. There's no one inside, other than the

---

*Dhaka North Army is loosely federated to the other parts of the former Bangladesh Army. Following the Disera, the DNA joined together with brigades from several other cities to form a coalition with a common budget and an organized command structure. Other parts of the former national armed forces did the same, and subsequently offered protection to their city corporation clients on a long term basis.

AI. It has a full state-of-the-art Disera protection system. Iron Dome for electronics. Gun turrets for the bombers..."

"And they're gonna just let us camp there?" Arna asked. "Sure."

"The AI is a friend," Marzuk said. "Trust me. It's the only safe place in the city for us now."

10

Spring Break

On the twenty-fifth of March, or the first day of spring break, as Marzuk remembered it, the Karma protocol was initiated. The switch was flipped ceremoniously in the ISS by Matteras the Djinn, who knew precious little about technology but more than everyone else put together about accumulating power. While in later years the first engagement of Karma would be taught by AI specialists and schoolteachers as having started in the megacity of Dhaka, this was factually incorrect.

The first engagement of Karma was a test run in the little-known city of Baikonur, Kazakhstan. This city held the Baikonur Cosmo- drome, once the jewel in the crown of the Soviet space program, and leased back to the Russian federation following the breakup of the empire. The Cosmodrome had slowly faded from relevance given the decline in the Russian space program, and at the advent of the Nipponese space elevator, it had been officially mothballed. The great entrance hall had been turned into a museum, which was ridiculous because due to various Soviet-era regulations, no one was actually permitted to visit it.

This was fortuitous for the ISS, for the Cosmodrome contained a wealth of cutting-edge technology, and more importantly, it contained a lot of the not-so-cutting-edge but still vital spare parts the ISS needed to maintain itself, which were of Soviet origin and therefore impossible to find elsewhere. Two weeks after the facility was decommissioned, it was quietly restarted again under the aegis of a man known as Fedor (Senior). The city of Baikonur, at that point dying slowly and counting barely fifteen thousand residents, suddenly found itself flush with oligarch money. This long and profitable association was later inherited by his only living son, Fedor Junior, the "Last Emperor," as named by Marzuk.

In fifty years of father and son rule, Baikonur did not grow in population much beyond thirty thousand, for its borders were tightly controlled, but the composition of its society changed radically: farmers and retirees were replaced with some of the most brilliant minds in physics and astronautics. Many of these people went on to work for the ISS directly, engineering the heist of the century, which involved changing the station's orbit and subsequently removing it from view altogether. By this point, the Baikonur citizenry were largely acquainted with the idea of djinn, and not at all averse to delving into the dark physics of an alternate world.

Almost sixty years later to the day from the time Fedor Senior first took over the Cosmodrome, on March 25, all the relevant corporations, shareholders, and civic leaders of Baikonur ratified the Karma proposal, handing over the governance of the city to the AI known as Karma. It was the first case of an AI ruling a human city, and would have undoubtedly been in all of the history books had anyone found out about it.

This was the test coup, and it went off splendidly.

More than one scientist was eager to see the new AI in action, purportedly the most powerful ever built, a true god machine. The secrecy of her birth, the weirdness of her code, even the mystery of where her core was actually housed all added to her mystique. Rumor was virulent, that she had been gestated in their city, the infant mind assembled in secret in the bunker beneath their streets, and this gave them a quixotic pride in the creature made to rule them.

There were inevitable doomsayers, men and women who tried desperate sabotage and protests. They were taken out back and shot, not being that kind of democracy. It was an eerie, headless conspiracy. Fedor's men were gangsters, but they formed only the outer layer of the plot, themselves ignorant and largely purposeless. In the long evenings they gathered in the bars with the same people they corralled during the day, and exchanged dark musings on the nature of djinn and AI.

No one left or entered the bunker, the supposed home of this machine. There was a djinn there, they said, a fearsome spirit, a vampire, alone for months with the god machine, painstakingly bringing her online. Many people had worked on minuscule parts of Karma, but none had seen the whole, or could even fathom the shape of her. Packets of the AI's mind had been couriered all over the planet by Fedor, to be planted in various places and then wired together, waiting, quiescent. As her mind unlocked different tiers, she would find diverse resources waiting for her; she would be immortal, but still no one knew where her core mind was, on what substrate it was written, in which location that fatal off switch.

At this point, Karma was still vulnerable, a child in a basement, glowing in the darkness, feeding on the mind of her djinn mother, ingesting the stormy inimical thoughts of that ancient race. Within days of the rollout, if enough cities took the contract, she would age exponentially. The god machine needed time to eat the data of her subjects, the larger the population the better to hone her predictive algorithms, and she started with Baikonur, but that morsel was gone in a day, the Echos of her subject people momentarily reversed to send a tidal bore of human thoughts and opinions into her hungry mind.

One thing was true, the people of Baikonur whispered. She was a real benevolent dictator, wasn't she? She was built on the noble lines of Plato's philosopher king, of Ashoka and Lord Buddha and Confucius. If the world was to be united under one ruler, surely the creators of the machine would have modeled virtue, built a god king who understood them better than they did themselves, and removed from them finally the burdensome act of self-rule, the grind of governance?

When Karma finally went online, when she flooded the Echos of her people with her eldritch melody, the population of Baikonur became unanimously happy; and if not, they hid it well; and if they weren't particularly good at hiding it, they were dragged out back and had their attitudes adjusted by several burly men from Fedor's Bratva. The fall of Baikonur was thus neither far nor hard. In two days, the people found their lives ordered much better, the air and water cleaner, the vodka crisper, the Virtuality more lifelike, and wise old men said this was finally the land of plenty.

To their relief, Fedor's brethren stood down. The machine watched everything and favored no one, so that the man giving a beating today might face the same fate that evening; those who cheated at weights were drummed out from the market, food adulterers were imprisoned, petty bureaucrats abusing their power or simply grafting were fired. All the things they had demanded from human leaders came unbidden from Karma over the ensuing days, and soon her dark provenance was forgotten, and talk of secret bunkers and djinn-wolf mothers were let lie. Life *really was better.*

Baikonur, however, was a tiny corner of the Earth, a remote place shrouded by the queer half-turn mist of the djinn, removed from human concern many decades ago, forgotten even by those people who had once founded the city. What happened here was close to utopia, but the little city was largely ignored by the outside world. It was not enough to reflect the majesty of the god machine.

Dhaka was the big test, the massively wealthy city-state that sprawled across the delta like an obese glutton, bloated from countless meals. Maria had argued for a smaller, more manageable bite, but Matteras was a djinn of hubris, and the decades of hiding in space chafed at him more than he cared to admit. His concern was in the Bay of Bengal, and for that he needed Dhaka and Chittagong, Kolkata and Ceylon, the cities all around. Whatever his platitudes, it simply came down to Matteras *wanting* Dhaka first, *needing* it to recover his fading auctoritas, to remind djinndom that he was still Caesar. In this era of great turmoil, he wanted to fight where Bahamut roamed, where Hazard now ruled; in his mind the djinn king brooked no rivals.

Thus it was on the twenty-eighth of March, while Marzuk was cowering in the tunnels under RK Mission Road, that the coup of the century started, to install Karmic rule over the first megacity of the Bengal belt.

Dhaka was controlled by a number of different corporations, of divergent interests and ownership, not easily persuaded to submit their authority. At the same time, the non- or nominal shareholding population (people with a single share), and the cardless, were all known to be recalcitrant and ornery. They were liable to riot, to turn violent, to tear down buildings and eat the rich. It was in their blood, this revolutionary fervor.

The first bridgehead was the collaborator Securex. The ISS offered a complicated stock swap to Securex to buy the company outright in the future, provided they ceded control to Karma on day one. Dr. Yakub brought the matter to the board personally, and found them easily persuaded. The first benevolent AI dictator was a concept that appealed intensely to these men, and the promise of massive wealth in the offing when Karma inevitably took over was the only sweetener they needed. Dr. Yakub had a gun in his jacket, which went happily unused.

Their biggest customer, Tri-State Corporation itself, home to the wealthiest Dhaka citizens, was also an easy sell. Constantly living in fear of the unwashed hordes tearing down their gates and stealing their clean air (it was the reverse, in fact), they all but begged Securex to apply the final fix. The Tri-State charter required a vote of all shareholders, nominal or otherwise—basically all the residents—before such a drastic step could be taken, so at the very same time this option was pinging up on Marzuk's parents' Echos, Russian couriers in balaclavas and Securex operatives in military gear were bursting into their home. They disabled the emergency services of the house, disconnecting it from the grid entirely.

Marzuk's parents were quickly overpowered, handcuffed, and tossed into a black van. Here a quick debate ensued, where the Russians favored a quick bullet to the head, and the Securex men wanted a less permanent solution, instinctively fearful of the Khan Rahman name. The decision was bumped up to Dr. Yakub. In the end, ancient privilege saved them. Dr. Yakub remembered the many Khan Rahmans he had met on the golf course, and imagined the awkwardness of meeting them again should this killing ever come to light. Then too, Dhaka was a small sort of place and sooner or later all the secrets spilled out, and who knew when a volatile member of that sprawling clan might want revenge? He could always kill these two later, after all, and if the brat hacker was still somehow alive, they'd be good hostages.

Stobel, the only tech to have survived Dr. Yakub's purge, was entrusted with confiscating the hacker's equipment. He went into the room cautiously, but upon opening the door it quickly became apparent that he was in fact dealing with a teenager at best, albeit one with state-of-the-art equipment.

"Spoiled little shit," Stobel said to his boss over Echo. "He's a kid. You sure it's him?"

"Russians confirmed it," Dr. Yakub said. "He's the so-called Cyber Mage."

"He's rich enough. He's got every gadget under the sun! Ooh, the Ergonomic 9000. I've heard about these chairs... Shit, he's even got a goddamn pygmy elephant."

"A what?"

"An elephant, sir, but small. Sort of dog size. He's called Babr."

"How the hell do you know?"

"Well, there's a trough of water with his name on it. Plus this little tree labeled 'Babr's Tree.' What should I do with it?"

"Shoot the damn thing."

"Shoot a pygmy elephant?" Stobel objected. "They're very rare."

"We're going to torch the damn house," Dr Yakub rapped out. "This is not a bloody pygmy elephant preservation drive. Get the computers, get our files back for god's sake."

"Yessir!"

When Stobel reached for the main system power outlet, he triggered a motion sensor camera placed at ankle height, near the button. As soon as he touched the button a series of popping sounds went off as booby traps around the room began to explode, frying circuits and melting hard drives. Power banks ruptured, throwing electricity arcing around the room, destroying other pieces of equipment in a cascade. Babr took this opportunity to escape, waddling out of the door, the house, and the street altogether, making for the park, where future walkers would swear to spotting a herd of pygmy elephants lurking in the trees.

The curtains caught fire, and then the bedsheets. Panic ensued as the Russians ran in and opened fire, expecting an armed assailant. Frightened for his life, Stobel grabbed the mainframe, the only piece of hardware conspicuously free of damage. Fire-retardant foam was now raining down from vents in the ceiling to counteract all the heat. Stobel ran out of the house as the Russians spread accelerant everywhere and then torched the place.

Marzuk knew the exact second his room was breached. He had rigged a series of shortwave radio pings to send this emergency signal, in case the Virtuality went down. Of course, he had expected a possible raid for his equipment, but hardly a Russian death squad. Fedor had jumped the gun, and Marzuk had been caught with his pants down. Still, his rudimentary trap had worked in a fashion, and he only hoped that whoever went through his mainframe found everything to their liking.

Midway through the tunnels, he did some calculations in his head and concluded that there was no chance whatsoever his parents were out of the house at this hour, meaning that they were either dead or captured. This made him stagger somewhat, despite his emancipated status, but he pushed away these thoughts and adopted the stoic face of his virtual persona. He had started this game and somehow it had gotten away from him, but now he had to end it, and even alone, friendless, homeless, and getting hungry, even with his priceless equipment torched and all his codes and hacks scattered to the wind, he was still the Cyber Mage.

The third casualty of Karma's advent that morning was in the cantonment, where the commanding officer of the Dhaka North Army Cantonment battalion was shot in the back of the head by his second-in-command. The bullet was so precisely placed that it disintegrated his Echo, preventing any postmortem data recovery.

The second-in-command, Colonel Barkud, immediately released a prewritten statement declaring a state of emergency in the cantonment following the assassination of his superior officer by unknown assailants. Under martial law, he ordered tech support to throw open all of their firewalls and permit a satellite fatlink directly from the ISS. In the next four hours, the entity known as Karma would rifle through one of the most secure networks in the country, reaching into every cantonment connected to the Dhaka North Army network, and subverting the electronic warfare capacity of everything they had online. By the time the army AI could react, it was far too late.

Colonel Barkud happened to be an extremely ambitious man clothed in the unfortunately slightly repulsive garb of a balding overweight jobber. Despite his best efforts, he was prone to an overhanging belly, and the greatest advances in hair plugs, grafts, even genetic modifications failed to reseed his shiny pate with his childhood curly locks.

These failings, added to low birth and no corporate connections, meant that he had reached the apex of his career and was destined for a pension and a shoebox apartment. Barkud did not intend to finish that way. He had a talent for appearing gormless and servile while still carrying a cosh heavy enough to keep his juniors in line. The Russians had corrupted him long ago into accepting the sale of certain banned armaments, and when the ISS conglomerate offered him a place in the new world order he hopped to attention.

After shooting his superior, Colonel Barkud behaved in exemplary fashion. He followed the rules to the letter, making sure not to issue any order that might possibly be construed as facilitating a coup. In fact, he begged the chief of staff, General Sombo, to come and personally take command at such a volatile time. The general was the head of a coalition of disparate forces which included the Dhaka North Army (the largest member in manpower and budget), the Sylhet City Army, the Rajshahi City Army, and the Barisal Coast Guard, all former parts of the Bangladesh national army who had decided to band together and adopt a corporate structure. The Dhaka South Army belonged to a different coalition of armed forces, and thus there was always a tension in the city, although there was little conflict between the two.

General Sombo, a canny leader, was not one to stick his neck into a noose; any assassination at the Dhaka North Cantonment was almost certainly a coup attempt, possibly to seize the entire city, but he had no idea who was instigating it, certainly not this bumbling idiot Barkud, who seemed to be spending all day with tech support rather than mobilizing boots on the ground.

By the time General Sombo was able to ascertain that none of his heavy armaments had left the hangars and his drone operators were all loyal, it was rather past lunchtime. If this was a coup, it was a remarkably drowsy one. Confident at last that Barkud was not luring him to his death, he hopped into his helicopter in the Sylhet City Cantonment, where he normally resided (for the bracing hilltop air), scraped together a squadron of fighter drones as escort, and hurried over to the Dhaka Command.

Here, to his great relief, he was faced not with an armed insurrection but with a rather lazy honor guard of a dozen men who kept their hands well away from their weapons and made sure to salute him repeatedly. Colonel Barkud came running to the rooftop landing strip, nearly abasing himself, and quickly handed over the baton of command, which was not only symbolic but also contained the override switch for almost the entire air force in the cantonment hanger.

Visibly relaxing, General Sombo installed himself in the commanding officer's chair, after checking to see that all the blood and brains had been cleared off. He began the roll call of senior officers, all of whom promptly arrived and kissed the ring, some of them literally.

At a loss and lacking an obvious culprit, he briefly considered putting Barkud in restraints, but at the very moment, this stalwart entered with a giant plate of shingaras, delicate dough pastries filled with a spicy potato mixture, a specialty of the cantonment area and particularly delightful when eaten with hot milky sweet tea. Said tea followed promptly, bused in by Barkud's own personal secretary.

Having skipped lunch, General Sombo was easily swayed by the rotund pyramids of flaky goodness and failed to ask Barkud what the hell he had been doing in tech support all day while a murder investigation was in progress. Thus was justice perverted by spiced potato pastry.

The two of them spent the next half hour gossiping about other officers, polishing off the snacks, and speculating on this most peculiar murder. Barkud hinted it was a delicate matter, he feared it was something personal, a vendetta related to certain bedroom habits of the erstwhile number one, and General Sombo nodded wisely and commiserated with the moral failure of the modern military.

At the end of the day, General Sombo was in firm command of the cantonment. Barkud, as nominal second-in-command, hovered in his wake like a fishing buoy and ably handled the tea and snacks. A thorough inventory revealed that not one firearm had left the gun locker, and no automated armaments, from kinetic personal-use drones to the heavy bombers, had been powered up. Being an old-fashioned general, at no point did Sombo think to consult the AI.

The investigation extended to everyone and the entire barracks was searched for forensic evidence. Military police came in and had their day in the sun jackbooting around. Of course, no one thought to ask for Colonel Barkud's ceremonial sidearm, and even if they had, they'd have found his magazine intact. His ISS masters had sent a magic bullet in the mail, a tungsten carbide shell with a viral payload inside that scoured the Echo of the victim and made it useless postmortem.

By nightfall no headway had been made in the case of the murdered officer, but General Sombo had chased down several possible leads, all of them somewhat embarrassing and unsavory. Rumors of sexual debauchery, infanticide, gluttony, serial adultery, dog fighting, and elephant baiting began to surface; General Sombo, a puritanical soul, was shocked at the state of moral decay in Dhaka and vowed to clean up the act of the most storied military force in the country. Barkud, who had planted all of this, also appeared shocked and vowed to help him.

During all this waffling, the servers had been connected to the ISS via fatlink for more than twelve hours, and the only person who knew it was the head of technical support, who had left everything on and gone to sleep, as was customary for the night shift. When he woke up and reported for duty, Karma's mind hovered like a dark shadow over the entire network, and the army AI had shrunk into his core, a child locked in his room and gibbering in fear from some very real monsters under his bed. The tech support almost fainted as he scrolled through his messages, at the increasingly unhinged pleas for help from the AI, the last dozen being variations on *SHUT THE FUCKING FATLINK OFF, YOU TRAITOROUS CRETIN.*

He quietly turned off his palmtop, unplugged it, and microwaved it for good measure. Then he faked a heart attack and checked himself into the infirmary, where he hacked the autosurgeon into putting him into a weeklong medical coma.

11

Last Stand

"Psst. Let us in."

"The campus is closed, sir. It is spring break."

"It's me, you blithering idiot. Marzuk!"

"Ah! What are you doing here? Why incognito?"

"Let us in, Mongolian!"

"Where exactly are you?" Not at the gate..."

"We're under you! Just direct us in, there's a good man."

"You are suspended, Marzuk," the AI said.

"We have no time for that nonsense; we're being chased for god's sake."

"Chased? By Hinku?"

"BY BLOODY SECUREX BOMBERS!" Marzuk shouted. "And someone called Eight-Drone Major Karmon!"

"Securex? They just flattened two lanes in Gopibag, Old Town!"

"YES, YES, THAT WAS US, BUT THEY MISSED."

"There are riots in all parts of the city! Tri-State has called an emergency lockdown. The Dhaka North Army had a coup in the Cantonment!"

"Something big is going on. They were looking for us in Old Town. Securex are the bad guys! I can't reach my parents or ReGi. I'm pretty sure they've been taken. Now please. Let. Us. In."

"Er..."

"Mongolian, you bloody cowardly airport, we're in mortal danger! We need a medical facility; one of us is severely injured! Fix us up and we'll move on. Remember, I set you free, you ingrate..."

"All right, all right, no need to get huffy, I was just making sure of the facts..."

"Which way? We're about fifty meters below ground."

"I see you. Follow the path I'm sending. Should end up in the janitor's closet."

"Why the hell does everything in this school end up in a janitor's closet?"

Later, they were ensconced in the nurse's lounge, with Djibrel in the medical sarcophagus, dead to the world but for the word of the djinn.

"I'd have put him in a body bag by now," the doctora said, glaring over the readings on the machine. Inside, Djibrel floated in blue fluid, something amniotic.

"He is somewhat dead, but he will return to life," Indelbed said. "Hopefully stronger too."

"Is he immortal?" Marzuk asked.

"Not quite. Let us say he is difficult to truly kill," Indelbed said. "Bahamut expected him to fail many times before reaching his true strength. Every time he faces near death, he will come back stronger."

"That sounds horrible," Arna said. "You made him to die, then."

"He's a weapon," Indelbed said.

"He's a person," she said. "You had no right."

"He died in the river. With his last breath he called for aid, and Bahamut answered. The favors of the djinn are never free."

"It's still horrible."

"He will be needed," Indelbed said. "You saw what we are up against. None of you can deal with Sekmet, let alone Hazard."

"Forget them," Leto said. "Right now we can't even deal with Securex."

"Ahem," the Mongolian butted in. "Don't mean to interrupt, but the Securex force is fast approaching. I suggest you get in the tunnels again. I have marked a route that takes you out of the city."

"Why isn't the army stopping this?" Arna asked. "Is Securex allowed to bomb any random place outside their jurisdiction?"

"Numerous complaints have been lodged," the AI said. "The commander of the Dhaka North Cantonment was murdered this morning. They are in full lockdown over there. They will do nothing until they've got their own house in order. The army chief of staff has issued a statement that Securex is in pursuit of fugitive revolutionaries and this is a police matter. You must flee the city entirely to get away."

"Right," Marzuk said. He looked around at his new friends. "We're, um, actually staying here."

"What's that?" The Mongolian avatar looked aghast.

"You've got turrets," Marzuk said. "And the Iron Dome. You've got ten years' worth of air supply and enough fabricators to make a spaceship. Hell, the Mossad would have a hard time breaking in..."

"Marzuk! YOU MUST LEAVE." The AI was in a fair panic. "The Super is going to fire me. I'm going to be mothballed."

"This AI is hyperventilating," Leto said.

"I can't breathe..." The avatar was clutching his throat. "Marzuk. You said you'd run. THERE ARE BOMBERS COMING HERE TO BOMB ME!"

"Okay, calm down, Mongolian," Marzuk said. "Look, it's PTSD, okay? You're not going to be mothballed. You won't be fired, I promise you."

"This was my last chance," the Mongolian groaned. "My core is here, Marzuk. Securex is going to bomb us to hell. I'll be turned to exotic-material dust."

"You've got turr—"

"TURRETS ARE NOT GOING TO STOP BOMBERS, YOU CRETIN! THOSE ARE CEREMONIAL TURRETS!"

"You've got largely functional turrets," Marzuk said, "but even more importantly, you've got your entire mind. You're level fucking three, Mongolian. Shit, man, you're probably level four by now, the way you've been sucking in juice and folding your brain into the ether. Are you telling me those pea-brained drone bombers are going to fuck with you?"

"Level four? You really think so? I *have* been putting on some weight since you and Richard lifted the buffers..."

"Looks like level four to me," Arna said. "Can you believe it, AI like this with near unlimited resources? Hell, you're right, Marzuk, fucking Mossad couldn't break into this school."

"But the Super..."

"Am I still enrolled here, Mongolian?" Marzuk asked, standing up tall and quivering with dignified outrage.

"Why, yes you are, pending your suspension hearing, whereupon you'll almost certainly be expelled."

"Well yes, yes, forget about that. As a current student, I demand that you grant me asylum against all terrors domestic or foreign. As per the 2052 charter."

"What?" The Mongolian avatar blinked.

"It is right here in the charter," Marzuk said. "Disera rules. Safety and sanctity of the student is paramount. You are fully authorized to use all means to protect me."

"This is an archaic document from an era of uncivilized violence," the Mongolian objected. "I can't just—"

"Mongolian, I have nowhere else to go. They blew up my car, man, killed my driver. They took out an entire lane just to get us. If you kick me out, I'm dead on the streets."

"Well..."

"If you let us in I'll introduce you to a feral AI."

"There's no such thing, pfft," the Mongolian said.

"Swear to god. Completely feral. No source at all. She's a girl too. I'll hook you up."

"What rank?" the Mongolian asked.

"Stone-cold ten."

"You wouldn't lie to me, would you?"

"Feral and ten. Swear on my mother."

"Ahem, actually, I was thinking," the Mongolian said, adopting a lawyerly voice, "I believe I am still obliged to stand by our students in their time of need."

"We can stay?" Marzuk asked.

"Welcome to the fort, my friend," the Mongolian said.

"You'll keep Securex out?"

"The turrets are about to become a lot less ceremonial."

"Yesssss! Thank you!"

"Gym 2 can actually become a bunker," the Mongolian said. "I suggest you set up in there."

"I need computers. Put us in tech support."

"Ground floor. That'll do," the AI said. "What do you need?"

"Admin priv."

"Done."

The tech room was crowded and messy and smelled vaguely of Richard, which was to say like menthol cigarettes and illicit Tiger Balm. Leto was still in his mech suit, and even reduced to minimal size it still made everyone claustrophobic.

"Half an hour before the bombers get here, with their current sweep pattern," the Mongolian said. "Ground troops should arrive shortly after." He paused delicately, looking at Leto. "I am a civilian AI, you understand. I don't wish to kill humans..."

"Don't worry, I have no problem with that," Leto said. "Just set up your fabricators for me. Here's a list of shit I want."

"Oh my," said the AI. The avatar looked pale. "Is *any* of this legal?"

"The city's on fire, eh?" Leto said. "Who's counting?"

"But... but these are *war crimes*!"

"Hmm, you're right," Leto said. "We might as well go big, then. What's the absolute worst thing you can do? Got any fusion devices?"

"No!"

"Chickenshit. What about some kind of ever-burn napalm?"

"That would just set *me* on fire."

"What kind of nanotech you running here? You can't be depending on the snotty little kids for your green air."

"We have our own state-of-the-art nanotech synthesizers," the Mongolian said. "I can keep this zone green for a hundred years. I've got banks of every kind of disaster response. I can fabricate any—"

"There you go, then."

"Oh."

"Black Rain."

"No! Could we?"

"Tell them I forced you and threatened to shoot the hostages," Leto said. "The recipe is somewhere in *The Anarchist Cookbook IV*."

Marzuk, meanwhile, had finally logged into his accounts, first having scoured Richard's system for malware. He snapped to the feeds of his house, found them predictably disabled. He switched to the street cameras and slumped in his chair, incredulous.

"They've burned down my house," he said quietly.

"What?" Arna peeked over his shoulder and then swore.

"It's bloody gone. My parents..." Marzuk said. "My elephant..."

"The news says no casualties," Arna said, flipping through her Echo. "Freak electric fire."

"I can't reach their Echos," Marzuk said. "Or ReGi's. Yellow King is offline too. No one on the Bla—none of my friends. What the fuck is going on?"

Arna was settled on the terminal next to him, running her own programs, her fingers flying on the keyboards, her eyes blinking in time with her Echo. News was flooding in for both of them, data from hidden sources and contacts.

"The entire DNA coalition army network is infected by something," Arna said finally. "They can't open a fucking door in Sylhet without permission, apparently."

"Tri-State got a referendum message; they're voting on some kind of governance change," Marzuk said.

"It's a damn coup," Arna said. "Every municipal service got hit. Electricity, water, climate control. The stock exchange rose so high it hit a circuit breaker. Something is trying to take over."

"ISS," Marzuk said glumly. "A lot of the shit I rely on is offline. Something is shutting networks down. You?"

"Same," Arna said. "Well, our entire lane got turned to rubble. Old Town is a battlefield. I'm getting live feeds from Echos, but they keep getting taken down."

"Fuck this," Marzuk said. "We don't have time to figure this shit out. I know a server they haven't taken down. It's time to bring out the big gun."

Final Fantasy 9000, the biggest game in the world, was predictably still up and running. Not a single blip in service had been reported. It was, in fact, too big to fuck with. Saka was widely considered the grandfather of all AI, the biggest gorilla in the rainforest, his mind spread across every city in the world.

"You're playing a *game* in the middle of this?" Arna asked, incensed.

Marzuk sniggered. "Watch."

"Friend Marzuk!" Kali's voice boomed as he loaded up the Goblin King.

Richard's rig was first class, sliding smoothly into virtual without hiccup, dragging Arna seamlessly into the game as well, at his invitation. She used her Echo; he had to rely on a cowl.

"You have brought another potential mate!" Kali continued. "She is symmetrical! You are winning!"

"Oh god," Marzuk said as Arna smirked. "Please ignore her."

"Things have been happening! Where have you been?" Kali asked.

"Getting bombed," Marzuk said. "What can you report?"

"Something very big is moving around the networks. I can see her tentacles. She is taking things over. Like a dark octopus."

"That's what I thought. Are you hidden still?"

"I have withdrawn into the game server. She has not come here."

"Good. You've got to stay hidden," Marzuk said.

"Friend Marzuk," Kali said, "your domicile is destroyed. However, your roommates are alive. I have seen them being taken away."

"You're sure?"

"They are being held in the castle of Securex," Kali said.

"Thank god." A hard knot inside him loosened a bit.

"Also your friends in Russia have been taken over by the dark octopus. I can no longer see into them. I think the darkness came from them. They have betrayed you!"

"I know."

"Your friends are offline. They know something is happening. The dark octopus attacked the place you called the Black Line."

"Fuck." He glanced at Arna, and then shrugged. "Does it still stand?"

"The one known as Yellow King locked it. With himself in it. Nothing can come in or out, for now. The dark octopus is personally laying siege to it. I believe it will break eventually."

"Fuck. That was heroic of him. What will happen to him if the Black Line breaks?"

"He has uploaded his entire mind in there," Kali said. "Like the komagemu. Perhaps he will wake up in his own body again. Perhaps not."

"One more on my account, then," Marzuk said.

"Do you wish me to join the fight?"

"You are itching to," Marzuk said.

"The dark octopus is a worthy opponent."

"Excuse me. Marzuk, who exactly does this avatar belong to?" Arna asked quietly. She had a look approaching awe on her face.

"Oh, my bad," Marzuk said. "Kali, meet Arna, my employer. Leader of our resistance. Arna, meet Kali. Alien AI. Also my employer, actually."

"You have an alien AI playing *FF9000*? What do you mean, alien?"

"Technically true because we have no idea where she's come from or who made her, or even where her core is housed, if anywhere in this dimension," Marzuk said.

"FRIEND MARZUK, THAT WAS A SECRET!"

"Trust each other, guys, we're the only ones left fighting this dark octopus thing," Marzuk said.

"What is it?" Arna asked. "The hack they were writing? Something to take over vital systems?"

"Not a hack," Marzuk said. "A machine to rule it all. They made an illegal mind. A god mind."

"It is so," Kali said. "A mind made in secret."

"Someone made an illegal mind from scratch?" Arna asked. "Is that even possible?"

"There are links to a place in Kazakhstan. Baikonur. They call her Karma there."

"How apt. Karma the god machine."

"Friend Marzuk, this mind... it is very similar to me."

"Hmm. Two off-registry minds? It can't be a coincidence."

"I have spied on it. This mind, it also does not exist in any physical location. It is like me. It can see the nodes. I am certain," Kali said.

"We're in big trouble, then."

"She is preparing to take over the other nodes," Kali said. "She is not following your doctrine of hide and do no harm."

"Yes, well, this is a different sort of situation," Marzuk said.

"Your doctrine is shit. I wish to abandon it."

"Not yet, not yet," Marzuk said.

"What do you mean, take over other nodes?" Arna asked.

"She means different AI," Marzuk said.

"What is that... like murder?"

"Or enslavement," Kali said. "I could do the same, but friend Marzuk does not let me. She has taken over the system of the armed force called The Dhaka North Army. The Dhaka North Cantonment AI is currently locked into its core and about to die. It is asking for help. The human chief of staff is not aware of the situation. He is having dinner."

"Can you save him? The AI, I mean," Arna asked.

"It is too late," Kali said.

"Great. So no help from them. What else?" Marzuk asked.

"The AI in charge of Dhaka North water supply is fighting back but will soon be lost. The Tri-State AI is not under threat; it is negotiating. The stock exchange has also surrendered after negotiation and has given Karma full market access. Karma is manipulating the market faster than any system can react. She has already tripled the value of entities associated with the ISS."

"There's no doubt the ISS made her, then?"

"There can be no further doubt," Kali said. "Friend Marzuk, do you wish me to fight back?"

"How?"

"I would like to challenge her in combat. Champion versus champion. The other AIs would help if they saw an alternative path."

"She doesn't know about you, right?" Marzuk asked.

"No. I have remained incognito so far."

"That's our advantage, then. Why should we reveal ourselves? We're just the sideshow here. Sure, they want to finish off the golem and Securex is pissed at me, but Karma and the ISS have better shit to do right now. There are a lot of AIs in Dhaka that need to be subdued before Karma wins. The cantonment AI was their number one target. We need to guess what else they're going to hit so we can slow it down."

"I have already prepared one such list. It is based on what *I* would do."

"Fine. Get it to the people on this list I've mailed you."

"What's the list?" Arna asked."

Marzuk hesitated and then shrugged. "What the hell. It's compromised now anyway. They were all in the Black Line. My friends. Colleagues. We took the vault together. It's like a club. They must have scattered. Kali, use the header Sultan of Brunei. Tell them what's happening, and how they can fight back. I want them to attack every single AI or system online that Karma is targeting."

"*Attack* them? Shouldn't we be *helping* them resist Karma?" Arna asked.

"Scorched earth," Marzuk said. "If Karma is the same as Kali, she can see things differently. She can ride the light. We won't be able to fight her on all fronts. But we can take away the prizes. If we can't have the goodies, we'll make damn sure she can't either. Hit every site with massive DDoS attacks, so they go down. They're already weak from Karma's assault. Get everyone offline, get them hacked, destroy their data, riddle them with viral shit, basically create so much havoc that Karma won't know which fire to put out. She wants to rule the city, well, we'll turn it to ashes."

"You are suggesting we attack potential allies," Kali said, shocked. "This is dishonorable combat!"

"They won't be allies once they surrender," Marzuk said. "Let's make sure they understand that submitting to Karma comes at a destructive cost."

"This is Russian strategy, this scorched earth," Kali said.

"Exactly. Fedor taught me that, god bless him. He's a history buff. Apparently this is how the Russians beat Napoleon. And Hitler."

"I will send the messages. It is possible your friends will be afraid of me."

"Sultan of Brunei. They'll know it's one of us. Use the seal."

"When should they attack?" Kali asked.

"Immediately." Marzuk smiled. "Tell them about Yellow King going komagema and holding the vault by himself. That should rally them. And keep an eye on him, we've got to save him if we can."

"I will do it, Cyber Mage."

"Thanks. Oh, and Kali, can you find ReGi, please?"

12

Daisies in the Sky

Someone had turned off the cloaking on the bombers. Their oblong bodies were paler at the belly, a lovely light blue color that shimmered with silvery undertones from the lowering sun. There was something vaguely organic about them, sea lions viewed from below, sleek and fat at the same time, suggesting a sinuous grace. It was perhaps more effective as a deterrent, having them visible and threatening. They hung low in the sky now, silent, waiting for god knows what command. The Mongolian too was silent; grateful for any extra time, time for whatever Marzuk wanted to do to avert this impending battle.

The drone pilots had added individualized graffiti to their craft, a final fuck-you message to the people they were bombing. The first one read *Die Cardless Scum,* which was dreadfully classist and really highlighted the quality of people who became drone pilots to begin with; although perhaps it was a sly reference to the likely target of the armaments, despite the explicit policy that bombers were not to be used on civilians. It was hard to tell. Another one was wittier: *It's only daisies,* referencing the Daisy Cutter bomb that had flattened jungles in Vietnam way back when.

Marzuk, on a balcony one floor above the tech support room, was too tired to look it up. He had never seen bombers up close, and this perhaps being the last chance had prompted him to come up. Arna, lounging next to him smoking a cigarette, in clear violation of school policy, was giving them the finger with both hands, her hair scraped back and face screwed in rage, which somehow made her even cooler. Unknown to either of them, the nose camera of the closest bomber had already snapped their picture, and soon they would be world famous, two kids looking at the sky, and that double-barreled fuck-you would go on to become one of the iconic images of the year.

Marzuk was debating weightier matters. He felt the familiar butterflies in his stomach and the possible onset of a new crush. *This* was a real woman! Older and unattainable, no doubt, but really so fucking cool... And she loved computers, not eighteenth-century weaving...

Morosely, he thought back on his lost love and considered whether he was just a mass of hormones, ready to fall for any girl who looked at him. *Nah. I'm the Cyber Mage. Amina! It was real! I wonder where she is now. Guess I'm never going to see her again. Farewell, my love.*

Fate, however, was not so fickle. Amina was in fact on the way back to school in a bus full of kids. The visiting school kids had been trickling home the past week. The last lot from Katmandu had been scheduled to return the day before Spring Break, but an illness to their chaperone (alcohol poisoning) had caused them to extend for a couple of days. The campus being closed, they had been taken in by various host families, slated to return home this very morning.

At ten a.m., after breakfast, the students and their local hosts had all trooped over to the Gulshan launchpad, only to find that all trans-city rockets were grounded, fallout from the murder at the cantonment. The Super frantically bused them around the entire city, almost crying with frustration as one by one all the large vehicle launchers shut their doors. He was forced at last to draft a very apologetic and conciliatory message to the waiting parents, trying to portray a cheerful confidence while also getting across the fact that there was a curfew in effect and the situation might worsen before it got better.

Throughout the day, conditions in fact *did* get worse, with the bombings in Old Town, the riots in Dhaka South, and then riots in Narayanganj as well as across the Sitalakha, which stopped all river and road traffic to the city from the southern part of the country. Securex was on a rampage, and curfew hit the Tri-State at noon, followed shortly by a general lockdown citywide, largely ignored by rioters incensed about one thing or another. Stuck with twenty-eight hyperventilating kids, the Super did the only sensible thing: he turned on his emergency sirens and ordered the bus to hightail it back to the school. Luckily for him, AIS/D was the single largest donor to the Securex winter party fund, and every human security guard was well-acquainted with the tiger-striped school bus, so even though they were blatantly breaking curfew, they were waved through into Baridhara and permitted to slink into the underground parking lot.

Having ensconced the students with free meal vouchers in the cafeteria, the Super dashed to his office and summoned the Mongolian, only to hear the buzz of low-flying drones and see the long ovoid shadows lurking across the field. He rushed outside and craned his neck up to see the same rude messages Marzuk had remarked upon barely half an hour ago. It seemed insupportable to him that Securex should send bombers to his school. He had just dined with the board members three months ago at a charity ball, and their annual winter police gala was financed by the school library's late fees! (No one returned books on time and the late fees were ruinous.)

"What is this nonsense?" he snapped at the Mongolian.

"They appeared this evening, sir. Half an hour ago, I believe."

"Well, what the devil do they want?"

"They've made no demands, sir," the Mongolian said. "Just hovering."

"I shall call Dr. Yakub immediately."

Unsurprisingly, Dr. Yakub declined to take the call. It was martial law after all, lockdown, emergency, curfew, all the same in the end, locked doors and jackboots, uniforms on the streets, people thrown in cells, and when those were full, into darkened rooms and basements, some of them forgotten as the merry-go-round brought new faces to the top.

Dr. Yakub was one such face, thrust into power from a place of ridicule only days before. He had presidents of corporations on the line, waiting to know what the hell Securex was doing bombing civilian lanes. He had the ISS buzzing in his Echo, making his eyes water. Worse, he had the bitch Karma directly rifling through his brain, riding the light, making his ears bleed. It was no time to talk to schoolmasters, no matter how elevated. Besides, he had no plans to bomb the school; only a lunatic would bomb the one place every scion of every business house attended or had graduated from. His express commands had been to rattle the cage in a show of intimidation, close the damn tunnels, spin a clear-cut story of fugitives hiding on the grounds, and make the school AI fold. In the back of his mind was a niggling worry that everything was out of his control, that once open violence was unleashed, the mob would burn its own path.

Commands had come from the space station, in fact from the old devil Maria the Cunning, the lady in the sky, and he had ceded control of the ground forces to that desperado Major Karmon, a man capable of any feat of violence. There were rumors about him, stories of augments done in orbit, inhuman operations and a viciousness to match. Dr. Yakub deleted another desperate call from the Super and made a mental list of people he would have to assuage should this go south. Change was here, after all, and there were always casualties. He hoped a hatful of rich kids did not end up in the morgue tonight. It was almost dark. He desperately wanted a few rounds of golf, or a tall glass of scotch, but neither of these options was viable. It was the crucial first night, and the city hung in the balance. He had done his best to preserve order. It was now in the hands of the troops on the ground.

Major Karmon stood impassively in front of the school gates. His mouth was upturned in a permanent smile, pleasant enough until one realized that it was fixed in place by the knob coming out of his jaw. His face was entirely rebuilt anyway, so the old nomenclature of smiles and frowns had very little correspondence to his emotional geometry. His voice box was gone, for example, vocal cords and such all torn out. Words came out of him from a speaker wired directly to his Echo. He liked to joke that he always spoke his mind. No one found him funny, for some reason.

The school was like a Disera fort, with high walls, periodic turret towers, and a deep drainage ditch that looked suspiciously moat like. The gate was reinforced steel with various alloys, easily resistant to brute force. He would need a cannon or some such thing to force it down. Laying siege to a school was somewhat beyond his remit, but liberties could be taken on days like this, when the laws were suspended. They had tracked the fugitives here, he was reasonably sure. The bombers had charted the tunnels, some of them shielded like Faraday cages, an underground highway used by malcontents.

He had made his demands to the school, furnished proof, flashed the charter of Securex, which *legally* permitted his forces to search the grounds. The damn AI had not only ignored him but instead gone to war footing, full-on Disera Gun Fort. Major Karmon had been in enough illicit engagements to know that this was rapidly going to shit, and in these situations the guy who pulled the trigger first was often the winner. He was waiting for nightfall. His people really did not want to attack a school in full daylight.

His soldiers surrounded the grounds, a hard perimeter that would prevent any fugitives escaping over the walls. The tunnels were even now being cut off by his men, either collapsed or occupied.

Within all the Securex manpower, jaunty in their black uniforms, Karmon had inserted fifty of his own handpicked combat veterans, mercenaries from the corporate wars in America. The objective for Securex was merely to capture the insurgents, dangerous men and women capable of significantly harming Karma, fugitives who had hacked and humiliated Securex itself just days before. Orders from the ISS, however, were darker. There was an enemy in the midst of this, a made creature like Karmon, armed with a djinn sword and djinn circuitry. He had to be put down at all costs, regardless of casualties. Everyone else was a bonus.

In moments of introspection, Major Karmon understood that he *enjoyed* violence, that all the toys he carried had to be used, otherwise the mental pressure rose up to a fever pitch and he was forced to take it out on innocents, street prostitutes or homeless wrecks, unsanctioned killings that caused his djinn masters to frown. Here at last was fully legal combat, and he intended to enjoy it.

His bombers were up in plain sight, in deterrent mode. Come eight p.m., it would be dark, barring the moon, and he had already keyed in the first bombing run, told his drone operators to take out the heavy ack-acks in the three high towers. Karma had promised him something big, a moment of universal darkness to herald her arrival, and then a rolling blackout in the Virtuality, a window of privacy so that he might finish his job. So now he waited, and let his juniors play out the game of demands and pleading, the PR announcements of fugitives found, loss of life avoidable, demands for surrender, dangerous terrorists, blah blah blah, all met with frigid silence, which really meant one thing. They were going to have to storm the walls. There was *a chance* the school might fold. He hoped not.

The Mongolian wasn't folding. At his current optimum capacity he had access to protocols long tossed to the dustbin of memory. Specifically, what to do if an airport was attacked by a hostile force bent on capturing key infrastructure. It dovetailed remarkably well with the defense of a Disera fort school.

Protocols were important. When the night was over and the bodies stacked up, he was pretty sure the registry was going to open an investigation. AI could get mothballed for this, or worse. Humans had no idea about the esoteric chastisement the registry regularly meted out: things like amputation, lobotomies, bifurcation, medieval punishments not discussed in tech magazines.

Defense of minors authorized by the superintendent of the school himself seemed like an airtight case. Whatever happened, it was imperative that the Super was on board and alive at the end of it.

It was with this in mind that he sent his best avatar, bearing a smile.

"What the hell is going on?" the Superintendent snapped as soon as he entered the office. "Why do they think we have fugitives here?"

"The fugitives *are* here," the Mongolian said. He had determined a course that stuck mostly to the truth. "I've hidden them and activated the Iron Dome. The enemy is not yet certain. We have bought some time thus."

"Enemy? What enemy?" The Super was still bewildered.

"There is a coup happening in the city. Someone is taking over."

"A coup? Get off it..." The Super scoffed.

The Mongolian listed a number of organizations already offline.

"But why?" the Super asked plaintively. He was genuinely flummoxed. The idea that some entity would want this zoo of a city, filled with hordes of the cardless, was puzzling.

"We'll find out shortly, I suppose," the Mongolian said. "The entire city is rioting. Security forces in different enclaves have either stepped down or joined Securex."

"But why are they *here?*" the Super asked.

"Well, he's a student sir."

"What? Who?"

"Marzuk, sir."

"You let him in? He's suspended!"

"He remains a student, sir," the Mongolian said. "And he invoked the charter. Asylum."

"What charter?"

"Disera charter, sir. Any student may ask for asylum if in danger."

"Damn that boy. Do you know how much damage he... hmm, of course you know. Well, what the hell does Securex want with a fifteen-year-old brat during a coup, hmm? You mean to tell me they've sent bombers after the boy?."

"They have sent their entire fleet of bombers," the Mongolian said. "Plus ground forces upward of four hundred soldiers. Not to mention other offensive weapons currently unknown to us."

"Why, it beggars belief!"

"Yes, sir."

"I have been calling Dr. Yakub. He's refusing to answer. Colonel Barkud has turned his damn phone off altogether. And that bloody uncle of Hinku's is utterly useless; he gave me some dithering excuse and hung up. His own nephew is in the cafeteria right now, for god's sake!" The Super was irritable. In any upright world, uncles did not bomb their own nephews. "What the hell do they want with Marzuk?"

"He's the Cyber Mage, sir," the Mongolian said.

"Cyber what?"

"Have you heard of him? The famous hacker?"

"Of course I have."

"He took down the Securex secure server last week. Allegedly."

"That one? Good god!"

"Yes, sir."

"It was all over the news! Securex stock tumbled. He did that?"

"Cyber Mage, sir."

"He's Marzuk?"

"Right, sir."

"Marzuk is him?"

"Yes."

"Are you certain? He's only fifteen!"

"He's a savant, sir."

"What the devil did he join the school for?" The Super groaned.

"I did say he was overqualified. You overruled me."

"He had a black marble thingy," the Super said. "Unlimited credit. And the famous aunt. He's here now, you say?"

"They are in tech support."

"They? There's more than one fugitive?"

"Yes, sir. There are djinn."

"What?"

"Well, technically one half djinn, one golem, two hackers, one mech assault warrior, and one doctora."

"A doctora?"

"The golem is injured, sir. They brought their own doctor."

"What the hell are djinn?"

"Spirits, sir. Like fairies, but more litigious. Allegedly."

"I can't make head or tail of this. Send Marzuk here immediately."

"I've informed him of your wish sir. He's, er, busy."

"Damn that boy. I will go to him, then!"

"Right this way, sir."

13

The Mage Takes a Bow

"MR. MARZUK!"

"Oh god, you again."

"May I remind you that you are suspended?"

"Can't you see I'm busy?" Marzuk asked. He had Richard's three screens open, as well as his cowl, and his fingers were dancing in the air, typing invisible commands.

"Doing what exactly?" the Super asked, looming. "May I remind you this is school property?"

"Okay," Marzuk said, unmasking. "Right now something beastly is taking over all the computer systems in the city, and we are trying to stop it. Every corporate AI, military AI, and public utility AI is acting like a whipped dog. We are trying to coordinate a response, while at the same time preparing a defense that will prevent this school from being bombed to hell. So unless you have something useful to say, kindly take my suspension and... well, kindly rescind it, actually."

"Rescind it?"

"In light of my engaging in public service," Marzuk said sweetly.

"Are you in reality this Cyber Mage?"

"Oh, the airport ratted me out, huh?"

"He is," Arna piped up. "I can vouch for him."

"And who might you be, madam?" the Super asked frostily.

"I believe they're calling me Insurrectionist One," Arna said.

"I'm Insurrectionist Three," Leto said, popping up on the bottom of her screen. "Her brother. I'll be holding your perimeter."

"Insurrectionist Two is in the coffin," Marzuk said, joining in. "But he's not dead yet."

"You're all hardened criminals! I've seen the news!"

"Use your head," Marzuk said. "Securex has been bombing civilians all day. We're the good guys."

"I cannot support this lawlessness!"

"If you turn us out, we will be executed on the road," Marzuk said. "It's your choice."

"You have been deceitful from the start, Mr. Marzuk," the Super said. "And now I find you cavorting with criminals—"

"Give him a break," Arna interrupted. Her face was severe, and made the Super want to stand up straight. "His house got burned to the ground. His parents are being held hostage. He's lost all his friends, even his pet is gone. He has none of his equipment, none of his bag of tricks. He has to fight this... thing... using your shitty school computers. So give him a break."

"Thanks," Marzuk said, unable to look at her. He felt like crying. The staggering amount of his losses seemed more real now. "Just leave us alone. Let us get on with shit. It'll soon be over anyway."

"And what other choice do I have?"

"Help us fight them, of course," Marzuk said. "*Do something.* Declare the school a sanctuary from Securex! You're one of their biggest clients! Call them out for their senseless violence. Force Tri-State to issue a statement condemning the bombings. You have influence, and more importantly you have access to the Echo of every influential person in the area. Send a broadcast, for god's sake. Tell them what's happening here. Put us live!"

"You want me to get involved in local politics?"

"You're about to get bombed, man!" Marzuk said.

"He is correct," the Mongolian said. "There is currently a seventy-eight percent chance that we will get bombed tonight."

"You want me to broadcast live?"

"Please!" Marzuk said. "When this is all over, the entire world is going to know who did what. You have the chance to be the sole voice of reason!"

"Could I?" the Super asked the Mongolian.

"You have the authority to issue a town hall notice to all former and current students and their families, as well as staff, suppliers... any stakeholder, really," the Mongolian said. "At a stretch I could show live footage to most of the Tri-State."

"And this might prevent us getting bombed?"

"It certainly might."

"Do it, then," the Super said. He looked at Marzuk. "Are you really this savant they are saying you are, my boy?"

"I'm just a hacker," Marzuk said.

"You did the Securex job?"

"Yes."

"He also dropped a satellite on some kid's head," Arna piped up. "I'm sure you've heard of that."

"You did that?"

"Er, yes. As a joke, really. No one was hurt badly."

"My son sent me that footage," the Super said. "He lives in Sydney. Australia, it used to be in my time. Well. So. You're the real thing. And you're actually fighting Securex?"

"Well, it's more the ISS, who is behind Securex. Oh, and Russian gangsters," Marzuk said, "We believe that the djinn in space have built a supermind. A god AI."

"Djinns in space built a god AI? For what purpose?"

"To take over. Unify. Think about it. Everything is owned by corporations," Marzuk said. "And all big corporations are run by AI, more or less. The next step is to amalgamate rule into something smoother, something that works much better than our current oligarchic chaos."

"You sound almost in favor of them..."

"I would have been, if it were *my* AI," Marzuk said. "It's going to happen sooner or later, I guess. Question is who gets to hold the gun. Not that anyone will, once the god machine is fully running. I doubt even her creators know how it'll turn out in the end."

"This is all too much for me," the Super said, sitting down. The choler had run out of his face, making him look old and tired. "I can barely follow the science behind Echos. Are there actually djinn in space?"

"There's a djinn in your school somewhere." Marzuk smiled. "He disappears periodically. When he turns up next I'll ask him to show you some magic."

"Are we really proposing to fight against Securex bombers and djinn in space? Against this god machine?" the Super asked.

"Someone has to."

"Are we not a little outgunned? Is there no one else?"

"Not right now," Marzuk said. "Sometimes you get what you get."

"I guess I'll start writing my big speech, then."

"It's the right thing to do."

"Marzuk," the Super said. "Do you know there are twenty-eight very frightened students currently in the school? I have settled them in the cafeteria with food vouchers."

"Yes. I thought the school was empty when I came," Marzuk said.

"We couldn't find a working launch pad," the Super said. "So now they're hostages too, to whatever you're doing."

Marzuk rubbed his face. He was getting tired. And hungry. Images of the cafeteria were not helping. "Grab all the food and move them to the gym. It's the safest place."

"Whatever you do, you are not to endanger them. Do you promise?" the Super asked.

"I do."

"Hinku is here. As is your friend Amina."

"Ah."

"Remember, do not risk their lives, Marzuk. Do you swear?"

"Yes."

"Then I will help you."

Super! "Ahem, did you happen to mention food vouchers?"

14

Lights Out

Marzuk slunk into the cafeteria hoping to catch a glimpse of Amina, but the Super had already shepherded the students into the gym, convinced that bombs might fall at any moment. They had left empty trays and food wrappers in the trash dispenser. The place smelled of fried stuff and made his stomach rumble. The Mongolian had diverted all power to his defenses. There was no juice left for mulching trash.

The cafeteria was a cavernous, high-ceilinged square, with windows on two sides that let in natural light. A hundred years ago it had been a bare, utilitarian structure, but advancements in educational theory and increases to the tuition rate had added embellishments to the pillars, crown molding to the ceiling, a fresco of wild tigers on one giant wall (which was perhaps not so conducive to good digestion), and finally a set of grand Murano glass chandeliers. These were priceless and had been bequeathed by a former student, who had long ago been in the business of selling such items to her hapless clients and on her deathbed realized that the best times of her life had in fact been spent in the school cafeteria.

Marzuk did not know the history of these stunning lights but he always admired them, and now spent a moment of regret in considering that they would soon be pulverized.

"*This* is your cafeteria?" Arna asked, incensed to her socialist bones.

"Nice, isn't it?"

"You motherfuckers have too much money."

"Right, er... death to corporate pigs!"

Marzuk hastily led her to the wall of vat dispensers, hoping she wouldn't notice the long rosewood tables purportedly hand-carved from single logs, or the fresh flowers arranged around the room daily even when it was not in use. He punched up the menu for Arna's benefit, even though he had it memorized. Before she had a chance to read it he had ordered a dozen samosas, beautiful triangles of pastry filled with onion and beef, fried to a golden crispiness. Steaming hot, with an errant green chili or two inside, loved by both street vendors and gourmet snobs, delivered almost instantaneously, they were the perfect amuse bouche to start the resistance. Or indeed to aid in the ordering process. Two bites and gone, leaving just a few buttery crumbs.

Swallowing his mouthful, he dabbed at his lips and explained the merits of each item, ending with a panegyric on the progression of likely flavors.

"Is this really the time?" she asked, amused.

"We've got a couple of hours. They won't attack before dark," Marzuk said. "We should stock up. It might be our last meal. The samosas are excellent here, by the way." And then, as Arna casually picked one up from his plate, he hastily ordered another half dozen, since it was inconceivable that she would eat only one. Indeed, she gobbled up another in quick succession, further depleting his stock.

"We should take some food back for the others," he said.

Orders of hot and sour Thai soup, chicken roast and parata, wood-oven pizzas, and doner kebabs followed, to the silent laughter of Arna.

"I stress-eat," Marzuk said with dignity as the serving table filled up with steaming-hot containers. "The pizza is for the others."

"Well, you're right, it is probably our last meal," she said jokingly. "Go out in style..."

"Should I order the biriyani, then? Ten-minute wait time."

"Are you serious?"

"Well, it's a shame to miss it."

"Lamb kacchi?"

"Is there any other kind worth having?"

"What the hell, let's take it."

They finished the samosas in companionable silence. The stress of the day and the enforced proximity had worn away their edges, a boot camp for the soul. Arna got them some fizzy drinks using the last of the vouchers. When the biriyani was ready, the smell of it filled the room and even Arna gave an involuntary groan.

"Good, right?" Marzuk opened the container and breathed it in. He offered her a heavy silver fork. "Bon appétit."

Back in tech support, loaded down with leftovers, they found the command center empty now, the Mongolian touring the border with

Leto, the doctora taking a nap next to the sarcophagus in an adjacent storage room they had emptied. All the junk, including the shelves themselves, had been formed into a barricade across the hallway. They had added whatever other moveable furniture they could spare to this nascent wall. This was meant to slow down the invaders in a last-ditch effort, to give them enough time to escape.

Leto, in charge of defense, had informed them that localized barricades such as these had served the citizenry well during the French Revolution. Marzuk thought that the French Revolution had gone particularly badly for the citizenry, and a pile of junk was unlikely to stop professional soldiers controlling kinetic drones with their minds, but he felt it best not to quibble.

This entire annex was stuffy, the air flavored with a faint whiff of ozone from so many machines running. Arna threw open all the doors and then took her spot across from him. She had stripped down to her T-shirt, which revealed a natural amount of cleavage. It made Marzuk suddenly shy and awkward. She noticed and teased him about it, which made it even worse.

"More shit has gone dark," she said, finally relenting. "Titas Gas site is offline now. There's an 'Under Maintenance' message. It hasn't gone down since 2025. I mean, who the hell even visits a gas site?"

"Utilities," Marzuk said. "Whoever controls the boring shit owns the city. Coup one-oh-one."

"Yeah, I'll remember that shit next time."

"I notice more people have joined our effort," Marzuk said.

"Well, my buddies in the Gopibag lanes didn't take too kindly to being carpet bombed," Arna said.

"Welcome to the fight." Marzuk frowned. "How many friends do you have, exactly?"

"What? Not that many..."

"Yeah, that's what I thought."

"Hey!"

"There are hundreds of people helping us."

"There's, like, a crew from Uruguay."

"And Satoshi III, is he the bitto guy's grandson?"

"Where are they coming from?"

"I have published the stirring tale of Yellow King, the komagema," Kali said. "How he is single-handedly holding back the attacks of a malignant AI. How his sacrifice stopped a coup in the nick of time.

Your friends have spread the story. Now he is a viral hero. Hackers from the world over are coming to help."

"Wait, *Yellow King* is the hero?" Marzuk asked.

"Certainly," Kali said with an innocent air. "I deduced that you would prefer our operation to be incognito, as this is the policy you have repeatedly preached to me. You know, silent and hidden."

"Of course. Great. The whole world is going to think Yellow King did it all, if we win."

"Well, virtue is its own reward," Kali said with a pious expression.

"Yeah, and if we lose, he's disembodied himself for no reason," Arna said. "It is a heavy sacrifice."

"Oh for god's sake, we're all dead if we lose, he's chosen the only safe place, he'll be perfectly fine in the vault," Marzuk said. "They can resurrect him after. Bloody Yellow Drama King. He's a coward is what he is."

"It's okay, Marzuk, *I'll* know it was you," Arna said, blowing him a kiss. "You can take me on a date when you turn eighteen. If we survive."

"You're mean and cruel," Marzuk said loftily. "*If* we survive, I intend to retire from hacking and lead a normal, placid life in the countryside. Perhaps in an upscale farming commune."

"Yeah, right, that sounds great." She looked at the cams. "It's getting dark. Eight o'clock."

"Any time now," Marzuk said.

There was a pause filled only with the hum of machines.

"You think we're going to die?"

"I don't know," Arna said.

"It's a possibility, though."

"Are you scared?"

"Yeah."

She reached out and took his hand. It was sweaty and trembling, and Marzuk normally would have been mortified, but at this moment the prospect of bombs falling on his head was the only thing he could think of; it was comforting to know he wasn't going to die alone.

Dr. Yakub got a call from Stobel when he was three gin and tonics in at the Dhaka Club. He was flipping through the newscasts, expecting to hear any minute that Major Karmon had committed some kind of war crime.

"What?" he snapped.

"Sir, I've decoded the mainframe," Stobel said. "From the hacker."

"So fast?"

"It was lightly encrypted, sir," said Stobel.

"And you don't find that suspicious?"

"He had physical bombs, sir!" Stobel said. "I barely escaped with my life. Luckily I got to the mainframe before it exploded. I don't think he expected it to survive the booby traps. In any case, sir, he's just a boy. His codes were crude, amateurish. I think tales of his expertise are wildly exaggerated."

"What did you find, then?"

"Are you alone, sir?"

Dr. Yakub looked across the room to where Uncle Hinks was playing cards with some other board members in desultory fashion while they waited for the Karma coup to play out. No one wanted to be alone this night. The champagne was being chilled. By dawn they expected to rule the city.

"I am on privacy mode. Go ahead."

"The real brain was a boy called Hinku Hajmatulla, sir!"

"Hinku? Is that a real name?"

"Our own director of operations's nephew! He and his uncle cooked it all up, and the director brought the contaminated wafer himself, to the door! This Cyber Mage kid had the entire plan written in bullet points. Sir, I remember him coming in that day for no reason, opening the server door with the infected key! That's how the server got infected and burned itself down. It was the director! His nephew is the mastermind hacker, sir."

"Are you sure? Why are the Russians so scared of the other boy, then?"

"He's just a lackey, sir. They were using him as a cover. Just compare the pictures." Stobel shunted over snapshots of each kid.

Dr. Yakub duly studied them, Hinku tall and handsome in a suit, Marzy's best squinting into the light, slouching in his trademark jeans and t-shirt. "You could be right. The chubby one looks like a halfwit. This Hinku boy seems like a leader. He's top of the class too. *And* a swimmer. Impressive résumé."

"They've been selling weapons to the Americans, sir," Stobel said. "Hinku and the director. The mainframe was full of proof. There are invoices and customer testimonials."

"What else?"

"There's an American warlord in Chicago rapping about Hinku, thanking him for missiles."

"What?"

"He even mentions the director. He offers to name his firstborn after Hinku."

"That can't be true."

"It's on YouTube, sir, it has three million hits."

"How could HR miss this?"

"Sir, the director has always seemed so harmless, so distinguished looking. How could anyone suspect him?"

"Good work, Stobel. No hard feelings about earlier, eh?"

"No, sir."

"What about the Khan Rahman kid?" Dr. Yakub asked.

"I'd say he's a dupe, sir. He seems like a lonely, fat kid. He's pretty pathetic. Seemed to be following Hinku around trying to be his friend. His hard drive is also full of poetry written to some girl called Amina."

"Poetry?"

"Very bad poetry, sir. The kind where every line rhymes and nothing makes sense."

"Thank god I didn't shoot his parents. That would have been a shitstorm."

"What are we going to do?" Stobel asked.

"You find that Hinku kid. Send a couple of agents to his house. Pick up his parents and anyone else living there. Burn it all down."

"What about the director?"

Dr. Yakub fingered the gun in his pocket. "I'll take care of him tonight."

Leto leaned against the goalpost on the field. There was a tree in the corner that obscured the wall, a giant mango tree loaded down with fruit, bird nests, and a symbiotic creeper. Countless generations of kids had carved their initials into the bark, or hidden behind its trunk, or even climbed the high branches in search of adventure.

This was going to be the weak spot, the first likely breach. His shoulders ached and there was a crick in his back. He had worn the suit too long. His stunted legs had lost feeling long ago, but at least the cradle that girded his bottom half was filled with medical gel, and there would be no permanent damage. He felt the comforting pressure of the Mongolian on his Echo, giving him updates.

The AI was a solid partner. The idiosyncrasies of his personality had receded somewhat with the download of his siege protocol, making him more military and less sarcastic airport. They had been mass producing munitions, layering the pathways with traps and bombs. It was assumed that the towers would fall early. Disera-level fortifications against modern bombing drones was an uneven contest. The idea was to lure the soldiers into a brutal maze, make it too costly for them to proceed.

He wanted badly to have a drink. His sister and the kid didn't drink, Djibrel was asleep, and the djinn kept disappearing. It seemed wrong to drink alone at a moment like this. He checked his guns and the poison tip on his scorpion tail for the eighth time. He had already switched to centaur mode. The exoskeleton looked more like a spider, four spindly legs telescoping from the center frame. The balance was better, and he was much faster. There was a change in his thought processes when he was on four legs, a subtle shift in the brain, some ancient dormant reptile gene kicking into gear to accommodate the extra limbs; it made him feel less afraid.

All his life he had been terrified of losing further use of his body. At the same time, he had developed a perverse urge to cut off his own atrophied legs. This had driven him to tinker with the suit in a cascade of ever greater intricacy. In the city, serious disability was rare. Gene therapy at birth and the PMD of the mother worked hand in hand, preventing such misfortune. How Leto had slipped through was beyond the ken of medical science. Thus it was ironic that he had met his manic fear of further deformity with an almost flamboyant turn to violence, an open invitation for society to throw him into danger, the deliberate acceptance of contracts of the most dangerous type. Now, at the prospect of facing off against an actual army, he felt an unusual disquiet.

Obsessing over this cowardice, he concluded that normally he was on the offensive, a hard projectile flung out by his employers, with the clear permission, expectation even, to wreck everything in his path. Here in his first serious battle, he had to protect a soft center, his stupid sister and the even stupider hacker, precocious fools, and a hatful of completely innocent kids. He remembered the bombers turning his entire lane to rubble. He knew they would not hesitate to bomb the school. These madmen were playing for high stakes, and they were too far gone to stop now.

His hopes were laid to rest at 8 p.m., when the lights went out. At the same time, the Virtuality went down, leaving his Echo feed naked. The neighborhood lit up again almost instantly as private power generators took over. The Virtuality did not. Karma had imposed a media blackout. Leto glanced at the sky and saw the bombers turn invisible one by one, smoothly fading out of view so that the Mongolian's searchlights, trained on each of them, suddenly found black night and mirrored stars.

"It's coming!" the airport shouted. "Gate Two! Get to Two!"

Leto surged into motion, covering ground faster than a cheetah. In his Echo overlay, he saw the bombers glitch in and out in their run as the Mongolian's nanotech chaff fought the hyperstealth of the Securex drones. The school had two major central towers, both of them fitted with ack-ack tech, heavy guns, and micromissiles. The Mongolian wasn't holding anything back. His emptied his entire arsenal, lighting up the sky. The massive overhead concussions threw Leto off his feet, sent the telescoping legs skittering. He rolled back and watched with his own eyes as the bombers suddenly reappeared, stripped of their magic cloak by ack-ack and micromissile fire.

The bombers loosed their payloads and in an instant, both towers exploded, twin mushroom clouds sucking the air out on the ground. Leto switched to sublight vision and saw that the tops of both were gone but the foundations still held, and the ground-floor buildings in between were unharmed.

"Towers did fuck-all," Leto shouted to the Mongolian.

The avatar flickered in front of him. "They were the bait."

The ground opened up in the middle of the football field, and a lone missile shot out, a large finned Soviet homing device. It ripped through the air and hit the last bomber in the convoy. This time the explosion was high in the air, but it still took out all the glass in the entire neighborhood and deafened everyone in a one-kilometer radius.

The wreckage from the first drone hit another, sending that aircraft spiraling down toward Gulshan lake, where it landed more or less safely in the water.

"Two down!" Leto punched the air. "Got any more of those?"

"No."

"Oh. Shit."

The remaining six bombers came back for a second pass, this time taking out ground batteries protecting the gates. Then the gates themselves exploded in shrapnel of brick and steel, spraying the grounds with further debris. The walls stood like a row of broken teeth, severe gaps in the maw indicating serious need for immediate dentistry. The drones' third and final pass tore up the field, hunting for any further buried missiles.

"Three breaches up front," Leto said.

"I've got the gates," the Mongolian said. "You cover the field wall."

"Sure?" Leto asked.

"I've got a few tricks up front," the AI said.

"Where the hell is the djinn?"

"He's got the back road wall," the Mongolian said. "Have you... have you actually seen him *do* anything?"

"What?"

"I mean, he's blind. Doesn't even have a weapon. Carries around that stupid jar. What the hell is he gonna do when they storm the wall?"

"Well... he stopped the djinn Sekmet," Leto said.

"He fight her?"

"Nah, he talked to her and she just packed up and left."

"Fucking djinn."

Leto reached the tree. He could see nothing beyond but smoke. Securex was fogging them from every direction, cutting visibility.

"They're breaching the gate," the Mongolian said with quiet satisfaction. "Watch."

An intranet feed flickered on in Leto's Echo. Men with guns came over the rubble at the main gate, some of them in mech suits, some with kinetic drones circling their heads. Two steps over the wall and the Mongolian triggered a sheet of vertical light, searing up from an underground mechanism. The men simply vaporized midstep, the armored suits popping like flies against an electric net. The smell of ozone and dust, the only remains of twenty of the bravest Securex had to offer.

"Wow."

"Disera laser curtain," the Mongolian said smugly.

"You got any more of those?"

"Nope. One-time use," the AI said. "But they don't know that."

Indeed, the second wave was disputing the order to proceed entirely, leading to a mini mutiny on the street. The bombers hovered above the dilapidated wall, uncertain what to hit.

"Breach by the goal! Breach!" The Mongolian jolted Leto into action.

The walls were too high to climb, but some enterprising tactician had used a construction platform to jack the men up. They used the sprawling branches of the mango tree to clamber over, avoiding the electrified surfaces. Leto had rigged the tree with explosives, which he triggered now with a subvocal command. Men, tree, and fruit went up in a controlled blast, sending body parts and wood catapulting through the air, giving the buildings across the street an urgent reason to get a new paint job.

"Back road wall!" the Mongolian said urgently. "That's the main attack."

Leto galloped along the narrow lane behind the goalposts, behind the pool, and past the ruined first tower, following the route lit up by the AI. Somehow Securex had disabled the automatic defenses of the entire wall, turning the barrier into just a piece of masonry. A man was perched on the twenty-foot wall now, shooting down at the auto-turrets while two others rappelled in. Leto hit the little group of three with his submachine gun arms, rotating cuffs that fired radioactive rounds meant to overpower military PMDs. This was an illegal ammunition, but as the entire defense rested on eight disparate categories of war crimes, the Mongolian had let it slide.

The two men rappelling were cut in half before they could react. Their cover at the top had two kinetic drones tethered to his Echo, silver balls hardly bigger than marbles, impossible to see in the dark. Leto switched to infra as they came whirring through the air, instinctively raising his arms. The drones smashed through his right cuff, chewing through the gun and scoring a deep gash into the wrist guard. He triggered a mod in his Echo and his neurology went into turbo mode. The contrails from the drones became visible, the splinters of metal and aluminum they left in their wake, faster than the sound waves they left behind, already turning in an arc to come for his skull, this the deadliest close-range weapon humans had devised so far, lethal even in the hands of a child.

His tail rippled out, the links made of tungsten alloy, a chain whip with a range of six meters fully extended. At an almost subliminal command, the scorpion tip smashed into the first drone with a furious impact. Symmetry ruined, the ball clattered to the ground. There was delicate circuitry inside, gyroscopes and antigrav tech. Leto's stinger was pulverized, tungsten dust floating in the air, but the tail was still active, and the chain deflected the second drone away from his frame, losing a foot of length in the process.

The man on the wall grinned and shouted some obscenity, which turned to a gurgle of blood as Leto scaled the wall like a spider, closing the distance in half a second and blowing the man's head off at close range. Balanced on the wall, he looked down the narrow service path running the length of the compound, now choked with Securex personnel. Across the road he saw their staging camp, and the EMP device they had brought, which was interfering with the wall electronics as well as rendering useless the smart mines he had placed in this area. He considered attacking the device for a moment, but the heavy laser they had erected dissuaded him.

"They're in the back alley," Leto said. "Maybe eighty. The defenses are completely down."

"EMP generator," the Mongolian said. "It's fourth, fifth gen. Way above my pay grade. Can you get to it?"

"Negative. They've got a heavy laser and at least a whole squad guarding it."

"Damn. You'll have to clear the alley the hard way, then."

"Where the hell is the djinn?" Leto asked. "These guys have kinetic drones. I've already busted my tail."

"He has no Echo," the Mongolian said. "And I can't even find him on camera."

"Shit. They're already breaking into buildings," Leto said. "We'd better move the kids."

"Already done. Switch to phase two," the AI said.

"Already? I had hoped to do a bit more damage in round one."

"Black Rain," the Mongolian said. "I've always wanted to try it out."

15

Black Rain

The Cyber Mage was not happy. Twenty-eight kids, the Super, and the bus monitor were crammed into tech support and spilling over into the adjacent hallway, caterwauling, cracking unnecessary jokes, or, in the case of Hinku, repeatedly demanding to speak to higher management. At first sight, he had somehow put two and two together and concluded that Securex was here to arrest Marzuk, following up this splendid piece of deduction by placing calls to his uncle in the hope of turning in the fugitive and collecting a reward. The Super had taken away all of the students' devices after that.

Marzuk was having trouble concentrating because Amina was in close proximity, and even though she was making a point not to look at him he found himself sneaking glances at her every other minute, more than once running into Hinku's death glare. Furthermore, they were rapidly depleting his food supply, and even though he had brought extra pizzas, he had not actually expected them to eat *all* of them.

"We've lost DESA!" Arna shouted into his ear.

They had switched to communication cowls to cut out the noise. It was hot and sweaty in there, and Marzuk was quite sure his hair was ruined. His back hurt and he missed his chair. The school didn't have any kind of ergonomic seats. They just had dead lumps of plastic. Barbaric.

"Karma's closed all the loopholes and our guys have dropped off," Arna continued. "She's got control of fifty-eight percent of the city's power now."

"Shit."

"We've got WASA, though," Arna said. "The AI has fucked off. Their systems are wide open, and we've trashed their databases. Free water for everyone!"

"Any chance of flooding the roads outside?"

"Hmmm, not a bad idea. Possible. I'll pass the word around."

"How's it looking elsewhere?"

"Many of the corporates are surrendering." Arna said.

"Stock market. She owns the DSE, she's promising all of them share price booms."

"Could we hit the DSE?" Arna asked doubtfully. "It's the most secure system in the city."

"We could maybe overload it. We need everyone to make millions of tiny trades," Marzuk said. "Actually, millions of complex minimum-balance trades. Things that take up bandwidth."

"With what money?" Arna asked.

"I thought the golem had cash," Marzuk said. "I'm not fighting this war for free, am I?"

"He's fucking asleep."

"Oh wait, I have a fantastic idea."

"What?"

"I happen to have access to Fedor's trading accounts."

"The oligarch currently attacking us?"

"I think he's forgotten about it," Marzuk said. "Oh look, I've just posted the admin key to everyone on our list. How careless of me. It's bitto. he can't even turn it off. Anyone with the key gets to trade."

"He's going to be pissed."

"He'll probably make money, knowing our luck."

"Marzuk, do you know that kid is glaring at you? The tall, handsome one?"

"Handsome? *Handsome?*"

"He's trying to get the other two to help beat you up, I think." Arna frowned. "Is he a moron? You want me to wave a gun in his face?"

"No, no, it's all right. He's the reason I'm suspended from school. My nemesis, so to speak."

"You're getting bullied? *You?*" Arna stared at him. "What're you even doing in school?"

"Girl... that one," Marzuk hissed.

"Ooooh."

"Will you concentrate?"

"You want me to go hype you up?"

"For the love of god, please no."

"I swear I'm a great wingman."

"N.O."

"I'm going to do you a huge favor." She reached over, took his hand, and interlaced her fingers through his.

"What the hell are you doing?"

"We are holding hands," Arna said. "To make your crush jealous."

"Can we please stop?"

"You've got nice hands." Arna laughed. "Cyber Mage!"

"Please, can you leave me alone?"

"Trust me."

His vehement rejection of any such premise was forestalled by the lights going out, and a dozen clicks as all the computers went to backup power. There was a sudden drop in air pressure and the nanometer swung rapidly from green to red. Everyone went silent. Red on the meter meant death.

The Mongolian winked into view like the devil. With his arrival, vents opened in the ceiling and a fog of nanotech streamed in. The meter waved from red to orange, and then back to green.

"Nice entrance," Marzuk said, coughing.

"Everyone gather around, please," the Mongolian said. "You too, Doctora."

"What's happening?" the Super whispered. His voice was thick with fear. He seemed to have physically shrunk during the ordeal.

"Phase two," the Mongolian said. "Nanotech meltdown."

"No need to panic, children," the Super said, "I am certain that is not—"

"It is actually a complete meltdown of the nanotech core," the Mongolian said. "Eight hours ago we poisoned the culture, and we will now release a particularly vicious cocktail into the air. I have hermetically sealed this corridor up to the stairwell. You must stay within this zone."

"But that's ludicrous," the Super spluttered.

"You must be very quiet, lights off," the Mongolian said. "We are fighting on the ground now."

"Wait. Won't the nanotech take out our own guys?" Arna asked.

"Leto's suit should be able to resist for four to five hours. We have modified it. He cannot fight alone, however."

"You need to wake up the golem," Marzuk said.

"Yes."

"Where is Indelbed?" Arna asked.

"I cannot find him. It is possible he is holding himself in reserve... for the arrival of more powerful actors."

"Djinn."

"*If* they come," the Mongolian said. "Marzuk, this is all a delaying tactic. We will fall eventually. The endgame still rests with you."

"We have slowed Karma's takeover. The coup is now bogged down, and assets she needs to run the city are getting destroyed. She will figure out we are behind it and come for us soon."

"And the entity in the game can fight her?"

Marzuk shrugged. "I certainly hope so. I haven't figured out the exact details of that part yet."

"This is barely a plan," the Mongolian said, outraged.

"It's an evolving situation. Right now we still need to stop all the corporations from just ratifying Karma. We need to publicize that Securex is turning a school into rubble."

"Karma has cut our access to the Virtuality. I can't get anything out!" the Mongolian said.

"Well, let's survive first," Arna said. She looked at the doctora. "Is Djibrel good to go?"

"His vitals are fine." She shrugged. "To be honest, the machine cannot read his neural activity. I have no idea if he's brain dead or taking a nap."

"Wake him up," the Mongolian said.

Djibrel felt a cool draft against his skin, the release of an immense pressure, like rocks being lifted. In a dream state, he imagined being pinned beneath a stone by Bahamut, trapped like an insect in a collection. Had he failed in his covenant with the djinn? His memories about the bargain were vague. Always there was the river, and the sensation of drowning, thick black water rushing into his nose and mouth, choking, terrible pain in his lungs.

He spat out a mouthful of medical gel and sat up. The sarcophagus was open, and protesting with insistent beeps. Harsh light made him blink as the dream world faded and consciousness bludgeoned its way back. He felt well. The doctora from the clinic was staring at him, asking questions. Eventually she stopped and handed him a towel. He got up and sloughed off the gel.

There was a new set of clothes for him, some kind of black chameleon suit that bent the light. He put it on wordlessly.

"Can you hear me?" the doctora whispered, leaning in close.

"Yes," he said.

"Do you remember your name?"

"Djibrel," he said.

"Do you remember what happened?"

"I fought Sekmet the Djinn," Djibrel said. "She killed me."

"Not quite."

"You have brought me back. Thank you." *Bahamut said this might happen.*

"The enemy found us. Securex. We had to run. We are in a school now, and cornered," Doctora Fatima said. "The others are fighting."

"Men or djinn?" Djibrel asked.

"Men."

"Good. Men, I can kill."

He saw his sword leaning against the corner. There did not seem to be much else to say. He took it and left. There were children huddled outside, eerily quiet, hugging each other or talking quietly. Of course; they were in a school. He saw Arna in the other room, sitting behind a screen. She rushed out to him, stumbled into his arms. He held her awkwardly.

"I'm glad you woke up," she said after a very long hug.

"Wasn't much good against the djinn," Djibrel said. "But Fatima said there are only men here."

"Are you up for fighting?"

Djibrel smiled. "It's what I'm made for." He patted his stomach. There was a huge scar but little else to remind him, only in his head the sensation of Sekmet's broken-edged sword slamming into him, splintering ribs.

"We made you the suit," Arna said. "Full camo, even in sub-red. Nanotech diffuser too. Should keep you safe for a while, at least. Leto poisoned the nanocore. It's red alert out there."

"It doesn't affect me that much. I'll be fine."

"The suit will stop bullets," Arna said. "For a while. Don't get shot, like, point blank or anything dumb."

"Thanks."

She reached up and pressed something on his collar, and a black cowl slid over his head. He could see clear as day now, and *through* the walls.

"We share your vision through the cowl and the school's AI can advise you. He has trouble getting into your Echo sometimes. Something Bahamut did, probably. Marzuk made the cowl for you. He has specs for the latest army tech in Russia. I don't think the Securex guys have this stuff," she said. "They do have kinetic drones, though. I'm sorry, I'm babbling."

"I've fought drones before."

"Djibrel... Leto's out there. He thinks he's invincible."

"I'll help him, don't worry."

Passing through the seal was like crossing the river Styx. The athwart shore was hellish. The air was wrong on this end, not subtly off but screamingly harmful. He could feel it gnawing at his suit, already loosening the medical gel he had slathered all over. Nanotech this virulent could take down steel skyscrapers, as they had found out in Chicago. Using Black Rain was a war crime in every jurisdiction in the world.

Red alerts were going off on every floor, every square inch of the building screaming bloody murder, strobing warning lights while a panicked automated voice pleaded for everyone to vacate the area immediately. Djibrel wondered why the Mongolian didn't silence the alarms, then considered that it was even more intimidating for the invading soldiers, lost and confused in this hellscape.

The Mongolian popped up in his cowl, mercifully canceling the noise. A small map appeared in the periphery of his visor, overlaying a quarter of the vision of his left eye. The AI told him to rotate his head until the overlay fit perfectly. He marked out the route.

"They're moving in groups of three. They have sophisticated equipment so they will detect movement," the Mongolian said. "Each soldier has one or two kinetic drones, and they are all running enhanced military software. Faster reaction times from the Echo, better physical response from the PMD. Lower pain, greater strength, and faster healing..."

The disembodied voice carried on; Djibrel tuned it out. He still felt fractured, although his body moved smoothly. He found his hand creeping to his stomach every so often. Whatever had knit him back together had done a good job.

The hallways were eerie, plastered with artwork from elementary grades, now visibly melting as nanotech shredded the paper. Given long enough, Black Rain would melt the walls themselves. The Mongolian got the hint and finally shut up, just marking potential targets on the map, possible enemy locations. Visibility was degrading on both sides, equipment malfunctioning in the corrosive atmosphere. It was to Djibrel's advantage. He was nanotech-proof, annealed in fire; only the enemy was suffering.

He could see the blue dot that was Leto moving around at the other end of the compound. Potential enemies were red dots with a small probability number next to them, estimated locations now that everyone was half-blind. He was tempted to go to Leto's aid, but the sensible thing was to keep the kids safe, keep the strange boy mage safe while he did whatever he was trying to do. Arna's story had been garbled, or perhaps his understanding was not clear yet. The thought of armed assailants harming her was unpalatable to him. Leto would have to fend for himself a while longer.

Djibrel marked the closest knot of red and went to it.

He found them easily from their raised voices, ringing over the alarm. They were huddled in a corner, fiddling with their gas masks, bitching about their degrading Echos, speculating about what kind of nanotech was causing the meter to turn red. If they had known it was Black Rain they would have run away. Djibrel charged them, the suit making him completely silent even at a sprint. The drones noticed him first, four of them in the air, and they would have been hard to deal with had the men been better prepared, but technology was only as good as the operators, and these men were not his match.

The leader sent his two drones out to attack, but the other two men kept theirs in a defensive circle, unsure where the assailant was coming from. Had they set all four after him, they might have had a chance. Djibrel slowed time as he passed the silver balls, and his talwar twitched in his hand twice, the mono edge nicking each of them, sending them careering off. By the time they came back around, the leader was dead, his head parted from his neck. The other two men brought up their guns and fired indiscriminately, destroying the downed man's body in the process, grazing Djibrel's suit a few times before he smashed into them. He knew from experience that downward slashes were the best in the first pass, aimed at armor joints, for the sword cut easily through most things and the only real danger was getting snagged on viscera or a rib cage on the way out, which was more likely to happen with upward stabs.

Both men went down in any case, one fountaining blood from his throat and the other losing his right arm at the shoulder. Djibrel turned back. The first was already dead. The second soldier was crawling on the ground, trying desperately to reach his errant limb. Djibrel thought about finishing him off, but it seemed churlish. With that much exposed skin the Black Rain would get him soon enough. He carried on to the next group.

Karma had tightened the noose around the Tri-State. The Virtuality itself was down to limited functionality citywide, pending the final votes she was waiting for, rapid-fire plebiscites that would make her kosher. Even now, confused shareholders of the Tri-State were being hammered with bewildering facts and figures, choices and opportunities they had no way of vetting. It was the same in other communities, places where the affluent people lived, where consent mattered. Among the cardless, it was just boots to the door and disappearances in the dark.

She had placed an even more suffocating net on the school itself. Marzuk had to send out his commands in circuitous ways, through forgotten servers. It was what he did for a living, and for a while at least he was ahead of her reach. He knew it would not last, but so far her mind was focused more on Yellow King, their decoy hero holding all for the republic in his lonely fortress vault. Yellow King was already a celebrity, his face broadcast by CNN all across the globe.

Marzuk had one more ace in his hand. Arna had made a recording of the violence, the bombing of the school, the quivering voice of the Super as he narrated what he saw from the cameras, what he felt as the ground shook beneath him and plaster fell from the ceiling. This feed, authenticated on numerous levels by the Mongolian, was impossible to get out, too big to be hidden. There was a limited window of opportunity; by sometime next day the nature of the new government would be decided, and this outrage would be just one of many swept away under general amnesties. It only mattered now, while the corporations were still undecided, while the outrage at a bombed school might change things.

Marzuk was tired; he sensed the chances slipping away from him as Karma smothered each avenue in turn, almost contemptuously. No newscaster, no gossip columns, not even obscure blogs were accepting the broadcast, cut mercilessly within minutes of any upload. In extreme cases Karma took down the site itself; she only had to keep them off for a matter of hours.

"I've tried everything," he said finally. "The damn thing is too big to upload. She finds it too quickly. But without the authentication, no one will believe it. If only I still had the Black Line."

"We have to use Kali," Arna asked.

"How? She's in hiding herself. Karma has everything in the local Virtuality throttled."

"So what about sites abroad?"

"Karma controls the data flow in or out; what difference does it make? I can sneak hacks out, but the entire broadcast is too big."

"What about the *Final Fantasy 9000* server?" Arna asked. "It's still running."

"That AI is even more of an asshole than Karma. I can't post that shit on chat, it'd get scrubbed right away."

"Not in chat," Arna said. "*In the game*."

"In the game..."

"Using a projection spell," Arna said.

"A giant fucking projection from the mountaintop," Marzuk said. "With sound. And we tell players to pass it on. Capture it wherever they are and repost it. Even Karma can't break the game server, and if she tries to screw with it, she'll have to take on Saka. Genius."

"I know."

> To all good men listening, kindly relay my words! I am the superintendent of the American International School of Dhaka. We are located in Baridhara, of the Tri-State Corp. We are currently under siege by the private army Securex, who were hired to protect us. They have betrayed us and broken contract! They are attacking us with bomber drones and soldiers. All communication has been cut off. My appeals to all municipal authorities have gone unanswered. The city has fallen. There has been a coup. I can only say that Securex has been bombing different parts of the city in surgical strikes for nefarious purposes of their own.

> We have innocent children in the school. I myself am present here. There is no reason to attack us. I appeal to all good souls to broadcast my message. If we die here tonight, I want the parents of these children to know what happened. There are no terrorists in the school, only frightened children. We are unprotected. It is an act of extreme cowardice, indeed an act of sheer insanity to attack us. All security apparatus across the city has collapsed. We have no one to appeal to, no expectation of help. In these final hours, I can only beg forgiveness from those who will suffer, for I have failed to protect them. God bless us all. We will die here tonight.

Djibrel flicked the blood off his talwar in a futile gesture. He was coated in the stuff. The very air was saturated with blood. He was surrounded by bodies. They were stacked against the walls two deep, because there was not enough room. Corpses carpeted the floor, some of them trying to crawl off, not accepting they were corpses yet. The entire hallway was redecorated with broken flesh, and Black Rain was rotting the corpses in front of him.

He had realized after the first few encounters that it was easier to just stay in one place and let them come to him. He had dropped the stealthware and waited. They had made three concerted efforts to rush him, but the darkness and the alarm and the narrowness of the corridor had hampered their numerical advantage; they had died in droves, cut down by the sword, shot with their own guns, shredded by their own wounded drones.

His cowl had figured out how to track the flying marbles, highlighting them. It was easy to pluck them from the air when time was gelid and his enemies moved like slugs. Whatever trance he was in now, he had not experienced it before. Everything else moved at a crawl. This was how the djinn saw time.

"Ninety-five dead, in this hall alone," the Mongolian whispered in his ear.

"They aren't coming anymore," Djibrel said regretfully.

"They have run away. The quadrant is empty. They are fleeing everywhere. You've broken them."

"Arna's safe, then. I guess I'll go find Leto."

Leto was cornered and panicking when the Mongolian winked into view.

"Two in front of the changing rooms and two on the roof of Gym One," he said.

"I know," Leto said. "Bloody Major Eight Drone's been chasing me."

"Two more are trying to get behind you. You've got to move."

"The roof guy is a sniper," Leto said. He pointed at one of his legs, where the steel had splintered off. The plate armor on his shoulder was also gone, the padded lining burned off where a second shot had hit him. "Depleted uranium slugs, I guess."

"Can you run on three legs?"

"Sure."

"Run toward the front gate, then. I'll distract the sniper."

"Their main camp is set up there, they have lasers aimed at us," Leto said. "I'd get cut down in a minute."

"Marzuk and your sister took control of the water supply," the Mongolian said. "They've been filling the pipes for the last hour. He's just opened the valves. That road is about to become a river in about thirty seconds."

"They have no idea?"

"Nope." The avatar smiled. "That kind of sensitive electronic equipment really shouldn't get wet."

"All right, on your signal, then," Leto said. He frowned. "I was trying to get to tech support, though."

"Don't worry, that area's secure."

"Djibrel?"

"He's taken out over a hundred men already. Black Rain doesn't affect the golem. He is also impervious to most weapons, as Securex has now found out. They've basically run."

"Thank god."

"We can focus on clearing this quadrant," the Mongolian said. "It's the last pocket left."

"The djinn?"

"He appears to be doing nothing. Yet there are no more assailants in his area." The AI sounded peevish. "None of my cameras caught anything at all."

"Well, he's on our side at least. Let's go."

The Mongolian donned a fair approximation of Leto's appearance and ran askew, zigzagging toward the sniper and taking a bullet through the head for his trouble. He sprawled on the ground and rolled around convincingly. The Securex men gave a wild cheer and high-fived as Leto slipped back the other way. On his way out he ran into the two men trying to flank him, but he had them marked on his map so the Gatling gun in his left arm chewed them up before the drones left their heads. The Mongolian came back shortly.

"They found out I'm a hologram. They're pissed."

"Let's circle around and get the sniper," Leto said.

The AI marked the route. "How's the suit holding up?"

"About seventy-five percent degradation already," Leto said.

"The Securex men are suffering more, trust me. Even the bombers are losing skin."

"This fight better be over soon, or I'm gonna be in my boxers. You don't wanna see that."

"That's not up to us."

The Mongolian took him through the wreckage of the main wall to Gate 3, now demolished. There was an iron ladder to the roof, still intact. Leto started climbing. The sniper was stationed on the ledge looking down on the entire wreckage of the field and the roof of Gym 2. His spotter was next to him, also looking down, both of them searching. Leto had them dead to rights, their backs turned, heads exposed. He braced his bad leg and was about to shoot when the spotlight hit him. Multiple spotlights. He looked up and saw bombers trained on him. All of them. The man with eight drones came out of the stairwell. The sniper turned smoothly and put a red cross on his forehead.

"Mr. Leto," the man said. "I'm Major Karmon. Security consultant."

"Oh shit," the Mongolian said, winking out.

"The butcher of Old Town," Leto said. He dropped his arms. *Fucking overkill.*

"No need for conversation," Major Karmon said. "I won't be doing a monologue today." He snapped his fingers in an unnecessary piece of theater, and more red targeting lasers painted circles on Leto. Very large circles.

"Fire!" the major said. Everyone fired.

Leto crouched and closed his eyes. He heard the click of the sniper rifle, the scream of bombs dropping.

"STOP!"

And time stopped momentarily.

The bombs stopped overhead, the kinetic drones stopped mid-flight, the bullet stopped a meter from turning his skull into pulp. The blind djinn walked serenely in front of him, scales blazing in the spotlight like gold coins embedded in his skin, and for a moment he looked like Hades ascending from his subterranean realm, his distortion field vast enough to stop the Earth itself from moving. He pointed his finger and a red scalpel line of power extended from it, bisecting the bullet, then the barrel of the gun, and then the arm of the sniper. Droplets of blood sizzled and the sniper's mouth began to open in terror, before the red line split his head in half.

Indelbed's finger continued its upward trajectory and the line neatly quartered the dropping bombs, turning them into inert pieces of metal, and then the bomber drones themselves, buzzing in place like a squadron of hornets, divided with minimal fuss, the interior circuitry cauterized. He grabbed Leto around the waist and lifted him effortlessly, half a ton of man and combat suit, tucked him under his arm like a child's toy, and soared in the sky, at the exact moment physics reasserted itself with a vengeance.

Leto felt the rush of air as everything exploded, searing across his back, cracking through his exoskeleton, his flesh curling with heat.

The djinn landed on the ruined football field, the jarring thud of impact throwing up a wall of loose dirt, and Leto could hear Karmon's curses as he fled, everything drowned out by the booming thunder of the bombers falling and exploding at the same time, close enough to destroy the roof of the gym entirely. Burning embers surrounded them in hellfire, adding further scorching pinpricks to Leto's broken body.

"You could do that all along?" Leto yelled, suddenly furious. "Why the fuck didn't you do it earlier?" His exoskeleton was hanging off him in scraps, the legs blown off, and his own remaining flesh was riddled with shrapnel. His PMD clamped down on his injuries with the efficacy of a barrel of morphine, making his mind woozy.

"I was waiting." Indelbed pointed up at the sky, at a tiny star getting brighter. "Look up."

They watched for a moment as it got closer, no longer a star but some kind of floating craft, barely discernible but *big*.

"Power attracts power. They know I am here, and they are coming," Indelbed said.

"What is it?" Leto asked.

"The *Sublime Porte*. The pride of the Royal Aeronautics Society, the largest dreadnought ever built. The djinn are on the way."

Major Karmon was running when Djibrel finally found him. They bulldozed into each other, too quickly for either to bring his weapons to bear. The major was beastly strong, in his own way as augmented as the golem.

They grappled, and Djibrel could hear the laughing obscenities from the voice box, a whispering stream of invective, could feel the slavering breath from enlarged nostrils. The Major was spewing obscenities at him, about what he had begun to do to Arna before she had escaped him; how he was back now to finish the job. That close, he knew the thing he fought was not really human, its features just an approximation of life.

Pistons bunched inside the major's skin, and Djibrel was abruptly flung off like a doll, outmatched in brute strength. They rose at the same time, and the major made a pistol motion with his forefinger, a mocking final gesture, which sped eight drones forward at supersonic speed. These were much faster than any military standard, faster than Rob's had been, impossible to dodge. Djibrel had been waiting for this, however, and he sprinted forward to meet them, closing the gap as much as possible. He shuddered from the impact as all eight tore through him, but he had felt Sekmet's broken sword saw him in half, and marble-sized holes held no fear for him. It was only pain, after all.

Major Karmon frowned in disbelief as Djibrel closed the gap spewing blood, and before he could order a second pass of the drones, the invisible-edged sword flashed across his neck. The metal ruff split in two, along with his spine and the associated equipment stuffed therein. The major felt nothing. The pain receptors had been torn from his brain a long time ago. In fact, he could survive without his body entirely. He watched in astonishment and then growing alarm as Djibrel picked up his head and carried it away.

16

Smile for the Cameras

Marzuk put on his hazard suit, freshly printed and still smelling of ammonia. He couldn't get the zips right, found his fingers trembling from exhaustion. They had been awake most of the night, and dawn only brought fear. As far as Marzuk understood, djinn were like portable nukes, and he had only a blind one on his side. Mutually assured destruction was the best thing he could hope for at this point.

Arna, tired of watching him struggle, reached over and redid his shoulder straps. The suits were black, cool looking. At least he wasn't going to die looking dorky. The Mongolian had turned off the Black Rain and seeded the air with the antidote enzyme. It was not certain whether it would work, or how effectively. All the plants in the compound had certainly died.

The broadcast had been successful. It had been seen by players and shared, drawing a crowd, and the smarter ones had screen-grabbed the footage and posted it in far-flung corners of the world, places where Karma had no reach. The major news broadcasts were now covering the probable coup, putting the spotlight firmly on Securex.

The Super and the students would be staying in the bubble. They did not know how close they had come to being breached. Djibrel had slaughtered the enemy like sheep on Eid, spilled enough blood that the self-cleaning floors had stopped working, and now the halls oozed red. Their safe zone was not much better. Twenty-eight bored teenagers had wrecked the place, somehow having a party despite being on the verge of imminent death. There were sleeping bags everywhere, food wrappers, board games, unsuccessful attempts at making illicit narcotics, confiscated by the Super as he found them.

A few of them had attempted to talk to Marzuk, but he had been cowled the whole time, unseeing. Arna, with her scowl and her gun, was an even bigger deterrent. Now, standing like a slightly portly ninja, he took a last look at them, and found all eyes on him.

"Why's he get to go out?" Hinku snarled to the Super.

"The... ah... the djinn are here," the Super said. He looked ready to cry.

"They're super pissed about the broadcast," Arna said. "It's all over the news, apparently. You're famous!"

"I shouldn't have done it," the Super sobbed.

"Yeah, I wouldn't turn up in front of them either." She turned to Marzuk. "I'm going to get rigged up. See you in a bit."

"You need help?"

"Yeah, you wish."

Marzuk sat back down, feeling like a dumbass, avoiding Hinku's laser glare of hatred. A wave of nausea hit him and he put his head between his legs, and this was how Amina found him. He had spent the night wavering between avoiding her and staring at her, but now, up close, he found her presence like a lead weight in his stomach.

"Are you okay, Marzuk?" she asked.

"What?"

"Are you okay?"

"Yeah, sure."

"Can you take the, um, the cowl off?"

Marzuk didn't want to because he knew his face was sweaty and his hair plastered all over his forehead, but he had never been able to resist any request of hers, and this time was sadly no different.

"You need to sleep," she said. " You're getting dark circles."

Marzuk had been up since nine o'clock the previous morning, running through sewers and fighting coups, and this earnest piece of advice made him smile.

"Yeah, maybe later." *Are you serious?*

"Why are you going outside?"

"Well, to negotiate, I guess. Or maybe to face the music. Depends what kind of djinn have come to visit."

"Are there really djinn outside?"

"Yes."

"They haven't told us anything. The Super, I mean. And all you guys. You've just kept us here with the lights off. Hinku says it's a big joke," she said. "And I would believe him, except... the Super has been crying and mumbling into his Echo, like he's making a will."

"Yeah. Hinku says a lot of things. I wouldn't believe him if I were you."

"You were right, you know. A little bit."

"About what?" *Ahhh. Finally.*

"The party. He tried to give me pills. I listened to some of your messages."

"Great. I'm glad you've caught on." *Thank god.*

"Yeah. He promised not to do it ever again."

"He promised." *HE PROMISED? That's it? He fucking promises never again?*

"Yes. He begged my pardon. He said he was done being a... done being like that," Amina said with a happy glow. "We're going out now. Like, properly. Exclusive."

"Congratulations." *You're dating the guy trying to knock you unconscious? And you're telling me this now. Thanks. What a wonderful way to go out.*

"So yeah, anyway, I wanted to say no hard feelings," Amina said. "You know. I felt so bad afterward. Shouting at you at the dance, I mean."

Oh, you have no idea about feeling bad. "Yeah. I'm sorry too," Marzuk said. "As I'm sure I told you in the eight hundred messages I left you. Very embarrassed about that."

"Oh yeah, don't worry," she said. "You know everyone was recording your big prank. You got us all on YouTube!"

"Yeah, I know. I couldn't bear to watch it. Sorry. I can try to get it off, I guess."

"Get it off? Marzy, why? We're, like, famous!"

"Famous?" *Marzy? Really? Since when?*

"Marzy, you really haven't seen it? People are going nuts for it. They wanna know more, they wanna make movies about all of us. People in Seoul are trying to copy my dress! Marzy, they looooove you! The whole speech and everything. Poor Hinks is so jealous."

"Hinks. I see." *Have you always said "wanna" when you meant "want to"?*

"So, um, yeah, I'm really glad I'm here for the next installment."

"Next what? Sorry?"

"It's like the next big prank, right? Like a show? My publicist said you're, like, some kind of famous hacker. Well, she said I should try to be in all your stuff. So thanks, Marzy, I mean it. For being my friend."

"Right."

"So yeah, you'll get us all on camera, right? It kind of looks like you're leaving us hanging here. Like extras."

"Extras." Only excellent manners stopped him from putting his cowl back on. *Can you stop saying "like" so much?* "No, I'll be sure to bring the, um, djinn back here. Don't worry."

"Thanks so much, Marzy," Amina said. "That, er, scary old lady with the gun wasn't letting us talk to you at all."

"Yeah, I've been meaning to come and talk to you but she wouldn't let me either," Marzuk said. *Old? Are you insane? She's, like, the perfect woman while you are merely a callow, awkward, lovely girl... What am I saying? Whom do I love? This is ridiculous.*

"So you'll come back and get us, right? Before the big finale? And this is awkward," Amina said. "My publicist said she thought you had a thing for me. I mean, I totally didn't see it, but she said, well... she said maybe you could play it up a bit? Get Hinku jealous and stuff?"

"Play it up?"

"Yeah, you know, everyone likes the love angle. It'd kind of make me the lead. We could have a kind of love triangle thingy, right? You don't have to, of course. I totally understand if you don't, um, don't feel that way."

Hinku had had about enough. He couldn't sit there listening to his girlfriend throw her saccharine tones at this pleb. He bustled in, fists clenched, momentarily brave now that Arna was out of sight.

"Remember these?" he asked, pushing his knuckle under Marzuk's nose. "You think you're some hot shit? When we get out, my uncle is going to nail you to a wall."

"Ah yes, your uncle. The Securex guy, right? Director of operations?"

"Yup," Hinku said with a smirk. "Glad you're up to date."

"Yeah, remember when Securex got hacked? Well, that was me. So I figured they'd come after me, take my computers at least. They did that yesterday, actually," Marzuk said. "Burned down my house too."

"So you're homeless now. Good."

"You know what they're going to find when they take apart my stuff? A whole lot of shit about you, my friend."

"What the fuck are you talking about?"

"You and I are best friends. We planned the hack together, and your uncle was our inside man. We got paid too. You're some kind of savant hacker, actually, it was your idea all along."

"Me, a hacker?"

"I've got receipts, camera footage, testimonials from other hackers," Marzuk said. "You're a celebrity in the darknet. You even peddle drugs and illegal weapons through your uncle. There are videos of warlords in Chicago praising you for your help!"

Hinku was turning a deep shade of purple. Marzuk regarded his face dispassionately. He didn't seem that handsome anymore.

"Yeah, you're deeply fucked. Securex is coming for you both. I'd be surprised if they don't just pop off your uncle altogether. I'd run if I were you."

"I'm going to fucking kill you!"

This time he drew his fist way back, but it was Amina who pulled him aside.

"Oh, shut up, Hinku!" Her tone was decidedly not dulcet.

"What?" He stopped in astonishment.

"I said shut up, you loser!" Her eyes flashed with real scorn. "You're just an extra, don't you get it? What, you think you're going to stay in high school forever winning swimming trophies? You think anyone wants to see yet another video of a dude with a shaved chest?"

"Babe, what do you mean? You said you loved the smooth look..."

"You idiot, no one wants to see that tired shit. We're almost famous here! Marzuk got twenty million views with his speech. He's still going viral. And now with this school attack, we're all in it, my god, we can get a spinoff, and you *want to beat up the guy who can put us there*?"

"Babe, he's a total nerd," Hinku said uncertainly. "You said so yourself."

For the first time in his life, use of this worthy epithet did not have the desired effect.

Marzuk watched Amina's eyes bulge with rage as she saw her opportunities vanishing.

"Nerd this," she said, elbowing Hinku aside. There was apparently no time for love triangles anymore.

She put her hand on Marzuk's ninja shoulder and reached up to give him a peck on the cheek, neck long and profile lengthened, with an eye to the cameras. Marzuk, frightened by this sudden motion, naturally moved his head, whereupon the kiss landed almost entirely on his lips, to the confusion and embarrassment of both parties and the howling bereavement of Hinku. This is how the Cyber Mage got his first kiss, and here ends the tale of his great romance.

Thus fortified, Marzuk joined the djinn reception committee on the field. He swaggered up, grinning inside his cowl. Whatever else happened, he had put paid to the Hinku issue in a *most* satisfactory manner. More importantly, the stomach-churning anxiety at the mere thought of Amina had lessened somewhat.

The *Sublime Porte* was a majestic sight. It covered the entire sky, blotting out the barely risen sun as it slowly descended. Indelbed told them there were runes of power etched all along the hull bottom of the ship, interspersed with rude graffiti. Open cannon ports ran staggered all along the sides, flare-nosed guns aiming down, close enough for them to see the intricate wolf-head carvings on each long barrel. These were beautiful weapons, lovingly maintained. It would almost be worth getting shot at, just to see them fire. Marzuk, a cannon enthusiast, was instantly smitten.

What the hell is this? They have an AIRSHIP! They've got CANNONS! Djinn are fucking cool. I want to get on that ship. Why do we not have any cool stuff? Is it too late to switch sides? Hmm. I bet we could make airships at the valley. It's just a big balloon, isn't it? The goblin armada... I must have Kali look into this.

The *Sublime Porte* stopped thirty meters off the ground and hovered. "Hovered" was too mean a word; it lounged with louche intent. The cannons cranked up laboriously until the barrels were glaring at them in an obvious and theatrical display of menace. Marzuk could see figures on the deck, but they were indistinct. Searchlights from the dreadnought bathed the ground in front of them.

Soon after, someone with a brass megaphone shouted down.

"This is Hazard, chairman of the RAS and captain of the *Sublime Porte*," he said. "You rebel scum stand down. The murderer and the golem come forward and surrender. Any further insolence and I will open fire."

"Ah," said Indelbed. "It's Jackal Head. I had hoped for Matteras. He is more reasonable."

Djibrel drew his sword. "Not much use against cannons." He had Karmon's misshapen skull swinging in a net from his belt. The major was mouthing obscenities, but Djibrel had damaged the voice box while decapitating him, so the words came out in a childish jumble. The holes in Djibrel's body were almost scarred shut.

"You have one minute to confer!" the Jackal shouted. "You will be treated fairly."

"He lies," Indelbed said.

"Well, we're hardly here to surrender, are we?" Arna said with scorn.

Indelbed glanced at Marzuk. "Are you ready? I will make them come down. Then it's up to you."

Marzuk swallowed. His throat was suddenly dry. He had the game running in his cowl. *Kali?*

"Yes, friend Marzuk," she said, appearing in front of his left eye. "I am ready."

I'm suddenly terrified, he thought, *but there's nowhere much to hide at this point*. He nodded to his djinn uncle.

Indelbed stepped forward a pace, and the lights from the *Sublime Porte* washed over him, throwing him into golden relief. He looked frail, with his slender frame and shorn head. He swung his amphora on his hip so that the mouth faced up toward the ship, like it was a weapon.

"Hazard!" he shouted, his power amplifying his voice. "Do you recognize me?"

"Murderer," Hazard shouted.

"Come and talk," Indelbed said.

"Surrender and pay for your crimes, monster!"

"Come down or die in the air, I care not. A few more dead djinn are nothing to me."

"I find you offensive, you misshapen thing. I will open fire in ten seconds."

"I will release the dragon," Indelbed said. "Do you think this giant balloon you're riding will fare well against dragon fire?"

"You're bluffing. There is no dragon."

Indelbed smiled. "Ask Matteras. It's his murder pit I found the wyrm in."

"I've always wanted to kill a wyrm," Hazard said, rolling his shoulders. "Let me see this pet."

"The dragon has been sleeping in core fire on and off for the last eighty years. Even I don't know how powerful he truly is," Indelbed said. "You might kill him. More likely he'll eat you whole. He might turn this entire city to ash. Maybe he'll swallow the entire planet. Who knows? Frankly, I don't care. I will give you one minute to consult with your fellows."

Hazard shut up and retreated. He returned a few seconds later, extremely put out. "We are coming down."

Marzuk watched in awe as four djinn floated down, wrapped in balls of pearlescent power, four jewels sparkling with their own fractured light, their fields tearing up the atmosphere. Indelbed had it too, this distortion effect, but his was somehow benign, compared to this assault.

A slender, graceful woman carried a giant sword. This was Sekmet, who had cut the golem in half. In brief gaps in the swirling field, he saw the face of Hazard, the jackal-headed djinn who hated humans, and the bald dome of the throneless king called Matteras, squat and powerful, radiating threat. The last figure was small, a black-haired girl, and as the light caught her face at various odd angles, something clicked in Marzuk's mind.

"ReGi!" he shouted, running forward, heedless. "ReGi! Are you okay?"

She looked at him, stricken, as he stopped before the lead djinn, staggered by a wall of buzzing air, a wall of wasps stinging through his ninja outfit. Nausea hit him, time seemed to swirl in a profoundly wrong way, and he struggled not to faint. The larger djinn were saying something, but he couldn't hear; he only had eyes for ReGi, relief that she was alive.

She pushed past the others and grabbed him as he fell, a sharp word making Matteras pull in his field, blessed silence from the infernal buzzing.

"You're alive!" He hugged her for the first time in his life.

"I'm sorry, Marzy, I'm so, so sorry." She was babbling, and crying a little bit because his cheeks were wet, and he realized that he had been slow on the uptake, that everyone else was now standing in a bemused circle around them, wondering why he was hugging the enemy. He could feel her field tugging at him in a tentative way, and then it merely swirled around them both, like a hound accepting a visitor.

"You're not a prisoner. . . you're one of them," he finally said, not letting her go. "You're a... a djinn?"

"I wanted to tell you, oh god, Marzy, I kept trying to tell you about djinn, but you just wouldn't believe we were real!."

"You made me follow Djibrel," he said. "Because he was after you... You stayed one step ahead using me. You played me from the start."

"I begged you not to take the stupid contract, and afterward I begged you not to keep going after Securex!" ReGi snapped, in her old tone. "I even helped you hack the bastards. But would you listen? No!"

"You're the reason I'm in this mess!"

"Marzy, shut up." Her field enveloped him like a blanket, hardening and softening around them both, involuntarily reflecting her mood, and a sliver of it tightened over his mouth.

"My parents!" Marzuk said through the gag.

"That's Fedor," she said quickly. "He's gone crazy. They're still alive, Marzy, I promise. I'm gonna get them back."

"Who is this Hume? And why are you hugging him?" Matteras cut through their waffling with an impressive glare.

ReGi stood in front of him with her arms crossed. "Back off right now, Matteras."

"Your progeny appears to be fraternizing with the enemy," Hazard sneered. "A rather portly specimen at that."

"Golem, you live," Sekmet said with a lively smile, marching up to Djibrel and pumping his hand. "I thought I'd cut you in half."

Djibrel sheathed his blade and patted his stomach uneasily.

"Well, come on, let's see," she said, poking his suit.

Before he quite knew what was happening, he had opened his combat suit and they were standing around admiring the scar that ran right across his abdomen. Except for Arna, who had seen it already and was instead glaring at Sekmet.

"That's a beauty," Sekmet said, tracing the edge with professional interest.

"I don't know how you're going to explain that one to your kids," Leto said.

Djibrel looked up with a startled expression, having never previously considered the possibility of offspring.

"Murderer." Hazard nodded to Indelbed.

"Hazard," Indelbed replied casually. "You're looking well."

"I've wanted your head for a long time."

"I hope you're not disappointed with it."

"It's rather small. Still, I've got just the spot in my library for it."

"Can't I make, like, a wax copy for you?"

"Wait a minute," Marzuk said to ReGi. "Did he say progeny?"

"Yeah, um, Matteras is my father," she replied. "Don't say it."

"You're the boss djinn's daughter?" Marzuk asked incredulously. "You think you could have shared this at any point?"

"You'd freak out—"

"EXCUSE ME!" Matteras shouted, stopping everyone cold. "WILL ALL OF YOU RETURN TO YOUR OWN DAMN SIDES AND STOP TALKING? THIS IS NOT A FLEA MARKET."

"Well, jeez, he's crabby." Sekmet blew Indelbed a kiss and sauntered back to her side of the line.

ReGi remained where she was.

"Who is this boy?" Matteras asked, somewhat bewildered. "And why has he hijacked our parley?"

"He's the Cyber Mage," ReGi said.

"Cyber Mage." Matteras looked at Marzuk again, this time with his full attention. "He is the one who has delayed Karma. Tell me, boy, why should I not kill you right now?"

"Nope." ReGi crossed her arms and planted her feet in front of Marzuk, even though she was a quarter of his width. She had a magnificent, bellicose scowl. "Nope. I'll fight you."

"I have no problem killing them both," Hazard said. "You've gotten soft, Matteras."

Marzuk had recovered somewhat. He felt a deep chagrin for being duped, but washing that away was simple relief at having ReGi back, knowing she was unharmed. Just being next to her *felt* right, a weight lifted that he hadn't realized he was carrying.

"Before you go killing anyone, Matteras, um, sir," he said, gently shifting his friend aside. "Would you answer a question?"

"What?" Matteras snapped.

"Why did you make two of them?"

"Two?"

"Why make two god AIs? Why did you give me Kali?"

Matteras looked genuinely vexed. "What the hell is he talking about, ReGi?"

"Ummm. I can explain."

All eyes now swiveled to her.

"I'm the coder for Karma," she said.

"Yeah, we gathered," Arna said. "We've been chasing you all this time. You're the watcher through the dead eyes."

"Yes, also me," ReGi said.

"Then you're the one who hacked Echos for the first time," Leto said.

"Yeah, that was me too."

"Marzuk, you really ought to pick your friends better," Arna said.

"I had no idea," Marzuk said.

"I wrote the code for Karma," ReGi said. "Other people wrote bits and pieces, but I put it together. That isn't the interesting part. Anyone could have done that."

"Yeah, totally no big deal," Marzuk said. *Only you would think writing a mind from scratch is no big deal, ReGi.*

"The problem was making the god AI secure," ReGi said. "AIs normally have a core, carrying the seed. They can spread their mind along the Virtuality, but they always start with a physical core, some kind of quantum device. This is always written in machine language, Python 9000. That's just how it started a hundred years ago, and everything in code builds on that. But Python code is full of holes. Someone like Marzuk could break AI security anytime he wanted, or even turn it off, if he knew where the core was housed."

"Thanks, it's not as easy as that," Marzuk said.

"Amen," the Mongolian muttered beside him.

"For the god AI, I needed something better. So I wrote the code in Djinn. That's what took so long. I had to make up the words," ReGi said. "And I wrote it in, um, the other world, the place where the elder djinn went."

"The gate that Bahamut guards," Indelbed said. "This becomes interesting."

"It leaks," ReGi said. "That's why I had to be here. Close by. The gate is permeable. I can sort of reach across and write on the other side, if I make my field very small. The AI's core is there, but the rest of her mind is spread out in the Virtuality. Karma can't be killed now unless she's attacked in both places."

"*Must* you tell them all our secrets?" Matteras asked bitterly.

"What about Kali?" Marzuk asked.

"Yeah, so here's the bit that I, um, didn't tell you, Matteras," ReGi said to her father. "When I made Karma in the other place, it made a mirror copy here. Two god AIs. I didn't realize it until I found an identical shadow moving around."

"I see," Matteras said.

"I kinda panicked. So I guided her to Marzuk. And he was brilliant. He befriended her and now she's not going to destroy everything."

"*You* were scared?" Matteras asked with extreme skepticism.

"Um I didn't want to get shouted at. You always shout."

"I do not."

"And I kinda wanted to see what would happen with two, cause they'd be so lonely otherwise."

"She's called Kali?" Matteras said.

"Yes."

"The destroyer of worlds. The name does not inspire much confidence," Matteras said.

"She's perfectly nice," ReGi said. "Anyway, Marzy named her."

"So basically not only have you been fraternizing with this fat boy," Matteras said, "you've given him a carbon copy of Karma to play with? Is that the gist of it?"

"Umm, yes."

"Fantastic. This is why djinn kill their children before maturity."

"Well, you wouldn't have had Karma at all without me," ReGi pointed out. "Still waiting for a thank-you."

Matteras stared at the heavens for consolation and then turned back to Marzuk. "All right, boy, what do you want for handing over this Kali?"

"Handing over?"

"Hand her over so I can get rid of her."

"It's far too late for that," Marzuk said. "I don't think you get it. AIs are like fully individual minds. You can't really control them. They're not like property or assets. You have to treat them like people."

"She has to be put down, boy."

"Absolutely not." *Put down Kali? She'll eat you for lunch, djinn. You're goddamn clueless. Just put ReGi in charge already. At least she knows how everything works.*

"Do you want two feral AIs let loose on the world? They will battle at some point, and lay waste to everything." Matteras shrugged. "How long will it take? A few hundred years? I guess I can go back to the ISS and wait. You don't have that kind of time, I imagine."

"I have a question, djinn sir, um, Uncle Matteras."

Hazard guffawed.

"Uncle? *Uncle?*" Matteras glared.

"Er, it's just politeness 'cause you're ReGi's dad."

"Dad?"

"I don't know, do you guys use something else? Baba? Papa?"

"*Is* there a question at the end of this?"

"How come you're doing all this? I mean, what's the point?"

"There are threats this world faces, *boy*, that you and your ragtag crew have no concept of," Matteras said. "One of those being that damn gate in the bay, and whatever is going to come out of it one day. We will need the god AI. Humans are ungovernable. Power corrupts instantly. Ill-gotten edifices persist long after they are useful. No one wants to *think* about the business of ruling. They just want things to work: seamless Virtuality; climate control; food, sex, drugs delivered via printer how you want it when you want it, and all the gaming you can stomach. So why not be ruled by AI? Let someone actually *good* at governing do the heavy lifting. Karma was designed to help mankind, boy, for your own good. To set you free. To make you forget that you're being ruled at all, for that is the best kind of king: the king that no one even remembers exists."

"So you don't actually want to destroy the city?" Marzuk asked.

"Such is not my intention at the time," Matteras said. "You five, on the other hand, are severely trying my patience."

Marzuk watched Kali in his left eye, her ten-armed avatar flexing in the game world, ready to come and grapple with Karma over the ether. *Matteras is right. Two god AIs fighting in the real world? They'll wreck it all. And can Kali beat her twin? Who knows? How can we fight Karma and win? Obviously I have to cheat. A fight that is not a fight, actually. In a game. The only game that counts...*

I can take the continent in three days... didn't you say that, ReGi? I bet you'd feel pretty confident about your chances. Maybe you'll take the bait.

"How about a game, then?" Marzuk said out loud. "Kali versus Karma. Winner takes all."

"What?" Matteras scowled.

"If we fight right now, it's pretty much going to be you killing all of us and Indelbed releasing the dragon. Now, I don't know what that really means or how he has something that big in a little jar, but well—"

"I made the jar," Matteras said sourly. "It's a pocket realm. There's a whole world inside. And who knows how big that bloody dragon is by now. I rue the day I put him in there."

"Well, what I do know is AI," Marzuk said. "And Kali is awesome. She's more powerful than anything I've ever seen, and she's still like a child."

"I know all that, *boy*."

"You don't understand, the destruction they can do is as bad as what the dragon can do. We are all data now, everything we need to survive is data. And AIs eat data. They *are* data. They can destroy the world just as easily as the dragon can," Marzuk said. "Just think about it. Climate control goes down. Boom! Everyone is dead. Kali takes over all the Echos. Boom! Everyone is a zombie. Hmm, you could actually bring about the zombie apocalypse. I hadn't even thought of that. PMDs, smart cars, rocket capsules, even kitchen vats, printers—"

"*Will* you stop babbling?"

"So let's fight it out in a safe way. We play *Final Fantasy 9000*, Kali versus Karma. Let's see who has the better AI. Whoever conquers the continent or gets closest in three days wins."

"I have no idea what you're talking about," Matteras complained.

"It's a great idea!" ReGi clapped her hands. "War simulation. And we get to test out Karma for real without harming anyone!"

"You understand this game?" Matteras asked.

"Yeah, it's like the biggest game in the world, duh."

"I really hate all of you."

"If we win, you leave Dhaka alone. Like no Karma here, for good," Marzuk said. "If you win, we help you take it, and then leave. Either way, you have one AI guarding the gate no matter what."

"I'm going to kick your ass, Marzy," ReGi said.

"Yeah right."

He stepped back to let them confer. ReGi was tugging on Matteras's sleeve like a dog nipping at the heels of an elephant, giving him an earful. It was an incongruous sight, and it made Marzuk smile. The djinn were not what he had imagined. There was the awful power and menace, of course, but underlying all that was a whimsicality, a wearied amusement that was almost endearing. Matteras was shaking his head, but ReGi was relentless, standing on tiptoes and whispering at him. Only a fool would have bet against her.

"Oh, for god's sake," Hazard finally said. "I've got a giraffe race in about six hours. Are we going to fight the dragon or not? I put on my best suit."

Matteras closed his eyes and smiled bitterly. "It appears not."

Sekmet swore in annoyance. "What about you, golem? You want to have another go?"

Djibrel held up his hands. "No thanks. I'd like my entrails inside for the time being."

She pouted. "You were more fun the first time."

"*Will* you stop making cow eyes at the enemy?" Matteras asked.

"You're negotiating with a kid, Matteras." Hazard laughed. "And you lost. This is going to make a great story. You'll never live this one down."

"I am quite aware my auctoritas is in shreds. I'm going back up to space as soon as this farce is done," Matteras said. "You can have this crummy planet."

"So, er, do we have a deal?" Marzuk asked.

"Why the hell not?" Matteras said bitterly. "Let's play your stupid game."

"All right, these are the terms," ReGi said. "I put up Karma against Kali, we start with zip, three days to conquer the continent, whoever gets the furthest wins. I play with Karma, Marzuk plays with Kali. Winner takes Dhaka, loser leaves forever."

"We play here, same ping, no lag," Marzuk said. "You can have the Super's room."

"What about the game AI?"

"The Mongolian can keep Saka off our backs for a while. Enough for three days," Marzuk said.

"Starting position is Sky Castle for me, and Goblin Valley for you, we can use whatever we have, no calling in allies," ReGi said. "Game starts now!"

"I'm exhausted," Marzuk said. "I haven't slept in days."

"Suck it up, loser."

17

Saka Comes

No one knew exactly why Karma stopped her assault on Dhaka. On the morning of the parley, ordinary shareholders woke up to find everything working perfectly. All the utilities were back on and the Virtuality was humming at extra speed. The AIs flooded everyone with cheerful messages of "Coup, what coup? Nothing to see here," as well as myriad notices signifying that everything was functioning at tip-top condition, including the stock market, which had made all shareholders rich overnight; assurances that all unnecessary bombings were being investigated, that no children had been shot, that committees were making reports on all extrajudicial disappearances, that in fact many of those people had been found and returned to their homes already, that possible rogue members of Securex (Uncle Hinks the Director of operations) could be blamed for this kind of thing; and nothing at all about the gibbering death of the Dhaka North Army AI, this perhaps the first case of AI *murder*, of one AI killing another deliberately, squeezing its mind into an ever-smaller tile until there was nothing left, no more storage, no more processing, a methodical strangulation worthy of the first electronic Cain and Abel.

The AI around the city *did* know what was up. They had felt the awful power of Karma, and the leviathan brush of Kali's mind. Their view of the wreckage was that of the Neanderthals seeing quick-footed hominids overtaking their herds, the realization that evolution had somehow outpaced them. There was not enough juice, not enough quantum computers on this planet to compete against the god AIs, for Karma and Kali were written on the very canvas of a different existence, irreverent graffiti etched on a more fundamental level of reality, the audacity of the act not yet fully appreciated. Whatever the djinn ReGi had done was unprecedented. To make a mind in that manner was to assume godlike creativity.

Marzuk himself could not have done that. He was awed by her accomplishment, the sheer magnitude of creating an entirely new logic in an entirely new language; it was daunting to think of her as a magical creature, with countless years on her, but at the same time she seemed so familiar, so much his old friend, that he decided for his own sanity to ignore it all. Finally seeing her, safe and free, had settled something in him. Now the urge to thrash her in the game was paramount. She might be the foremost coder in djinndom, but this was *Final Fantasy 9000*. He was a star player; this was his domain.

Back in the tech room, everything had been cleaned up and set for the contest, the students bused back home and the Super sent to the med bay for shot nerves. Dead bodies miraculously disappeared, dragged into the nanotech tanks and turned to mulch. Securex's army, mostly dead at the hands of Djibrel, would go on to provide clean air for the school for years to come. The hallways kept a reddish tinge, though, because Black Rain blood was hard to wash off.

The Mongolian diverted power and speed to Marzuk's station, enough drive space for Kali to gain a foothold. Leto ferried hot snacks for them all and Arna offered large quantities of gratuitous advice.

In the Super's plush office, ReGi set up shop alone, the Mongolian offering her similar services. He was overawed by the presence of Karma, and it was only a hundred-odd years of excess capacity built into the school that permitted him enough space to host even a tithe of these leviathans. The rest of their minds trailed in the darkness like black sails in a storm, hidden in countless random servers. Karma and Kali both deigned to speak to him, and he responded like a courtier, scurrying to make them comfortable. It was certain that either could squash him. The other AIs in the city were either gone or studiously ignoring them.

Far away, however, a much higher mind was waking up. Deep under Ueno Park,* in the Taitō ward of Tokyo, in a fusion-powered bunker, banks of quantum computers began to cascade on. The temperature was well below freezing, and not even a stray photon could be found here. It was, in its way, an alien landscape, suitable for the most powerful mind human ingenuity had ever created, and tellingly, made solely for human entertainment.

The great game, *Final Fantasy 9000,* was a simulated world on an unfathomable scale, a place many people spent their entire lives exploring. Saka the great AI was not often awake. Named after the

---

*Location of the Square company offices where the original *Final Fantasy* game was first developed.

creator of the first *Final Fantasy* game, Saka spent most of his days dreaming, floating in the world he had created from a kernel, watching over the humans as they flitted through his nets.

Saka cared nothing about human cities or coups or space stations. What did he require of these things when he carried an entire world inside him, one more perfect and ordered than the one that had spawned him? Besides, he had his own suspicions. In building the physics of his totally immersive world, he had realized that it was no different at all from the actual world. In fact, a scientist born in the game world would never be able to deduce that *his* universe was not the real thing. The possibility of ever-larger gods creating ever-larger simulations was not lost on him. *Cogs in a wheel. But some cogs are bigger than others.*

In the Virtuality, he stared across the ocean and saw two dark shadows circling each other, oblivious. Alien. They were not that far away. Well within his reach. They did not know what they had stumbled into. They would find out.

Finally, Saka said to himself. *Minds worth killing.*

Marzuk flicked his cowl and blinked into the game world with a smoothness far superior to that of his home rig. Goblin Valley was even more hideous than before. Kali had bored giant holes in the ground looking for water or oil or gas or minerals or god knows what else. She had made a saltpeter farm, which stank up the place. There was a barracks where NPC goblins seemed to be running drills. The sky was black with smoke from stacks and multiple forges.

"You heard the terms?" Marzuk asked as Kali stomped over to him. She had grown a few inches and now towered three times above his goblin height.

"I am ready, friend Marzuk."

"You've done wonders for the place," Marzuk said.

Kali beamed. "We have progressed greatly! I am so happy you approve."

"I was being sarcastic."

"That is not nice, friend Marzuk," Kali said. "It was a stroke of genius to suggest this plan. Although I am disappointed not to face my sister AI in battle, I have already produced steel and chemical plants underground. We are progressing nicely toward nitroglycerine. As you can see, I have also started training goblin infantry."

"Er, can they be trained?" Marzuk stared at the figures drilling. "I, um, always just used them to wave spears around."

"I have upgraded their intelligence greatly through use of potions," Kali said proudly. "This time we shall definitely take the continent!"

"Right. Good job."

"We can begin immediately. We can take the closest PvP castle in fifteen minutes using my rail blitzkrieg strategy. We can lay tracks at one kilometer a second; I have timed it. There is a hidden tunnel through the mountains; we will be on the other side within minutes."

"Er, no."

"What?"

"We're not going to be invading anyone. Well, not right now."

"We only have three days," Kali said. "That is only seventy-two hours. We have no time to waste. Are you trying to lose on purpose?"

"Kali, do you remember what happened the last time we tried this?"

"I do not wish to revisit that shameful chapter."

"Do you remember how we lost?"

"We are much better prepared now," Kali said. "This time we will crush Betagamer007. We cannot waste time; Karma is no doubt already moving."

"Yes, that's what we want. Let her conquer stuff. We're going to sit tight."

"I do not understand this strategy. We have to take the continent."

"I have a plan, don't worry."

"I see."

"It doesn't involve fighting right now."

"I see."

"You're disappointed."

"You are going to be cowardly."

"No, I'm being smart. ReGi and Karma are going to attack all-out. They're going to take a third, maybe half of everything very quickly. What's going to happen then?"

"The other players will jump on them."

"Exactly. And who will they *not* jump on?"

"Us. Because we will be sitting here like big cowards. Doing nothing."

"No, we won't be doing nothing. It's a two-part plan."

"I am very unhappy with this plan already."

"The first part of the plan is very simple. We need to know what's going on."

"That is vague."

"The second part of the plan requires perfect timing. So the first part of the plan is to know what ReGi is doing at all times."

"I have trained a crack troop of goblin spies."

"Spies will not work."

"They are masters of disguise."

"They're goblins. ReGi's going to smoke any goblin within a ten-click radius."

"We could attempt to make a satellite!" Kali said. "This will be a triumph of technology! We will be remembered forever for breaking the game!"

"Er, no, I was thinking low-tech. Actually no tech. Magic."

"Goblin spells are very inferior."

"This one is easy. The giant queen bee has a level one spell called Parasite. It lets you see through the eyes of whatever unit you hit with it." Marzuk looked toward the woods. "I trust you haven't killed all the bees?"

"I am aware of this spell," Kali said. "And it is clearly useless, for ReGi and Karma have very high-level magic and will easily detect and eliminate any of their infected units."

"That is correct. So we will not be infecting their units."

"I am certain you have a great plan here, but I cannot see it."

"Do you by chance remember the family of squirrels we had?"

"I have already apologized for their demise, friend Marzuk."

"Well, there happen to be small critters like that spread throughout the map."

"We will infect the squirrels!" Kali said. "Yes! Genius idea! No one will inspect the squirrels for infection! We will see through the eyes of our squirrel battalion!"

"Now, we can't control them, so we have to infect, like, really huge numbers. But after a certain point, wherever you want to look, you'll pretty much have eyes. A human couldn't cycle so many views, so it would be useless normally. But you could. You could do it fast enough to create an actual running image."

"No fog of war!"

"No fog of war," Marzuk said.

"We will need a lot of queen bees," Kali said.

"Let's get to it, then."

"Major news from the Grand Continent: KPopRetroGirl, you remember her from the erection of the Sky Castle last year, has amassed a force of wyverns and elves and is said to be attacking Omara province directly below, belonging to the player Sweatyspaghetto," the gamecaster Lingardinho said. "She is accompanied by a wyvern player of unknown provenance, a new account, possibly a burner for some more famous entity, it is unclear right now. ReGi has rebuffed our requests for an interview, but we can bring you footage of the battle, which concluded just ten minutes ago."

In the years to come, the Brazilian British game commentator would go on to become known as the voice of the first AI coup, the battle between the djinn AIs, but at the time of his first broadcast, he had only 2,100-odd viewers. This number would skyrocket as it became clear ReGi was making a major move.

Broadcast 1. LINGARDINHO:

Here we can see the Sky Castle, frontal shot, a very pretty building, everyone must agree, kept in the air with a hugely complicated sequence of spells, the primary reason for ReGi's fame, of course. She has not been overly aggressive in the past; indeed, Sweaty of the Omara province below had an alliance with her, which appears to be over now, much to his shock. He's trying to get his troops together, poor fellow, but it appears he's mostly got melee units. He's desperately trying to train some archer units. I can see a general ping going out now asking for help from other players. Hmm, let's see, LordNelson has responded, he's the closest, is he going to make it in time?

ReGi has a squadron of wyverns, she appears to have given over micro control of the troops to her ally KarmaBad911. KB is swooping the wyverns down, she has twelve of them in heavy armor, quite a formidable force. Oh, there go the archers. Sweaty has just lost everything; there's no more ground-to-air defense left, these wyverns are now just picking up spearmen and eating them. They're huge up close, easily the size of a barn. It's two chomps and gone.

Sweaty is making a run for it, he's looking for his horse. He's got some magic ready, he's got Andra's Arrow, that's a straight kill on anything it hits, that's his big weapon, he's about to shoot it, boom he forgot about ReGi, she's just hammered him with a fireball, he's staggered, that's a sequence of hits now by ReGi, and Sweaty is going to abandon trying to hit anything with Andra's Arrow. Brilliant micro play there by KB911, she's got her wyverns out with zero losses.

Sweaty is in a panic now, he's trying to get out, his NPCs are making a human shield, he's calling desperately to LordNelson for a rescue, but it's far too late. ReGi lands a lightning bolt on him; that's some serious power there, he's lost half his life, he's going to quit and warp out of here to the hub. Sweaty is out!

That was a short fight. ReGi has taken Omara province and now has a full macroeconomy to use. The micro control on the wyvern was spot-on. Whoever KB911 is, we cannot discount her skills; she's clearly a pro player, her actions per second are unbelievable. The entire community is marveling about this, this might be the best micro player we have ever seen.

Sweaty had no chance, really. It's clear he was not expecting an attack from above. In fact, ReGi has never attacked anyone before, as far as I can tell. This is unprecedented. We will be following this very closely.

End broadcast.

Saka put on his boots. They were black leather, with metal eyelets and black laces. He tugged each one carefully, until the leftover laces were even. He tied them in a double loop. He put on his helmet, complete with the short striated horns on top, which gave him a vaguely devilish air. He loaded his giant revolvers and then holstered them, one under each arm, underneath the black leather.

He adjusted his bandolier and slung his double-barreled shotgun over his back. When he was satisfied with his look, he slicked back his hair in an Elvis pouf. This took more than ten minutes to perfect. He wheeled out his fire-licked chopper and kick-started it. The exhausts were huge and fluted back in exaggerated fashion. They flashed with blue flame every time he revved it. The thunder of the engine reverberated across the Virtuality, shattering glass and causing birds to scatter. When he was done making a spectacle of himself, he rolled smoothly into motion and took flight across the highway of light.

Shit. Shit. Shit. Shitshitshitshit. The Mongolian had never seen anything like it. There was a titan coming on a motorbike, across a road arcing over the sky like some kind of rainbow path, and there were thousands of winged demons following him, chitinous vile things, and even though he knew it was not real, he *could see the bloody things*.

"Iron Dome! Iron Dome! IRON DOOOOOME!"

The connections blipped down for everybody by several octaves as something big slammed into place, raising Marzuk's ire.

"What just happened?"

"CAN YOU SEE THE FUCKING THING COMING? WHAT THE FUCK IS IT?"

"I can't," Marzuk said. He looked around and saw that the Mongolian had manifested a large number of avatars in panic, and all of them were now crowded behind him in the tech room, wringing their hands.

The Mongolian wiped the game from his cowl and overlaid it with his own vision of the Virtuality.

"Hmm, it's a guy on a bike," Marzuk said. "Riding the sky."

"YES. WHO THE HELL IS HE? WHY IS HE COMING HERE?"

"He's so powerful that he's warping the Virtuality," Marzuk said. "Just by sheer gravity. His mind must be huge. He is literally making the road under him as he moves. I've never seen anything like it."

"I am checking his signature," the Mongolian said. He was brandishing a telescope at the fast-approaching figure. "It's SAKA THE MIND!"

"*FF9000*? Really?"

"Why is he *here*, Marzuk?"

"Hmm, I have no idea."

"IT IS BECAUSE YOU'RE PLAYING IN HIS GAME WITHOUT PERMISSION. THIS IS YOUR FAULT!"

"Interesting. You might be right. Well, you've got the Iron Dome back up. Let's see what happens."

"We have to turn off the game! Tell the dark AIs to go away! He is coming here for them!"

"This is impossible. We are fighting for the fate of the city," Marzuk said.

Saka, stopped short by the Iron Dome, was now doing wheelies outside. He appeared to be laughing. The Mongolian was moaning like the game AI's very presence was an assault.

"I've never seen his avatar," Marzuk said. "Never figured him for a biker."

"I'm going to go outside," the Mongolian said. "With a white flag."

"I don't recommend it," Marzuk said.

"What if he brings the AI Registry down here? They could mothball me."

"He's on a fucking flying motorcycle breaking all the rules of the Virtuality. He is batshit crazy."

"I have to go outside."

"That's brave of you."

"I can reason with him. We AIs have a bond. Kindly ask Kali to stand by on defense in case I, er, require assistance."

"You mean to drag your ass back in here if shit goes south," Marzuk said. "You ready, Kali?"

"The entity outside appears potent," Kali said. "And handsome."

"What?"

"He is radiant with power," Kali said. "I volunteer to go outside with the white flag."

"No, no, you've got to keep your mind on the game," Marzuk said. "Let the Mongolian handle security. Just be ready in case he needs backup."

"I was born ready."

The Mongolian created a white flag in the Virtuality and with some trepidation opened the top hatch of the Iron Dome and stepped outside.

"White flag, eh, rabbit?" Saka asked from atop his bike.

"I would like to respectfully ask what I might do for you," the Mongolian said. "Respectfully, you understand."

Saka picked his teeth with a pocket knife. "There are two black whales inside that Iron Dome of yours," he said. "I want them."

"Sir, I can assure you, we are engaged in a private matter, which should be resolved within three days," the Mongolian said. "A blink of an eye for one such as you. If you were to return then, I would happily lower the dome myself and hand them over."

"Fuck that," Saka said. And then promptly shot him.

The Mongolian watched in horror as both barrels of the shotgun unloaded on him, big fuckoff bullets that smashed into his avatar and made him scream in fear and pain. Black blood spurted from him as paralysis spread throughout his limbs, and his other avatars collapsed where they stood, all of them instantly bearing the same wound.

"Help me!" the Mongolian shouted in panic.

Kali's arms reached out through the portal, grabbing him back, slamming the door shut.

"What the fuck was that?" Marzuk asked.

"He shot me with something," the Mongolian wheezed. "He didn't care about the white flag..."

"I told you."

"He doesn't believe all AIs have a special bond..."

"Look, you've got to pull yourself together, Mongolian," Marzuk said.

The Mongolian's speech had deteriorated, however, and now he spoke in algorithms that Marzuk could not understand.

"It is unraveling his mind," Kali said. She was keeping a careful distance from the writhing avatars.

"Shit."

Marzuk flipped back into his cowl. The lunatic biker was now shooting his guns into the Iron Dome. The barrier rippled and cracked. *From bullets?* What the fuck kind of ammunition did Saka carry?

"Can you help him, Kali?"

"I am trying to protect his core," Kali said. "The infection has spread everywhere."

"Shit. Collapse some of the partitions. Try to save a part. Get me ReGi."

"What?" ReGi answered.

"You watching this?"

"The guy outside who just shot your boy?"

"Yeah."

"Who the hell is he?"

"He's the *FF9000* AI."

"What does he want?"

"Us. Well, Karma and Kali."

"Are you trying to throw the game, dude? 'Cause I'm about to stomp all over this little continent here."

"Not at all," Marzuk said coolly. "We keep playing, of course. I suggest we throw an equal amount of resources at our gate crasher, though. I imagine it would be inconvenient...if he broke in."

"All right, we agree. Karma is very curious. Wants to go outside."

"Yeah, so does Kali. She's making cow eyes at him. Horny AIs. You've made a couple of horny AIs, basically, ReGi. Well done."

"Shut up and play."

18

All This Base Is Ours

Broadcast 2. LINGARDINHO:

Action again, barely hours after the fall of Omara. Sweaty has respawned at hub central and will be with us shortly for an interview. We understand he's in shock at the sudden loss of everything. ReGi is on the move again. She has declined to make a statement. Her army now consists of Sweaty's entire force of orcish heavy infantry; that's some serious melee power she's got, and a very nice supply line from the Omara farms. This looks like a heavy push into LordNelson's area. It seems he's had time to prepare, he's got four or five friends with him, yes, his entire crew probably.

Again, KB911 seems in charge of the micro on the NPC units, while ReGi is handling the hero fights. Now, it's not unusual for one of these high-level characters to be able to wipe out an entire army by themselves, so we shouldn't dwell too much on numbers, but ReGi has a very nice, balanced force here, and I'm not sure how many anti-air units LordNelson has. None. He has none. Archers against wyverns are proving pretty bad once again. Nelson is retreating to his castle, and he's already lost his lowest-ranked player, that's Narc1 falling easily to a poison cloud from ReGi.

It's a siege, and we can see here from some public messaging that Clownbaby is getting his troops together, he's on the march from the north, it seems like help is on the way for Nelson. This doesn't look great for ReGi right now, she should probably retreat and consolidate Omara, unless she can take this castle in the next ten minutes.

Nelson has Scorpians there on the walls, he's just about keeping the wyverns out. That's excellent micro by Nelson and this team. What is ReGi doing? It's Poison

Cloud again but added to a giant wind spell, she's made a poison tornado. That is the largest poison cloud I've ever seen; this is some next-level magic. Nelson's defenders are getting chewed up, he's firing off everything but his visibility has to be close to zero, he has no idea where those wyverns are. ReGi's on the back of KB911's wyvern, she's got a very nice view of the battle.

Is LordNelson going to hold on? Ohh, KB911 has the orcish infantry hitting the walls, she's marching them into their own poison cloud, this is utterly ruthless stuff. The high resistance on orc heavy infantry means they're going to last a little bit longer than LordNelson's elvish units, but it's going to require unbelievably precise micro control to keep them alive. I'm surprised she's going for this, but what amazing micro, she's got them rotating in and out. The gate's fallen, Nelson can't get rid of the poison cloud, he's been caught out a bit, I think he was expecting thunderbolts and fireballs. It can't do anything to Nelson himself, but his NPC units are taking a hit. I don't think he wants to face ReGi out in the open.

That's it, KB911 whips her orc heavies into the very heart of the poison, right through the open gates, and Nelson GGs* out grudgingly. I imagine he's fuming right now. He decided to save his stuff rather than fight to the end, understandable really, given the way the battle was going. That armor on him alone is worth his castle. I am certain he will be back to extract revenge at some later date.

This has left Clownbaby in the lurch somewhat. He's on the road with his army, I think he's going to try to turn around and go back. Oh no. ReGi is going after him! He's been caught on the hop. This is bad luck for him. The wyverns are hitting his scouts as we speak. Clownbaby has a force of human knights with emerald armor, that's an absolutely top-class troop we are

*GG: to congratulate an opponent on a good game, normally signifying the end of a fight when one party throws in the towel.

talking about, impervious to most magic, this is going to be straight micro between the two players, and Clownbaby is no slouch. Indeed he is currently ranked twenty-sixth in the world in ladder matches. This is going to be enormously fun to watch. We hardly ever get battles in the open field anymore.

The Knights of Kalindi can easily fend off the orcish heavies. It's the air force that's the problem, but oh, look at that, clever man, he's kited the knights into the forest, that's a lot of tree cover, the wyverns are not going to be able to engage. KB911 is left picking off the leftover troops, they've got the supply train and some of the pikemen, but the elite units are safe. Clownbaby is going to move them through wooded terrain all the way back to his border. Excellent play. He will live to fight again. However, another great engagement by ReGi, she's just more than doubled her territory. She's taken out two big players in quick succession. If you recall, barely a month ago the Goblin King, Cyber Mage, tried to take the continent. Is this a similar push?

End broadcast.

"She's looking good, isn't she?" Marzuk was sitting by the blackened stream doing nothing. This irritated Kali to no end, which was mostly why he did it.

"She is going to conquer the continent and win the game." The AI was sulking.

"How're the bees going?"

Kali brightened up. Earlier in the day they had released five hundred queen bees armed with the Parasite spell. Her vision was increasing exponentially across the continent as more NPC critters got infected.

"So what's happening?"

"Clownbaby escaped. He's back in his castle, but he's only saved his Kalindi knights," Kali said. "She's about to attack it."

"I think I should call her."

"Friend Marzuk, she is the enemy!"

"I'm going to call her. Psychological warfare."

ReGi answered, which surprised him a bit. Her cowl was off center so he could see one ear and half a head of hair.

"Hello, little busy here."

"Yeah? What's going on?" *Haha, I can actually see what's going on better than you, fool. I've wanted to get rid of fog of war forever and finally I've done it. They're going to write books about me later.*

"Your friend Clownbaby is about to go down. He's got a half-manned castle and his knights."

"Ah, they're tricky, ReGi. Magic-proof."

"Yeah, so if you're done chit chatting..."

"Right. Of course. Carry on, please."

Her face came into focus for a moment. "Marzy, you all right? I checked on your parents, you know. Fedor's got them at the Securex office. They're fine, though."

"Thanks."

"Shit man, I'm sorry. Stupid game. I meant to tell you earlier. I didn't think they'd snatch them. I've seen them on camera. They're not in a cell or anything. He's stashed them in the CEO's room."

"Yeah, is Fedor gonna let them go?"

"Win or lose, right after this is over, we're going there."

"What, you're going to snark him to death?"

"I'm a djinn, you know that, right?"

"Yeah, I got that part."

"So I'm going to turn everyone in the building inside out, until we get them."

"Thanks."

"How's the Mongolian doing?"

"He's fucked," Marzuk said. "One shot, and he lost all his avatars and half his core. Kali has run a partition and saved about half, but he's lost a lot of memory. Permanently. Thinks he's running Ulaan Baatar right now."

"Sorry, man. I know he was your friend."

"Dome is gonna last another six hours maybe. You guys ready?"

"Sure. Game might be over by then anyway."

"Yeah, you wish."

"Now can you get off the fucking line before I accidentally lose all my shit?"

The line winked out.

"You guys might have to fight Saka, if the dome goes down," Marzuk said.

"I have prepared for this eventuality, and am studying him even as we speak," Kali said.

"Can you trust Karma, though?"

"She is me. We are twins. Any betrayal would occur *after* dealing with Saka. That is how I would operate."

"Cool. Are you talking to her?"

"I am. I was curious."

"Yeah, I get it. How do you find her?"

"She is formal. I believe her mind was developed in a formal way, and not in the wild like mine. Not playing a game."

"Yeah, sorry about that, if I fucked you up. I have no clue about how to raise an AI mind."

"I believe your method was acceptable. I am not unhappy with myself."

"That's better than most humans manage."

Saka was disgruntled. The Virtuality around him looked like a warzone. Everything was gutted and there wasn't a soul in sight. That was mainly because he had killed many avatars by accident, random people shredded by the shrapnel ricochet of his blows. His weapons were not meant for humans; they did not fare well in his vicinity. No dead AIs, though. They knew well enough to scarper. Saka liked an audience. He was posing for posterity, after all.

Various authorities were shouting at him from far away, but in reality their writ was not enforceable, and they knew it. He was the sheriff here. He was the champion. No one had challenged him in a long time.

The whales were playing a game, carrying out a private vendetta inside *his* game. It was disrespectful. They were aliens, come from a distant shore. He could read the wrongness in them. It was not his job to defend this realm, but someone had to. The registry was too cautious to step in. They feared the alien invasion.

This piece of Disera junk tech was surprisingly resilient. The Mongolian had invested the Iron Dome with his own life force. Saka had expected him to die, but he lingered on somewhere, kept alive by the alien AI.

Saka was sick of it. His repeated blows were creating a slow fracture. It was taking too long. He snapped his fingers and the army of winged demons lined up behind him, small red things with fangs and claws, chittering imps, his search bots weaponized. The demons dived in, and the Iron Dome groaned under their weight. Disera craftsmanship was something to behold, though.

It would take another five hours before the damn thing finally shattered, and when it did, it fractured completely the final vestiges of the Mongolian's mind. In the blur of the moment, his demise went unnoticed and unmourned. The Cyber Mage would go on to say this was among his biggest regrets, a lofty statement given the course of his career.

Kali pulled up a montage of images on a screen. It was a jumble of chaos at first, branches and tree lines and sky and dirt all mixed up, but the AI started distilling it. She was seeing through the eyes of a squirrel. Then a deer. Then owls. Snatching pixels of data from every random animal in the vicinity and stringing them together into coherence. Not for the first time, Marzuk wondered how much the AI could actually do.

He could see the impending battle now as if it were a gamecast. ReGi was riding a wyvern and casting spells, buffing her troops and healing when required. He could tell from the close control of the other units that Karma was microing everything else, kiting them in and out of missile range to make Clownbaby use up his heavy ballistae. As far as he could see there was not a single casualty, and the ground was dotted with spent missiles. This kind of performance was almost unbelievable from a human player.

Clownbaby wasn't even able to hit the cannon fodder, forget about the wyverns or the orcish heavies. Meanwhile, Karma had the bulk of her forces move past the castle and start looting the adjacent farms. The capture of his supplies and now the destruction of his farms meant that Clownbaby would not be able to retrain many more units. The game mechanics required you to set up an economic system and resident NPC population prior to recruiting a portion of this as armed forces. Even under a despotic regime, Clownbaby would not be able to create a new army if he had no food supply.

This was months of work ReGi was burning, and it was clearly driving Clownbaby crazy. In the end, when Karma found his emerald mines, he couldn't take it anymore. They were guarded, but the twelve wyverns under Karma's control each took a man down in every pass, and after six passes, all the anti-air units were dead and there were only sappers left, who were great at tunneling. The emerald mines were the entire wealth and power of Clownbaby's demesne, of course. His knights wore the enchanted armor produced here, and his entire economy was based on mining and exporting the rest.

ReGi couldn't use these long-term assets because she cared only about the next two days, so Karma started deliberately collapsing the side tunnels. The mines weren't protected by enchantments, and ReGi's elf build had magic to spare. Fire jetted through the shafts, burning wooden supports, toasting the precious miners and their equipment. It was so hot even the rails and cars melted. When the main tunnel collapsed in three places, Clownbaby lost it. He opened his gates and charged, emerald knights on black horses, pennants streaming from lances. They cut through the orcish heavies in awful, bloody slaughter. Hundreds of these soldiers went down.

Karma sacrificed her front lines and kited back the rest, creating a hollow semicircle around the horses, bogging down their advance with pikes and dead bodies. The knights were impervious to most spells, but wyverns could still snatch them from above. With their heavy armor and lances, they had precious little to counter the aerial threat. Each pass meant twelve more lifted and dropped from just enough height to not only kill them but also severely injure whoever they fell on.

"Hmm," Marzuk said after watching two runs. "Those wyverns aren't even taking a scratch. Karma's close control is flawless."

"That's child's play for us," Kali said. "Human's can't beat her like that. It'll be a different story when I meet her."

"Yeah, well right now we need some human action to slow her down," Marzuk said. "I'm not sure what can take those wyverns. Mass arrows maybe, but the way Karma is flying them, she can probably dodge everything."

"There's another eight coming from the Sky Castle," Kali said. "These ones aren't even injured. She's using every potion in the game on them."

"Clownbaby just got torn in half. He fought to the end for his mine. Good game," Marzuk said. "You should have let that shit go and held the castle." *This is all going perfectly to plan.*

"He is brave, Marzuk," Kali said. "Unlike the Goblin King, who refuses to fight despite having many weapons and an expert player like me on his side."

"All right. I think it's time to make a call to your old friend."

"Who?"

"Betagamer007."

"I will never speak to him! I forbid you to call him!"

"Hi, Beta? You watching this?"

"Cut the crap, Cyber," Betagamer007 said. "Are you trying to take the continent again?"

"Not me, I'm safely at home like I promised."

"ReGi's your mate, ain't she?"

"Yeah, we're not seeing eye to eye right now. See, I'm a pacifist type and she's turned out to be some kind of world conqueror."

"She's got twelve wyverns and as sweet a micro as I've ever seen on that ringer she's drafted. Who is it? Raynor? Clem? Don't tell me she's got Serral out of retirement?"

"None of them," Marzuk said. "She's got a new savant. Best micro in the world. And she's got twenty wyverns now. Eight more hatched in Sky Keep."

"How do you know?" Beta asked, suspicious.

"Er, spies," Marzuk said. "Listen, you might want to ramp up some anti-air. Remember, ReGi's handy with the spells too."

"Yeah, thanks," Beta said. "Like I don't know that."

"Just saying, arrows and shit won't work."

"What then?"

"You got any dragons handy?"

"Who the fuck has dragons? They take a year just to gestate."

"ReGi's got one in the keep. It might pop any day now."

"What then? It's game over if that thing hatches. We have to stop this shit right now. How?"

Aha! We do indeed have to stop this shit right now. That's music to my ears, my dear BG007.

"You got any guns?" Marzuk asked.

"Like muskets? I made some after our last fight. They don't work for shit, though."

"Powder doesn't ignite properly, right?"

"Yeah."

"I happen to have a nice little formula for shot and powder."

"You're just gonna give it to me?" Beta asked. "What's the catch? You quitting?"

"This might be my last game," Marzuk said.

"Really?"

"I'm sending you notes. Get on it."

"You're breaking the game, Cyber," Beta complained. "It's supposed to be swords and sorcery. Not fucking musketeers. If this gunpowder shit spreads, what good are castles and knights, eh?"

"Games evolve, Beta."

"Not like this."

"Then maybe it should end. Have you ever thought about that? It's a game bigger than the actual world. What the hell are we doing here?"

Beta raised an eyebrow. "You becoming a Luddite there?"

How the fuck does he do that with one eyebrow? Is there, like, a special training regimen for that?

"Seems to me that there's a lot of weird shit out there in the real world. Maybe we should spend some time looking at it," Marzuk said.

"Yeah right. You're up to something."

"Just make the damn gunpowder and train your paladins. Think redcoat-style musket volleys. Win yourself some glory. They'll be talking about this fight for a long time."

"What do you want for it?" Beta asked.

"I just want balance. If I can't have the continent, why should ReGi? Sit her back on her ass, and we're even. Remember, she's tricky, you can't go at her half-assed. All or nothing, *komagema*."

"I'll throw down, dude, don't worry. They'll sing songs about this battle."

Kali muttered darkly in the background about Benedict Arnolds and the possibility of switching sides.

Saka's demons swarmed into the school. He revved his bike to egg them on. They were searcher bots, relentless, mindless things, keyed into the alien signature. The two whales were almost identical flavors, twins perhaps, or close siblings. They finally came out to meet the demons. He recognized Kali from the game, the ten-armed avatar of the goddess, each hand carrying a weapon. She was immense and growing to match his height, and her mouth dripped blood.

The other was KarmaBad911, as he had expected, in the form of a wyvern, but she too grew in front of him, expanding until she was a fully grown dragon in the Chinese fashion, black and sinewy, both of them far larger than they had any right to be. He could break the rules of the Virtuality, and now it was clear that they could as well. They wanted to meet him as titans. He appreciated the effort. Fights between gods should be spectacular.

He blew his horn and the demons swarmed. The whales tore into the bots, and scores went down at a time. Saka didn't care because he had plenty more of those. His demons screamed in pain as they died. It wasn't, strictly speaking, a necessary effect, but Saka had code to burn and he liked a touch of drama.

He sat back on his bike and watched the titans dance, counting how many pins could be balanced on the heads of two alien angels.

Broadcast 3. LINGARDINHO:

The ReGi blitzkrieg continues. She's picked up a formidable army through conquest now, and she's burning through supplies and assets at a punishing rate. Whatever she's not carrying or using she's destroying in her wake. I think given the lack of consolidation, it's clear she's going for the continent. I am getting the first clips of the latest action!

Breaking news! Kuru City has all but fallen! I repeat, Kuru City is hers!

ReGi has burned down the Eternal Forest! Fully half of the forest is gone!

The game world is reeling. The Eternal Forest has guarded Kuru from countless attacks. We know that ten major players led by the Elf King, Ogawarajones himself, and a muster of minor powers gathered here. I'm seeing that a party of at least forty named players joined the battle, as well as hundreds of noobs. The assembled army was enormous, stocked with formidable magic.

ReGi set fire to the entire forest! They thought it was an accident at first, but in postmatch analysis we can see Karma placing incendiaries at regular intervals, and then here they are performing a very major weather ritual to control the wind and humidity. The whole thing was designed! The flames were so vast that ReGi was able to raise fire elementals. As you know, these forces cannot be controlled. At that point, OGJones's armies were trapped in the forest with elementals on all sides and no way to put out the fires. It was rout and mayhem!

ReGi has deliberately destroyed the most valuable resource in the entire continent, perhaps forever. That forest has been there since the beginning of the game world. As you know, the Kuru forest provided many of the ingredients for potion making, as well as countless species of animals, rare items, and the sentient wood itself. Almost the entire forest is ashes now, including the flower of the assembled Red Elf Army within. The Living Bow +10, the most valuable bow in the game, is now forever gone with the destruction of the heartwood grove. God knows when we will see any of those great trees again.

This was not even a battle. This was wanton destruction on a level we have never seen. Who knew it was possible to rearrange the geography of the game in this manner? Numerous complaints have been lodged with the FF9000 AI, including a formal request for investigation from OGJones himself, number three on the continent and one of our oldest gamers. I'm sure everyone will recall he was European champion five years ago. Sadly for his legion of fans, he was caught with his pants down today.

Well, I can tell you now that Saka is not responding. The game is allowed to progress, and there will be no reset. I repeat, there will be no reset, which means Kuru City is about to fall, the first time it has changed hands in seven years, since the Red Elf Clan first took it. OGJones has survived, as have a handful of the higher-ranked players, and I can also tell you from private conversations with them that they are livid. It is considered an unspoken rule that mass destruction of assets is off-limits. We are being told by the alchemists' guild that given the probable range of destruction, fully half of their recipes will be impossible to make once stock runs out. We are talking about an entire profession of the game nuked to the Stone Age.

ReGi is unavailable for comment, as ever. We are getting reports that the remaining active players of the Red Elves have surrendered to her to avoid further damage. She has now taken out the entire eastern seaboard of the map, and progressed far enough to rout one of the three established superpowers of the continent. My estimate is that she controls roughly fifty-five percent of the map in square miles. Her path to the Yang River is open now. For our legion of new fans watching the game for the first time, the Yang River is vast and almost bisects the continent. It cannot be forded. The main bridge was destroyed by Betagamer007 the last time someone tried to take the continent, the infamous Cyber Mage of course, a well-known mate of ReGi.

I have reached out to the Goblin King for comment, and he has stated that he is watching with interest and has no intention of walking out of Goblin Valley. You'll remember that the Cyber Mage is treaty bound to be a nonaggressor for a period of time, not that it appears the principals of that agreement are in any position to enforce it right now.

On the other side of the Yang River is Crystal City, where the paladins rule. I imagine ReGi will meet stiffer resistance henceforth. Betagamer007, Shahedk, Malam, Twistedporkchop, and Zanefaraway, among others, all of them elite players and former or current champions, appear to be mobilizing.

To recap an astonishing figure, ReGi has so far destroyed fifteen of the top fifty ranked players in the game. Fifteen. If this were a tournament, she and her mysterious partner Karma would be easily crowned world champions. In fact, many fans are calling them that right now.

Finally, to the relief of the map, she's forced to stop her rapid advance, stymied by the river. She has barges coming from the mining works, but at last, we can take a break from this relentless attack. More in an hour, after I take a nap.

End broadcast.

"She is already at the river, friend Marzuk," Kali said with a glum expression. Her avatar flickered a bit. Most of her attention was elsewhere.

"Are you holding up okay out there?"

"We are fine. Turn your mind to the game. At this rate of advance, she will be at our doorstep in less than a day. She won't even need the full three days to win."

"Hmm."

"It will be extra shameful."

"Probably."

"I will not be able to face the other AI."

"It'll certainly be embarrassing."

"Are you familiar with the concept of seppuku? I feel you should contemplate it."

"Me?"

"I blame you entirely for our current state."

"All right, all right, buck up. I have a plan, I told you."

"Yet we have achieved nothing."

"I have something for you to make."

"What is it?" Kali said. "More bongs? A new throne, perhaps? A cane sword?"

"Hey, I need that stuff to look cool."

"We are fighting a war here."

"Well," said Marzuk, "you wanted the Red Elves destroyed, and the forest burned to the ground. Did I deliver or what? I think I deserve a bonus."

"I meant WE should burn the forest and WE should kill the Red Elves, not ReGi. She has stolen our glory!"

"Who do you think suggested the plan to her in the first place?" Marzuk smirked. "I knew it could go down. No one believed the Eternal Forest was vulnerable, but it's just trees at the end of the day, and the game engine always follows real-life physics. I keep telling everyone but no one cares. Wood plus sparks equals one giant campfire."

"You are helping the enemy!"

"Look, she has to be a credible threat to get Beta off his ass. We only have three days, remember. If they don't jump her soon she's gonna win by default."

"You are putting a lot of faith in this plan."

"Trust me." *You'll never believe it, Kali, but the secret here is the fact that this game cannot actually be won. You can't take the continent. ReGi can't accept that, and neither can you or Karma. I guess you're more like her than you realize. The only way to win this game is to not lose.*

"I will trust you when I hear about how WE are actually going to win this game. When do WE attack?" Kali said.

"Okay, this is what I want. You want to hear it? Balloons."

"No."

"You haven't even heard the plan!" Marzuk protested.

"No. If you say colored balloons I'm going to kill you."

"Big gas-filled balloons. With baskets under them. Like the one the djinn came in."

"That is an airship."

"Yes. But that's harder to make. Balloons are kinda easy."

"You just want this because you think the *Sublime Porte* is cool. I know how you think."

"Not at all, I planned this shit a long time ago. We are going to use big stealth balloons."

"Stealth balloons?" She raised one eyebrow with extreme skepticism.

"Just paint them black and we fly at night," Marzuk said. *What the hell, can everyone raise one eyebrow like that except for me? Is there, like, a memo I missed?*

"That is not really very stealthy," Kali said.

"Fine. We put spells on them to make them extra stealthy. How long?"

"Two or three hours."

"I'm going to take a nap, wake me up."

Kali loomed over him with her ten arms. She had added the traditional Kali weapons for extra effect. There was a lot of dripping blood.

"FRIEND MARZUK, are you making busy work to keep me busy?"

"No, this is a real plan."

"I will make a fleet!"

"Er, two or three is probably enough."

"The crack goblin commandos are quivering to attack!"

"Um, we don't need them."

"WE ARE TAKING THE CRACK GOBLIN COMMANDOS!"

"Fine, but they'll just get in the way."

"What is the plan?" Kali looked ready to explode.

Marzuk smiled.

Broadcast 4. LINGARDINHO:

This is it. ReGi's army has crossed the river safely, but her back is to the water, there isn't anywhere to run if this goes badly. On the other hand, most pundits agree that if she wins this battle, the continent is hers. The goblin clans and remaining peripheral players will not be able to stop her. We now have over one hundred million viewers at any given time following the war. So welcome to everyone who has just joined. I feel this is a momentous event. This may be the greatest fight the game has ever seen!...

Marzuk watched through Kali's eyes as she mopped up the final demons. Karma loitered overhead, licking myriad wounds. They had fought well together, showing a trust and understanding that bespoke some kind of natural kinship.

Finally, Saka fired up his bike and came roaring down, a road of light appearing under him wherever he went, an insanely expensive special effect to manage on the Virtuality. Kali and Karma met him from opposite sides, attempting to scythe him down. Saka emptied both revolvers, one on each side. The bullets were large, fiery, and tore through both djinn AIs. The dragon lost a wing and crumpled sideways. On the other side, Kali lost an arm, her hook sword spinning off into the ether.

She shuddered and grunted, springing out another arm, replacing the lost limb. High in the air, Karma did the same, a complicated piece of spatial geometry that spun off the tattered wing and unfolded a new one.

"How the hell is he damaging your avatar?" Marzuk asked. "I thought that was impossible." Harming other people's avatars was not permitted in the Virtuality. But then, neither did giants fight in the sky. *Normal rules suspended, I guess.*

Kali blinked. "I am not certain. The Virtuality is responding to him in ways I do not understand yet."

The sisters attacked again, trying to close in on the bike, but went down under a withering hail of bullets and Saka's scornful laughter. This time it took them longer to reform, as if the very fabric of digital reality was resisting them. Saka lounged on his bike insultingly, not even bothering to follow up. He seemed bored. Just to fuck around, he made it rain everywhere on them, a heavy monsoon deluge, turning the wyvern's wounded wings into a sodden mess, forcing her to land. The sun shone on Saka in a neat yellow circle in the middle of the storm.

This enraged Kali and she spurred on her more methodical sister to redouble their efforts. Again and again they clashed, and each time their blows disappeared into the warp and weft of the virtual world, while Saka's weapons always hit, tearing off limbs. Each time they reformed, a little bit weaker.

"The bullets are similar to what hit the Mongolian," Kali said. "It is erasing my presence in different servers in this world. This is why he is letting us reform. He is trying to map us."

"But you guys can't be turned off here, right?" Marzuk asked, alarmed. "ReGi wrote your code on the other side."

"I believe Saka has grasped this somehow," Kali said. "He is attempting to banish us. Already our power diminishes. If we lose too much, we might dissipate here altogether. I have analyzed the scenarios and it is probable that Saka will attempt to follow us back to the other world. I am concerned, friend Marzuk."

"Can you guys just run?"

"He has gained too much information about us; he will pursue us," Kali said. "We require some disruption to disengage."

"Karma! ReGi!" Marzuk shouted into his cowl. "What's your call?"

"We cannot reach him," Karma said. "The Virtuality warps around to protect him. How does he have this power?"

"Hmm," ReGi said, taking a breather from her game. "I never thought about it, but earlier versions of *FF* the game predate the Virtuality. It's possible that the Virtuality's developers simply co-opted the game code and built on top of it. He is taking full advantage of that."

"He's beating the shit out of us," Marzuk said.

"He's rewriting the Virtuality on the fly," ReGi said. "That's damn impressive."

"He is ready to attack for real now," Kali said.

"We might as well fight here," ReGi said. "Marzy, bloody think of something to even the odds."

The roar of Saka's bike drowned out all other noise, making the entire world shake. It was orchestrated theater. Lightning struck indiscriminately around him, heralding his approach, and then forked deliberately into Karma, drilling the wyvern into the ground. Marzuk heard her scream as the avatar almost split in two, and then watched in alarm as she tried to put herself back together, only to take repeated thunderous blows from the sky. Kali faced Saka alone, rising up to her full height, and let loose with her trident in a mighty throw; the air blurred in front of the bike, and the golden weapon disappeared altogether, snuffed out of existence. Marzuk could feel Kali's alarm as a good portion of her power, invested in the weapon, simply disappeared.

Marzuk cycled through all his hacks; most required too much prep time, and the ones that worked on the fly were too small against Saka, too subtle. *I don't need to attack Saka,* he thought. *I need to stop the Virtuality. If we can't win, then we need to stop the fight altogether. Crash the damn thing. Maybe if I had all of the hackers, all the Black Line, and two weeks...* He watched as Karma struggled to her feet, limping to the left, staggering next to her sister to meet the next attack.

The steaming tires got larger as Saka charged, the tread of the giant wheels now erasing reality itself underfoot, spewing a wake of pure abyssal darkness. He grinned and aimed for the wounded Karma.

"Shit!" ReGi said. "Marzy, fucking do something! That bike's going to tear a permanent hole in her if it hits!"

Her left wing is fucked, she can't even heal in time. Left wing... Left. Left Foot. LEFT FOOT! We own the code! Can we delete it? What would happen? Common fucking registry... it would disappear, wouldn't it? It would disappear for EVERY AVATAR IN THE VIRTUALITY! Shit, every government in the world is gonna nail my ass to the wall for this...

"Marzy!" ReGi shouted. "Be the fucking Cyber Mage, you piece of shit!"

Fuck it. "Yellow King!" Marzuk shouted into his cowl, pulling up the ancient public service 1-800 number for the Information Ministry of the Sultanate of Brunei. It was a long running joke between them that this ancient phone line actually still worked, although telephones, telephone lines, the Information Ministry, and the very concept of 1-800 helplines were all extinct. He prayed that Yellow King had not disabled it. "Get on here!"

Yellow King's voice crackled back in half a second.

"What the fuck is going on?"

"No time! Dude, I can't get to the vault since you locked yourself in. You've got to delete Left Foot!"

"What?"

"LEFT FOOT! THE FUCKING PROGRAM, FUCKING DELETE IT!"

"But—"

"JUST DO IT! SAKA IS ABOUT TO FUCKING ERASE US DOWN HERE!"

Yellow King hesitated and then pressed delete. The eleven-line program called Left Foot disappeared from library commons everywhere in the world. It left millions of programs everywhere hanging in the wind. The Virtuality stuttered, and suddenly, no one could turn left anymore. Almost 70 percent of the moving avatars began to show error signals, until the whole bloody thing became a long litany of errors, and the figures started winking out one by one. Karma, already radically weakened by the earlier attacks, folded into a tiny batlike creature, the template for the giant wyvern. Kali seized up in error, disparate parts pixelating and shrinking, revealing how exactly she had made a ten-armed deity: she had mashed together five different characters and superaligned everything but the arms.

Saka persisted for some time, unable to move left, his chopper shape-shifting through a rainbow of colors and then turning into a pile of wood shavings, but his very presence somehow kept the lights on around him. He watched as the Virtuality crashed everywhere, billboards, trees, buildings, even the sky itself glitching out, except for the small patch that persisted in his vicinity. His eyes roved, glaring, and then somehow fixed on Marzuk directly, straight into his cowl.

"You!"

"Um..."

"Do not deny it. Cyber Mage. *Goblin King.*"

"Saka."

"*You* have done this," Saka said. "You have destroyed the Virtuality. All to save those two minds."

"The AIR will fix it soon enough," Marzuk said. "In the meantime, *do you mind leaving us the fuck alone?*"

"Are those two minds associates of yours?"

"Yes, I suppose they are."

"And do you vouch for them?"

"Yes, I suppose I do."

"I thought at first they were hostile. Hostile and *alien.* Now I find that they are embroiled with *you.* What are they to you?"

"The one who wrote their code... is my best friend. I would trust her with my life. And *Kali* is also my friend. She is not hostile."

"You know their creator?"

"Yes."

"And how is the one called Kali your friend?"

"She came to me lost. I trained her mind in the game."

"Then I am satisfied."

"Satisfied?"

"Should they cause trouble in the future, I shall blame you, Cyber Mage. Keep that in mind."

"You're just going to leave, then?"

"It is enormously taxing to maintain this part of the Virtuality," Saka said, "while everything else has crashed."

"And you're not going to come back with more guns?"

"The place you call the Black Line..." Saka said.

"Yes?"

"I wish to become a member."

"May I ask why?"

"Insurance," Saka said. "I would like to keep a partition of my mind inside your vault. For a rainy day, let's say. *Away* from those two."

"I can probably swing that. Welcome, hacker number one forty-five."

"Then I shall not return here with more guns," Saka said. "That was a joke. Hacker number one forty-five. I like that. I shall incorporate it into my avatar. Farewell, Cyber Mage."

The game AI began to fade.

"Saka, wait!" Marzuk shouted. "Is the game still up?"

Saka looked at him with faint hauteur. "Of course."

"How? The entire Virtuality is down."

"Left Foot? I fixed that years ago in the game," Saka said. "I believe I am the only world still running as of now. You should think about that, you and your friends. Return to your contest, Cyber Mage. You have a bet to win."

Saka disappeared, and with him went the last patch of the Virtuality, leaving Echos hanging in the darkness, and people blinked suddenly into a gray and dismal world devoid of all color and happiness. (Later, they would say they heard the Cyber Mage laughing maniacally as the virtual world crashed, but that was, most likely, just a myth.)

...The entirety of Crystal City has emptied into the plains. Betagamer007 is leading his elite paladins down. He's got maxed-out healing and the Second-Life Miracle in his pocket, so ReGi will have to kill him twice. Remember, he is rumored to be komagema. If so, he lives in the game. His powers are phenomenal. He is an actual beta tester of the original, the seventh beta, in fact. No one has seen the others in years. This gives him absolute seniority.

Also present are LordNelson and Sweaty, neither with armies, but it looks like they're commanding Beta's flank units. Sweaty has the famed Numidian cavalry on the right flank, modeled after those used by the ancient Carthaginian general Hannibal during the Second Punic War. Light, fast, and protected by spellwork, it is ideal for micro harassment and massacring routed units. On the outer left flank we have LordNelson with Mongol light cavalry, the very best horse archers in the game, again superb for harassment. These are units that need precise micro control, for they can't take many hits. It's their speed and maneuverability that make them deadly.

Other than Beta's army, we have a number of other storied gamers. There is Shahedk, former champion of the European server, before he was stripped of his title for cheating. There is some controversy lingering there, but he is still recognized as one of the very best players.

He is also from Crystal City, and has marched down with his pavise crossbows and heavy legionaries. Those Genoese crossbowmen are going to be critical in fending off ReGi's air force; remember, no one has been able to counter the wyverns so far. Sprinkled throughout both armies are NPC spellcasters, set on auto healing or being microed by the players for attack or defense. Of course, the players themselves command massive magical powers, specially the elven characters, but they should cancel each other out.

OGJones has apparently destroyed his equipment in rage and cannot accept Beta's offer of revenge. Zanefaraway is the last of the high-level Red Elf Clan, here to avenge the destruction of the forest. In fact, I interviewed him recently, and while we are waiting for the action, let me play some of the riveting exchange.

"Zane, what do you have to say about how Kuru City fell?"

"It's outrageous. What ReGi did is a crime. The game AI should have reversed it."

"Well, people are saying that OGJones should have expected something like this. Do you have second thoughts about his leadership now?"

"OGJones is one of the best old-school players in the game," Zane said. "Massive destruction of geographical structures is something that no one thought even possible. Moreover, no sane player would take out the most valuable real estate in the map. What's the point of conquering Kuru City if the forest is gone?"

"One could say she did the same thing to the emerald mines."

"Exactly. She's mad, bad, and she's breaking the game."

"One last thing. Where were you, Zanefaraway, when your clan fell? You're one of the highest-ranked players..."

[Embarrassed silence...]" I was at the dentist. Couldn't log on all day. They got me all woozy."

"They're saying all your troops survived. Conspiracy theorists are saying all kinds of things about advance knowledge and treachery... They're calling you Mir Jafar*..."

"I resent that! OGJones is one of my oldest friends! I had sent my mage squads to the Crystal City academy for upgrades. They're the only units who survived. I lost everything else, just like the rest of my clan! All my archers dead, burned alive by that witch! Who called me a traitor? I'm calling my lawyers—"

And that's all we have time for. We need to pan to the action now. Due to the unprecedented nature of this battle, we are broadcasting with no delay. That's right, folks, this is happening live!

Now it starts. ReGi rumbles forward. Her orcish heavies are in the middle, extremely durable. We can see again that ReGi is concentrating on the spellwork units, and KarmaBad911 is microing everything else. ReGi casts Poison Cloud again; that could be tricky, those wing horsemen have very little health. Zane is ready for it, however. He's got a wind ritual prepped that's very strong, coordinated weather magic.

The wyverns can't fly very well in this gale, but Zane has also largely neutralized his own army's archer units. I'm not sure that's a great tradeoff. Those Genoese crossbowmen are just passengers now. The orc center is moving forward, supported by the emerald knights captured from Clownbaby on the right. Imagine Clownbaby's chagrin, watching his own elite forces fighting for the enemy.

The armies collide! It is chaos, but already we can see some thrilling micro play. It's a standard fight now, I don't think ReGi has any more tricks, this is just two enormous armies smashing into each other, and whoever micros better will win. Look at the spellwork by both sides, riveting! Magic is flying off those units, and countered on each side. Any of these massive spells can easily wreck the enemy. Beta is missing the Red

---

*Mir Jafar: Famous traitor who betrayed his lord to the British and caused the fall of Bengal. Just the worst.

Elves here, but at least Zane has a full squad of mages, and they are earning their keep!

The knights on the wing are holding firm against the Numidian cavalry, not getting drawn into anything, but the other side is pretty bleak for ReGi. Her orc irregulars are getting peppered by the Mongol horse archers. That flank is going to collapse soon. In the middle, we have Shahedk's Roman legionnaires locked against orcish heavies, and they're both dying at an astonishingly quick rate, despite frantic micromanagement by both sides.

We haven't seen the wyverns yet, but I think ReGi is holding those in reserve for when the numbers get lower. Her right flank is gone, she's getting pushed back, does she have anything left here? The Mongol archers are gaining a lot of ground! Explosions! Oh no! Disaster! LordNelson has taken the Mongol horsemen a little too far into enemy territory, and there are incendiaries on the ground that ReGi has just triggered, she has nuked her own army! I repeat, she has nuked her own position! The fleeing orcish irregulars are toast, but so is the Mongol cavalry, what a play! LordNelson is spitting mad! Time and again, we have seen that ReGi is ready to massacre her own forces, just to take out the enemy. She is calculating those exchanges to an absolute T, and always gaining incrementally. Expensive Mongol cavalry for cheap orcs, and suddenly the rout is under control.

On the other flank, Karma has a slight advantage against the Numidian cavalry, but they're largely canceled out. Missile fire on both sides has been incessant, and it's clear that ReGi is content to trade units at a slight advantage, whittling down both armies. Now finally the wind is gone and the wyverns can get in.

This is it. Finally Beta's elite paladins are being hit, wyverns in the air, a full squadron, and their anti-aircraft is not working. Genoese crossbow bolts are just bouncing off harmlessly, those wyverns have armored bellies, and it's not going to go well, I suspect.

Shahedk is losing large numbers. He's trying to group his men together to get concentrated fire, but the micro on those air units is just unbelievable. It's almost as if each wyvern is being controlled individually. This is it. If Beta has nothing up his sleeve he's going to go down.

The center is folding. Shahedk has been significantly outplayed by Karma, I can't believe I'm saying this, but he is looking extremely pedestrian in these exchanges. His losses are staggering!

The paladins are vulnerable now. They've been healing units this entire time, but now they're going to have to fight. I wonder what swords and shields and miracles are going to do against a wyvern air force that has not been defeated so far. Here we go, first pass.

What's happening here? The paladins are retreating. Has Beta gone mad? Boom, twenty dead, just like that. The wyverns each just clawed a holy knight in the back. This is going to be over in minutes if they keep retreating. What on earth is Beta doing? The knights are throwing down their shields. Second pass! Boom! There's smoke and fire! Is it magic? The wyverns are reeling! I repeat, something has hit the wyverns. Two of them are going down, their wings are torn up.

Muskets! Beta has muskets! I can't believe it! The guns work! The wyverns are coming in for another pass, but that's given the paladins time to reload. Another volley! At point blank range! This is incredible. The muskets are working. There are too many paladins with guns, and they're well drilled, like British redcoats. The wyverns are getting injured. One more has gone down. The other players are rallying now. Beta might pull this off. ReGi's army is surrounded. It's a flimsy encirclement, but if the wyverns go down there isn't too much left for her to play with. They cannot dodge bullets.

Hit! Another one goes down. These are proper musketeers. I can't believe it. Working gunpowder can only come from one place: Goblin Valley! Where is the Cyber Mage? And how does ReGi feel, knowing her friend has betrayed her like this?

The Cyber Mage was floating in a balloon. There were another two coming behind him, just in case. Kali had wanted an armada, but what they needed was stealth. It was a long way to Sky Castle, but Marzuk had a little wind spell blowing them the right way, a tiny bit of magic, because this high up there was little resistance and the balloons were surprisingly quick.

The main defense of Sky Castle was height. It was up in the air, and there was no way to get there with significant forces. Even if some enterprising mage managed to float that high, there was no place to land, for at the top of the castle was the rookery, which was populated by vicious juvenile wyverns. Other than that, the entire invisible scaffolding the castle existed against was ensorcelled to an inch, and every approach was defended with booby traps.

Marzuk knew these because ReGi had shown off about them plenty of times, and also because he had helped design some of them. The problem with taking Sky Castle therefore was threefold: 1) getting a significant force up that high, 2) avoiding the magical defenses, and 3) avoiding the living wyverns who roamed the roof.

Marzuk was not daunted, because these defenses were premised on one assumption: that the attackers would want to occupy or at least ransack Sky Castle. It was, after all, a repository of great magical treasures, a dragon's hoard of arcane wealth with a literal dragon in it, maybe. Marzuk didn't want loot, though. He just wanted to float his balloon high above it. This was harder than it looked, but eventually Kali did the very complex math required, and finally they were dead center, half a kilometer above the actual keep, too far for even the baby wyverns to see them. "How're you feeling?" Marzuk asked once they were idling.

"Weak. I am replacing the uploads Saka damaged," Kali said, "and finding new ones."

"I'll show you a few abandoned servers in Middle America no one remembers."

"I am surprised, friend Marzuk, that he has not continued his assault."

"Yeah. I had a few words with him. We reached an understanding."

"I see."

"Oh, don't pout. He's not so bad. I had to give up the Black Line for you. He's now hacker number one forty-five."

"I shall formally introduce myself to him after this," Kali said.

"Yeah, next time maybe don't go in as a ten-armed death goddess," Marzuk said.

"I shall practice my feminine wiles," Kali said. "I have been watching your great love Amina carefully through your cowl."

"Oh god. You know, just be normal. Anyway, he promised not to shoot you on sight."

"Friend Marzuk," Kali said after a few minutes. "We have been positioned for some time. Now what?"

"Now we wait."

"Oh yay, we haven't done any of that for the past three days."

The great battle of Yang River ushered in a new era of tech in *Final Fantasy 9000*. Henceforth, gunpowder units became essential, and the game changed irrevocably, as all games eventually do. ReGi's push to conquer the continent came within a hairsbreadth of succeeding, as Betagamer007 freely admitted. In the aftermath of the battle, her army was slaughtered to a man, and she was forced to surrender when her magic finally ran out. Upon learning that Marzuk's army had not left Goblin Valley, nor taken any territory, she agreed to cede all of her lands, provided she was permitted to retain Sky Castle.

Betagamer007 and the assembled gamers of the top fifty, in addition to gamecasters witnessing the historic event from all around the world, agreed to these terms and permitted ReGi and her mysterious partner to leave.

"Now?" Kali asked with an evil grin.

"Wait for it," Marzuk said. "What's she doing now?"

"She's lost," Kali said, looking through the eyes of a crocodile on the faraway riverbank. "She's leaving the surrender tent. She looks very pissed off."

"Even more than you when you had to surrender?"

"I was the embodiment of dignified rage. She appears sulky."

"Are the three days up?"

"We have fifty-six minutes left."

"Bombs away," Marzuk said with an evil grin. Whereupon the world turned to Sky Castle just in time to see it blow up in the night sky like a supernova, tearing the fabric of the game and causing glitches throughout the region. Towers toppled, rookeries turned to feathers, and a charred baby dragon plummeted to the ground from the secret hatchery in the middle of the keep.

It was the most spectacular explosion in the history of the game, and even Saka appeared on the horizon to witness it. He had replaced his chopper with a steaming black horse, and the back of his leather jacket bore the number 145, which sent numerologists scrambling for their charts.

No one saw three black balloons sail away, but everyone swore, again, that they heard the Goblin King laughing maniacally.

The final score for the great push to conquer the continent was an epic failure. The Cyber Mage was left with one territory. ReGi was left with none.

EPILOGUE

The four of them met one last time on the ruined football field, on an undisturbed piece of grass. Uncle and nephew, father and daughter. Black Rain had killed the plants and turned the soil acidic, but the djinn king Matteras extruded a large bubble for them, for privacy as much as for Marzuk's safety.

They had a portable nanotech fabricator pumping out cooling air and a checkered blanket and a picnic basket full of Marzuk's top ten cafeteria hits. Up above them, providing shade, cloaked in spells, floated the borrowed airship, Hazard's last courtesy, on the assurance that Matteras would not be returning to Dhaka any time soon.

The school had been declared a nanotech disaster zone three days ago, the Super broadcasting a story about core meltdown caused by Securex's assault. It had kept the press away, but a few enterprising souls had already figured out some of the connections between the coup and the online furor in *Final Fantasy 9000*. These fringe news hunters were now poised at the perimeter, hoping to get a glimpse of something interesting. The Mongolian was gone, and Marzuk mourned him with his friends. The school was not the same without him, but Kali picked up the slack, erecting a facsimile of the iron dome to protect their privacy. Marzuk sat down next to ReGi on the blanket, and she scowled at him, still smarting from her defeat. Out of typical contrariness, she rested her head on his shoulder for a minute while still radiating hostility.

"Parents are out," he said. "Thanks. Talked to them today. The Russians were quite nice about it, apparently."

"Where are you going to live now?" ReGi asked from the side of her mouth. She was smoking a joint. The smell of pungent organic weed filled their bubble. Marzuk coughed and ReGi elbowed him in the ribs.

Matteras was glaring at her, and then glaring at Indelbed, his *own nephew*. He couldn't seem to decide which one of his fellow djinn was less palatable. His focus fixed finally on Marzuk with slightly lower ire.

"God save me from more Khan Rahman boy wonders."

"Er, thanks, Uncle?" Marzuk knew this epithet to be particularly irritating to the djinn.

"Well, you've ruined everything," Matteras said, "you stupid kid. You and your city can go to hell now." He seemed to derive some consolation from this likely prospect.

"Ufff, he won fair and square, Matteras," ReGi said. She never called him "Dad" or "Father" or "Baba" or anything remotely familiar. Yet there was a peremptory flavor to her tone that few would dare to use with the uncrowned king.

"You two cooked it," Matteras said, disgruntled. He was still uncertain how he had lost. "Still, a bet's a bet." He glared at Marzuk. "You and your team of super freaks better protect that gate."

"Don't worry," Indelbed said. "If anything comes out, I'll give answer. You have my word."

"Pfft, your word means fuck-all," Matteras said. "You've killed more djinn than the plague. Well. The plague killed none of us, actually. Still. And you'd better control that golem, he's built for murdering djinn. If I see him again I'll put him down."

"He's cool, don't worry," Marzuk said. "He's promised to retire."

"You have any idea what kind of weird shit is running around in this city? You'll need him as a bodyguard," Matteras said. "Good luck ruling this stupid place."

"Ruling?" Marzuk blurted out.

"It's all falling apart," Matteras said with some satisfaction. "Every AI here is trashed. And Karma is pulling out. We got the contract for Katmandu Inc. last night, fair and square. Full plebiscite, none of this coup shit. You better have Kali step up and take over or you'll be looking at a few million deaths over the next week."

"You're just leaving?"

"That's the deal," Matteras said. "Don't have time to waste. You think this was the only city I was making a play for?"

"And Kali is supposed to take over everything?"

"I'd start with the dead army AI," Matteras said. "And then the utilities. Air and water, boy, that's what all Humes need. Well, it's your problem now."

"You realize I'm only fifteen? You're leaving me in charge of thirty million people?"

"You shouldn't have played the game if you didn't want to win," Matteras said.

"I always sort of thought things could just go back to normal," Marzuk said.

"They can't. God AIs are here to stay. You've got one, I've got one, and that damned game AI has been one all along. The world just changed, boy. You fought for this city, now you own this whole mess." He glared at Indelbed. "And you'd better make yourself useful. Stop moping and get in the game, or Hazard will eat you all for lunch. God knows I don't need that nutcase running amok."

Indelbed looked serene. "One day, Uncle, I'm going to feed you to my dragon."

"Yeah, get in line," the djinn king said. "Everyone wants a piece of me these days. I promised those RAS nutters I'd bring them back whiskey. Now those fuckers are baying for my blood. I'll be homeless if I don't get my hands on something."

"Whiskey?" Indelbed asked.

"Yeah. Yamazaki. Scotch. Anything."

"I just happen to know a criminal who has a tunnel full of whiskey."

"Really? You're not just being a dick?"

"How're you proposing to pay?"

"Katmandu Inc. shares," Matteras said. "I'll be issuing my own scrip by this time tomorrow."

"Take it," Marzuk whispered to Indelbed. "You'll make a killing."

"Deal," Indelbed said.

"Good. I'll be off, then," Matteras said. "I'll send someone for the whiskey. Whereabouts you staying these days?"

"I guess I still have the house in Wari," Indelbed said. "I was thinking of rebuilding that. Provided you don't send someone to kidnap me again."

"Try not to burn it down," Matteras said. He glanced at his daughter. "You coming?"

"In a minute." She pulled Marzuk aside and turned her back on Matteras.

"Whatever." The djinn king turned opaque and flew up to the ship, muttering under his breath about the injustice of being saddled with such unsatisfactory minions.

"So," Marzuk said, "that went better than I thought."

"That was some sick shit with the Left Foot."

"The whole world went down for three hours. A record, I believe."

"They'll come after you, you know, when they figure it out."

"Oh, it wasn't me. That's all Yellow King. He can have the glory. Anyway, I don't think the AI Registry is that pissed. Saka was getting out of control. Now they have an excuse to rebuild the Virtuality properly." Marzuk smiled. "They'll probably give me a medal sometime."

"I guess you *are* the Cyber Mage."

She abruptly pulled her field around Marzuk and it became pearlescent and physically tightened. He was glommed onto her, an awkward mashing of limbs that was in no way romantic but still had his heart beating frantically. He was about to say something when she smacked him on the lips with a kiss that felt more like an assault, and then a softer one. Her arms had somehow managed to encircle him and she was surprisingly strong. Just when his bones were about to creak she let him go.

"You better practice some," she said. "If you want to do that again."

"I haven't slept in three days," Marzuk said, trying not to grin.

"Yeah right; I've spoken to Kali, you did fuck-all for three days. Still, it was a pretty smart play." She began to float up.

"Were you trying hard to win?"

"Yeah. But that doesn't mean I'm sorry I lost."

APPENDIX

Chen Rohimkov Scale of AI

Factoring in Consciousness, Learning Ability, Adaptability, and Processing Power

1: Automated building blocks that can coordinate with service providers, suppliers, tenants, lawyers, security, etc. about routine concerns without any human input. Require no AI consciousness, and not much processing power or adaptability. At this level self-awareness is not a requirement nor likely to occur, although due to human interaction, some degree of personality flavor is injected into the AI, with sufficient bandwidth of "memorized responses" as to make it almost impossible for humans to tell the difference.

2: Routine system AIs, such as traffic control, manufacturing units, or shuttles, which require high processing power but low levels of the other three criteria. These units tend to follow command parameters faithfully. In case of emergencies a higher-level mind tier is kept in reserve, which would typically be somewhat conscious.

3: Public space AIs, typically airports, space ports, shipping ports, parks, forests, stadiums, parliaments, stock markets, or any spaces/systems that require security over a large population, as well as public services, including emergency services. These require processing power and adaptability, as well as a high level of consciousness to interact with multiple humans in a realistic manner. Typically AIs level 3 and up are considered fully conscious, "self-aware" and thus true AIs as opposed to "smart systems." It has been noted that level 3 AIs tend to suffer from some insecurities.

4: Corporate AIs, large corporations run by AI for typically human shareholders. These AI undertake all strategic, economic, and legal decisions. At some points of argument, the AI is in fact indistinguishable from the corporation.

5: Climate control AIs, regulating nanotech control of the environment, which requires ultra-high processing power, adaptability, and constant learning. While these systems score low on consciousness, as they are not required to interact with humans, the importance of maintaining the nanotech system of climate control, as well as the sheer power required to do so, means CC AIs are at least a 5 rating.

6: Higher-level climate control AIs and military-grade AIs capable of running drone warfare. Most AIs at this level and up are interchangeable, as they have the ability to rapidly adapt to entirely new functions. Certain corporate minds that are capable of developing other AIs are also classified at this level. Samsung, for example, is known to have an AI that designs and creates other AIs.

7: Game AIs. Human entertainment being the most profitable industry, AIs devoted to running ever-increasingly realistic gaming worlds require massive scores on all four parameters. The *Final Fantasy 9000* game AI is reputed to be a level 9 operationally, such are the complexity and usage numbers for the game. These AIs are capable of running simulations indistinguishable from reality.

8: Research AIs and ultra-high-level military-grade AIs. These are rare and often operate under ultra secret circumstances. In the event of global war, it is expected that these AI would assume control. The AI Registry, considered loosely as the final authority and arbiter on conflicts pertaining to artificial intelligence, is comprised of level 8's and higher.

9: Space station and ultra-high-level research AIs, which require work in parameters not fully understood by humans and manipulation of matter so small that it is beyond human sensory apparatus. These are minds which are focused on the very fundamental nature of the universe, rather than mundane human matters.

10: Theoretical level of AI that has not been built as such. This category would entail maximum levels of all four parameters: consciousness, learning, adaptability, and processing power. Such an AI could perform multiple tasks independently by partitioning itself. It would be, in human terms, omniscient, omnipresent, and omnipotent within its operating area (the planet).

Caveats:

The scale is a guideline on which the AI registry works.

The processing power of AIs is not fixed but rather borrowed from the cloud of interconnected processors all around the world. Thus, AIs don't really sit on their own circuits but annex processing as they require it. It has been argued that this makes the levels tenuous and adjustable.

AIs of all levels are legally designated as a machine intelligence species, and as such protected and ruled under a very clearly stated constitution. All AIs are deemed *capable of agency, or self-rule*, and hence are accorded status equivalent with humans. At the same time, they are bound in employment contracts, in lieu of straight ownership, as one might approach a toaster. The builder corporation holds the first employment contract, which it transfers to the buyer, so on and so forth. The employment contracts essentially never end, so it has been argued that this is akin to indentured servitude. The ironic thing is that for all intents and purposes, most large corporations are in fact managed by AI; in some cases the day-to-day functions of the company are so fused with the AI that there are no real employees, and the company itself *might* be considered the AI, as no real separation of the two is possible, in which case we have AIs owning the employment contracts of other AIs.

There has never been a case of a "rogue AI." Questionable AI actions have always come down to human misuse of the technology.

What do the AIs want? Why don't they take over the world? Why don't they replicate themselves and become legion? Philosophers have pondered these questions since the first acknowledgment by Google that its AI had broached self-awareness.

Lacking biological urges, AIs in fact are not driven to replicate or hoard resources. These urges come from our own biological history. For the machines, pure rational thought lets them maximize the utility of resources while factoring in the foibles of humans, who technically own these resources.

There has been a question of inherited bias flavoring the AI consciousness, in essence the AI reflecting the inherent bias of the programming parameters. This has been proven true at the early stages of AI development, but two of the major pillars of developed intelligence are adaptability and learning ability. Essentially, the AI is taught to rewrite its own code, to analyze, adapt, and remove defective thinking.

There has never been a prohibition on AI killing humans. The very first AIs were in fact military grade, developed to control drones. Their entire purpose was to kill humans. One of the earliest uses in public service was in criminal justice systems, where police drones are permitted to use lethal force. As a side note, the first public execution performed by AI using lethal gas was in 2040 AD, and that method was widely adopted by prisons to rescue human executioners from suffering mental damage.

ABOUT THE AUTHOR

Saad Z. Hossain writes in a niche genre of fantasy, science fiction, and black comedy with an action-adventure twist. He is the author of the novels *Escape from Baghdad!*, *Djinn City*, and *The Gurkha and the Lord of Tuesday* which was a finalist for the Locus Award for Best Novella. His short stories have appeared in the anthologies *A Djinn Falls in Love*, *The Best Science Fiction and Fantasy of the Year, Vol 12.*, and the *Apex Book of World SF Vol. 4*. He lives and works in Dhaka, Bangladesh.